Praise for the Novels of Cindy Miles

Highland Knight

"Spunky Abigail and typically gruff but warmhearted Ethan (and his rough and tumble kin) are sweetly entertaining." —*Publishers Weekly*

"When it comes to delivering charming, funny, and tender romances, Miles is at the head of the class. Not only are the primary characters wonderful; the secondary characters are engaging and bring depth to the story. This warmhearted book is guaranteed to leave you with a satisfied smile!" —*Romantic Times* (top pick, 4½ stars)

"This is a book to fall in love with and to read over and over. Cindy Miles has written a surefire winner for . . . fans of Scottish heroes."
—*Affaire de Coeur* (reviewer's pick, 5 stars)

"Cindy Miles completely captivated me with *Highland Knight*. . . . I was glued to the story line and loved how the characters interacted with each other . . . downright sexy." —Romance Junkies

"An enjoyable ride, start to finish."
—*The Romance Reader*

Into Thin Air

"Another sweet paranormal featuring a sparkling lead couple and a supporting cast of ghostly charmers . . . this adorable, otherworldly romp is sure to leave readers feeling warm and fuzzy." —*Publishers Weekly*

"Filled with humor, romance, mystery, and a lot of ghosts, *Into Thin Air* is a book that is hard to put down." —Romance Junkies

continued . . .

Spirited Away

"Absolutely delightful! Cindy Miles outshines the genre's best, writing with a charm and verve sure to captivate readers' hearts. *Spirited Away* is pure magic."
—Sue-Ellen Welfonder, *USA Today* bestselling author

"A sparkling debut, reminiscent of favorites like *The Ghost and Mrs. Muir*."
—Julie Kenner, *USA Today* bestselling author

"This charming paranormal debut heralds an exciting new voice in the genre. Warm, humorous, fun-filled, magical, and spiced with deadly danger, this ghost story has it all."   —*Romantic Times* (4½ stars)

"Cindy Miles's love for the genre shines through in her endearing, quirky heroines and her larger-than-life heroes. As a reader, I was *Spirited Away* by the magic in each and every word."
—Jolie Mathis, author of *The Sea King*

"This is the most charming story I have come across in some time. It has such a wonderful plot, characters, setting, and dialogue; I eagerly await the next book."
—Romance Readers at Heart

"A charming tale that mixes best what readers enjoy in medieval fantasy and contemporary romance. The less common ghostly theme will appeal to paranormal fans looking for variety, and the quirky, lovable characters will leave readers wanting to revisit the knights of Dreadmoor Castle."   —*Booklist*

"An energetic, amusing ghostly romance starring a likable, intelligent mortal and a somewhat frustrated ghost."   —*Midwest Book Review*

For Brian, because *we made it*.
I love you.

And for Kim, Betsy, Molly, and Rita-Marie,
for all the reading and encouragement for
MacGowan's Ghost.
This one's for you.

Prologue

Odin's Thumb Inn and Pub
Northwest coast, Scotland
October, midnightish

"Hurry, before Himself returns!" Friar Digby whispered, glancing about the dimmed room. "Make haste!"

"Well, move your robe-garbed arse over, then, so I can see!" Captain Catesby elbowed in next to the friar and squinted at the computer screen. His eyes widened. "Damn me, but she's fetchin'."

Three more souls sifted into the small stone-walled office and hovered behind the captain. Mademoiselle Bedeau gasped. The two fatal duelers, Christopher and Baden—both English—followed with like noises.

Friar Digby sniffed and lowered his voice still more. "I daresay the very last thing to be concerned about is her beauty, sir."

"Aye, although she is a lovely maid," said Christopher. He cocked his head and stared even harder. "Think you she will try to oust us from our home?"

Captain Catesby stared at the smiling face on the screen. "Nay. She willna."

Mademoiselle Bedeau sighed. "How can you know that, sir?"

A slow smile pulled at the captain's mouth. "I can

see it in her eyes, lass. This one's a wily lamb, but no' a threat to us." He rose and grinned at his fellow ghosts. "I have a feeling Himself will get far more than he bargains for with this gel, truth be told."

The heavy tread of boots in the corridor made all of their heads snap up.

"Himself returns!" said the friar under his breath. He shooed the duelers, frantic. "Quick, begone! But just inside the wall, there, so we can listen whilst he makes the call to the lady."

The spirits scrambled and hastily seeped into the stone. With a much-stifled chuckle and a shake of his head, Captain Catesby followed, and waited.

Chapter 1

"Thank you so much, Ms. Morgan. I don't know what we would have done without you." Mrs. Zolaster glanced around with unease. She lowered her voice to a whisper. "Are you sure they're gone?"

Mr. Zolaster, a middle-aged man with a strip of brown hair encircling his crown, shifted his gaze from one side of the living room to the other. By the pinched expression, he didn't look very convinced.

Allie slid a glance over the heads of both Zolasters and straight into the naughty, smiling, and nearly transparent faces of three youthful spirits.

One of them winked and waggled his brows.

Allie ignored the playful gesture and met the expectant gazes of the Zolasters. "They won't be causing you any more trouble." She smiled. "I promise."

Relief washed over both of their faces, and Mrs. Zolaster held out her hand. "I can't thank you enough. Now, if I can show you out?"

Allie thought the woman was more than happy to see the last of her, too. "Absolutely." She stepped through the door of the Zolasters' 150-year-old brick manor house and into Raleigh's crisp night air. No sooner had she made it to the end of the drive than the three young ghosts materialized beside her. Three teenaged brothers who, on a warm July day in 1861, fell to their deaths at the First Manassas.

They'd made their way home. Eventually.

But without the first memory of what had happened.

"Aw, Allie, come on. Don't leave," one brother said in a North Carolina drawl.

"Yeah, the Zolasters seem nice and all, but they ain't no fun," the other said.

"Not fun like you," the third and eldest offered. "Please?"

Allie stopped and looked each brother in the eye. She sighed, then smiled. "Listen, guys. Now that you know how, where, and when you died, you're free. I found your family's history, you know what happened to your parents and the the rest of your siblings, and you're no longer forced to haunt the halls of your old homestead." She waved her arms. "Go out, explore, have a little fun." She narrowed her eyes. "But not too much fun. And please, leave the Zolasters alone. I promised them, you know."

The three brothers grinned.

One scratched his forehead. "Can we come visit you sometime?"

Allie studied the three boys. All wearing drab gray uniforms of the Confederacy, their ghostly eyes revealed nothing more than hope. She gave them a wide smile. "I'd be upset if you didn't. Now stay out of trouble."

"Yes, ma'am!" they all three hollered at once.

Then they disappeared.

Allie shook her head, made it to her trusty old Wrangler, climbed in, and started for home. A half hour later, she pulled into the Waterloo Apartments complex, growled when she saw a visitor had parked in her spot, found another, and climbed to the fifth floor. She pushed her key into the lock and let herself in to her one-bedroom corner abode.

And immediately met the ghostly stare of her long-time friend.

"Well, I see by the satisfied look on your lovely face that you have completed yet another successful de-haunting." He gave a curt nod. "Congratulations once again, love. How go the lads, then? Are they content?"

Dead for more than a hundred years, Alexander Dauber made himself quite at home in Allie's presence.

She loved that about him. "Yes, they're content. Mischievous, but content."

"Excellent. Now that you've finished another case for the eve, why not consider wandering down to that rather lively establishment on the corner, hmm?" Dauber said. " 'Twould do your soul good to mingle with—"

"The living?" Allie interrupted. "Come on, Daubs, we've had this discussion at least a hundred times. I don't want to mingle." She glared at the tall, lanky, somewhat bony Irishman clothed in a soft hat, suspenders, and black wool trousers that hung just a bit too high over ankle-high boots. He was one of the very first spirited souls she'd ever encountered. "I'm not a mingler." She grabbed her dinner dishes, which she'd left on the table, crossed the tiny kitchen, and loaded them into the dishwasher.

"Young lady, I happen to know you have a most cheery personality that any mortal with half a wit would enjoy to the fullest, if given a chance." Dauber grinned, the corners of his mouth pulling far into his cheeks. "I'm sure of it."

Allie crossed her arms and leaned against the sink. She stared at Dauber until his face turned a bright tomato red. She chuckled. "I am completely content doing what I'm doing, Daubs. Honestly, you sound like my mom and sisters. I don't need to hang out at the bar in hopes of meeting someone." She shrugged. "That's just not my style."

He quirked a reddish brow.

Hitching up her jeans, she walked to the part of the kitchen she referred to as her office, opened the one spare drawer, and pulled out a handful of papers. She held them up and shook them at Dauber. "See? All new cases. I have so much work to keep me busy I don't have *time* for mingling." She narrowed her eyes. "Even if I were a mingler."

Dauber made a tsk-tsking noise under his breath. "I daresay, young lady, that is the poorest of excuses." He peered at her. "You need a nice holiday, methinks. You're looking a bit peaked. Didn't your sister invite you for a bit of frolicking in merry old England?"

Allie frowned, but before she could respond, her laptop made a tinkling bell sound, announcing incoming mail. She raised her brow at Dauber. "See? Another inquiry." She sat cross-legged in the straight-backed chair and clicked the mouse over her in-box. She blinked.

"What is it, love?" Dauber asked.

Allie stared at the screen. "My first international inquiry." She continued to read. "Gabe MacGowan apparently has a few naughty spirits disturbing his pub and inn."

Before she could read further, the phone rang, and Allie picked up the cordless. "Morgan Investigations."

A deep, graveled, somewhat unsure voice came over the line. "Er, Allison Morgan?"

"Yes. Can I help you?" Allie glanced at Dauber and shrugged.

"Right. I'm Gabe MacGowan. I, uh, sent a post to your e-mail."

Allie smiled. *Nice accent.* "That's right. Scotland. I

just received it, actually. So what sort of disturbances have you been experiencing, Mr. MacGowan?''

The line went silent for a moment, then, ''Eh, well, I've had these, um . . .'' He cleared his throat and muttered something unintelligible, then, ''Oy, damn. I'm sorry for wastin' your time.''

''Wait, you're not—''

After a muttered something in a strange language, the line went dead.

''Another disbeliever, miss?'' Dauber asked.

Allie set the cordless on the counter beside her laptop. ''He'll call back.''

Dauber gave a winsome smile. ''They always do.''

Exactly eight minutes passed before the phone chirped.

With a quick peek at the caller ID, Allie smiled and answered the cordless. ''Hello again, Scotland.''

''I can't sell my bloody pub and inn because the lot of spooks living here run off every potential buyer who shows interest. They're drivin' me bloody crazy.'' A pause. ''Can you help me?'' Another pause, followed by another unknown word. ''I'll pay your airfare, your room and board, and your fee once I sell.''

Allie glanced at the stack of pending inquiries for her services. Twelve cases in all. Twelve irate and fedup humans trying to exorcise spirits from their homes or businesses. Not all of the claims were legit, but Allie's services included a thorough investigation. Not that she ever performed the first exorcism. While the mortals were the ones doing the hiring of her services, she actually used her skills of communicating with the dead to help the ghosts. She simply interpreted, helped the unsettled soul or souls with whatever issues they might have, find out just what made them haunt.

But pass up the chance to go to Scotland? Even with twelve cases pending, who in their right mind would do that?

"Ms. Morgan?"

Snapping out of her thoughts, Allie glanced at Dauber, who lifted a brow, and then she cleared her throat. "Yes, Mr. MacGowan. I'm sure I can help you. But first, I need you to send me the link to your pub and inn. You have a Web site, don't you?"

"Aye."

"Great. Just e-mail me the link, and I'll be in touch."

Mr. MacGowan sat silent on the line for a moment, then, "Your Web site describes you as a paranormal investigator. Does that mean you oust unwanted spirits, Ms. Morgan?"

Allie thought a moment. "I communicate with unsettled souls, Mr. MacGowan. It's been my experience that they haunt for a reason, and usually it's a reason even they aren't fully aware of, and I try to find out why. Haunting is all the control they have left in a mortal's world. I work with them to resolve whatever unsettled matters they may have. More times than not, their souls become mended and they move on."

Again, momentary silence. "I'll be waiting to hear from you, then."

They disconnected, and Allie sat for a moment and stared at her laptop screen. Wow! What an opportunity! She'd always wanted to encounter souls from the medieval era, not to mention a crumbly castle or two.

"You're going, then?"

Allie gave a nod. "I'd love to, but we'll have to see. I'm not so sure I sold my services to him. First, I'll check out his Web site, just to make sure the inn and pub is what he says—and that he's indeed the proprietor and not some sort of serial killer." She rubbed her chin. "I get the feeling he's pretty desperate. And legit."

Dauber mimicked Allie's movement and rubbed his

pointed chin. "I daresay those unsettled souls must be stirring up quite the mishmash. I wonder why."

Allie met the questioning gaze of her ghostly friend. What would she do without Dauber? She'd met him on her very first unofficial case in Raleigh. God, what was she? Nineteen? A sophomore in college, she'd stumbled across the willowy ghost sitting on the corner pew in the small campus chapel. A handful of other students was present. No one saw Dauber but Allie, and it was the first time she recognized the fact that she had a gift. *After her accident.* Their gazes had met, and Dauber had blinked several times in what Allie could only believe was dismay over having a mortal actually see him.

And they'd been fast friends ever since.

Allie pulled her thoughts back to the present. "I don't know, Dauber, but I bet it's going to be a lot of fun finding out just what's up in the Highlands of Scotland."

Odin's Thumb Inn and Pub
Sealladh na Mara
Northwest coast, Scotland
October, a week later

"Right. Fifty quid, then, lass."

Allie Morgan blinked. "Pardon me?" Quid? What the heck was that?

The cabdriver, a tall, lanky guy, around thirty, with a pair of soft brown eyes, grinned. "Your fare. Fifty sterling pounds." He winked. "Quid."

With a smile, Allie nodded. "Gotcha." Digging in her backpack, she pulled out the bills and paid the man. "Thanks for a spectacularly wonderful drive."

The driver's grin widened. "Aye, and thank you for

the spectacularly wonderful tip." He stuffed the bills in the console and inclined his head. "Stayin' at Odin's, then, are you?" he asked.

Allie gave a nod. "I sure am."

The cabbie studied her for a few seconds, then shook his head and grinned even wider.

"What?" Allie asked, gathering her bags. "What's so funny?"

The driver chuckled. "Oy, lass, I'm sorry." He lifted a brow. "Do you know much about Sealladh na Mara, then?"

Allie met his stare. "Nothing at all, actually. Why?"

The cabbie smiled and rubbed his hand over his jaw. "It has a reputation, you see. 'Tis cursed."

"Cursed? What do you mean?"

A mischievous grin tipped the corners of his mouth. " 'Tis a place for the ghosties, lass. They're drawn to it."

Allie smiled. "Is that so?"

The cabbie inclined his head to Odin's Thumb. "Have you met the owner yet?"

"Gabe MacGowan?" Allie shook her head. "Not in person. Why?"

He studied her a bit more. "Damn me, but he'll no' be expecting the likes of you."

Allie opened the door. "He's not expecting me at all. I'm a week early. That's why I just paid you a hundred American bucks to drive me here from Inverness."

The driver laughed. "Right. Let's get your bags, then."

Allie shook her head, pulled her knit cap over her ears, and stepped out of the cab. A fierce gust of coastal October wind hit her square in the face and she shivered. So Sealladh na Mara was cursed. *Perfect.* Slinging her pack over her shoulder, Allie grabbed her overnight bag, the camera bag, and shut the door. At the back of the cab, the driver pulled out her one suitcase.

"I'll take this in for you," he said.

"No, that's okay. It's not heavy." Allie grasped the handle. "Thanks, though."

With a shake of his head, the cabbie slid back into the front seat. He glanced at Allie and cocked a brow. "You understand that it's full of spooks, aye?"

Allie gave him a big smile. "I sure do."

"If you need a ride back to Inverness, you just give me a shout." With a laugh, the cabbie waved and drove off.

After a deep breath of crisp, briny air, Allie quickly took in her seaside surroundings. A slender green sign with the name SEALLADH NA MARA stood just at the top of the lane. Gaelic, she supposed, and she'd have to remember to ask Gabe MacGowan what it meant. White, traditional croft-style buildings, and others of weathered stone, lined the single-lane Main Street that rambled down to the wharf. Each establishment had a weather-beaten sign outside noting its business: a baker, a fishmonger, a small grocer, a post office, a few B and Bs. Halfway down the walkway stood one of Britain's landmarks: a red telephone booth. With the notion to explore later, and to call her mom and sisters to let them know she made it safely now, Allie turned and stared up at the sign hanging high above the single red-painted door of the three-storied, white-washed inn and pub. ODIN'S THUMB was written in Old English script at the top of the sign, with a colorful picture of an imposing Viking longboat, the sail a deep red with black stripes, the long wooden mast a big ole *thumb*. The words INN AND PUB, EST. 1741 were at the bottom. She smiled. *Perfect*.

After balancing all of her gear onto both shoulders,

Allie opened the door to the pub and was all but blown into the dim interior of Odin's Thumb. She set her suitcase off to the side and plopped her bags down beside it—

"I'm not staying here another moment!" a woman's voice shrieked.

Allie jumped, then stood there, against the wall, and took in the scene. Had she been any other woman, she'd probably have run screaming, too.

It was, after all, quite an interesting scene to behold. She almost had to pinch her lips together to keep from laughing. Instead, Allie simply watched.

Amidst the muted lamplight of the pub, flickering candles floated overhead in midair. A lady's old-fashioned parasol opened and closed rapidly, also in midair. Beer mugs and wineglasses zipped—yep, in midair—from one side of the room to the other, coming precariously close to the head of the shrieking woman. A suspicious-looking mist slipped around the bar stools, over the head of the woman whose face had turned dough-pasty, and at the same time the chairs began lifting and slamming back down on the floor.

"Arrrgh!" screamed the woman, who batted at the mist swirling about her and ran for the door.

"Wait, Mrs. Duigan, dunno go," a deep, graveled, and heavily accented voice said, the tall figure hurrying after her. "I can explain."

Mrs. Duigan paused briefly.

Then the dozens of fish appeared in midair, their tails flapping back and forth.

She let out one final scream and pushed her way out of the door.

The tall man—pretty darn good-looking, too, Allie thought—followed the frightened woman.

Allie peered out the door and watched Mrs. Duigan slam her car door and peel out. The man stared after her. With his back to Allie, he tilted his head, as if looking up to the sky, shoved his hands into the pockets of his dark brown corduroy pants, then looked down, staring at the sidewalk.

"Oy, we're in for it this time, aye?" said a male voice behind her.

" 'Twill be worth it, no doubt," said another.

"I dunno," said yet another, "he looks powerfully angry, he does."

Allie turned, and noticed the fish had disappeared, as had the floating candles and eerie mist. A handful of mischievous-looking spirits stood in a half circle, staring at her. A very much alive young boy stood in their midst. His little auburn brows furrowed together over a creamy complexion.

"Who are you?" the boy asked.

Allie looked each ghost in the eye. A friar. A pair of rather cute English lords. A dashing sea captain. A noblewoman wearing a large powdered wig . . . attached with a chin strap?

The sea captain's mouth quirked into a grin. "We've been waiting for you, lassie."

The heated look he gave her, from the top of her head to her feet, then slowly back to meet her eyes, left little wonder just what he was thinking. Allie could already tell he was going to be a handful.

"Allison Morgan?"

Allie turned and came face-to-face with the man who'd just chased after the fleeing woman. "Allie," she said, preferring her nickname. Now, up close, she blinked in surprise. Good-looking? No way. Not even close. *Ruggedly beautiful* fit more closely. Tall, at least six foot two, with close-clipped dark hair, a dusting of scruff on his jaw, green eyes, and generous lips, he was broad-shouldered and . . . utterly breathtaking.

His eyes held hers, intense, studying, evaluating. A

muscle flinched in his jaw, and Allie thought she'd never been more intimately weighed in her entire life. Her mouth went dry, and she finally cleared her throat. "Mr. MacGowan?" She smiled and held out her hand.

He glanced behind her briefly, and when she looked, she noticed the ghosts and boy had gone.

Ignoring her hand, the man gave a short nod and grabbed one of her bags. "Aye. And you're early," he said. Without asking permission, he reached down and grabbed her suitcase. He inclined his head. "This way, Ms. Morgan." He headed toward the back of the pub. Not once did he turn around to see if she'd followed.

"I could have gotten those," she said, but he paid no attention and kept walking. Hurrying past a long, polished mahogany bar, complete with the high-backed stools that had moments before lifted and slammed against the wide-planked wooden floors, Allie glimpsed the barely there figure of a bartender wearing suspenders and dark trousers, wiping down the tables with a white cloth. He tipped his soft hat by the bill and grinned, and she returned the smile and shrugged.

When Allie turned, she plowed into the very broad back of Gabe MacGowan. "Oops. Sorry."

Gabe stared down at her, those green eyes hard and set. He didn't frown, nor did he smile. He remained completely aloof. "Dunna make friends with them. I'm paying you to make them leave."

Allie met his stare, unhindered by its intensity. Instead of frowning, or telling him to stick it where the sun don't shine, she gave him a wide, friendly smile. "I'll keep that in mind."

He stared a moment longer, scowled, then turned and headed up the narrow staircase, the old wood creaking with each of his heavy steps.

Allie followed, thinking things could be a lot worse than walking behind Gabe MacGowan's grumpy ole self as he climbed a set of stairs. She wondered why such a gorgeous guy had such a somber, unfriendly personality.

She'd tell him later that the one thing to remember when dealing with the unliving is you can't make them do anything they don't want to. Especially leave.

Allie turned and glanced over her shoulder. The ghosts from before stood at the bottom of the steps. Grinning.

The sea captain, a tall, swarthy guy with sun-streaked brown hair pulled into a queue, and a swash-buckling goatee, gave her a roguish smile and tipped his tricorn hat.

Throwing him a grin, she turned and hurried after Gabe. Allie decided right then and there that the decision to cross the Atlantic to oust a handful of mischievous spirits from their old haunt had been the smartest one she'd ever made.

Getting to know the ghosts of Odin's Thumb would be exciting. But deciphering just what made stuffy ole Gabe MacGowan tick would be something else altogether . . .

Chapter 2

"This place is fantastic. Did you grow up here?"
Gabe didn't turn around. "Aye."

"Great. Then you should have plenty of experiences with the souls residing here. Have they been here long, as well? Oh—better yet, did you grow up with them? I can't wait to hear all about it."

No doubt. Giving little more than a grunt of acknowledgment, Gabe continued to the end of the hallway and stopped at the last door. He fished the key from his pocket, stuck it in the lock, turned the knob, and pushed open the door. "Your room, Ms. Morgan."

"Thank you," she said. "You can call me Allie."

Gabe simply inclined his head toward the open door.

As she started to pass, she paused and stared up at him a moment, head cocked and with the sort of mischievous light in her eyes that suggested a thorough feminine once-over, and then turned and stepped into the room.

Gabe followed and set her belongings in the corner. "The toilet's across the hall."

"Okay." Walking over to the window facing the loch, Allie Morgan parted the curtain and peered out. She stared a moment, and just as Gabe was about to speak, she said, "This place is truly breathtaking. Why

on earth do you want to leave, Mr. MacGowan?"
Turning, she leaned against the windowpane and
crossed her arms over her chest.

Gabe stuffed his hands into his pockets and studied
her. A ridiculous amount of untamed blond hair spilled
over her shoulders, and her wide blue eyes didn't show
the least bit of intimidation. Elegantly slender, she certainly didn't look like a paranormal investigator.

The photo on her Web site had caught his eye.
Pleasant enough, aye. But there was something else,
something in her eyes, maybe.

She looked far more fetching in person.

That made him scowl.

He cleared his throat. "No offense, Ms. Morgan,
but that's none of your business." He gave a nod.
"Supper's at seven. We'll talk then."

Just as he turned to go, he noticed one corner of
her mouth tip upward in an amused grin. Or a smirk.

Closing the door behind him, Gabe stormed down
the corridor, stopped, and turned back. He'd forgotten
to give her the bloody key. He reached the door and
without much thought, opened it.

Just as Allison Morgan had her sweater pulled over
the top of her head.

She froze, arms up, sweater covering her face, a
black bra with pink dots her only covering. With each
breath, her chest rose and fell.

Gabe's scowl deepened.

"Your key," he said, and set it down on the mantel.

"Thanks," Allison Morgan replied, her voice muf-
fled by the heavy wool.

Gabe's gaze lingered for a moment; then he left and
shut the door.

He didn't make it to the end of the corridor before
abruptly pulling up short. 'Twas either that or walk
through the bloody spirit blocking his path.

Gabe met the sea captain's stare but didn't say a word.

Captain Justin Catesby lifted one brow. "Fetching lass, that Ms. Morgan." He leaned in, his brows pulled close and making a fierce crinkle in the space between his eyes. "Aye?"

Gabe said nothing.

The captain stroked his chin. "I'd watch me steps, were I you, boy. 'Tisn't becoming to take advantage of an unsuspecting maid."

Gabe stared and almost didn't give the cocky ghost the satisfaction of a reply. 'Twas a sight to behold, for certain, but he hadn't meant to. Quite the opposite, actually. The girl should have locked the bloody door.

The very last thing he wanted or needed to do was engage in anything other than what he'd hired Allison Morgan for. A business transaction. Nothing more.

"So she's who ye hired to oust us, aye?"

Gabe looked Justin in the eye. "Unless you've decided since an hour ago to stop chasin' away the buyers?"

The captain gave a crooked smile.

With a glare and a nod, Gabe stepped round the captain and started down the stairs. He'd screwed up enough of his life—and Jake's. No more. His decision was made.

He really had no other choice.

"Ye canna run away from yer problems, lad," Catesby called behind him. "They'll just catch up with you."

Gabe ignored him.

Reaching the bottom of the stairs, Gabe made his way to the kitchen. The usual patrons would be in soon for supper—including the not-so-new one unpacking upstairs. Not only did he have to help prepare the cod and chips, but he had to prepare himself. For *her*.

No doubt the American would talk his bloody ears off. *As long as she does her job* . . .

Allie dropped to her knees and pushed the empty suitcase under the bed.

"I take it you had a satisfactory flight?"

"Whoa!" Allie said, jumping hard enough to bonk her head on the wooden bed rail. She sat back on her heels and rubbed the back of her head, glaring at her unexpected friend. "Dauber, how on earth did you get here?"

Dauber scratched a place under his cap and shrugged. "Difficult to say, actually." He gave her a crooked grin. "Ghosts do what they do for no good reason. I suppose I must have desired it powerfully bad, aye?"

Allie stood. "Yeah, you must have just wished yourself here." She sat on the bed. "I'm not so sure you'll be well received, though. The owner is quite determined to get rid of his own mischievous spirits, although I haven't gotten to the bottom of why, exactly. I doubt he'll want another addition."

Dauber perched upon the chest of drawers. "So you've met them, then? The others?"

"Briefly. And in that short amount of time I can tell at least one of them is some kind of naughty."

Crossing one bony leg over his knee, Dauber met her gaze. "Mischievous spirits you can handle. But what of *him*?"

Allie rose and walked to the tallboy chest she'd placed her clothes in and pulled out a black turtleneck and a clean pair of jeans. "*Him* who?"

"The mortal, love. How difficult will *he* be to manage?"

With a sigh, Allie laid her clean clothes on the bed. "I'm not sure, Daubs. He isn't the friendliest of guys. Grumpy, really, and about the only expression I've seen on his face is a frown."

Frown or no frown, she purposely left out how *dead sexy* the proprietor of Odin's Thumb was. *Good grief.* The intensity of that green stare unnerved her—although she thought she hid it quite well. Nice, strong jaw, though, and that heavy Scottish brogue, which at times completely puzzled her, was made even more appealing by the deep, smoky pitch—

"Allie?"

She blinked, turned, and grabbed clean panties and a bra from another drawer. Tossing them both on the bed, she glanced over at her nearly transparent friend. "Yes?"

"Tsk-tsk, love. Lost in your thoughts, hmm?"

Allie mock frowned. "Mind your beeswax, pal. I was just thinking about what I might learn tonight."

The crooked grin on Dauber's face stretched deep across his cheeks. "Indeed."

"Well," Allie said with a clap. "I am going to shower and then rest before dinner." She cocked her head. "What are you going to do? Tell me you're not going to sit in here and watch me sleep."

Dauber flicked an imaginary bit of something from his sleeve. "Whilst a favorite pastime of mine, indeed, the watching over of you, I think instead I shall wander down to the wharf. Quite an interesting town, so it seems." He gave a nod and another smile. "Until later, love."

Dauber faded until he disappeared.

"Bye," Allie said to herself. She smiled at the space of air her friend had just occupied, scooped up her overnight bag containing shampoo, conditioner, razor, lotion, soap, and other girl stuff, and stepped out into the hallway. She scooted across to the bathroom, anxious to wash the ten hours of airport/airplane germs from her hair and body. Then, she thought, a nice cozy nap before dinner . . .

Slowly, Allie cracked open first one eye, then the other. At first foggy, her vision adjusted to the dim, hazy late-afternoon light in the room.

As well as to the small figure standing beside her bed. A young boy. Staring. *Scowling.*

Allie blinked, and for a split second the outline of another figure—a woman?—stood directly behind the boy. It quickly vanished.

"Are you here to oust me mates from my home?"

Allie turned on her side and propped her head on the heel of her hand. She studied the boy. Auburn hair, with an adorable cowlick just off-center at the forehead, a creamy complexion, and the widest, bluest pair of eyes she'd ever seen. A half dozen tiny freckles trekked over his nose.

At present, those very blue eyes scrunched into an accusing stare.

"Well, are you?" he said in a strong Highland brogue.

Allie looked him directly in the eye. "I wouldn't think of it." She smiled, sat up, and stuck out her hand. "My name is Allie."

The young boy, who looked to be about six or seven, gave her another in-depth inspection, and gripped her hand in a surprisingly strong shake. "Aye. And I'm Jake." He cocked his head to the side. "Are you going to stay here, then?"

"For a while." Allie rubbed her jaw. "You're the boy I saw downstairs when I first came in. Do you live here?"

"Aye." He toed a knot in the wooden floor. "Me

mates says you are here to oust them." He narrowed his eyes. "You're no', are you?"

"What do you think?"

One narrow shoulder lifted in a shrug. "Me da says aye."

"Indeed, miss," a voice said from out of nowhere. "We do know for a fact your employed intentions."

Had Allie not been completely used to ghosts and spirits materializing out of thin air, she would have yelped when the two young spectered gentlemen sifted through the wall and came to stand before her. Instead, she gave a short nod and smiled. "How do you do?"

Both gave a slight bow, and the shorter one, who still topped her by several inches, met her gaze. "I fear I've seen better days, miss. Himself has indeed employed you, aye?"

"Himself?" she asked.

"Gabe MacGowan," the other answered. "Proprietor of this inn and pub."

Allie nodded. "Right. Well, yes, he did."

"So you *are* here to oust them?" Jake said.

Allie turned to the young boy. "Well, no—"

"Run along and wash up, lad. Supper's ready."

At the deep, gruff voice, Allie turned. The two ghostly men had vanished. Gabe stood in the doorway, arms crossed, expression stern. He didn't make eye contact with Allie.

Jake looked at Allie, closed his eyes briefly, and gave a very grown-up, very aristocratic nod. "Until later, miss." Then he scrambled from the room.

Allie rubbed her arms. "Cute kid. Your son?"

Gabe studied Allie for several seconds before answering. His face revealed nothing but indifference. "Aye. He willna be botherin' you again." He turned to go. "Supper's ready. We'll discuss your employment matters afterward."

"Wait," Allie said, rising and walking toward the door. "He wasn't bothering me at all."

Gabe stopped. Green eyes regarded her, and finally, he gave a nod—very similar to Jake's. "Verra well." He glanced at her arms, which she continued to rub with vigor. He frowned. "I'll show you where the peat is kept so you won't bloody freeze to death up here."

With that, he left.

Allie stared after him, shook her head, and blew out a gusty sigh. "I just don't get him. He's so, so . . ."

Stodgy, a deep, amused voice whispered in her ear.

Allie shrugged. Maybe. Or maybe not . . .

With that thought in mind, she left the room, her prepaid phone card in her pocket, to call her mom and sisters before the time grew too late.

Chapter 3

"I dunna want to leave, Da," Jake said. "Captain Catesby and the others are me best mates."

Gabe inspected his son's face in the mirror. They'd been Gabe's best mates as a lad, as well. Still were, truth be told, but he'd never say it out loud. "You missed a spot." He inclined his head. "Just there, at your chin."

Jake took his washcloth and scrubbed at the smudge. "I dunna want to leave Sealladh na Mara, though. Da—"

"Stop your whining, lad, and finish up here. We'll talk about this later."

With a scowl, the boy met his gaze with eyes that reminded Gabe every day of Jake's mother. "Aye." And with that he hurried off.

Gabe stared at his own face in the mirror. Rubbing his eyes, he thought he looked as though he hadn't slept for a solid week.

Actually, it'd been a bloody month. Ever since the dreams had returned . . .

He rubbed a hand over his jaw. Paler than usual skin. Scruffy cheeks. Dark circles beneath his eyes. He looked like the living dead.

He wondered what the American thought.

That thought pulled his mouth into a frown.

After a quick wash, he stomped out of the two-room apartment he and Jake shared on the second floor of Odin's Thumb and made his way to the kitchen.

As he entered the dim interior of the pub, his gaze landed on Ms. Morgan straight away. Perched on a bar stool and cast in the amber glow of the Victorian lamp beside her, with that blond mass of curls pulled back and standing out stark against the black jumper she wore, she spoke with her hands as she animatedly talked to Willy, the grumpy fishmonger from next door who never spoke more than a few grunts of acknowledgment to Gabe.

Just then, old Willy barked out a laugh. Gabe blinked. Willy *never* laughed.

"Come, lad, and give me a hand with this, aye?"

Gabe broke from his thoughts at the request and turned to his aunt, Wee Mary—preferring Wee rather than Aunt—whose gray-shot red head poked through a crack in the kitchen door. "If ye can stop ogling the lass long enough to help us with this cod?" With a devilish grin, Wee Mary stepped back into the kitchen.

Gabe pushed open the door and followed his auntie, who came no higher than his ribs. She threw him one of the heavy canvas aprons hanging on an iron hook against the far wall. Slipping it over his head, he tied it round his back. "I'm no' ogling, woman."

Wee Mary simply grinned. "Fetch me that stack of cod, lad, and aye, ye were, too, ogling, and I'll take no arguments from you."

Gabe did as she asked and ignored her fun. Grabbing the large cutting board of fresh cod fillets, he set them next to the stove where his aunt had a large cast-iron kettle filled with hot oil for frying.

"Your mum tells me she saw a lady screaming in terror from the pub this afternoon," Mary said. She pointed to a stack of plates. "Pull those down, will you, love?"

Gabe did so and nodded. "Aye. Fifth one this month. The captain and his lot and their dodgy tricks."

Battering several fillets, Wee Mary lowered each piece into the hot oil with a pair of tongs. The resounding sizzle and crackle waved through the room. "Have you ever thought you might verra well be making the wrong choice, lad?"

Gabe gave his aunt a frown. "Dunna start with that, aye? We've been through it enough times." He set the fry screen atop the pot and resisted the urge to let out a long sigh. Aye, he thought he made an abundance of mistakes. Every bloody day. Where Jake was concerned, he was always questioning himself. But this decision was *right*. His son needed lads his own age to play with, not a lot of old ghosties.

And Christ, the nightmares. They had returned, plaguing not only his nights but his days, as well. And he knew why . . .

Wee Mary tsked. " 'Tis a hard head ye have, nephew. A hard one, indeed." She sighed, then pointed a wooden spoon toward the door. "Your ghost buster out there seems to have charmed that stodgy old fishmonger." She elbowed Gabe in the ribs. "Quite a feat, wouldna ye say?"

Gabe grunted in agreement.

"I'd bet my knickers she'll charm your grumpy self before it's over." She lifted a brow. "Does the lass know just what she's getting into here at Odin's?" Mary asked. "Has she met the lot?"

With a heavy set of steel tongs, Gabe settled large fried slabs of cod on the inn's plain white plates. "Aye, she knows, and aye, she's met most of them, I think.

Including Jake. And she's no' from a dating service, Wee. She's a paranormal investigator. A professional."

"Och, that scalawag Catesby no doubt has his eye on her already. She's quite bonny, and you know how the captain is with the lasses," she said, ignoring Gabe's comment.

Again, he grunted.

From another boiling pot of oil, Gabe lifted the screened basket of chips and clicked it into place to drain. A minute later, he released it and heaped a mound onto each plate of cod.

"Now shoo, and get those patrons their dinner. And wipe that scowl off your handsome face before you frighten someone."

Gabe grabbed several plates of food, balanced them across his forearm, and lifted two more with his free hand. "How long is Katey going to be out?" The girl was much more efficient with serving than he was.

"She had a baby, Gabe MacGowan. It'll be several more weeks."

Stifling a curse, Gabe pushed out of the kitchen and started across the dim interior of Odin's. The usual patrons greeted him as he set down their food, including Jake, who sat by Chadrick Ferguson, Sealladh na Mara's postmaster, and by Gabe's third trip out, he had served everyone. Except Allison Morgan, that is.

Glancing around the room, he found her sitting in a corner alcove, alone, and staring out the window. He stepped back into the kitchen, grabbed two more plates of fish and chips, and made his way through the dwindling crowd toward her. As he walked up to the table, she turned and smiled, as if she had not been in deep thought. Gabe knew better. 'Twas a big, bright, sincere smile, he noticed, with lots of white teeth showing, and for some reason that irritated him.

Setting the plates down, he eased into the seat facing her and gave a nod toward her food. "Supper." He couldn't help but remember their encounter earlier, when he'd walked into her room.

"Thanks." Lifting her fork, she stabbed a single plain chip and popped it into her mouth.

Gabe shook his head, grabbed the brown sauce and vinegar from the caddy, and gave a generous squeeze of both to his chips. He set the condiments before her. "Try that."

She did, and nodded her approval. "Dee-lish." She dug into her fish. After a few bites, she wiped her mouth, tipped her head to the side, and studied him. And 'twas with far too much intensity for his liking. The glow from the lamplight made her eyes twinkle mischief. "So, tell me, Mr. MacGowan, just what sort of trouble are your Odin's Thumb tenants stirring up? They seem to be rather friendly, actually. And more importantly"—she leaned forward and met his gaze— "why are you losing sleep over it?"

An intense, smoky look came over Gabe's face, complete with narrowing of eyes and clenching of jaw. He didn't look away when she continued to stare; instead he set down his fork, finished chewing, and took a long pull of water from an icy mug. Green eyes met Allie's over the rim of that glass before he set it down and wiped his mouth.

She found it odd that he was about the only Scotsman in the pub who wasn't drinking a pint of beer.

"There's no' much to tell, Ms. Morgan. The inn and pub are haunted—you've met the spirits, and I want them out."

Allie rather liked how his *out* sounded more like *oot*, and how his r's rolled around *spirits*.

She sipped her soda. "Why?"

Gabe blinked. "They're making a bloody nuisance of themselves by scaring off the potential buyers."

"Why?"

He frowned. "Why what?"

"Why do you want to sell the pub and inn?"

The smoky look returned. "That's none of your business, lass."

Allie studied Gabe's face. Fading dark half-moons lay just beneath both eyes, evidence of too little sleep, or none at all. She couldn't help but wonder what had made such a vibrant, young, good-looking guy so uptight and aloof.

She threw him another smile. "How badly do you want them out?" Not that she could make them leave, of course. But she needed to know his reasons anyway. It would help when interacting with the Odin's Thumb gang.

She had a feeling Gabe might be too stubborn to acknowledge all those reasons.

Then Gabe surprised her.

With a resigned sigh, he leaned back in his chair, studied her for a moment, and scrubbed his jaw with his hand. An unintelligible word emerged on a frustrated exhale, and he met her gaze. "I'm raising Jake alone. He's young and impressionable, and needs a more stable environment than living in a pub with a ghostly lot of bad influences. Those are my reasons, Ms. Morgan. I need the ghosts out. Or at least to keep bloody quiet. I canna move if I dunna sell." He leaned forward, his stare penetrating. "I need your help."

It was the first time in a long while Allie didn't have an easy comeback. What could she say to all that? Gabe's sincerity—and desperation—struck her hard, although she still thought he was keeping something from her. Why wouldn't he? It wasn't as though they were friends, or that they'd even known each other for a while.

They hardly knew each other at all.

That struck her, too. Gabe MacGowan was putting quite a lot of faith in her abilities.

Damn.

With a fork, she pushed a bite of fish around her plate, stabbed it, and popped it in her mouth. As she chewed, she stared at the man across the table. A dusting of dark stubble the color of his short-clipped hair covered his jaw, and green eyes bored into hers. Great lips, and she could only imagine how those lips could form a fantastic smile.

She'd not seen him do that yet.

She hoped desperately that she would.

With a napkin, she wiped her mouth. "I'll help you, Mr. MacGowan, but I'll need to know a little more about the pub and inn, including all the inhabitants." She grinned. "A little about your history with them wouldn't hurt, either. The more I know, the more I'll be able to do my job. Savvy?"

Gabe stared at her for several seconds, no blinking of eyelids, or averting of gazes, or twitching of lips, before finally giving the briefest of nods. "Fair enough. What exactly do you need to know?"

Chapter 4

Gabe scratched his chin. He studied the American sitting across the table with close scrutiny.

She'd just polished off the last of a fried Mars bar. Her second one.

Where the bloody hell did she put it all?

No doubt if Wee Mary brought the girl out another, she'd eat it, as well.

Allie Morgan licked the spoon, met his gaze, and grinned. "Those are the best things I've eaten in my entire life."

Gabe grunted. "I can tell." No' shy about eating, that one. Quite different from most females he'd encountered.

If she heard the comment, she ignored it, and instead set down the fork and leaned back in her chair. "So you've grown up with Captain Catesby and the rest. They've lived here for how long?"

"Centuries."

She rubbed her chin with her index finger. "And the whole village knows about them?"

"Everyone in Sealladh na Mara has grown up with them. They're like family. We've sort of a reputation."

"For being cursed?"

Gabe shrugged. "I'm no' sure *cursed* is the right word, but it's well known in the Highlands that Sealladh na Mara is a haven for spirits."

Allie cocked her head. "Why is that?"

He gave an indifferent shrug. "Who knows? 'Tis an old pirates' cove, wi' plenty of lore and mystery shrouding it."

Allie rubbed her chin. "And everyone simply . . . accepts it?"

Gabe met her gaze directly. "You seem to."

"It's what I do."

" 'Tis what we do, as well."

Leaning back, Allie studied him with those wide blue eyes. "Well then, if they're like family, and everyone accepts the spirits, and you've grown up with them, why do you want to move away? Why do you want to sell Odin's?" She held up her hand. "And don't say it's none of my business. You hired me to help you. So it's all my business."

He hardly had anything to say to that.

He wondered briefly what her response would be if she knew his dead wife was haunting him every single night . . .

"Mr. MacGowan?"

Snapping from his thoughts, Gabe looked at her straight-on. "As I said before, my son needs a more stable environment. 'Tis bad enough he's without a mum. He deserves to be with children his own age."

Allie cocked her head. "Isn't he with children his own age at school?"

Gabe frowned. "Aye. But at home, his best mate is a three-hundred-year-old pirate." He pinched the bridge of his nose, then stared at Allie Morgan. "You have my reason for wanting to move. I hired you to convince the Odin's lot to at least keep bloody quiet whilst I show the place. Anything else you need to know, ask them. They can all speak for themselves."

Before Allie Morgan could answer, Wee Mary came

through the kitchen door and made her way to the alcove. She stopped, patted Gabe on the shoulder, and gave Allie Morgan a large smile. "Well, loves, 'tis time for me to call it a day." She glanced down at Allie's empty plate. "Quite an appetite you have there, lass, although I canna see where you put it all. You're as thin as a reed."

"I stuffed myself," Allie said, grinning. "They were fantastic."

Wee Mary nodded. "Aye, and 'tis this sulking brute here ye can thank for that. 'Tis his specialty."

Gabe thought he'd choke his beloved aunt later.

Allie Morgan simply lifted a dark blond brow.

"Right. Well, I'm off," Wee Mary said. "I'll be here early in the morn, Gabe, along with your mother." She winked at Allie. "Tomorrow's Sunday. Traditional pot roast with potatoes and peas. Scrumptious."

Allie smiled. "I can't wait."

Mary glanced at him. "With young Katey out on maternity leave, we'll be here about sevenish, then." With a wave, Wee Mary left.

Leaving him and Allie Morgan alone.

He briefly wondered where the others were. 'Twasna like them at all to stay invisible for such a lengthy time. Usually, they were mingling amongst the dinner patrons.

"So your parents live here?" she asked.

"Aye."

"Any siblings?"

Gabe looked at her. "A brother and a sister, both away at university. My da is an offshoreman. My grandda lives just up the shore a ways. Wee Mary is my auntie." He lifted a brow. "Anything else?"

Allie shifted in her seat. "So all your family lives here, the spirits have resided here for centuries, and

they're like family. Seems like a pretty stable environment for a kid to me." She studied him hard. "I think
there's another reason and you're just not sharing."

Gabe frowned.

Allie lifted a brow.

Neither said a word.

Finally, she sighed. "Are you shorthanded?"

Gabe blinked.

"You know." Allie smiled. "Low on staff?"

Gabe nodded, relieved that she'd dropped the uncomfortable subject for now. "Right. For just a wee
bit longer."

Allie nodded, then glanced at his glass. "I don't
think I've ever heard of a Scotsman who doesn't enjoy
a pint or two." Her lips quirked.

He couldna help himself. He stared at those lips.
They looked verra soft and with a sexy curve, just at
the corners. Quickly, he cleared his throat. "Mayhap
you shouldna stereotype the Scotsman, aye?"

Her gaze dropped to his own mouth. "Aye."

"Lo, what have we here, then?"

"Och, methinks they call it a *date* nowadays, aye?"

Gabe pinched the bridge of his nose. From the far
wall emerged the duelers, followed by, well, the rest
of the bloody specters of Odin's Thumb.

"Fetchin' lass, MacGowan," said Ramsey. He conjured a chair and plopped himself into it. "I hope
we're not interrupting?"

Gabe frowned. "Of course not."

"Stand up and introduce yourself properly, young
man," the friar said, frowning. He whispered, "Remember your manners."

Ramsey jumped up.

As the Odin's Thumb spirits gathered round, Gabe
nodded toward Allie, who casually leaned back in her
chair, meeting each ghost's gaze without hesitation.

"Ms. Morgan, meet the very reason you're here, and I pray to Christ you can talk sense into them. Friar Digby, Mademoiselle Bedeau, Lords Ramsey and Killigrew. Captain Catesby you've already met."

That swashbuckling fool made a big show of throwing his arm across his waist and giving Allie a low bow. The sea captain—a pirate to Gabe's way of thinking—glanced up and smiled at her. " 'Tis beyond my pleasure, lass, a score of times over. Welcome to Odin's Thumb. And call me Justin."

Gabe thought he just might be ill.

Allie smiled, and for the first time Gabe noticed a small dimple in her right cheek. "Thank you very much."

The duelers pushed their way to stand before Allie and take their turn. "Baden Killigrew, ma'am," the one said. "Glad to make your acquaintance."

"Indeed," the other said, giving a bow, "and I'm Christopher Ramsey."

The friar approached and gave a short nod. He pushed his cowl down and ran a hand through his hair. "Drew Digby, lady," he said with a smile. He turned, grasping the mademoiselle's elbow. "Come here, love. She's not here to exorcise us." Under his breath, he said, "At least I hope not."

Mademoiselle stepped forward, pushed aside a bit of that enormous silk dress, and dropped a formal curtsey. "Lovely to meet you, *chère*. I am Mademoiselle Bedeau." She winked. "You may call me Elise."

"And you may call me Allie," Allie Morgan said. "Nice to meet all of you. I have loads of questions to ask."

Gabe took in the scene before him. Five spirits surrounded a modern-day lass who sat and grinned and carried on conversation as though 'twas all quite normal.

To him, it was.

But to see another, an *outsider*, someone no' from

Sealladh na Mara, taking it all in as though 'twas everyday life made him pause and consider. He ran his hand over the back of his neck. Odd, indeed.

Standing, he nodded to the group and glanced down at Allie. "Ms. Morgan, I'll leave you to this motley crew for the night. You can leave the peat as it is. 'Twill die down on its own." He turned to leave.

"Good night," Allie said behind him.

With a quick glance over his shoulder, he gave a short nod and continued on his way.

"Aye, good night," said a masculine voice struggling to sound exaggeratedly high pitched and feminine.

The group burst into laughter.

Crossing the pub, Gabe locked up for the night. At the stairs, he turned and glanced back at the alcove.

Allie must have sensed that he'd stopped, for she glanced in his direction, and smiled.

Gabe held her gaze for a moment—unable to bloody help himself, actually—then he turned and started up the stairs.

Mayhap an outsider such as Allie could talk some bloody sense into the Odin's Thumb lot.

He could only hope.

Allie watched Gabe MacGowan's big self lope up the stairs. A funny sensation started in her stomach, and whether it was the big cod fillet, heap of potatoes covered in brown sauce and vinegar, plus two fried Mars bars that caused said sensation, or . . .

No. It was definitely all that food.

She was *not* attracted to a virtual stranger.

Not, not, not.

Especially one who lived an ocean away. One could think another was attractive without *being* attracted. Right?

Captain Catesby slid into the chair very recently

vacated by Odin's Thumb's proprietor. With ease, he leaned casually back and stared at her with a long, alluring gaze. "So, lass. Are you spoken for, then?"

Groans went up all around.

Allie studied the captain, who must've been quite the rogue in his day. Tall, lean, early thirties, with that wavy, sun-streaked brown hair that hung to his shoulders, a sharp goatee the same color, and dressed in a garnet shirt that tied at the neck (but which wasn't tied at all and left a chiseled chest exposed), a long leather overcoat, and a pair of silver pistols tucked into a wide leather belt. Earlier, she'd noticed dark pants and wide-cuffed leather boots.

A *pirate*, she thought.

A sexy one at that.

A wide grin stretched across the captain's face, exposing straight white teeth, and Allie wondered if he could read her mind.

"I'd say by that inquisitive way you're perusing my person that's a nay, you aren't spoken for, then?"

Allie narrowed her eyes to slits. The others chuckled.

The gleam in Captain Cates' eye was nothing short of devilment.

"Do not let that rake trouble you, love," Mademoiselle Bedeau said. She pulled at a dangling earring. "He tries to intimidate all the females he encounters."

"Aye, but it doesna always work, I'm afraid," the captain replied. He grinned, wolflike and predatory and slam-packed full of sex appeal. "Or does it?"

"Is anything amiss here, Allie?"

Allie turned to find Dauber sifting through the kitchen wall. He walked over to the group and met Allie's gaze. "Are you all right?"

"Bloody hell, she brought her own ghostie," Lord Ramsey said. "I daresay Himself knows nothing about it."

Justin Catesby half rose, nodded, and introduced himself. "Catesby of Aberdeen, sir. And you are?"

"Alexander Dauber, at present of Chicago, previously of county Cork, Ireland," Dauber said, returning a nod. "I came here of my own accord."

"Dauber is my close friend," Allie said, giving the older ghost a smile. "He's like a father to me."

"Well then, sir," the friar said, conjuring up a chair, "you are most welcome here amongst the likes of us. Take your reprieve with us, if you will. I'm Drew Digby, by the by."

"And I'm Elise," said the mademoiselle. "Welcome to Sealladh na Mara, sir."

Dauber gave the woman one of his cheek-to-cheek smiles. *The flirt.*

Lord Killigrew leaned forward, elbows resting on wide-spread knees. "We were just about to discuss the issues at hand, Dauber." He looked at Allie. "What plans do you have, Ms. Morgan?"

Allie glanced at everyone in the room. Expectant, ghostly eyes blinked, waited. She drew a deep breath. "You all know why Mr. MacGowan hired me, so let's get down to the business of you telling *me* just what's going on, okay?" She looked directly at the captain. "I'm not a ghost ouster; I'm an interpreter. An investigator. But I can't help if I don't know everything, and Gabe MacGowan isn't telling me much. So let's start with you, Captain Catesby."

He gave a nod. "Indeed. What we have here, Ms. Morgan, is a bullheaded man wanting to not only leave but take with him his son, Jake, who doesn't want to leave." He leaned back. " 'Tis the wrong decision. It's that simple."

"And so we're taking precautionary steps to make sure the lad doesn't make that wrong decision," said Lord Ramsey.

"Aye, although it doesn't seem to be working quite the way we wanted," said the friar. "Young Gabe is determined to sell Odin's Thumb and take Jake to Inverness to grow up amongst the living."

A sniffle escaped Mademoiselle Bedeau, and she fretted a white lace hanky between her hands. "*Oui*, and I could not bear to see the little lad go, or his father." She dabbed at her eyes. "We've loved Gabe since he was a babe. I've become so"—she hiccupped—"attached."

A round of "ayes" sounded in the room.

"I dunna want to go!"

Everyone turned to see young Jake scampering down the stairs. Dressed in long blue pajamas and socks, his hair at the cowlick standing straight up, he must have waited for Gabe to go to bed before sneaking out. He hurried across the room and scooted into the chair next to Captain Catesby.

"I'm no' goin' anywhere," he said, his western Highlands' accent as thick as his father's. He put both hands on the table and leaned forward, eyes clapped on to Allie's. "Please, lady, dunna let my da take me away."

Allie glanced at the semitransparent faces staring at her. All of them pleaded with her for help.

"Please help us," the friar said. "We could not stand it without the lads."

"Aye, Himself knows not what he's doing," said Lord Killigrew. "He's grief-ridden, and ever since—"

"Shush now, Baden," Mademoiselle Bedeau warned. " 'Tisn't our place."

Allie glanced at the captain. By the look on his face, he knew something. Something *she* needed to know.

And yet somehow she could tell that the conversation needed to be dropped. *For now*.

The subtle nod the captain gave her confirmed it.

She'd have to find out in private just exactly what it was that the mademoiselle thought wasn't *their place* to speak about. In front of Jake wasn't the right time.

"Can't you do *something*?" Jake said once more. "Please?"

Five ghostly faces pleaded with her. Even Dauber carried the same expression.

How could she refuse?

Besides, they knew the MacGowans much better than she did. They'd been here for centuries. They'd watched him grow from a baby to the man he was now.

Something was definitely up, and Allie was determined to find out what that thing was. *Eventually*.

She stood, scooted out of her chair, and paced around the expecting souls. All from different centuries. All with one obvious common denominator.

They loved Gabe and Jake MacGowan and didn't want them to leave.

Before she said anything at all, she glanced at Justin Catesby. A slow smile spread across his handsome face. Damn him, he *knew* her answer.

"Stop looking so smug, Catesby."

The rogue threw back his head and laughed.

"So you'll help us, then?" Friar Digby asked, rubbing his hands together and smiling. "Truly?"

Allie massaged the back of her neck and blew out a gusty sigh. "I hope I don't regret this. Part of me feels like I'm crossing the line into business that's not my own. But . . . yeah." She smiled at little Jake. "I'll help."

Before she knew it, the kid launched out of his chair, ran straight to her, and threw his arms around her waist. With his head to her belly, he muttered, "I'll never forget this, lady!"

She smoothed the cowlick at his forehead down

with her fingers, but it sprang right back up. Allie smiled. "I'm sure I won't, either. Now come on. Let's get you back to bed before your dad wakes up and finds you gone. Then we'll both be dead meat." She glanced at the Odin's lot. "This little get-together isn't over yet. If you want my help I'll need a complete history of your life—and unlife—from each and every one of you. Fair enough?"

Five "ayes" met her ears.

As Allie and Jake, with Dauber right behind them, started up the stairs, she looked over her shoulder. All five Odin's Thumb souls stared after her. Grinning.

One more than the others.

Captain Catesby gave her a knowing nod and a wide smile.

Allie prayed she'd just made the right decision.

After all, what did she have to lose but airfare and a few bucks?

Chapter 5

Just as Allie and Jake reached the room, the door flung open and Gabe stood there, wearing nothing more than a pair of faded jeans and a frown. *Scowling*.

Allie noticed Dauber had disappeared.

Gabe glanced down at his son and inclined his head. "Go to bed, lad."

Jake scurried into the room.

In the dimmed corridor lamplight, Allie met Gabe's hard gaze—a difficult task, truth be told, when the man had a six-pack of chiseled abs bared to the world. She cleared her throat. "Sorry. We must have woken him up. I was just on my way to bed—"

In the shadows, his rugged face took on a sharp angle. "That ghostly lot of busybodies has him taking on crazy notions of staying here. Dunna undo everything I've worked for to have Jake see my reasons for leaving Sealladh na Mara, Ms. Morgan. I beg that of you."

He didn't give Allie a chance to answer. He glanced away and gently closed the door.

She stared at that wooden door for a few scant seconds, then turned and headed to her room. Only in the Highlands for less than twenty-four hours and her host/employer was already ticked off at her.

And she felt guilty about it.

Probably because she knew she was conspiring to sneak around behind his back and aid little Jake and the gang to prevent Odin's Thumb from being sold.

Somehow, as wrong as it seemed in logic, in her *heart*, Allie felt helping them was the right thing to do.

Just as she reached the landing to climb one floor up to her own lodgings, a hand encircled her arm. When she turned, Gabe stood one step below.

"I didna mean to snap at you." He dropped his hand and rubbed the back of his neck in that sexy way guys do. "Jake—he makes me dim-witted, that boy." He looked at her, and in the shadows of the corridor the light from a wall lamp turned his eyes glassy. He pushed his hands into the pockets of his jeans. "I'm, er, sorry, then. I suppose."

Allie's gaze dropped. Barefooted, bare-chested, and dead sexy? What? *What* on earth was she to say to that?

With a wide smile, she shrugged. "No problem at all. He's a great kid."

Just then she glimpsed a small figure slink back into the shadows, behind Gabe.

A sneaky, covert little great kid, rather.

"Right, then. Well, good night, Ms. Morgan."

Allie looked down at him. His gaze had lowered a fraction, to her mouth, and the sensation of it caused butterflies in her stomach. As soon as Gabe caught himself, he flinched.

The fact that he continued to refer to her as Ms. Morgan amused her. She pretended she hadn't noticed. "See ya in the morning, Mr. MacGowan."

With that, she turned and headed up the stairs.

She felt Gabe's gaze on her the entire way, but when she reached the landing and turned, he'd gone.

Allie sighed and headed to her room.

She could barely wait to see what tomorrow would bring.

Gabe jerked awake and sat up. Sweat covered his brow and his heart pounded hard in his chest. He glanced at the small digital clock on the bedside table. One a.m. It had been less than an hour since he'd fallen asleep.

Another bloody dream. Of *her*.

Rolling out of bed, Gabe crossed the floor to the bathroom. He flipped on the light, turned on the faucet, and splashed cold water on his face. As he rubbed his eyes, his jaw, he looked at himself. A month ago, the dreams had started again. At least, he thought they were dreams. They were so damn real. Christ, what was happening to him?

With a hand towel, he dried his face, laid the cloth across the sink, and turned out the light.

In the living room, he stopped. A streak of moonlight shot through the picture window facing the loch, coating everything in silver. The steady *tick-tick* of the wall clock above the hearth seemed to be only in his head.

Without thought, Gabe moved toward Jake's room. The door was cracked, so with a slight push, he eased it open. The lad lay completely relaxed, flat on his back and out of the covers. Gabe crossed the floor, pulled the duvet from beneath Jake's narrow body, and tucked him in.

"I dunna want to leave, Da," Jake muttered.

A lump formed in Gabe's throat. He smoothed his son's cowlick down, watched the hair pop right back up, and leaned over to drop a kiss onto the top of his head. "I know, lad. Now go to sleep."

Gabe turned and eased out of the room.

Instead of going back to bed, he found himself perched on the window seat in the alcove, staring out at the loch. The same silvery beam that bathed his face streaked across the black seawater, catching every ripple, every turn of a wave against the pebbled shore.

The very same sea that took Kait's life.

Now she came to him, whether in sleep or in that gloaming of wakefulness that doesn't quite seem real, she came. She reached for him, but she was not as he remembered. Chunks of hair were missing, as well as an eye, and her skin was pale white, waterlogged, and fish-nibbled . . .

As he scrubbed his eyes to rid himself of the vision, another one replaced it straightaway.

Untamed blond curls, blue eyes, a wide smile with the smallest of dimples to her right cheek. And as he recently noticed at the stairwell, inviting lips that curved just right and would fit against his perfectly . . .

Swearing in Gaelic, Gabe pushed from the window seat and paced. He stared at the ceiling and rubbed the back of his neck with both hands. What the bloody hell was he doing? Having nightmares about one woman, fantasies about another?

Christ, he'd known the lass but for half of a day. Why could he not get her off his mind? 'Twasn't simply because he'd seen her with her jumper over her head. He'd seen breasts before. Loads of them. He hadn't even really seen hers, yet he couldn't bloody get the alluring sight out of his brain. 'Twas something else, as well—something about *her*—and he couldna put a finger on it.

He didna want to, either. He had no room for such in his life. He owed everything he did to his son. He'd taken Jake's mother from him. And he'd spend the rest of his days trying to make up for it—even if it killed him.

Gabe blew out a heavy sigh. Two in the morning and he knew if he tried to sleep, he wouldna. He might as well stay up and occupy his time.

Pulling on the jeans he'd discarded earlier, he slipped on a T-shirt, a long-sleeved shirt over that, and pulled on socks and boots. Quietly, he eased out of the room and made his way to the small workshop off the kitchen. A single bench, a single lamp, and a single wooden chair, along with his chiseling set and several chunks of marble in various sizes and colors, filled the small eight-by-eight chamber. Against the far wall, a long wooden shelf ran the length of the room, a place to set whatever finished thing he'd made. The room had once been a place to cure meat.

It now served as Gabe's escape.

One of his escapes, anyway.

He couldna help but wonder if leaving truly was the answer.

Or if by leaving would he truly be free of his dead wife . . .

Choosing a small chunk of white marble streaked with obsidian, Gabe settled into the chair, pulled the lamp close, picked up a small hammer, chisel, and file, and set to work.

As Allie tiptoed down the third-floor steps, all was quiet within Odin's Thumb. No ghosts, no mortals— nothing. Not even a sign of Dauber. Quarter till seven on a Sunday morning, overcast, and she'd bet anything it was colder than a witch's tutu outside.

Perfect.

Once she made it to Odin's front door, Allie buttoned her black wool peacoat, pulled on a striped skully, and stepped outside. The cold, late October wind took her breath away, but the air smelled clean, a bit salty, and with a tinge of something Allie just couldn't seem to put her finger on. She liked it.

Taking a few moments before starting her morning walk, Allie seized her surroundings. Every one of her five senses snapped to life as she became familiar with the small coastal Scottish village.

Above her, the Odin's Thumb sign creaked on iron hinges, swaying softly back and forth with the wind. Quite eerie, actually—the empty street, no noise pollution—only the sound of that creaking sign and the ebb and flow of the sea. The cold coastal air against her skin, the salt of the ocean in her nostrils and on her tongue—all of it felt like a burst of life. How could anyone willingly leave this place?

On somewhat of an incline, Odin's Thumb perched at the top, looking down the single lane of white-washed buildings that rambled to the sea loch at the bottom. Turning in that direction, Allie began to walk.

The building next to Odin's was the fishmonger, McMillan's. Allie had met him at the pub the night before. Willy. Pretty funny guy. Looking into the storefront window, she found the large slab empty of display fish. She supposed on Sunday, Willy had closed shop. She'd make it a point to come see him when he opened for business on Monday.

As she ambled down past the stores, she discovered all of them closed, save one: the baker. And she'd smelled it long before she reached it. A large picture window with the words BREAD AND PASTRIES painted at the top in red letters displayed loaves of fresh bread and, well, pastries. A smiling woman with brown hair pulled into a ponytail met her gaze through the window and waved her inside. Allie pushed open the door where a bell tinkled her arrival.

"Aye, come on in out of the cold, gel," the woman,

who might have been in her early forties, said in heavy Highland brogue. "Have you had your breakfast yet, then?"

The scent of dough and baked bread made Allie's stomach growl. "Not yet, but I think I'm about to." She scanned the cases, found a stuffed-to-the-gills meat pie, smiled, and pointed to it. "That looks too good to pass up."

"Och, you must be MacGowan's American ghost buster. I'm Leona, and I see you've good taste in meaties," she said. Leona opened the case, and with a sheet of waxy paper, grabbed the meat pie, pushed it into a white paper sack, and handed it to Allie. "Coffee?"

"Definitely." Allie wondered just how many folks had heard of her arrival. She'd be willing to bet *every-one.* It was a small village. Funny, how Leona didn't seem to think Allie's presence an abnormal thing, not to mention one of her neighbors hiring a *ghost buster.*

Leona handed a steaming cup of coffee over the counter. "Condiments are in the corner, just there."

"Thanks, and I'm Allie," Allie said. She stepped to the corner and dumped in several spoons of brown sugar and cream.

"Aye, Justin's told me all about you. Smitten, that one is."

Allie nearly dropped her pie. "Justin?"

Leona nodded, her ponytail swishing back and forth. "Aye. You've met him, no doubt. That swarthy sea captain?" She snorted. "More like a rogue pirate if ye ask me. Quite the flirt. He told me all about you."

Allie set her breakfast on the condiments counter, dug in her jeans pocket for a few pounds, and handed them to Leona. "Yes, I've met him. Mr. MacGowan told me the village was sort of a . . . haven for spirits.

I guess I'm still just surprised. I'm used to dealing with people who are frightened by ghosts, not friends with them."

"Aye, the whole Odin's lot is well known in Sealladh na Mara. Have been for as long as I can remember. They go back centuries—our parents' parents' grandparents' played with the lot when they were lads and lassies." She shrugged. "I suppose having Justin and the others around at every birth, every celebration, from the time we enter the world—it doesn't seem overly strange to us. Like family, they are, more than anything." She leaned on the counter and met Allie's gaze. "I suppose, for whatever reason, they felt drawn here all those years ago, and didna want to ever leave."

Allie resisted the urge to shake her head in wonderment. She was used to people *thinking* they were seeing ghosts—and wanting her to get rid of them. But this small village thought of the Odin's spirits as family? New one on her. She rather liked it.

Leona turned to the register, punched in the numbers, the drawer popped out, and she handed Allie the change. "You know, one legend goes the way of a spell. Centuries ago, before the spirits ever showed up, a band of pirates cursed Sealladh na Mara to keep their hidden treasures safe. They figured if the outlying villages feared the ghosties, they'd stay away." She smiled. "Funny, how no' everyone can see those from the other side. So maybe there's a bit o' truth to that ole legend, aye?" She winked. "You must have a wee bit of Scot's blood runnin' through you, lass, for you to see ghosties the way you do. 'Tis a fine ability, indeed."

Allie grinned. "Maybe I do." She held up the meat pie. "Thanks. I'll see you around, Leona."

"Aye. Why not come round next Saturday? We're

having a ceilidh. They're always loads of fun. My husband plays the fiddle."

The questioning look must have been evident on Allie's face, because Leona grinned. " 'Tis a dance, love. A party. Quite informal here, I promise you." She inclined her head toward the wharf. "We'll gather just there at about sixish. Bonfire, music, food, and plenty of dancing."

Allie smiled. "Thanks. I hope I'm still here."

Something sparkled in Leona's brown eyes. "I've a feeling you will be, gel. Now shoo. Enjoy your breakfast, and I'll be seeing you."

With a wave, Allie left Leona to her baking. With her meat pie wrapped tightly in the waxed paper, she sipped her coffee and continued her walk down to the wharf. As she passed the other establishments, one red building stood out amongst the other whitewashed traditionals. It had a single sign that read ROYAL POST. She'd have to remember to stop by and send her mom and sisters a postcard.

At the wharf, several benches lined the walkway to the water. Allie chose one, set her coffee beside her, and opened the meat pie. Flavors of chipped beef, onion, spices, and cheese popped through the flaky pastry shell as she took that first bite. Her eyes closed as she chewed. *Heaven.*

The sounds of the sea, the wind against her cheeks, drowned out any approaching noises. Which is why she nearly jumped out of her skin when Gabe's deep brogue interrupted her breakfast.

"I've yet to meet a lass who can eat quite as much as you," he said, suddenly behind her.

Allie jumped, her mouth full of pie. She finished chewing, swallowed, and nearly choked. "Don't sneak up on me like that!" she said, wheezing. "Is something wrong?"

Gabe walked around and faced her. Leather jacket, jeans, boots, and a black skully made up his attire. He hadn't shaved yet, and from the looks of it, he hadn't slept much, either. Still. *Dead sexy.* "Aye." His green eyes bored into hers, lingered a moment as he studied her with an intent and profound stare, before answering— almost as if he wanted to say one thing, but *couldn't.* "I've a potential buyer coming to look at the place in two hours and I need you to keep the others busy." His gaze didn't waver. "That's what you were hired for, aye?"

She took a sip of coffee. "You should know by now that no mortal can force spirited souls into doing something they don't want to do. But I'll see what I can do."

Gabe looked a second or two longer, then out across the loch; then he kicked a pile of pebbles with the toe of his boot. Then, without even a glance back, he shook his head and walked up the lane.

Allie took another bite of pie and stared after him. She couldn't figure the man out. She just needed more time. It'd only been a day. Not even a day, actually.

There was something bothering Gabe MacGowan, and it was a lot more than misbehaving spirits and wanting to sell Odin's. As a matter of fact, she would bet her life that he didn't truly want to sell Odin's at all. She still needed to have a speakeasy with the others, find out just what brought them to Sealladh na Mara.

She sighed. Gabe was attracted to her. She could tell that for sure. She could also tell he would fight that attraction tooth and nail.

Her job to keep the others busy?

Oh, I'll keep them busy all right . . .

Chapter 6

Gabe shoved his hands deep into his coat pockets and made his way back to Odin's.

He couldna quite figure out why Allie Morgan burrowed under his skin so much. He hardly knew her.

Yet somehow, for some odd bloody reason, he found it completely endearing when she'd turned toward him, cheeks stuffed with pie.

He'd never admit it to anyone.

The reason he felt to continuously snap at her failed him, as well. He'd snap, she'd smile. Snap, smile.

'Twas madness.

The cold sea wind beat against his face, and for a second, he stopped and faced the loch. Inhaling a lungful of salty air, tasting it on his tongue, Gabe allowed it to revive him after another sleepless night.

After a moment, he continued on, stomping into Odin's just as Wee Mary and his mother were setting up the kitchen to begin lunch. Both women, sisters who looked nothing alike, looked up. He slipped his coat off and hung it on the rack.

"Well, good mornin' to you, son," his mother said. "What's gotten inside your knickers this time, lad? That horrible mug seems to be your usual of late."

Wee Mary laughed. "Oy, Laina. You'd only have

to lay eyes on her once to understand." She winked. "Your boy there has been ogling the American."

Gabe pulled off his cap and set it atop the coatrack. "I've no' been ogling, woman."

"Och," his mother said, ignoring his innocent plea. "You mean that lovely girl he hired to oust the ghosties?" She tsked. "Gorgeous blond locks the girl has, wouldna you say, Sister?"

"Aye, indeed."

Gabe shook his head, unable to completely smother the grin pulling at his mouth. "You both are crazy."

The sisters giggled.

His mother cocked her head and studied him. "You look like death, boy. Have you no' been sleeping again?"

Tying an apron about him, Gabe moved to the cutting table and began preparing the pot roast. "I'm getting enough." 'Twas a lie, but he didna want to worry his mother over something so insignificant. Besides, he'd brought it on himself. "I've someone coming to look at the pub today, so be on your best behavior and stay in the kitchen." He glanced at them. Their faces revealed nothing as they busied themselves with the peas and potatoes.

"I need a bit of help mending one of the fences, lad," his mother said. "I dunna want to leave it for your da when he comes ashore. Do you think you could go over this afternoon sometime?"

Gabe stared at his mother hard. So hard she finally blushed and looked up.

"What?" she asked.

"I'll go over once I've shown Odin's." He wouldn't put it past his mum or auntie to consort with the Odin's lot in keeping it from being sold.

His mother shrugged. "That'll do, then. Mary, pass me that paring knife, eh, love?"

Together the sisters continued their work. While he paid them both well, he more than appreciated the help. Wee Mary and his mum were the best of cooks, and people came from neighboring villages just to have their Sunday pot roast dinner. Which was exactly why he had one stipulation with the selling of Odin's: Wee Mary and his mum remained on as cooks.

Setting aside his carving knives, he scrubbed his hands on a dish towel, walked over to the sisters, and put an arm around each. He bent down and planted a kiss on each cheek. "I dunna know what I'd do without either of you meddlesome hens."

His mother kissed him back, then popped him on the backside with a towel. "Full of compliments, I see. Oh, go on with you. We've work to do, and 'tis work we can do without your bothersome self."

"Aye, you cocky lad," Wee Mary said. "Go."

They both beamed at his praise as he left.

Somehow it made him feel more like an idiot than he already did.

An hour later Gabe felt somewhat refreshed.

A shower, shave, clean clothes—even a tie—had him looking and feeling more like a proprietor ready to do business.

He sincerely hoped he could pull off such a farce.

Tightening the knot, he glimpsed Jake in the mirror, staring at him with a scowl that stretched clean across his scrunched-up little face. Arms folded and head down like a sulking vulture, his son was the epitome of piss 'n' pout.

Gabe would never let on he felt the verra same way.

Trouble was, he felt more selfish than ever—especially since Allie's arrival. So many questions—for most of which he had no solid answer. Was he making the move for Jake's sake, or was he running from the tormenting dreams of his dead wife? He knew the answer, but somehow, not saying it out loud made it not quite as foul. Or as true.

But Christ—he felt as though he were losing his bloody mind . . .

He met his son's accusing gaze in the mirror. "Stop glaring at me so, boy, and get your shoes on. Your granny's waitin' for you downstairs."

With an exaggerated harrumph, Jake jumped off Gabe's bed and stomped to his room. By the time Gabe had brushed his teeth and put on his own shoes, Jake was ready.

And was giving quite a good show of the silent treatment.

Deciding it best to just ignore it, Gabe inclined his head to the door. "Let's go."

Wordless, Jake stomped to the door, opened it, and stomped out.

Once downstairs, Jake ducked into the kitchen. Gabe pushed open the door and stuck his head in. The smell of pot roast filled the air, making his stomach growl.

He figured it would have the same effect on Allie.

With a frown at the random thought of her, he met his mother's stare. "Thanks for watching him. I'll be along in a bit to mend the fence and pick Jake up."

His mother waved him away. " 'Tis fine, son." She pulled Jake into a brace—one his son was resisting. "We'll have a grand time, aye?"

"Aye," Jake muttered, frown still fixed to his brow.

Gabe pointed at him. "Behave, lad. I'll see you in a bit."

Jake stared but didna say a word.

Wee Mary passed on her way to the fridge. "Dunna worry about him, lad. He'll be fine. We're all but ready to serve—just waitin' on the roast to finish up.

Go see to your sale and we'll set up for lunch when you're done, aye?"

"Right." Gabe glanced once again at Jake, whose expression hadn't changed, and stepped back into the pub. The mahogany bar gleamed, the lamps were dusted, the floor scrubbed.

He couldna see how anyone looking to buy a pub and inn would possibly refuse Odin's.

With a quick glance around, peering into darkened corners and shadowy alcoves, he heaved a sigh of relief. So far, no signs of the others.

He could only hope it stayed that way.

Rather, he could only hope Allie Morgan *made* it stay that way. Surely, she'd talked some sense into the ghostly pain-in-the-arses . . .

An abrupt thought suddenly hit him. He glanced around once more, then let his gaze travel upward, toward the stairs.

Where was the ghost ouster, anyway?

Approximately forty-five minutes passed before a white two-door compact pulled up and parked in front of Odin's Thumb. A middle-aged couple climbed out. The man, portly and wearing quite a lot of tweed, hurried round to open the door for his companion— a woman, taller than he and also favoring tweed. As the blustery wind picked up, they both grabbed their tweed hats and huddled close.

With a deep breath and a final glance behind him, Gabe walked out to meet who could possibly be the next Odin's Thumb proprietors.

"If he finds out I'm in on this, I'm gone. Fired. Back to the States," Allie said, meeting each of her cohort's gazes. "I just don't know."

"Pardon me, miss," said Friar Digby, pacing in his old woolen cloak and rubbing his fingerless-gloved hands together. Friar Digby actually wasn't old at all— only thirty-five years at the time of his demise, which had occurred in the year 1586 after a band of thieves jumped his wagon in hopes of finding coin. Instead, they'd found a large shipment of mead. They'd taken it, along with Drew Digby's life. He also claimed not to have yet been a full-fledged friar at the time.

A somewhat comforting thought when conspiring to commit . . . whatever they were about to commit.

The almost-friar continued. "We were pulling tomfooleries long before you arrived. 'Tisn't anything new, I assure you."

"Ah, that's where you're wrong, Drew," said Captain Catesby. He glanced her way, a dangerous glint in his eye. "We've never had such gloriously gruesome ideas as the ones in which the lovely American has thought up." He glanced at Mademoiselle Bedeau. "Can you recall?"

The mademoiselle shook her powdered-wig head. "*Non*," she said, her French accent especially potent. "Not once, Capitan Catesby."

Lord Killigrew stood by the hearth, arms folded over his chest. A wicked grin spread from ear to ear. "I say we do it. 'Tis a wondrous plan, Ms. Morgan."

"Well, we'd best hurry, then," Lord Ramsey said. He peered out of Allie's window. "I think the hopeful proprietors have just arrived."

All ghostly eyes turned to Allie. She shook her head and rubbed her temples. "I'm used to dealing with unsettled souls," she said, glancing out the window at the couple emerging from the car. She looked over her shoulder, back at the others. "Not conspiring with them."

"Well then, lass, your mission hasna changed a bit," said Captain Catesby. "Yon MacGowan is the most unsettled of all souls here in Sealladh na Mara."

"I really don't know," she said.

But it was too late. The Odin's lot had most assuredly decided to go ahead with the plan. And like it or not, Justin had made a solid point.

Maybe Gabe MacGowan was the most unsettled soul in Sealladh na Mara . . .

"Well, MacGillan, you've quite a place here."

Gabe stifled a growl. "MacGowan."

The man, *Stover*, and his wife, *Mrs. Stover*, chuckled. Stover shook his head. "So right you are. Come, show us the rest of the place. It's bloomin' freezing out here."

"It smells a bit fishy," Mrs. Stover said, waving a hand in front of her face. "Does it always, Chester?"

Gabe wondered if her nose always pointed skyward.

"Of course not, Millicent. Come, now."

Stepping ahead, Gabe held open the door and allowed the Stovers to enter. "Right on in," he said, then followed.

"It's quite dark in here," Mrs. Stover announced. "I can't see a thing."

"We could fix that right up, love," said Mr. Stover, bending over a lamp and twisting it about. "A few overheads would do wonders for this place."

Gabe simply stood to the side, stuffed his hands in his trouser pockets, and allowed them to look around. He already knew there was nothing he could say that would sway their minds one way or the other.

Overheads, his arse.

Mr. Stover eased behind the bar and ran a hand over the mahogany. He made a face of disdain. "Needs stripping, I'd say. Wouldn't you, Millie? Come feel. It's rather rough and faded."

Mrs. Stover found her way next to her husband, and ran her fingers over the wood. Again, the nose jutted skyward and she sighed. "I'm afraid he's right, Mr. MacGiven."

Before Gabe could correct their slip of his name, the one thing he was *not* expecting happened.

And performed by the least likely soul of the bunch.

Out of nowhere, Mademoiselle Bedeau's lovely powdered-wig head began tumbling from the far end of the bar, rolled and rolled until it came to a halt directly in front of the Stovers.

An odd, bizarre noise sounded from deep within Mr. Stover.

Mrs. Stover simply gasped, eyes wide, mouth open.

With a squeak, Mademoiselle's head turned and faced them both. "*Oui*, I would say that, indeed, this is the smoothest of mahogany. No need to refinish."

Just then, the lamps all began flashing.

"As for the lights, monsieur, *non*. As you can see they work just fine. Only a nincompoop would desire a brightly lit pub."

A slow, low sound began low in Mrs. Stover's throat.

It didna take long to escalate into a full scream.

"Mr. MacDowan!" screamed Chester Stover, pulling his wife close and patting her with one of his big beefy hands. "What is this foolishness? Stop it at once, I say! You're frightening my wife!"

"Oh, *he* cannot do a thing, monsieur," said Mademoiselle's head. "We do as we please here, *oui*!"

Gabe sighed, pinched the bridge of his nose, and barely peeked as Mademoiselle's headless body came stumbling into the pub, arms outstretched, and, Christ . . .

she'd conjured the illusion of blood spurting from her neck. She ran straight for the Stovers.

"Arrgh!" screamed Millicent Stover, slapping and batting at the headless body as it came toward her. Jumping up and down in place, she waved her hands. "Chester, get me out of here!"

Gabe almost didn't notice Wee Mary, peering through the crack in the kitchen door. And he nearly missed one Ms. Allie Morgan trotting down the stairs.

"Wouldna you care to at least see the kitchen?" Gabe asked, feeling like an arse even as he spoke.

"No!" both Stovers said in unison.

They pushed their way past Mademoiselle's ghastly body and Chester shouted over his shoulder, "You'll be hearing from our solicitor, MacGowan!"

Funny, how they *now* finally got his name right.

Gabe watched as the Stovers stuffed themselves into their car and sped away.

The second potential buyer in less than twenty-four hours. That was a record, even for him.

Gabe turned to find Allie Morgan standing before him.

She gave him a weak smile. "Oops."

He frowned, felt the space between his brows bunch, and all he could do was brush past her without a word.

Leaving Allie Morgan to stand alone.

Chapter 7

Allie rolled over and stared at the green illuminated numbers on her bedside clock. One a.m. She fell back with a sigh.

She hadn't slept a wink.

Guilt probably played some small part in her sleeplessness. While she felt bad for coming up with the head-rolling-down-the-bar act, she could definitely see where Gabe MacGowan had an issue or two.

And that he might be making a drastically wrong decision to leave Odin's Thumb.

Not that it was her business to meddle.

Even in just the few short hours she'd spent with Captain Catesby and the others, she could tell, could *feel* how much they cared for Gabe and Jake. It was why she communicated so well with the unliving. She had a way with souls—living or not.

And she could certainly tell Gabe MacGowan had a troubled soul.

And she aimed to help him.

He hadn't spoken to her during lunch, and then he'd disappeared right after and she didn't see him for the rest of the evening.

Not that she blamed him.

But one thing she could tell about Gabe MacGowan was that he loved Odin's Thumb just as much as he loved the ghostly lot who resided there. So what was making him want to leave? It was far more than desiring a stable environment for Jake. She could tell that, too.

She buried under the covers and stared at the hearth. The fire had nearly died out, and she'd used the rest of the peat earlier.

Easing out of bed, her teeth chattering, Allie went to the dresser, pulled out an extra pair of sweatpants, pulled them over her long underwear, and found her NC State University sweatshirt and pulled that on, too. With a big pair of thick wool socks on her feet, she eased out of her room and into the corridor.

Down the stairs she went, creeping as quietly as she could, until she reached the second floor. Glancing down the corridor, toward Gabe's room, she paused. Maybe he'd be awake? She should try to explain herself . . .

Again, she paused, listened, but didn't hear a TV, a stereo—nothing. With a sigh, she rubbed her arms vigorously and continued to the first floor.

Only a few lamps burned in the pub, throwing the room into an even softer light than usual. She liked Odin's. Masculine, yet with a slight touch of femininity by way of the Victorian lamps. Comfortable. Welcoming.

She wondered why a great-looking guy like Gabe didn't have a girlfriend.

Or maybe he did?

She headed toward the back hall, close to the kitchen where Gabe had shown her where to get peat for the hearth in her room. *Boy, if he does have a girlfriend, she is one strong woman to handle that veritable powerhouse of grumpiness . . .*

As she drew closer to the peat closet, a noise caught her attention. At the kitchen, Allie paused and listened. A strange scraping—no, tapping—sound seemed to be coming from close by. As she glanced around in the shadows, her gaze landed on a door, ajar, at the far end of the hall, next to the kitchen. Easing closer, she noticed a small line of faint lamplight spilling out into the hall.

Gently, Allie placed her fingertips on the wood and pushed.

Gabe sat at a workbench, an iron lamp with a bendable neck tilted toward something he had in his hands. He wore an untucked white, long-sleeved button-up shirt and jeans, and was barefooted, with one heel resting on the rung of the chair, the other leg sprawled out before him. He worked intently on . . . something. Head bent, he either ignored her or had no idea she was watching . . .

And she certainly watched. She couldn't help it. Intrigued by his rough, aloof behavior yet obvious love for his son, she now learned another interesting fact: he had a hobby. And it was one he kept a secret.

Various chunks of stone, perhaps marble, sat against one wall. A long shelf ran the length of the other, with small pieces of . . . She stared but couldn't make them out. She squinted and stepped a bit closer.

Just then, an iced chill raced up her spine and raised goose bumps on her skin. Out of nowhere, a fierce gust of wind blew the door shut right in her face.

Allie stifled a squeal and stumbled back. Her heart raced, taken aback by the unexpected *something*.

What had just happened?

Wrapping her arms about herself, she eased away from the door. Best Gabe didn't even know she'd been standing there—

Just then, the door cracked open. Gabe leaned against the jamb and crossed his arms over his chest. He stared at her with that potent stare for an uncomfortable amount of time before inclining his head. "Come in."

"Thanks." Allie scooted past him, but not so fast that she didn't feel the heat coming from his body. She swallowed and ignored how the sensation had made her heart flutter.

Gabe stepped in and pushed the door, leaving a small crack open.

The room was small, and a space heater in the corner kept the area nice and toasty. It didn't take long for Allie to warm up. Although interested in the pieces sitting on the shelf, she turned to Gabe instead.

"I think things have gotten off to a bad start," she said. "About today—"

"Today's forgotten."

Allie blinked. "Why?"

The very smallest of smiles tipped one corner of Gabe's mouth.

It completely changed his appearance.

And it made her heart skip a beat.

She couldn't fathom what a full-blown grin would do to her.

"Because. Whilst I seek to find a buyer for this place, I dunna want to turn it over to a horse's arse who wouldna appreciate it." He scrubbed his jaw. "I'm fairly sure the Stovers wouldna fit in well at Sealladh na Mara, aye?"

Allie couldn't help but smile. "I'll have to agree with that." So he really did care about Odin's. She cocked her head and studied Gabe in the dim light. Never before had she thought much about a Highland brogue, but hearing it on Gabe's tongue? Good Lord. Sexy didn't quite sum it up.

"I'll work a bit more with the others. You know," she said, easing toward the shelf against the far wall. "They really care about you and Jake—"

"If it's all the same to you, we'll leave your employment as you were hired," he said. "I didna ask you to come here and be my personal counsel."

That stung. "I know," she said, covering up the sting. Deciding not to push, especially before she had the chance to sit down and get every ounce of information possible from the others, she glanced down at the small pieces of marble and lifted one. It appeared to be a miniature medieval warrior, complete with a sword. "What are these?"

"Chess pieces," Gabe said, right behind her. So close, she could once again feel the heat from his body.

"Such intricate work." She glanced up and over her shoulder. "You made all of these?"

He shrugged. "Passes the time."

She inspected the dark circles beneath his eyes— and not for the first time. "You don't sleep much, do you?"

Again, he shrugged.

His eyes didn't move from hers.

After a too-long moment of silence, Allie moved to set the chess piece back on the shelf, but it fumbled in her fingers and dropped. She jerked down to catch it and her forehead bopped against the wooden shelf. "Ouch," she muttered, and when she lifted her head, it smacked right into Gabe's chin.

They both stared at each other, rubbing their injured body parts.

She gave him a half grin as he scrubbed his jaw. "Sorry." Carefully setting the chess piece down, Allie folded her arms over her chest. "Well. I suppose I'd better get that peat and head off to bed."

Gabe said nothing. He just continued to watch her.

"Okay, then," she said, easing by him. "I'll see you tomorrow—I mean later, I guess."

She had nearly made it to the door when he spoke, that smooth brogue washing over her.

"Why do you do it?"

She rubbed her still-aching forehead. "Do what?"

He gave her that smoky look. "Hang out with specters."

She mimicked his shrugging. "Why not?"

Gabe glanced down, lifted one shoulder, and then met her gaze again. "Why no' with real people?"

She looked Gabe directly in the eye. "They are real people, Mr. MacGowan. They are the exact same souls they were when they had a live body to live in. Being dead doesn't destroy the soul. Just the live flesh." She moved past him and out the door. She paused and glanced over her shoulder. She smiled. "They're just as real as we are. Remember that."

With that, she turned and left.

At the back corner alcove, the Odin's Thumb lot sat. Justin sat quiet for a moment, and then met his ghostly mates with a sincere gaze. "That Allie is some gel," he said. He glanced at Dauber. "Has she always been that way?"

Dauber gave a nod. "Yes, indeed. A good soul, through and through, that one. I've yet to see her unable to help settle those who needed settling."

"Aye, but has she ever tried doing the like with a mortal?" asked the friar.

Dauber scratched a place under his cap. "I can't say she has, although she seems to have a way with them, as well." He looked up. "There's something there, between those two. I can sense it."

Justin frowned. " 'Tis been naught but two days, man. That canna possibly be so."

Lord Killigrew grinned. " 'Tis bothersome to you, the joining of those two, aye?"

"Of course it's not," said the friar. "We've known Gabe since he was a baby." He glanced at Justin. "We desire the very best for him, and for young Jake."

Everyone was silent for a moment.

"At least we've thwarted another buyer," said Lord Ramsey. He grinned at Mademoiselle. " 'Twas a fine showing, miss, with your head rolling atop the bar and your body flailing about."

Everyone chuckled.

"I say we stay close to Ms. Morgan and follow her counsel. She's quite bright," said the friar.

Everyone muttered an agreement.

"I'm no' convinced our young Gabe would have sold to that overstuffed pair of tweed peacocks anyway," said Justin.

"And I'm not quite convinced he really wants to sell to anyone," added the mademoiselle. "The poor lad is torn."

"I'm sure Ms. Morgan could use the full extent of her capabilities if she knew the entire tale," said the friar.

"Aye, but 'tisn't our place to tell her," said Mademoiselle Bedeau. She shook her head. "*Non*, it would not be right."

"Now, Elise," said Justin. "It happened more than five years ago, love. We should tell—"

Mademoiselle Bedeau shook her head again. "*Non*. I'll hear no more of it."

Dauber glanced about. "I'm sure my Allie could help, indeed. You should trust her."

The Odin's Thumb lot looked at each other; then the friar spoke. "Indeed we trust her, sir, but for now, what happened those many years past shall remain silent. Mayhap in time, we can discuss it. Mademoiselle is right. 'Tis young Gabe's place to tell, and his place only."

Dauber gave a nod. "Fair enough, then. I'm sure she can help in other ways."

Mademoiselle Bedeau rose and smoothed her gown. "I must say, though, that the key for our very livelihood, such as it is, here at Odin's Thumb may well lie in the hands of the joining of those two." She smiled. "*Oui*. I think that would most certainly assure our homestead."

Dauber rubbed his jaw. "I don't know your Gabe, but my Allie is a strong-willed girl. Much stronger, even, than the women of my time."

"And of ours," said Killigrew and Ramsey in unison. They glanced at each other, and Killigrew stroked his chin. "Methinks 'tis passing agreeable, that trait."

Ramsey nodded. "I have to agree."

"Enough of this," said Justin. "We canna force two people together. They're either in harmony, or no'."

"Well," Mademoiselle said, a sly smile stretching across her ghostly features. "We shall certainly see, then, *non*?"

"Indeed, we shall," said Justin, frowning. "Indeed."

Allie stared up at the ceiling, turned once, then flipped back. She was sleepy, but sleep wouldn't come.

Not as long as Gabe MacGowan stayed on her mind.

Two days. *Two days!* How could she possibly be attracted to distraction by someone in so little time? When she was around him, she fought to keep her eyes off him. When she was away, her thoughts strayed to memories of that unique accent, green eyes, and . . . *damn*. That silent power he had, the way he just stared, looked so intently at her, as though peering all the way through to her soul.

He *mystified* her.

Turning her head, Allie watched the peat burn in

the hearth. It gave off a deep, clean, earthy scent that she found very appealing. That same scent seemed to cling to Gabe, adding to the already alluring scent of soap . . .

She blew out a gusty sigh. "See?" she said out loud. "I can't even look at peat burning without thinking of him."

A vision of Gabe came to mind, of him rubbing his chin while she rubbed the back of her head, after they smacked together. He'd had a slight, barely there grin lifting one side of his mouth. She'd also noticed that when he talked, his mouth was just a fraction crooked.

She liked it.

Finally, her eyelids grew heavy, and she began to drift. Before she fell asleep, she briefly wondered if Gabe planned to go to that ceilidh on Saturday.

She supposed she'd find out soon enough . . .

Chapter 8

The sound of an engine roused Allie from sleep. The barest sunlight streamed through the window and across the bedcovers. Sitting up, she rubbed her eyes and waited to get her bearings.

Scottish Highlands. Odin's Thumb.

Proprietor of Odin's Thumb.

"Good Lord." Flinging back the heavy duvet, Allie climbed out, padded over to the window, and glanced out. In the distance, a small yellow school bus ambled down the lane. *That must be Jake's bus.* She'd forgotten the little guy was in school.

Turning, she crossed the room to the highboy chest of drawers and pulled out clean undies, bra, socks, her favorite olive green khaki carpenter pants, and a long-sleeved, cream-colored cotton T-shirt with the tattoo design of a Celtic dragon in navy on the front. Her sister had bought her the T while on a trip to Wales and Allie loved it.

After a not-too-long shower, leg shaving, and hair washing, Allie stuffed her heavy wet hair into a towel, wrapped it turban-style atop her head, lotioned her legs, and dressed. She applied a small amount of makeup, deodorant, brushed her teeth, and then walked to the window seat, plopped down, and set to the task of towel-drying her hair. God knows if she blew it dry with a hair dryer, it would stand on end and she'd never get it tamed.

The *curse of curls*, her granny had always said.

"Can I come in, love?"

The voice just *happened*, as if floating about the room. Allie smiled. "Yes, Dauber, the coast is clear."

Dauber sifted through the wall, walked over to the bed, and perched on the chest at the footboard. His famous ear-to-ear grin spread quickly. "Good morn to you, then. You look lovely, as always."

Allie narrowed her eyes as she rubbed her hair with the towel. "I saw that."

Dauber feigned a surprised look, glanced around the room, and then cocked his head. "Saw what?"

Shaking her head, Allie giggled. "What's with the compliment this morning, Daubs? You've seen me a thousand mornings drying my hair in these very same plain-Jane casual clothes." She pretended a frown. "What are you up to?"

He blinked. "Nothing, of course."

"Hmm."

Dauber flicked an imaginary bit of something from his trousers. "The others tell me there is a dance of sorts in a few days." He looked at his nails. "Are you going?"

Allie continued to study her old friend. "If I'm still here, I am. Leona, the baker down the street, invited me."

With outstretched arms above his head, Dauber yawned. "I wonder if Mr. MacGowan will be there, as well."

She lifted a brow. "I don't know. He doesn't seem the partying kind."

"Oh, I wouldn't say that for sure," Dauber said. "He may well surprise you."

Dropping the wet towel in her lap, Allie stared at Dauber. "Don't. Do you hear me? Do. Not."

Dauber again blinked innocently. "Do not what, young lady?"

She rose, carried the towel out the door, across the hall to the bathroom, hung it on the rack, and then returned to the room. She shut the door. "You *know* what, smarty-pants. No matchmaking. The man has issues—"

"As do you."

She stopped. "What?"

Dauber gave her an accusing glare. "You're afraid of having your heart broken again."

Turning her back, Allie ran a comb through her tangled hair. "That's not true at all."

"Yes, love, it is," he said, gentler this time. "I was there when it broke the first time. Remember?"

Allie stopped combing and sighed. "Okay, so maybe that's it a little." She turned and leaned against the dresser. "But there are many other reasons—"

"So you admit you like him?"

Allie frowned. "I'll admit nothing. What I'm saying is that I was hired to come here and bring to heel a motley crew of naughty souls. It's not working, in case you haven't noticed. I've been here two days and already they've coerced me into working *against* my employer."

Dauber smiled. "You're never coerced, my girl. And you never do anything unless you truly, fully believe in it."

Her frown deepened, despite the fact Dauber was right. "That may be, Alexander Dauber, but my life is an ocean away from here." She glanced out the window, and at the beauty of the sea. "Once this job is finished, I'll go home."

Dauber sighed. "I suppose it's too early to decide anyway, I imagine." He grinned. "But we've still time enough."

Allie shook her head. "You coming?"

"Where are you off to?" Dauber said.

"First, down to the bakery. Leona makes the best meat pies ever. Then the post office. I want to send mom, Emma, Boe, and Ivy a postcard. Then"—she grinned and grabbed her peacoat—"I'm calling to order a ghostly get-together with the Odin's lot. Interested?"

"You mean," he said, scratching a place under the bill of his soft cap, "just walk into the bakery and post office with you?"

She smiled. "Cool, huh? This is a very open-minded village when it comes to ghostly souls. And you'll love Leona—she's really nice. Now come on. My stomach is growling and you know how I get when there's no food in my belly."

"Coming right along, then," said Dauber.

Together, they left the room and headed downstairs.

The pub was empty, and Allie couldn't help but glance toward Gabe's workshop door. She couldn't tell if the light was on, but the door was closed fully, so she suspected Gabe had finally gone to bed. And since the pub didn't open until eleven for lunch, he might very well be catching up on sleep.

As she and Dauber made their way out into the crisp October air, she couldn't help but wonder just what kept the man awake so much. He had to be exhausted.

With that curious thought in mind, along with the plan to ask the others about it later, she and Dauber set off down the street toward Leona's.

Gabe pushed out of Odin's front door.

And nearly took off Allie's nose in the process.

She stumbled back, and Gabe reached out and grabbed her arm, steadying her.

She grinned. "Thanks. What's the big rush?"

Christ, the girl was beautiful. A wee bit of October morning sun had slipped from behind the clouds, reflecting off the loch and throwing all those glorious curls into a yellowish glow. Her eyes were bright and they sparkled when she smiled. He felt all bloody tongue-tied around her, which usually led to him just saying nothing at all.

Not that he'd ever tell anyone that. He'd never hear the end of it. He sounded like a witless arse as it was.

Gabe cleared his throat. "Wee Mary is sick this morning, and me mother's gone to the doctor in Inverness, so neither can come over to help." He glanced behind him. "And I've just burned lunch."

With both hands, she grabbed his forearms. "Calm down, MacGowan. Why didn't you call me earlier?" Her smile, bright and confident, widened. "I'll help. No problemo." She jerked a thumb toward the pub. "So what'd you burn?"

"Soup."

The woman had the nerve to laugh.

He fought not to join her.

"How on earth do you burn soup?" she asked. "Never mind." She pushed her way into the pub. "Let me see what else you have."

"Er, wait," Gabe said. "No offense, lass, but I'll have about twenty or so folks in for lunch in approximately three hours—"

She held up a hand. "Step off, Scotty. And stop worrying." She narrowed her eyes. "I can see it in your face—you don't trust me in the kitchen. Well, I'll have you know that my mother and sisters—and me at one point—run a fabulous B and B on the coast of Maine. I can cook." She grinned. "And I've *never* burned soup before."

Damn. He would have taken the time to laugh, but

he wasna used to being the sole cook. He was the proprietor, did the books, the figures, helped out when short-staffed. But Wee Mary and Katey did all the cooking and serving.

He was desperate. He had no choice but to accept Allie's offer.

Rubbing the back of his neck, he blew out a frustrated breath. "I hired you to bring to heel that meddlesome lot of spirits—who I'm fairly sure are watching us both right now. Not cook for the pub." He stared at her. "Right. Search through the pantry and see what you can find. I'll be right back."

"What are you getting?" she asked.

"Potatoes, milk, and crab. Can you do something with that?"

"Absolutely. And some onions if you haven't burned those, as well." Allie stepped into the pub.

"Hey," Gabe called. She turned and looked at him. He felt his bloody knees go weak. "Thanks."

Another wide smile and Allie Morgan disappeared into the shadowy depths of Odin's Thumb.

And Gabe could do nothing more than trust the girl.

And pray she couldna tell just how much she'd started to affect him.

Twenty minutes later, Gabe hurried into Odin's. He pulled up short when he reached the kitchen.

He blinked.

Allie, with her mass of curls pulled up into a clip at the top of her head and one of Wee Mary's aprons tied on, surrounded by every single Odin's Thumb ghostly resident—and one extra soul, he believed— perched on counters and chairs, had cleaned up the mess he'd made earlier *and* had several ingredients pulled from the cabinets and pantry, lined up neatly on the counter beside the stove. Baden Killigrew said something and the whole room burst out laughing.

Allie, Gabe noticed, looked just as easy and at-home comfortable in his kitchen, with his ghosts—as if it were all a natural and everyday occurrence, to be laughing and carrying on amongst the dead.

He supposed, to her, it was. It had been some time since he'd allowed himself the same easiness.

Their souls aren't dead, Mr. MacGowan. Just their live flesh. Remember that.

"Hey, 'tis the soup burner, returned," said Christopher Ramsey. "I say, lad, how does one burn soup, by the by?"

Everyone roared.

Allie just grinned.

Gabe set his bags on the counter and glanced at Allie. "We've a new soul here now?"

She began looking through the bags. "He's with me. Alexander Dauber, and I promise to take him home when I go."

Gabe cast a look in Dauber's direction. The older ghost tipped the bill of his hat but didna say a word.

Gabe returned the nod.

With very little time before the lunch crowd arrived, he decided to wait until later to ask Allie Morgan why she'd brought her own spirit to Scotland. He wondered if Alexander Dauber was as mischievous as the Odin's lot. He glanced over, and Dauber's left brow raised. High.

That answered Gabe's question.

"Okay," Allie said, interrupting Gabe's thoughts. "We need to get busy here. And since it's just me and you physically doing this, how about you chop the onions? I'll peel the potatoes."

Gabe just stared at her.

She'd already found a paring knife and had started peeling. "What?" she asked.

He shook his head. "Are you always so bossy?"

"You don't know the half of it, sir," Dauber answered.

The Odin's crew laughed.

Allie simply shrugged. "I grew up in a houseful of females. We're used to running the show."

"I can tell," Gabe said under his breath.

Together, with the spirited and lively souls of Sealladh na Mara, plus Alexander Dauber, looking on and adding advice wherever they deemed necessary, Gabe and Allie prepared the afternoon meal. In between chopping onions and wiping the tears streaming down his cheeks from the fumes, he watched her. Deft fingers moved over the potatoes, and the whole while not once did Gabe notice a smile not affixed to Allie's face. One of the lords would tell a raunchy joke, they'd all laugh, and Allie would come back with one even raunchier.

Finished with the potatoes, she dumped the whole chopped lot into the large pot Gabe had burned the last bit in, added water, and set it to boil.

Then she started cutting up various vegetables to cook fast over the flame. For the crab cakes, she said.

Forty minutes later, Gabe had pulled the plates and bowls from the cabinet. Allie was just finishing up the last of the crab cakes when the first of the lunch crew came through Odin's door.

Within minutes the pub was mostly filled.

Allie wiped her hands on her apron, stood before Gabe, and looked up. "Okay. No menus, right? People just come in, pay one price, and they get whatever it is you're serving for the day. Right?"

Gabe looked down at her. "Right."

Allie grinned.

"What's so funny?" he asked, and started dipping the bowls full of potato soup.

"You have a great accent. The way you roll your r's—I like it."

For some reason, Gabe liked that *she* liked it.

But he shrugged it off. "You Americans—you all like this," he said, waving a hand about.

"What?" she said, exchanging her apron for a clean one.

"The Scottishness."

She grinned. "Hmm. I can't say how much I liked it before." She lifted a tray laden with three large pitchers of water. "But I like it now."

And with that she left the kitchen.

Chapter 9

Allie hadn't run so much since she'd waited tables in college. All the patrons were locals—plus a few from the neighboring village—and everyone was genuinely courteous and patient. While Gabe served up the plates in the kitchen, Allie had run from table to table, pouring tall glasses of water. Once finished, she helped him serve. Bowl of soup, two crab cakes, hard roll. It was really quite simple. No menus, except for the one outside the pub. And that one listed daily what was being served at lunch and at dinner.

Dinner. She hadn't even asked what it was. No doubt that as soon as they had everything cleared and cleaned from lunch it would be time to start preparing for the next meal.

"Lass, dunna tell Wee Mary this," said Willy Mac-Millan, the fishmonger. "But those were the best crab cakes I've ever eaten." He squinted. "Canna quite place the difference—"

"American," she whispered, and wiggled her brows.

Willy laughed, shook his head, and pulled on his cap. "So it is, then. Good day to you, Allie."

She watched him go through Odin's front door, the last patron to leave. The ghostly souls had dispersed, going their own way and doing whatever it was they did when not in the presence of mortals. Even Dauber left with Captain Catesby, off to see something at the wharf.

"I canna believe you have that old grouch eatin' out of your hand in just three days," Gabe said, suddenly behind her.

She glanced at him over her shoulder and grinned. "I had him eating out of my hand the *first* day, sport." She grabbed a tub from beneath the bar and started loading up the dirty dishes from the tables. Gabe followed suit.

And every time Allie would look up, she'd catch Gabe watching her. Together they loaded all the dishes in silence, but the glances were still there. Finally, Allie set a bowl in the tub, tossed in the silverware, and met his gaze. "What?"

He looked away. "Nothin'."

Gabe grabbed the heavy tub and headed to the kitchen. Allie followed. "So, where do they go?"

Gabe set the tub next to the sink. "Away."

Good Lord, getting information out of Gabe Mac-Gowan was like pulling teeth. "Away *where*?"

He began to load the dishes. "I dunno. They visit others, go to places from their life before." He shrugged. "For the most part, the Odin's lot stays in Sealladh na Mara, where they have freedom."

Before Allie could comment on that, the front door swung open and Jake came barreling through.

"Hiya, Da!" the boy said, and ran straight to Gabe and threw his arms around his waist. "Captain Catesby says you and Allie made lunch for everyone."

"Ms. Morgan to you, lad, and aye, we did. Wee Mary was sick today," Gabe said. "Have you homework, then?"

"A wee bit," he said. "Can I do it later?"

"Nay, boy. You go straightaway to your room and do it now. After, I'll make you a snack, aye?"

"Aye," Jake said grudgingly. He turned to Allie. "Al—I mean, Ms. Morgan, do you wanna throw pebbles in the wharf with me after homework?"

Allie studied the pair of MacGowans. One big, one little. One with dark hair, the other auburn. Jake had that adorable little cowlick right at the hair line, a few freckles trekking across his nose, and the bluest eyes.

Eyes completely unlike Gabe's green ones.

"Ms. Morgan doesna want to be bothered, lad—"

"Well," Allie said, "here's the deal." She gave Jake a stern look—probably a lot like the one her mother used to give her. "You get your homework finished, your snack in your belly, and I'll get busy cleaning up this mess." She glanced at Gabe. "If it's all right with your dad, I'll go throw pebbles with you before we start dinner. How's that?"

Jake squirmed where he stood. "Canna, Da?"

Gabe met Allie's gaze for a long moment, then nodded. "Aye, I suppose so."

Jake took off up the stairs.

"Dunna hurry through your homework, lad," Gabe called after him. "I'll be checkin' it."

"Aye-aye," said Jake, his voice growing fainter as he raced up the steps and disappeared down the corridor.

Gabe gave her a direct look. "You dunna have to entertain my son, Ms. Morgan. 'Tisna what I hired you for."

Although Allie knew it was meant sternly, she decided the best way to handle Gabe and his grumpy mood swings was to laugh them off. Something greater than anything she'd imagined weighed heavy on Gabe's mind, and perhaps she'd find out just what that was. Until then, she could only be her usual, chirpy self.

She threw him a big grin. "You didna hire me to cook and do dishes, either," she said, mimicking to the best of her ability Gabe's Highland brogue. "Yet here I am, apron and all, me hair a mess"—she blew a loose strand and it flew skyward—"and potato all over me trousers."

And then it happened.

It nearly knocked her over where she stood.

Gabe threw back his head and *laughed*.

Allie didn't think a man could look so beautiful.

Gabe shook his head and scrubbed his eye with the heel of his hand. "You are crazy, woman." He looked at her and shook his head again. "Bloomin' crazy."

Allie shrugged. "Maybe so. I've got a meeting with your lot of spirits tonight, Mr. MacGowan, and I'll try to see just what's going on with them and their hauntings. I now have a pebble-throwing date to get ready for, so if you don't mind, I've got to get busy getting this mess picked up." She lifted an empty tub and started past him.

With a firm yet gentle grip, he stopped her. She glanced up, his jaw flinched and his eyes bored into hers, and her mouth went dry.

"Thank you, Ms. Morgan," he said, his gaze dropping briefly to her lips. "Again."

"Absolutely," she replied, thankful the sound didn't come out as a squeak. She started for the dining area, and it wasn't until she was there, and he was in the kitchen, and dishes were clinking together as Gabe placed them in the dishwasher, that Allie took a long, deep, steadying breath.

What in God's name was happening to her?

Somewhere deep inside, so very deep that it wasn't even a clear and consciously formed thought, she was afraid she knew.

And she, Allie Morgan, for the first time in quite a long while, was absolutely petrified.

*   *   *

Allie followed Jake. He'd changed from his school uniform of a white collared shirt and blue trousers to a pair of rough and tumble little boy jeans, a sweatshirt with a Celts logo on the front—a *football* team, apparently—and a blue jacket with yellow piping. They walked down to the wharf, over the rocks to a small tidal pool. Jake squatted down, scooped up a handful of pebbles, and dumped them into Allie's hand.

"Do you have a husband?" Jake asked, tossing a pebble into the water. "Back in America?"

Allie laughed. "I sure don't. Why do you ask?" She tossed in a pebble, too.

Jake shrugged and threw a couple more. "Why are you here all by yourself?"

Allie studied the boy. The late afternoon light had faded, the air had grown colder, and a gust of wind ruffled Jake's hair.

She suspected the little sneak had lured her here to question her about Odin's Thumb.

Smiling, she picked a few choice pebbles and skipped them into the water. "I go everywhere by myself. Why?"

Again, he shrugged. "My mother died."

Allie froze. Damn, she had no idea. When Gabe had mentioned he was raising Jake alone, she thought he'd meant that Jake's mom had simply run out on them. He'd never mentioned being a widower. Leave it to a six-year-old to be brutally honest and spill the beans.

She took in a breath. "I'm sorry, Jake. How long ago?"

"I was little. I don't remember her, really." He peered up at her. "I have a picture by my bed, though. She's pretty."

Allie smiled and smoothed his cowlick. It sprang back up. "I have no doubt about that." She wondered how Jake's mother had died, but she didn't want to ask. Perhaps after he got to know her a little better, he'd tell her.

Or perhaps Gabe MacGowan would.

Glancing up, she studied the cliff to the right of the loch, and could make out a building of sorts on the top. She'd meant to ask someone about it but had forgotten.

She pointed. "What's that up there, Jake?"

He followed her finger. "Och, that's the old keep." He wiped his nose with the back of his hand. "My da says it once belonged to our ancestors."

"Can you go up there?" she asked.

"Aye," Gabe's voice sounded from behind them. "But only with someone, right, Jake?"

"Aye," the boy agreed. " 'Tis dangerous up there, you know, with stones falling and such."

Allie met Gabe's gaze. "I see."

"Can we take her up there, Da? She's from America and they dunna have castles and such there," Jake said.

"Another day, lad," Gabe said. "Right now Ms. Morgan and I have a dinner to prepare." He scrubbed his son's head. "And you have a bath to take, aye?"

Jake frowned. "Aye, I suppose." He looked at Allie. "Tomorrow, then?"

"If your dad says it's okay," she answered.

"Great!" Jake shouted, his r's rolling like his father's.

And with that, he took off.

"Go straight to your bath, lad!" Gabe yelled after him.

Jake waved, hollered something that sounded like "aye, aye, aye," and kept on running.

Leaving Allie and Gabe alone.

Allie shifted her gaze to the ruins on the cliff. "So. Your ancestors used to live in a castle, huh?"

Gabe gave a half grin. "What? And yours didna?"

Allie laughed. "No. Mine didna." She turned and looked at him. "Look. I'm sorry about Jake's mom. I had no idea—"

He lifted a hand to stop her. "Dunna worry about it. 'Twas before the lad can remember."

"What about you?" she asked. "Is that why you can't sleep?"

Just that fast, Gabe's demeanor changed. His jaw tightened, he rubbed his chin, and he glanced out over the loch. The aloofness had returned with gusto. " 'Tisna your concern, Ms. Morgan."

She looked at him. Maybe she'd crossed the line, but sheesh. She just wanted to help. Apparently, though, Jake's mom was an off-limits topic. Maybe, eventually, he'd open up. Thinking to try and lighten the mood, she gave a slight smile. "My name is Allie, by the way. My mother's name is Ms. Morgan," she said, and smiled. "Let's go get dinner started or we'll never have it ready in time."

With that, she turned on her heel and began to climb from the rocks. Her rubber sole hit a particularly smooth, wet stone and she pitched forward. She turned to try to right herself, and found herself falling backward.

A dirty word slipped from her mouth.

Just as she fell into Gabe's arms.

Breathless from the adrenaline rush, Allie could do little more than lie there, supported by Gabe as he stared down at her. That jaw still clenched, and those eyes bored into hers, weighing and measuring.

She could barely breathe.

"Does your mum know you swear like a man?" he asked.

Allie blinked.

A smile started at the corner of Gabe's mouth.

"She's worse than me," Allie said.

"I should have guessed."

Allie stared up into Gabe's green eyes.

She'd known him less than a week.

He made her heart flutter.

"Are you ready to go now?" he said.

"I think so," she answered. "Yes. I'm definitely ready."

"Great," he said, the r rolling. He continued to stare.

"Great," she mimicked.

Finally, Gabe lifted her upright. Neither said a word as they made their way back to Odin's Thumb.

After a few feet, Gabe spoke. "Your brogue needs a bit of work."

"Aye," Allie agreed.

And for the second time, she heard Gabe MacGowan laugh.

And as they walked past Leona's, the Royal Post, and Willy the Fishmonger's, Allie wondered briefly just how many more times she'd hear that deep, throaty laugh before she had to leave for good.

More important, how long it would take her to forget it.

"Are you nearly finished with those?" Allie asked, pointing to the chips sizzling in the deep fryer.

"Aye," he answered. "Are you nearly finished with those?" Gabe pointed to the cubed beef she'd been frying on the stove top.

"Yep."

"I daresay they look scrumptious, love," Dauber said. "Reminds me of my own mother's cooking."

"My mother didn't have to cook," said Lord Ramsey. "The servants did all of that."

Allie glanced at him while she flipped the meat. "What a little snot you must have been," she said.

"Must have been?" said the friar. "Sounds as though he still is."

They all laughed.

" 'Twas the times, as you know," Lord Ramsey said with a nod.

Gabe listened with curiosity. He'd hired the lass to help boot out—or at least force to stay quiet—the quirky lot of spirits who now took each and every opportunity to be around the American.

Not that he blamed them.

He'd been invited to the meeting tonight, and he hoped some sort of agreement could be met.

Not that he'd ever admit it, but he loved the irritating ghosts. They'd been a part of his life his *entire* life.

If only things could be different . . .

"Look you at how young Gabe there is gathering wool," said Lord Killigrew. "I cannot fathom what consumes his thoughts of late."

Gabe frowned at him.

"*Oui,*" Mademoiselle Bedeau agreed. " 'Tis something powerful, no doubt, to give him such a look."

Allie looked around. "Where's Captain Catesby? I haven't seen him today."

"He'll be back tonight," the friar said. "He made a short trip up the coast to see an old friend."

Allie cocked her head. "So he can just zap back and forth to and from wherever?"

Lord Killigrew grinned. "We all can. We sort of just . . . think it, and we're there. You see, we move about in the mortal world, but on our plane of existence."

Allie nodded. "That makes sense." She rubbed her chin. "Can other mortals, outside of Sealladh na Mara, see you?"

The friar nodded. "At times, aye, for a certainty. It's been our experience, though, that those who are especially receptive can fully grasp our presence, whether we want them to see us or not."

"Aye," said Lord Ramsey. "And there are those not so receptive who perceive us merely as that certain something that makes one glance over one's shoulder."

"Interesting. So Chester and Millie must have been relatively receptive?"

The lot laughed.

"Well," Allie said, glancing at Gabe and grabbing the platter of water pitchers. "Let's get this food served and then we'll both work the bar." A gleam lit her already gleaming eyes. "I've always wanted to do that."

Gabe watched her push through the kitchen door, only to hear a rousing, cheerful greeting from the patrons in the lobby as she entered.

How had the lass become such a well-liked fixture at his pub in such a short amount of time? Mayhap 'twas that cheery sort of personality she had. Everyone, spirited or no', responded to it.

He glanced up, and all of Odin's souls, Dauber included but minus Justin Catesby, had ridiculous smiles pasted to their ghostly faces.

Right then, Gabe knew he was in trouble.

Deep, deep trouble.

With that, he began loading the plates.

He had a feeling this would be a long night, indeed.

Chapter 10

Eight thirty, and the last of the dinner plates had been washed. Another successful meal without a problem or complaint. At least now Gabe was not surprised. Allie handled herself just as well with the live folk as she did with the dead ones. They all loved her. For Christ's sake, Willy MacMillan loved her.

And the lass could bloody well cook, too.

Amazing.

He tossed the dish towel onto the sink, dried his hands on the apron, and slipped it over his head. A few patrons remained in the pub, having a pint or two before heading home for the night.

Deciding to check on Jake and put him to bed, Gabe left the kitchen, peered into the pub, and then headed up the stairs. Opening the door to his room, he heard voices. Rather, one voice. A feminine one.

Allie's.

Quietly, he slipped closer to Jake's bedroom and listened at the door.

"How did you find out your da had died, Allie? Do you remember?" Jake asked.

Gabe's insides tightened.

"Well," Allie said, "I was about your age, I think. My father worked during the night, so he was gone a good bit of the time, and when he was home, he was sleeping."

Silence, so Gabe placed his fingertips on Jake's door and gave it a slight push. Leaning against the frame, he watched as well as listened.

Jake scratched his nose. "And so what happened?" he asked.

A somber expression crossed Allie's face, and she tried to smooth the cowlick at Jake's forehead. "My mother got a phone call during the night. My father'd had an accident at work and they'd called to tell her she needed to come right away to the hospital."

"Do you remember all of that, then?" Jake asked.

"No," she answered. "I was asleep. But I remember my mom waking me and my sisters to tell us Daddy had been in an accident." She thought a moment. "We had to bundle up and get dressed to go stay with our aunt that night."

"Do you remember burying him?" Jake asked. He was getting sleepy, rubbing his eyes and turning sideways in his favorite position.

"Yes, I do," Allie answered.

Jake thought for a moment. "My da has verra bad dreams. I think he's dreaming of my mother after she was dead. He wakes up screamin' sometimes, and he leaves and doesna come back for a long while. It scares me."

Gabe again froze. He didn't know if he should interrupt or let his son tell Allie what was obviously bothering him so badly. He chose to wait.

"Have you told him?" Allie asked Jake.

Jake shook his head and yawned. "Nay. I dunna want to make him upset." He looked up at her then, and reached out with his hand and grabbed hers in a tight grip.

"Can you help him, Allie? Captain Catesby says

you have a way with ghostly souls. He says you mend them. Do you think you can mend me da's soul? Even though he's alive?"

The lump that formed in Gabe's throat was nearly too big to swallow past. He eased away from Jake's door, not wanting Allie to know he'd overheard the conversation. Once out the door, he pulled it closed and stepped down the corridor. When he heard the door open, he walked toward it again.

When Allie stepped through, her eyes widened in surprise. "Oh. I'm . . . sorry. Jake came and got me and asked me to put him to bed." She glanced over her shoulder, toward his and Jake's small apartment, then shrugged. "I hope you don't mind?"

Gabe forced a half smile. "Nay, o' course no'. I thank you—"

"Gabe, come quickly," Ron, a frequent patron at Odin's, called up the stairs. "Your mother needs you on the phone in the kitchen straightaway. I couldna find the bloody cordless."

Gabe turned and hurried down the stairs, and he could hear Allie's steps right behind him. He made it to the kitchen and picked up the receiver Ron had laid on the counter. "Aye, Ma, what's wrong?"

His mother's voice was laced with worry. " 'Tis your auntie, Gabe. Wee Mary's in terrible pain. Her stomach. I dunna know what's wrong with her."

"I'll come straightaway," Gabe said. He hung up the phone and turned to Allie. "I'm sorry to ask this of you, but can you stay with Jake? Wee Mary's sick—"

"You both go, Gabe. I'll stay here and watch after Jake and Odin's," said Laura, Ron's wife. "Go. Hurry, and dunna worry about us."

With a quick look at Allie, who nodded and was pushing him toward the door, Gabe grabbed his keys to the Rover from a hook on the wall and hurried out the door. Allie was silently right on his heels.

In minutes, they were at Wee Mary's. Gabe jumped out and hit the gravel lane leading to Mary's cottage running. He swung open the front door and found his mum, sitting beside Mary on the sofa. Mary was doubled over in pain.

Gabe knelt on the floor and put a hand to Mary's forehead. Her skin felt hot and was flushed. "What's wrong with you now, you wee troublemaker?" he asked, trying to keep his voice from shaking. "Have you gone and had some bad fish?" He glanced at his mum. "She's burnin' up."

Allie came round and knelt beside him. She reached over, picked up Wee Mary's slender wrist, and held it for a moment. "How long have you had a fever?" she asked his aunt, then smoothed back the hair from her forehead.

"Just since earlier today, I suppose," she said, her voice weak. "Och, me stomach is killing me." She pressed low and to the right. "Just here. And I didna eat fish today, lad."

"Do you have your appendix?" Allie asked.

"Aye," Mary answered, then moaned.

Allie turned to Gabe. "I'd be willing to bet it's her appendix. How close is the nearest hospital?"

"Too far to wait for the ambulance service to arrive," he answered. "Mary, love, I'm going to pick you up and put you in the Rover, aye? We're goin' to the infirmary. Allie here will ride in the back with you." He glanced at his mother. "I'll call you once we get there."

His mother, whose face had turned ashen, nodded. "Aye, lad. Hurry."

As he scooped up his wee aunt, he noticed Allie grab the pillow and wool throw from the back of the sofa, then bend down and grab Wee Mary's house slippers. They dashed to the Rover. Allie ran just ahead, opened the back door, climbed in, and Gabe placed his aunt on the seat, her head on the pillow in Allie's lap. He jumped in and they took off.

Eighteen minutes later they arrived at the small local infirmary. Luck was with them as the emergent room was empty. With his wee aunt in his arms, he ran straightaway to the first exam room he saw and placed her on the gurney.

"There, you wee witch," he said to Mary. "The doctor will see you shortly. And dunna be rude to him. I know you hate doctors."

When he turned, he saw Allie speaking to one of the nurses, who in turn called for the doctor. A short man in a white coat came hurrying out of another room and headed straight over to Mary. After several questions, he started barking orders. A nurse came over, started an IV, and drew some blood. The next thing Gabe knew, Wee Mary was headed to X-ray.

"She'll be right back, lad," the doctor said, following Mary's gurney.

As soon as Wee Mary was out of sight, he immediately turned to look for Allie.

She was standing right behind him.

Gabe rubbed the back of his neck. "Christ."

Allie touched his arm. "She'll be okay. You made really great time getting here."

Gabe nodded. "I dunna mean to act like a baby. Mary's like me other mother."

Allie smiled. "You sound far from a baby, Mr. Mac-Gowan. Apparently you didn't hear the words that flowed from your mouth on the way over here."

He grinned. "Sorry for that."

"Oh, call your mother."

Gabe nodded. "Right." He pulled his mobile from

the clip on his belt and dialed his mum's number. Before he finished the update, the doctor came rushing in to the waiting area. Gabe handed the phone to Allie.

"Your aunt needs emergent surgery, I'm afraid. That appendix has to come out." He scratched his bald head. "She's mighty lucky it hasna burst yet."

Gabe nodded. "Right. What do I need to do?"

"She's signed the permit but wants to speak to you before we take her back. This way."

Gabe nodded at Allie, who waved him on and continued talking to his mother, and hurried after the doctor.

In the holding area, Gabe eased over to Wee Mary and leaned over, planting a kiss on her forehead. "You'll be fine, woman. The doctor will take grand care of you."

"Och, I know that," she said, and Gabe could tell she was still in pain. "What about Odin's?"

Gabe shook his head. "Dunna worry. Allie's helping out and doin' a fine job."

Through her misery, Wee Mary gave Gabe a slight smile. "I'll just bet she is, love."

"Sir, we need to prep her now," a young nurse in blue scrubs said.

Mary patted his hand. "Go now. I'll see you shortly."

"I'll be here when you wake up," he said.

Gabe watched the nurse wheel his aunt away. When they turned a corner, he made his way back to the waiting area.

Allie was sitting in one of the plastic chairs near the exit. When he approached she stood. "Call your mom back. She's so worried."

He did, spoke with her for a moment, and then promised to call once Wee Mary returned from surgery.

Nearly two hours later, she did.

The doctor found Gabe and came right to him. "Your aunt did fine, lad. Luckily, we were able to do the surgery laproscopically. The appendix hadn't burst, thank God. She'll have to stay a couple of nights, but she'll be fine."

"Can we see her?" Gabe asked.

"Aye, although she's quite out of it," the doctor said.

Gabe and Allie went to the recovering unit, and as soon as Gabe lifted his aunt's hand, she opened her eyes. "See, laddy? I'm fine. Now go home. I just want to sleep."

Gabe dropped another kiss on her forehead. "I'll see your wee bossy self tomorrow, then. Aye?"

Mary was already back to sleep.

After a few words with the doctor, who assured Gabe Mary would indeed be just fine, he and Allie left.

They drove in silence. Comfortable silence, Gabe thought, and he was thankful for it. He waited for Allie to bring up the conversation she'd had with Jake, but blessedly, she didn't.

He couldna answer questions he himself didna know the answers to, like why he'd been having horrid, vivid nightmares about his deceased wife.

What would he say if Allie asked him about it?

More than once, Gabe felt her gaze on him while they drove, and finally, she spoke.

"Your Odin's lot doesn't want you and Jake to leave," she said.

He glanced at her. "I suppose I never wanted them ousted anyway. Just hushed whilst I show the place. I tried everything and they'd no' listen to me."

Allie nodded. "I'm used to dealing with people who can't interact with them. They simply want the spirits gone." She shrugged. "The thing is, usually, spirits haunt because their souls are troubled and need mending."

"What do you mean?"

Allie shrugged. "Most of the time, the spirits have pieces of their life, or death, missing from their memory. Perhaps they don't know how they died, or what happened to their loved ones after their death. And it's been my experience that the souls who linger here on earth were the ones who died an untimely, or unnatural, death."

He regarded her. "What do you do to help?"

"I research the names, places, dates, and find out what sort of information I can." She gave a winsome smile. "I counsel. Sometimes they're consoled just to be able to communicate with a mortal, and in a positive way."

Gabe nodded. "Makes sense."

She scratched her brow. "You see, the mortals pay me, but it's the unsettled souls who are actually helped." She looked at him. "Do you see?"

"Aye." And he did. He'd grown up with the Odin's lot, as did his mum and da and Wee Mary and most of the villagers.

"How did the Odin's souls come to be in Sealladh na Mara, anyway?" she asked.

Gabe studied the reflection of the Rover's headlamps on the road. "Aye, well, they each have their own tale to tell, but they all have one thing in common."

"What's that?"

He gave her a quick glance. "Sealladh na Mara is where each of their bodies washed ashore, at one point in time or another." He shrugged. "I believe the friar was the first to arrive."

"Wow. Amazing. Not at all what I expected when I took the job."

Gabe gave her a quick glance. "I think what you're tryin' to say, lass, is you scammed me."

"Ha-ha, no. No, that's not what I'm saying at all, smarty-pants." She half turned in her seat and faced him, and although he couldna keep his eyes on her, he knew she kept hers on *him*. "What I'm saying is I've been in Sealladh na Mara for almost a week and from what I can tell, the Odin's lot is not the problem." She sniffed. "It's you."

Gabe stared at the road ahead. He didn't look at her. "Is that so?" he asked.

"Yes, it is."

"How do you figure that?" he said.

Allie was quiet for a moment, then heaved a big sigh. "I'd be able to help the situation a lot more thoroughly if I knew the whole story. Everything. As in why, exactly, you want to leave." She waved her hand. "You know—all that stuff you keep telling me isn't any of my business?" She patted his hand. "Well, sorry to burst your bubble of privacy, but that's the stuff I need to know in order to help." She straightened and stared out the windscreen. "*Everything*, in other words."

Gabe slid a sideways glance at her, then set his gaze back to the road. The lights of Sealladh na Mara flickered up the hill, and beside him sat a woman he'd known less than a bloody week.

Yet he felt as though he could trust her with his life.

And that thought scared him worse than the nightmares.

What terrified him even more than either of those things was the overwhelming urge to put the Rover in park, pull her onto his lap, and kiss the mouth he seemed unable to stop thinking about.

Instead, he blew out another breath. "Let's see what happens, aye?"

A very satisfied grunt escaped her throat. 'Twas one of victory, Gabe thought.

"Aye, indeed," she said.

Gabe shook his head and pulled into the lane leading to Sealladh na Mara.

He'd been right.

Deep, deep trouble.

Once inside, Gabe thanked Ron and his wife for staying with Jake, and when they left he locked the front door to Odin's. When he turned, the keys slipped from his hands, and he bent to retrieve them.

Allie, standing right beside him, did the same.

Their heads knocked together.

"Ow, sorry," said Allie, rubbing her forehead.

Gabe stared at her and rubbed his own. "Aye, me as well."

The low light from the single lamp turned on in the lobby fell over Allie's face, and the beauty of it gave Gabe a lump in his throat. He felt like a daft lad of sixteen, unable to speak without tripping over his own bloody tongue. So he simply stared.

Allie did the same.

And for a moment or two, they stood. He couldna help but notice the curve of her lower lip, the shape of her jaw, and the depth of those blue eyes. The smallest of freckles crossed over her nose, and . . . damn, he couldna stop looking at those lips . . .

"I, uh, hope Wee Mary will be all right tonight," Allie said. She gave a hesitant smile. "If she needs someone to stay with her I'll be more than happy to go back."

Gabe blinked. "Right. Thank you verra much for offering." He rubbed his jaw. "Er, good night, then."

She smiled, and the sight of it nearly buckled his knees.

"Night." And with that, she turned and headed up the stairs.

Gabe watched her go until she disappeared round the second-floor landing. He continued to stand there, like a dolt. Staring.

Deep, *deep* trouble, indeed.

Chapter 11

Three days passed with not much activity at Odin's Thumb at all, really. Allie continued to help with the meals, and each night they'd gather at the pub. There were a few regulars from Sealladh na Mara who made it part of their evening ritual to stop by and have a pint or two before heading home. Afterward, once they closed up the pub, Gabe would hastily say good night and head up to his and Jake's apartment.

He was avoiding her. She could tell.

And for some crazy reason, she could think of very little save that night they'd stood in the foyer near the lobby. Staring.

She could hardly get Gabe's face out of her mind.

The man had studied her—maybe he hadn't even known she could tell. But she could tell.

And she'd liked it.

Good God, she hadn't been able to help herself. Never had she encountered a man like Gabe MacGowan. So intense, so brooding.

So sexy.

Allie slapped her hand to her forehead. "Ugh, get a grip, Morgan. You didn't come here to lust over your employer . . ."

Since Gabe was avoiding her, that would leave Allie

each night with five nutty spirits, plus Dauber, to contend with. So they talked. They played cards.

They *conspired.*

Wee Mary had returned from the hospital and was doing well. She hadn't returned to work yet and wouldn't for a few weeks. That was fine with Allie. She rather enjoyed working at Odin's.

Especially alongside Gabe MacGowan.

"Your play, love," Dauber said, interrupting her thoughts.

"I can tell by the look on her lovely face just who she's thinking of," said Lord Killigrew. "Lucky bastard."

Allie threw down a card. "There is no look on my face, you silly nobleman." She glanced at the pile of cards on the table. Some were real. Others were conjured. Allie soon realized that the souls of Odin's Thumb had a fantastic knack for conjuring. Lord Killigrew had produced a conjured deck of cards that only the spirits could touch, while Allie had used cards from a real deck. Perhaps not the most accurate of hands, she thought, but it worked close enough.

She grinned. "I just wiped you out. Full house, Lord Killigrew. Read 'em and weep!"

Lord Killigrew grinned. "Indeed you did, you wily lass."

"So, is young Gabe still avoiding you?" the friar asked. "I daresay he's getting quite good at it."

Allie nodded. "Yes, I'm afraid he is, Drew."

"He's more the fool for it, says I," said Justin. He gave Allie a wink.

"He'll be at the ceilidh, though, won't he?" Mademoiselle asked. "He hasn't been to one in quite some time, come to think of it."

Allie leaned back and stared out the window. "Maybe he'll come to this one?"

Lord Ramsey blew out a breath. "I wouldn't count on it, miss. But if anyone can draw him out, 'twill be you for a certainty."

"Aye, she'd draw me out," said Lord Killigrew.

"It doesn't take much to draw you out, boy," said Justin.

Everyone laughed.

"So, tell me," Allie said when the chuckles died down. "How is it you all came to be here?"

At first, everyone was silent. The souls glanced at each other, possibly waiting to see who would start. Justin took the lead.

He leaned toward her. "Strangely enough, we all know how we died. 'Tis a mystery, though, how our bodies all washed up on Sealladh na Mara's shores." He shrugged. " 'Tis a good thing, methinks. Still, 'tis puzzling." He inclined his head. "The friar there arrived first, not long after his wagon o' mead was set upon by highwaymen. Then myself, after a rather dodgy fellow shot me in the back and then pushed me overboard my own bloody ship. Next came the lovely Elise, which, as you can tell by the fetching bow she uses, had an unfortunate date with Madame Guillotine."

"I was quite innocent, mademoiselle," Elise said to Allie.

Allie nodded.

Justin waved a hand. "And then those two dolts," he said in the direction of Lords Ramsey and Killigrew. "Bloody fools took to a duel—"

"Aye, and over a lass," said Ramsey.

"I daresay she wasn't worth it," said Killigrew.

They all laughed.

Allie shook her head. "You shot each *other*?" she asked.

Killigrew grinned. "While I, too, fell to my demise, I've no doubt, miss, that my aim hit its mark first."

"My arse it did," said Ramsey.

"Enough, lads, enough," said Justin. "You're boring the poor maid to tears and I vow I cannot bear to hear the tale again."

Allie rubbed her chin. "Leona told me that Sealladh na Mara was possibly cursed, and that's why everyone can see and interact with all of you."

Justin gave her an arrogant smile. "Doesna sound so much like a curse, then, aye?"

"I remember the first time I discovered a mortal who could actually see me," said Drew Digby. " 'Twas a small lad from the castle on yon cliff." He inclined in that direction with a slight nod. "A MacGowan, to be sure. A fine family, even back then, although the wee troublemaker tried his best to get me to participate in his antics."

"Like what?" Allie said.

"Oh," the friar said, smoothing his hair down, "frightening his sisters, for starters, and I promise you, I only conjured a small hedgehog or two to scamper from beneath their beds."

They all chuckled.

"That's something else that fascinates me," said Allie. "How exactly do you conjure?"

"*Oui*," said Elise. "Justin taught us to simply concentrate on whatever it is we wish for the mortal to behold, then voila! It happens!"

Allie glanced at Justin. He wagged his brows. She wasn't sure she even wanted to know how he learned.

Allie leaned back and smiled. "So, how did you first meet Gabe?"

"Oh, he was such a sweet little dear," said Elise. "With those chubby cheeks and green eyes and darling little crooked mouth."

"Och, he was a fine little lad, indeed," said Justin. "Although from the moment he could walk, he was quite the handful."

"We all followed to the infirmary when he was born," said Killigrew. "We stayed invisible, but there he was, lying in the nursery with a dozen other babes."

"Aye, but his holler was indeed the loudest of them all," said Ramsey. "Dandy set of lungs, that young Gabe."

"So much like his own da," said Justin. He gave a winsome smile. " 'Tis strange, at times, to think of Gerald as a wee babe. But we watched him come into this world, too."

Allie watched the spirits of Sealladh na Mara with a newfound respect. They'd watched so many babies mature into adults, only to lose them at some point in life. To grow to love someone so dearly, only to watch them die. How very sad . . .

"So you can see why we dunna want the lads to leave us, aye?" said Justin.

Allie regarded each soul, and the very same thing shone in each of their ghostly eyes.

Love for Gabe and Jake.

"Yes, I certainly can," she answered. "And the only way I think I can help is to find out what's truly bothering Gabe." She met Justin's gaze. "Jake says he has bad dreams of his wife."

He nodded. "Indeed, I can see how—"

"Shht!" said Elise. Her face softened when she looked at Allie. "I don't mean to sound so crude, but 'tis Gabe's tale to tell and no one else's. 'Twould be wrong of us to tell it behind his back, *non*?"

Allie nodded. "You're absolutely right. I'm sure with a little time, he'll open up."

She just hoped it wasn't too late when he decided to do it.

Allie stretched and yawned. "Well, I'm off to bed." She stood and faced the lot. She started for the stairs. "Good night, then."

A round of good-nights sounded in the room, and Justin rose from his seat. "I'll walk you to your chambers, lass."

Allie led the way across the lobby and to the stairs, Justin just behind her. As they reached the third-floor platform, Justin fell into step beside her.

She glanced at him, noticed he was looking down at her, smiled, and shook her head.

"What is it?" he said.

"You. You're like, what, six foot two?"

"Four."

"Okay, six foot four. You're walking beside me, you tower over me, you're swaggering in that arrogant way guys walk, with your overcoat swishing around your legs, and although your physical matter isn't really there, *you're* really there." She looked at him. "Your soul. The thing that *really* counts." She looked away and shook her head again. "I guess that's what fascinates me so much about the unliving."

Justin chuckled, a low, deep sound in his throat, and as they reached Allie's door, he turned to her. "Well then, lass, let me say that I've never been more bloody thrilled to be amongst the unliving." He winked, and gave her a sweeping low bow. "Until the morn, Allie Morgan."

He rose, gave her a lopsided grin, and swaggered off down the corridor.

Allie watched him until he disappeared.

Literally.

With a yawn, she let herself into her room and readied herself for bed.

Gabe could hear the moan, and somehow, he thought he was awake.

And that the moan came from *someone else*.

Yet he lay there, unable to move, unable to fully

rouse. His heart slammed against his chest, and sweat beaded his forehead. A vision appeared, foggy, unclear, and tendrils of icy mist slipped about his throat and squeezed, and the breath left his lungs in a rush of forced air . . .

"No!" he shouted, and Gabe found himself sitting straight up in bed. He blinked, trying fiercely to clear the awful vision.

But before it faded, it changed. He was awake now, not half asleep. The tendrils of mist became dank hair, auburn hair—*Kait's hair*—and the place where her face should have been remained dark, shadowy, hollow. From a body that wasn't fully formed, a long arm rose, and from that, a finger.

It pointed straight at Gabe.

Make her leave . . .

"No!" Gabe shouted. His eyes flew open. This time, he truly did sit up. He glanced around, peered into every darkened corner, and found nothing. He wiped his forehead that was indeed beaded with sweat, and tried to calm his ragged breath.

He couldn't tell which time he'd risen was real.

Swearing, he pushed the duvet from his body and walked to the window, lifted the pane, and let the cold air drift in. It cooled his face and bare body, and he closed his eyes and inhaled, tasting the salt of the loch on his tongue. Familiar things that haunted him yet soothed him at the same time.

Christ, he was daft.

Although he knew what he'd find, he checked the clock. One a.m. Just as he thought.

After brushing his teeth and washing his face, he pulled on a pair of jeans, a long-sleeved shirt he left unbuttoned, checked on Jake, who blessedly was still asleep, and slipped out into the darkened corridor. At the landing, he stopped and looked up.

It took everything he had not to take the next flight of steps and go wake Allie Morgan. Why he had the insane urge to simply talk to her, he didna know. Christ Almighty, he was losing his bloody mind . . .

He shook his head and started down, toward the kitchen. Adrenaline pumped through his veins, and he felt as though he wanted to run as fast and hard as he could, just to make the dreams go away. He'd lose his mind alone. He wouldna drag anyone else along. Especially a virtual stranger.

A stranger you're powerfully attracted to . . .

With an intensity building within, the need to release the pent-up frustration of what was happening to him, Gabe hurried through the dark. Just as he neared the kitchen, he slammed into a body. He reached out and grabbed a pair of arms that seemingly reached for him at the same time.

Allie gasped and covered her mouth. "Oh, gosh, I'm sorry: I—Gabe, what's wrong? Are you okay? Is it Jake?"

Gabe realized only then how tightly he held on to Allie's upper arms, and he could only imagine what his expression looked like.

He loosened his grip, but didna let go. "Nay. No' Jake."

"Take a deep breath, Gabe," her calming voice spoke just above a whisper. "Close your eyes and breathe."

He did as she asked, and with that deep breath Allie's scent wafted up, soft, feminine, a bit flowery, and clean. When he opened his eyes, he could barely see her, and only with what the small amount of light shed by the single lamp in the lobby allowed. She was mostly in shadows, but he could tell her hair was down, and that she wore something dark, thin, and soft. And although her words were soothing, calm, her breathing told a different tale. She was either nervous or scared. Maybe both.

"Look at me," she said, her fingers tightening around his forearms. He hadn't even noticed right away that she'd held on. "Focus, Gabe, breathe again, and *look* at me."

Again, he did as she asked. He opened his eyes and looked down, and the amber glow from the lobby's lamp made her blue eyes appear dark, glassy, and fathomless. She said nothing else. She simply stared up at him, breathed with him, waiting.

And it was more than he could bloody take.

Locking in on her gaze, Gabe eased one hand up and threaded it through the heavy mass of Allie's hair—just as soft as he imagined. He watched with fascination as one long curl coiled around his finger as though it had a life of its own.

Slowly, he slid his hand to her jaw, tilted it just so, and held her chin as he lowered his head. His mouth settled over hers, soft, full lips that seemed to fit his perfectly. They stood there, mouths pressed together, and *breathed.* Gabe edged closer, cupped the back of her head with one hand, slid the other to her waist, and barely opened his mouth. When his tongue touched hers, he groaned, a sound he felt deep in his chest, a sound he had no control over.

Allie moved then, and where she'd been still as a statue before, her hands left his forearms and slid up to his neck, encircling it and pulling his mouth closer to hers. She kissed *him* then, hesitant, yet willing, and Christ, she tasted so good, he wanted more. Leaning into her, he pressed her against the wall, felt the softness of her body beneath whatever thin slip of something she wore, and pulled her closer still. Their mouths moved together, his hands held her head at just the right angle, and there, in the dark and without words, they kissed.

Allie's soft fingers trailed his jaw, slid close to their mouths, and held on tightly as he pulled her closer still. One hand moved over his chest and slipped round to his back. The sensation of her skin brushing his drove him mad. Christ, it'd been forever since a woman had touched him . . .

"Ahem!"

Gabe and Allie both jumped at the same time, efficiently clunking their heads together. Gabe held her at arm's length, and then let go and stepped back farther. He kept his eyes trained on hers. She rubbed her forehead. He rubbed his.

He didna trust his voice at all.

"I do believe 'tis time for the young lady to return to bed," said Friar Digby with more severity than Gabe remembered ever hearing. "She's spent way too long out here in this drafty hall"—he peered at him through his ghostly cowl—"with *you*." He smiled at Allie. "Miss? Shall I accompany you?"

Allie glanced at Gabe, the corner of her kiss-swollen mouth lifted into a tiny smile, and she nodded. "Sure. Thanks, Drew." As she stepped around Gabe, she looked at him once more. "Good night."

"And to you," Gabe said.

He watched them both leave.

Turning, he put his back to the wall and rested his weight there. With one hand, he rubbed his jaw, then scrubbed his eyes.

Christ Almighty, what had he just done?

He was damned lucky the only spirit to have seen them was the friar. One never knew where they lurked.

Pushing off the wall, Gabe made for the kitchen,

filled a large glass with water from the tap, and drank it down in two, three gulps. Wiping his mouth with the back of his hand, he set the glass down and stared out the window. The loch gleamed in the moonlight, and somehow it *looked* cold outside. Just what he needed.

Without another thought, he walked to the side door, opened it up, and stepped out. A blast of icy air hit his bare chest, his throat, his face. He stood there for several minutes—maybe longer—until his heated body had cooled, and his heart had slowed to normal.

As he glanced at the cliff in the distance, and at the remnants of his ancestor's keep, he wondered briefly if his bloody heart would ever beat normal again.

As long as Allie Morgan was around, he doubted it.

With that gloomy thought in mind, Gabe eased back inside and closed the door.

Allie closed her door, then turned her back to it and rested her weight there. Briefly, she closed her eyes.

And that brought back every memory, every sensation of Gabe's hands moving over her skin, his mouth tasting hers, his weight pressing against her.

And the absolute power and desperation the man had bottled up inside. Allie knew it had taken nearly all his strength not to unleash that power and desperation— she could feel it simmering just below the surface of his skin, feel it in his kiss, and in how his hands had clung to her.

Opening her eyes, she heaved a hefty breath and moved to the alcove window seat, lifted the glass, and stared out over the loch. Cold and windy, the air touched her skin, cooling it, somehow soothing it, and bringing her back down to earth just a little.

Enough to realize something else.

Desperation and power weren't the only things she saw and felt in Gabe MacGowan. After the friar interrupted their kiss and Gabe had stepped back, he'd not broken his stare. But Allie recognized something immediately in the depths of those green eyes.

Fear.

Fear of what, she had no idea. Gabe MacGowan was not the type of man who feared much of anything. His entire being radiated confidence, strength, power. She'd noticed it right away, from the second she'd met him at Odin's.

No, scratch that. To be perfectly honest, she'd sensed that during their short phone conversation.

The briny scent of the sea washed over her as the breeze slipped over the loch, and through the tiny beam of light cast by the moon, the ebb and flow of the tide lapped against the pebbly shores and rocks of Sealladh na Mara. She could see the outlines of the boats anchored close, and across the loch and to the right, the craggy cliff and Gabe's ancestor's old castle. She and Jake hadn't made it up there.

Allie suspected they just might never get to.

Leaning her head against the cool wood of the jamb, Allie continued to stare out. What was she doing here? As soon as she had arrived, she knew Gabe was fighting a losing battle with the Odin's lot. They had their mind set to keep the ones they loved close by—and that meant doing whatever it took to keep Gabe and Jake from selling Odin's and leaving the village. She'd been here less than seven days and was pretty sure nothing had changed. So much had happened in the short time she'd been around that there hadn't been much of an opportunity to have everyone sit down and talk things over—Gabe included.

She highly suspected it wouldn't happen any time soon. But it certainly needed to. And she'd make it a point to call that meeting to order that next night.

Again, memories hit her of that kiss, of that man, and worse than any of those things, the way he'd made her *feel*. It wasn't love—they'd known each other way too little for that. But it was *something*. A *connection*.

A connection that went far above attraction.

Allie's eyes drifted shut, and the last thing on her mind before consciousness shut down was Gabe's mouth against hers, the way his body trembled so slightly she nearly missed it, and the urgency in his kiss . . .

Chapter 12

The alarm went off and Allie awoke, strangely enough, in the bed. She didn't remember leaving the alcove, but subconsciously, she must have started to get too cold and moved to the warmth of the duvet.

As she gathered her bearings, her gaze traveled to the fireplace. A nice blaze crackled there, making the room warm and toasty.

She certainly hadn't done that in her sleep.

Climbing out of bed, Allie gathered clean under-stuff, jeans, her favorite black *Raiders of the Lost Ark* T-shirt and her toiletries, and crossed the hall to the bathroom. After a quick shower and a fast towel-drying of hair, she pulled a comb through several times, put on her boots, grabbed her peacoat, and headed downstairs. She'd go to Leona's first, as had been her habit after that first day, and then head back to Odin's to start on the lunch meal.

She'd already made her mind up to smile, laugh, and do her best to put Gabe at ease about last night. The last thing she wanted was for him to feel obli-gated. They'd shared a kiss. Okay—it was way more than a kiss. It was something more and Allie couldn't put her finger on it, yet she was pretty sure Gabe didn't recognize it. Either way, she'd had enough ex-perience with guys to know Gabe probably would avoid her like the plague this morning. If she laughed and pretended nothing bothered her, maybe he'd loosen up.

Or not.

Butterflies of nerves hit her stomach as she slipped downstairs. She knew it was always weird, the initial encounter with a person with whom something had happened for the first time. She hadn't experienced the feeling in quite a long while, but was positive it'd never been as bad as now.

But when she reached the first floor, the very first person she laid eyes on was Laina, Gabe's mom.

Laina, dressed in a pair of khakis, a dark blue sweater, and sneakers, gave her a big smile. *"Ciamar a tha sibh?"*

Allie blinked.

With a laugh, Laina patted her arm. " 'Tis Gaelic, lass. It means *How are you*?"

Allie smiled in return. "Oh, that's lovely. And I'm fine, thank you." She tried to repeat the question in Gaelic but failed miserably.

Laina, though, took it in stride. "Nice try, love, and I'm fine, as well." She heaved a sigh. "Looks like 'tis me and you for the next couple of days, then, lass. Are ye up to it?"

Allie glanced around. "Where's Gabe?"

"Oh, he has business to tend in Inverness. He'll be back by Saturday."

Wow. She'd expected Gabe to avoid her, but not to the extent of leaving Sealladh na Mara. She forced a smile. "Oh, okay."

Laina studied Allie. "You've really helped him out of a bind, you know. Usually 'tis Wee Mary and Katey runnin' Odin's meals. Without you here Gabe would be in a terrible mess, aye?"

Allie smiled. "I'm glad to be of some help." She

inclined her head. "Do you want something from Leona's? I'm headed there now."

Laina shook her head. "Och, no, I had me porridge early this morn. Thanks, though."

With a wave, Allie set off. No sooner had she paid Leona for her pie and coffee and had started off to the wharf than she picked up company.

"I like a woman who can eat. Shows her confidence, methinks. And from what I've seen, you've loads of it."

Allie jumped, only because she wasn't expecting a voice so close. She looked up into the ghostly dark eyes of Captain Catesby.

He gave her a wicked grin and a slight nod. "Have you missed me, lass?"

Allie grinned. "You mean since yesterday? Well, Captain Catesby, yes, actually, I have. Where'd you go off to the other day, anyway?"

"Please. Call me by my Christian name."

With a nod, Allie made the correction. "Justin. Where'd you go?"

A slow smile spread across the handsome spirit's face. "Much better. And to answer your question, off to the North of England to see a friend."

Allie looked at him. "What sort of friend?"

Justin clasped his hands behind his back as they walked. "Och, a fierce lad with an ornery mortal for a curator." He leaned his head toward her. "Methinks the sweet old woman is tryin' to be a matchmaker."

Allie blinked. "A match between who?"

Justin shrugged. "Well, 'tis just my observation, but the sweet old wily woman who watches over the castle ruins has a bonny niece from the Colonies on her way for a wee visit." He winked. "I've no' seen a more cunning woman than that old curator."

Allie stopped. "A match between your friend, who I am suspecting is a spritied soul, and the niece?"

He grinned. "Stranger things have occurred, lass."

She supposed he was right. The thought intrigued her, though.

They passed the last few establishments and then made their way to the wharf. While Allie picked her way over the rocks and pebbles, Justin seemed to glide.

"Glorious day, aye?" he asked as Allie settled onto her usual bench. He inhaled, but shook his head. "I do indeed miss the salty air. 'Twas one of my most favorite scents, the sea."

She smiled. "Mine, too. Sit with me?" she asked, nodding to the space beside her.

"There'd be no greater pleasure," he said. "Well, I could think o' one, or mayhap two."

"No doubt." Allie rolled her eyes, sat down, and glanced out over the loch. The sun peeked through a cluster of clouds, making the water sparkle. The air was still crisp and cold and the breeze wasn't quite so fierce. "It is a beautiful day."

Justin Catesby did sit then, leaving a decent amount of space between them. Allie studied him closely—enough to make him cock his head and grin.

"Why do you inspect me so, lass?" he asked.

Allie shrugged and opened the heavy wax paper sealing her pie. "You're not very old, are you?"

Justin barked out a laugh. "A good bit older than you, I'd warrant."

Taking a bite, Allie chewed, swallowed, and wiped her mouth. "No, I don't mean how old you are *now*. I mean how old you were when you passed." She looked at him. "You seem so much more . . . experienced than what you should be."

Justin leaned forward, elbows resting on knees spread wide in the fashion that guys do. "I was thirty-one to answer your question." He gave her a grin that was surely meant to flirt. "Experience? Aye, I've plenty o' that, love."

Allie glanced at him while she ate. "You big flirt. I knew you were naughty from the first moment I laid eyes on you. I bet the girls in your day didn't have a chance."

"Not even a smidge of one, I'm afraid." He turned to her, wavy brown hair brushing the tops of his shoulders. The leather tricorn hat that made him appear all the more roguish. Although a bit transparent, his brown eyes gleamed of mischief, danger, and something else Allie couldn't place. His large hands were clasped, thick veins crossing the tops, and he wore a ring on his left forefinger.

Allie bent close to study it. It had a half-moon and what appeared to be a . . . tooth? A large, pointed fang of a tooth.

"Interesting ring, Catesby," she said, rising and looking him in the eye. "What's it mean?"

Justin smiled, flexed his hand, and glanced at it. "Och, nothin', lass. Just some trinket I won in a game of bones."

Sipping her coffee, she lifted a brow. "Looks ferocious if you ask me."

He laughed, and shook his head. "I've heard you've made a bit of progress with young Gabe."

Allie's thoughts turned to the kiss they'd shared, and she nearly choked on her coffee. She wondered if the friar had ratted them out. She wiped her mouth and crumpled the wax wrapper. "Er, not really—"

Justin's eyes narrowed as he studied her face. "You've no' a poker face, lass, 'tis a certainty." He lifted a brow. "If I didna know any better I'd say you were guilty of something."

Allie frowned. "I'm not guilty of anything."

With an intense stare that all but made Allie squirm,

Justin searched her face, from her chin, to her lips, nose, and then eyes. "Hmm. I'm no' sure about that, lassie, but 'twill be immensely enjoyable to wrench the information from you."

"My granny would call you a perv-o."

After a moment more of studying her, Justin threw back his head and laughed. "Aye, no doubt she would." He rose, glancing out to sea. "Are you plannin' on goin' to the ceilidh Saturday?"

Allie blinked. "Yes. Why?"

A slow smile with much anticipation spread across his handsome face.

And with that he faded into the sunlight.

Over the next two days, Allie and Laina saw Jake off to school, opened Odin's for lunch and dinner, and everything went off without a hitch or glitch. As she and Gabe's mom prepared the food, Lords Ramsey and Killigrew sat close by on whatever empty countertop they could find and flirted with gusto. Laina giggled and would scold them, but Allie could tell she thoroughly enjoyed it. Mademoiselle would stay close by, taking great interest in how to prepare the meals, and the friar would sit quietly in the corner with Dauber, discussing only God knows what.

And then there was suave Captain Justin Catesby, who always seemed to be going the very same direction Allie was going. He was full of charm and Allie fully believed the women in his day had no chance whatsoever of repelling him.

Allie sat back and closely regarded the souls of Sealladh na Mara. She quickly decided the MacGowan case was by far the strangest case she'd accepted. Employed to quiet the determined spirits so Gabe MacGowan could properly sell his establishment, she hadn't needed very long at all to see that the problem didn't lie with the spirits, but with Gabe MacGowan himself.

She'd told him as much, too.

She'd fought hard not to question little Jake. But she withheld, hoping Gabe would tell her just what it was making him run from his family and friends.

And Sealladh na Mara.

Each night, after the last patron had left Odin's, Allie would sit in the pub with Justin, Drew, the lords, Dauber, and Elise. Story after story was told, and before long, Allie felt as though she'd known them all her life. She also realized Odin's Thumb's spirits were the most contented souls she'd ever encountered. They weren't haunting the pub and inn. They weren't haunting Sealladh na Mara. They looked at the quiet little seaside village as their home.

Their home in the afterlife, so to speak.

They loved it, and they loved Gabe and Jake Mac-Gowan.

And didn't want them to leave.

So, it seemed, while Allie was hired to do one thing, the task at hand had turned into something else altogether.

She had to get to the bottom of Gabe's distress and change his mind.

Jake was adorable, full of energy and questions and really, a continuous sponge. He'd ask all sorts of things about America, life in general, and was especially interested in science—Allie's specialty was astronomy, and Jake was more than enthusiastsic about sitting outside to stare at the sky once it grew dark. After school, though, she'd walk to the wharf with him, the Odin's crew plus Dauber in tow, and in the wade pool they'd discover new creatures with each fresh tide. The nobles, being younger, she supposed,

had loads of personal experience from their own childhood to offer on how to capture a small fish, or any
other urchins lying just below the surface of the water.

At night, before he went to bed, Jake would ask Allie
to tell him a story. That, of course, was a cover for
his grandmother's benefit. What Jake really wanted to
know and asked all sorts of questions about was *death*.

Particularly about her own personal experience with
her father.

Allie didn't want to pry and ask things of Jake she
knew might upset Gabe. And God knew Gabe himself
was experiencing something awful, and apparently almost every night of his life. The night they kissed?
Just before that he'd been in a terrible state, eyes
wide, nostrils flared—it had been all Allie could do to
get him to come back to the present.

Jake had told her of the dreams Gabe had, and
she'd assumed that was what had happened that night.
She wondered what they were. Obviously, they were
pretty horrific to shake Gabe up so badly. Jake had
mentioned they were of his dead mother. She wondered if he was right.

Either way, it troubled the little guy. Troubled the
hell out of the big guy, too, but he'd left soon after.
Allie had a feeling Gabe would clam up tight if she
ever brought it up.

She'd have to let him come to her.

Pulling herself from her thoughts, Allie inspected
herself in the mirror. She considered her appearance.
The ceilidh was a casual dance, so she'd chosen a pair
of dark jeans, a gauzy white long-sleeved button-up
blouse, a black leather jacket, and black boots. Adding
just a touch of makeup, because makeup usually made
her break out, some lip gloss, and a small squirt of
vanilla, she admitted to herself that she was hoping

beyond hopes Gabe MacGowan would make it back in time.

And that he wouldn't ignore her.

She dug in her bag, found a silver clip, and pulled part of her hair back to the nape of her neck and secured it. Cut in layers and parted in the middle, her boingy curls sprang whichever way they wanted. Luckily the long bangs in the front stayed out of her eyes.

"You look adorable as always, love," said Dauber, perched behind her on the chest. "Are you ready?"

Allie turned and smiled. "Thanks, and yes. Let's go."

Outside, the sun hung low in the sky, the tide was high, and the wind minimal. The crisp air brushed Allie's cheeks, and she inhaled the ever-present brine of the sea. She found she rather liked that scent. It reminded her of Maine, and her mom's B and B.

Music wafted uphill from the wharf, and from the outside of Odin's Thumb Allie could see a large bonfire. As she and Dauber strolled down the sidewalk, laughter reached her ears.

"Sounds like a lovely time down there, don't you think?" Dauber said. "I wonder if Gabe MacGowan will make it back before it's too late."

Allie glanced at him, the fading light sifting through his already transparent self. "Too late for what?"

His grin dug deep into his cheeks. "Why, before the other lads in the village snatch you up."

Allie shook her head and grinned. "You're crazy, Alexander Dauber." But she loved the old soul as if he were her own father. "Come on."

Down at the wharf, the entire village and surrounding crofts had turned out for the get-together. Long tables with lanterns and chairs were set up on the perimeter, with a wide square area on the higher bank lit by a string of twinkling lights stretched between four poles. A few people danced to a small band of musicians. Allie remembered Leona saying her husband played the fiddle. She'd make it a point to meet him later.

As they drew closer, Allie caught sight of Wee Mary, sitting at a table with both Lords Ramsey and Killigrew. Walking over, she placed her hand on Mary's shoulder. "How are you feeling?"

Wee Mary glanced up and gave her a wide smile. "Och, good as new, love. You and Dauber have a seat and join me and this fresh lot of boys."

Once again, Allie considered the fact that Sealladh na Mara was haunted, and the people of the town completely accepted it. It fascinated and bewildered her at the same time. She wondered if the small coastal village had a reputation throughout Scotland.

Dauber eased into a chair. Allie sat next to Mary, grinned at Christopher and Baden, and lifted a brow. "Have you two no shame?"

Wee Mary giggled. "They've none, I'll say. Flirting with an invalid. Tsk."

Baden Killigrew barked out a laugh. "Invalid, me arse." He smiled at Allie and leaned forward, and she thought just how handsome the ghostly lord was. "I've been trying to coax her into a wee slow dance, but she continues to say my nay."

Wee Mary blushed.

Allie glanced around. "Where's Jake?"

Christopher Ramsey inclined his head. "Just there, at the water's edge with the friar and Justin."

Allie watched the boy as he interacted with Drew Digby and Justin Catesby. Other than Drew being slightly transparent, and wearing a fourteenth-century woolen cowl, and Justin in his usual sea captain's gear, they seemed perfectly normal together with the boy. Jake would stop, look up at Drew and Justin, and pay close attention to whatever it was they were telling him, and then Jake would drop to his knees, fish around in the water, and lift something up and show it with excitement.

"You know, that used to be young Gabe," Wee Mary said. "All excited and busy, not noticin' that his best mates were spirited souls who'd lost their earthly flesh."

Allie glanced at Gabe's aunt.

Mary gave a winsome smile and sighed. "That boy— Gabe, I mean—would trail after Justin"—she inclined her head to Baden and Christopher—"and these two, as well, askin' question after question, beggin' for stories of the high seas. Which, of course, the scalawag did just that and with unabashed pride and joy." She gave another winsome smile. "Justin would tell young Gabe stories at bedtime, would take him all about Sealladh na Mara, taught him many a nautical task, just by talkin' him through it." She shook her head and glanced out over the loch. "Things certainly have changed."

"Aye, no doubt Gabe would resort to fisticuffs with the lot of us, if we had substance," said Baden. "Always seems to be at odds, he does."

Mary met Allie's gaze dead-on. "For some reason, lass, I have a feeling deep in me bones you'll be the one to change him back."

Baden and Christopher both nodded in agreement.

Allie studied Wee Mary. The smallest of lines fanned out from the corners of her eyes. "What makes you think I can change anything?"

Mary's smile touched her eyes. "Hope."

Allie looked down at her feet, laced her fingers together, and glanced back up. Before she could utter a word, Wee Mary cocked her head and spoke.

"He's no' told you about Jake's mum, aye?"

Allie shook her head. "Not yet."

A slight curve lifted one corner of Wee Mary's mouth. "When he does, and I do belive he will, you'll discover where Gabe's troubles lie." She reached over and patted her hand. "Help my nephew, if you can. He's a good lad and deserves a bit o' peace in his life."

Allie turned her gaze to Sealladh na Mara's sea loch and sighed. She sincerely hoped she could help Gabe MacGowan.

If only he'd let her . . .

Chapter 13

As the hour grew late, Allie couldn't help but glance out, away from the crowd, in hopes of seeing Gabe return. So far, he hadn't. She'd be lying if she said she wasn't disappointed.

She looked over at the dancers. That Baden Killigrew had finally convinced Wee Mary to honor him with a *wee slow one*, and in his defense he seemed to be making good and sure it was indeed slow and that Mary didn't overexert herself. They were doing some crazy-looking dance from Baden's time—a dance that could be pretty darn seducing if done properly. Of course, there could be no bodily contact, but in Lords Ramsey's and Killigrew's days, there couldn't be. So they moved in sync, circling each other, dipping one way and then the other, maintaining eye contact and nothing more.

She had a suspicion Baden knew just what he was doing.

Introductions had flowed all night. Leona and her husband, their seventeen-year-old twins, Alex and Aida, old Angus, once a longshoreman who, at eighty-three, spent his days, no matter how cold, in a straight-backed wooden chair on the small pier, whittling sailboats out of chunks of oak. The epitome of Scotland, Allie thought, with a weathered face, wool sweater,

and soft hat, complete with a pipe. He even had a
faithful old dog that sat at his feet. Bones. The dog's
name was *Bones*.

As many people as Allie met at the ceilidh, not one
single person mentioned Gabe's wife. Not one. Allie
knew she'd died, but that was the extent of her knowl-
edge. She'd asked Wee Mary, but the sweet older
woman had simply shaken her head, saying 'twas
Gabe's tale to tell, and that he wouldna like his business being told. Wee Mary's eyes had misted over,
and Allie hadn't pushed the subject any more. Jake,
the cute little guy, had never elaborated, and God
knows Allie wouldn't ask. Maybe Gabe would eventually open up.

She wondered if he ever would.

As the song wound down, Baden and Wee Mary
passed where Allie stood watching, grinned, and
moved toward the tables. Another song kicked up,
this one a bit livelier, and several couples hurried to
find a spot.

"I see you've been waiting for me, lass," said a
deep voice.

Allie turned to find Captain Catesby, a mischievous
sparkle in his eyes.

"Dance with me?" he asked, inclining his head in
that direction. "If you think you can keep up?"

Allie grinned and nodded. "All right, big guy.
Let's go."

As they neared the dance floor, Justin bowed, indicating Allie step out. She did, and he joined her,
standing close and staring down at her. She followed
his moves, something from his time, she guessed, and
although she didn't know the dance it was easy
enough to keep up with Justin. Or so she thought.

The rogue smiled when she took a misstep, and
leaned his head toward hers. " 'Tis my sincerest regret,

lady, that I am in such a flimsy and paltry state as to be completely unable to put my hands on you." His grin widened. "To lead you properly, of course."

"Hmm," Allie said. "No doubt."

He moved around her in a slow circle, keeping his gaze directly on hers. She smiled. "Are you flirting with me, Justin Catesby?"

The corner of his mouth lifted. "Is it working?"

Allie giggled and mimicked his circling. "Nay."

He laughed, and abruptly changed directions, brushing so close to her that Allie felt a tingle at the spot they would have touched. Without much thought, she took her hand and swiped it through Justin's arm. Another tingling sensation, this time stronger. When she looked up, Justin was watching her closely.

"What does it feel like, lass?" he asked.

Allie, keeping in step, shrugged. "Sort of like when you've been sitting with your foot under your bottom for too long."

Justin changed directions and nodded. "Aye, and it starts to prickle once you get up." He grinned that cocky grin. " 'Tis quite an intimate thing, the swiping of a mortal's limb through that of a spirit. Did you know that, lass?"

Allie turned, dipped, and narrowed her eyes. "You are flirting again, Catesby."

One corner of his mouth lifted. "Again, is it working?"

Allie lifted a brow.

Justin laughed. "Then I shall strive harder to accomplish the feat."

"Rogue."

"Tease."

They both laughed together.

Keeping in step, Allie cocked her head. "I just can't get over how the entire village of Sealladh na Mara accepts all of you. Do you ever think of how unique it is?"

Justin glanced away, shrugged, and then met her gaze. "Aye, and nay. When I visit other places, I do realize how fortunate we are here to have the entire village accept us. Of course," he said, ducking his head and drawing close, "we've been here since their fore-fathers' forefathers were bairns. They've known us all of their lives." He gave a winsome grin. "I remember the verra first time I stumbled up the cobbled path"— he inclined his head in that direction he spoke of— "just there a ways. I didna realize just yet that I had died. I simply thought I'd been lost at sea for a spell." He glanced down at her and shrugged. "I stumbled right upon a MacGowan. I suppose 'twould be young Gabe's great-grandfather's great-grandfather. Or something o' that nature."

Allie looked at him. "What was his name?"

"Luke. Luke MacGowan, and he was one big, or-nery lad. He'd just anchored his fishin' boat and was makin' his way to Odin's when I sort of walked through him." He shook his head. "We stared at each other for a long bloody time." He met her gaze. "And then the bloody fool tried to take a swing at me. After that, it didna take long to become friends."

Allie could see how that had happened. Justin was just about the most charming soul she'd ever encoun-tered. She felt sure he could be stern if he had to, but his personality was so confident and easygoing, she just bet he was able to coerce his shipmates into fol-lowing command without too much force.

She grinned. "And you met the friar not long after arriving here?"

Justin nodded. "Aye. We each knew what the other was the moment we clapped eyes on each other." He waved a hand in the air. "Drew is an easy lad to get along with, so we, too, became fast friends. And 'twas nice enough to have a soul in the same . . . shape as myself. Aye?"

Allie nodded. "Definitely aye."

The music wound down, and Justin gave Allie a low bow.

Just as a slow, haunting melody kicked up. Winsome and Celtic, it sounded as though it were snatched straight from the movie *Braveheart.*

Justin grinned; then his gaze lifted and rested on something behind her. His expression faded into something *else.* Wordlessly, he bowed and backed away.

Strong and purposeful fingers encircled Allie's upper arm and pulled her around. She was surprised to be face-to-face with Gabe MacGowan, his green eyes a mixture of accusation and desire. How she could tell that, Allie didn't know. But she *could.*

Just as she knew they connected on a level far beyond anything she'd ever experienced. Her heart thumped erratically as he stared at her, his jaw tense, eyes searching her face. It all but unnerved her, and Allie wasn't one to normally become unnerved. She was now.

Without a single word and without breaking his stare, Gabe loosened his grip on her arm and found her hand, lifting and placing it around his neck. Her other hand, he took in his, raising it to rest on his chest. With his free hand he found her hip, and tugged gently to pull her closer. The warmth she felt from his grip through her clothes, strangely enough, made her shiver.

Allie found she could barely breathe.

The haunting pipes and strings of the melody drifted over the loch with the slightest of sea breezes, and while not exactly the sort of music to dance to, Gabe and Allie somehow managed anyway. They moved together, she following his slow, surprisingly easy lead. The twinkling amber lights strung above their heads entwined with shadows, casting planes of darkness across Gabe's jaw, the side of his nose, beneath his eyes, across his lips. It mesmerized her, the shadows on his face, and she found she couldn't quite get her fill of the sight.

Or of Gabe.

For the first time, she noticed something different about him. He looked *rested*.

"I canna stop thinking about you," he said, his heavy Highland brogue making *about* sound like *aboot*. "And I'm no' sure I like it."

The blunt honesty of his comment struck her. She sighed, then shrugged. "I have that effect on most people. Terrible trait of mine."

The smallest of grins lifted the corner of Gabe's mouth.

Allie found it sexy beyond belief.

His hand inched from her hip to the small of her back, and her skin tingled beneath the thin gauze of her blouse.

He leaned his head toward hers to whisper in her ear. "I can still taste you," he said, his voice deep, a bit gritty—almost as if he smoked, but he didn't. He inhaled. "I've thought about that night over and over and it's drivin' me crazy." His words brushed against her hair; his tongue rolled with each r.

Both made her shiver some more.

Allie caught her breath. "Me, too."

Gabe stared at her for a moment, the muscle in his jaw flexed, and she could tell he wanted to say something, but just wouldn't. Finally, he muttered something under his breath, glanced away, and then once more met her gaze straight-on.

"I want to show you something," he said. "Come with me."

Allie looked up at him and blinked. "What about Jake?"

His brow lifted. "I've already seen Jake and he's staying at my parents' for the night."

"It's late," she countered.

"We're grown-ups."

"I'll just say this and then off with you both," said Friar Digby, suddenly beside them. "Whilst I won't be a complete bother and a ninny, I can assure you, I'll know what goes on." He eyed Gabe. "They'll be no taking advantage of this maid, is that clear, lad?"

Gabe pulled Allie along. "You dunna have to threaten me, Friar. I wouldna take advantage of her or anyone else."

"Lad?" the friar said, this time more stern.

Gabe looked over his shoulder as he led her away. "You have my word, Drew."

That must have satisfied the friar because he didn't follow behind.

"Where are we going?" Allie asked as they made their way through the dwindling crowd of ceilidh-goers. They received quite a few good-natured stares, but Gabe didn't seem to notice. Or care.

He glanced down and grinned. "You'll see."

She supposed she would.

Gabe handed her a helmet. "Here. Put this on."

Standing behind Odin's, with only a streetlamp and the moon to cast any light whatsoever, Allie paused. "Why?"

Gabe reached down to the mound he stood next to, grabbed the end of what appeared to be a dark tarp, and whipped it off. Allie thought she'd find a large grill, maybe.

No grill. A motorcycle.

One that looked *fast*.

She laughed. "Ha-ha, you're kidding me."

Gabe turned to her. "You scared?"

Allie rubbed her chin and mimicked his accent. "No, I'm no' scared."

He grinned and nodded toward her helmet. "Great. Then put that on. I promise no' to go fast."

Allie stared at him a moment, weighing.

Gabe stared right back.

"Who *are* you?" she asked.

Gabe simply nodded once more to the helmet.

With an exaggerated sigh, Allie pulled on the helmet, waited for Gabe to start the bike, and then climbed on behind him.

Over the hum of the motor, Gabe flipped up his visor and leaned back. "Put your hands about my waist, lass. I swear, I willna bite."

She did.

And could have sworn she heard Gabe say "yet."

She trusted a virtual stranger with her life.

Had she lost her mind?

Within seconds, they pulled away from the pub, down the lane, and out of Sealladh na Mara, where the bonfire near the wharf still blazed, a few dancers still moved to the reels of the musicians, and where Allie could just make out the haunting strings of the melody over the purr of the bike.

Although Gabe felt like opening the bike's engine up and blazing across the moors, he didna. Mainly because the deer tended to be out and about after the sun went down and the last thing he wanted to do was hit one with a motorbike.

Allie's arms encircled his waist and she held on

tightly, even taking her hands and wadding them up into his shirt.

He'd told her the bloody truth. He'd no' been able to get her off his mind at all. No matter what he tried.

And he did try.

Winding along the single-track lane, he made their way toward the cliffs. At the base, he slowed and flipped his visor. "Hold on tight, lass. We'll be uphill for a bit."

He thought she said "Great." And had said it like him, with r's rolling.

Flipping the visor back down, he grinned behind it. A lass with humor. He liked that.

Turning up the gravel path that led to the top of the cliff, Gabe drove slowly, Allie held on tightly, and within a few moments, they'd reached the crest. He pulled the bike a safe distance from the path, stopped, and killed the motor. He took off his helmet.

Allie didna move an inch.

"Lass?" he urged.

"Oh," she said, throwing her leg over and stepping down. She pulled off her helmet and Gabe watched that mass of curls spill out.

"Wow," she said, glancing out across the flat span of grass and rock. "We're at your ancestors' castle on the cliff."

"Aye." He dismounted, set their helmets on each handlebar, pulled a rolled blanket from the back, and inclined his head. "Ready?"

In the moonlight, she grinned. "For?"

Gabe stared at her, thinking he'd never seen anything more lovely than the American ghost ouster standing there, bathed in silver. "The view of your life."

"Lead the way," she said.

And he did.

As they walked, he eased his hand down and took hers, threading their fingers and pulling her close. It seemed such a natural thing to do, yet it felt foreign, just the same.

It scared him. Liking Allie Morgan scared him.

He'd decided to tell her a few things about himself, and he prayed she'd not judge him on the person he used to be.

He suspected she wouldna.

But just in case, he'd brought her to a place where she couldna run. Childish? Sneaky? Aye. 'Twas all of those things. But had he not felt such a powerful connection with her, he wouldna have bothered wasting her time. Or his.

But he *had* felt it. And she had, too. He could sense it. And he could ignore it no longer. She was makin' him bloody witless.

In silence, they crossed over the grassy outcropping, closer to the edge of the cliff. The MacGowan keep rose toward the sky, more feeble than it had been in its heyday but still strong and proud. The main entrance was a yawning cave of shadows. Allie pulled closer.

"How do you know there aren't any serial killers or bears in there?" she said, ducking her head and peering in.

Gabe smiled and shook his head. "No serial killers, Allie Morgan, and the only bears in Scotland are at the zoo."

She turned and looked at him, the moonlight glistening in the depths of her eyes. "Wildcats?"

He nodded. "Aye, now, there may be those. Best you stay close, then."

She blinked.

He smothered a grin.

"Come on," he said, tucking the blanket under his arm, taking her shoulders in his hands, and turning her about. "Over to the cliff's edge we go."

Gabe led her closer, stopped, and shook out the blanket, spreading it over the damp, dewy grass. He inclined his head. "Sit with me?"

With a smile, she did. "Whatever you say."

Gabe, keeping a modest distance between them, sat beside her. He looked at her, the silver light of the moon sliding over her skin and hair. She moistened her lips and smiled.

And he prayed mightily he could keep his hands to himself.

Chapter 14

It was just sitting, for Christ's sake. *Sitting.* Yet Gabe knew that nosy friar was lurking somewhere close by.

Probably, 'twas a good thing.

Pulling his knees up, he rested his forearms atop them and stared out across the sea loch. 'Twas cool, but no' windy. The moon offered just the right amount of light.

Allie had remained silent, which to him was a surprise. She stared out before her, a soft smile to her lips. "It's gorgeous."

He looked at her. "Aye. Indeed."

Taking a deep breath, he looked seaward and started before he changed his bloody mind. "You said you could help if you knew more." He glanced at her. "And I need your help. So mayhap, if you know everything, you can."

She simply nodded.

"I met Jake's mum whilst at university in Glasgow. We were both young. She was twenty-two, I was twenty-six. I was nearing my last term in law school when she found out she was pregnant. We'd been seeing each other for no' quite a year."

Allie sat silently, listening.

Gabe didna glance at her. Not yet.

"I was so bloody angry." He sighed. "I felt as though me life had been swiped out from under me legs. I couldna stay in school and raise a baby, so I dropped out, as did she, and we moved back here, to Sealladh na Mara. My uncle—Wee Mary's husband—had died a few years before. Mary offered to sell Odin's to me, so I could make a decent living for Kait and the baby. I drained my savings and took out a loan and bought it from her. Then we married." He breathed, feeling an anxiety build within him, and let out a long breath. "Jake was born six months later."

They sat silent for a few moments. Allie said nothing. Just sat there, content to allow him to go at his own pace. For that he was grateful.

He hadna spoken about any of it in years.

To anyone.

"We were both unhappy. I resented the hell out o' Kait, and she hated me for stealing her youth. She hated Sealladh na Mara, hated working the kitchen, and we fell apart quite fast. It was a bloody awful situation."

From the corner of his eye he saw Allie nod.

He took a deep breath. Opened his mouth, then shut it again. He swore in Gaelic.

A soft laugh escaped Allie. "Your mother has taught me a few words. That's one of them."

Damn his mother.

And that soft laugh, and that small admission, somehow made it easier for Gabe to go on.

"I started drinking—more than usual, anyway. I'd always partied with me mates, stopped by the local pub for a few pints. The usual. But this was excessive. And I started smoking like a freight train. My escapes, I suppose. I still held things together, though. For quite some time, actually. I ran Odin's, alongside Wee Mary. By then, Kait had given up."

Again, Allie nodded.

"The night she had Jake, I was too drunk to drive her to the infirmary. My da drove us. I vaguely remember Jake's birth."

The suffocating sensation that always accompanied all of the events surrounding his and Kait's short-lived marriage threatened to choke him like an unseen hand to the throat, squeezing. He rose, simply standing, eyes locked on the sea. It was all he could do not to shout.

"Both of us were lousy parents to wee Jake. I was a functioning drunk, spending all of my time at the pub to avoid my wife and infant, and she simply withdrew. My mum and Wee Mary looked after Jake mostly, whilst Kait sulked about, depressed, angry. She began to drink, as well, and sleep a lot."

Gabe could hear his own voice quiver, and he hated it. His eyes stung, for he knew how horrible a father he'd been to his infant boy. He'd never forgive himself. *Never.*

With a final heaving breath, Gabe finished. "The night Kait died, we'd fought terribly. I was mostly drunk; she probably was, too. I canna completely recall." He stared up at the crescent moon and blinked. "But I can recall what happened next. She screamed that Jake wasna really mine, and that she hated us both and wanted to die." He closed his eyes. "I remember telling her I wished she would, too. *Just go on and die, then,* I told her. *Just bloody do it.*"

Suddenly, Allie's presence shook him from the past. She stood beside him, her fingers linking through his and squeezing tight. Finally, she spoke, her voice soft, reassuring, unaccusing. "Her death is not your fault, Gabe. It's just not."

He pulled his hand free. "It is my fault, Allie Morgan." He moved from her then, a few steps away, and rubbed the back of his neck. "I drank like a fish during Kait's pregnancy and Jake's entire first year of life. I am a recovering alcoholic who doesna even remember his son's birth!" Old anger built inside him, anger from Kait, anger from his own stupid self, and all the mistakes made in between. He glared at Allie. "Do you know much about recovering alcoholics, Allie? Nay? I'll let you in on the bloody secret, then. It's always here, Allie." He tapped his chest. "Trapped inside. Waiting to be let out again. I have to be on guard all the bloody time."

"No, it's not," she said, and moved closer to him. She reached for his hand, and he slung it away.

And she grabbed it back, looked at him, her voice even, steady, and still soft. "You beat it."

"I killed Jake's mother," he said, the sound a low, menacing growl. "I did it. Dunna you see why I have to move Jake from here? Too many bad memories, Allie Morgan. And too many mistakes." He rubbed his hand over his eyes. "I canna afford to make any more. Jake deserves it."

She bravely took a step closer and looked up into his eyes. She still didna know everything, and by God, he'd no' tell her. She knew everything she needed to know. 'Twas enough.

The rest would make her think him a lunatic.

She stared, her eyes hard now, her mouth drawn into an angry frown. "Do you think you're scaring me with all of this, Gabe MacGowan? Honestly? I appreciate the soul-bearing, but I don't scare that easy." She pushed his shoulder. "Do you hear me? You don't scare me! And I don't care what you think you did, you didn't kill your wife and I will never agree with you! Do you understand? And do you honestly think running away from your past is the answer? Are you telling me that selling Odin's and leaving

your family—the souls of Sealladh na Mara who love
you and Jake—is the answer?" She shook her head.
"This was your home and your ancestors' home long
before you brought Kait here, Gabe. And you hired
me to oust those loving souls, just so you can sell an
establishment that's been in your family for years?"
Her anger exploded. "I wouldn't have accepted this
job, had I known what was really involved, Mr. Mac-
Gowan. Knowing what I know now? I think you're
making a huge mistake moving Jake from Sealladh na
Mara. And just so you know—not *everything* revolves
around your past!" she screamed. "Ugh!"

She turned on her heel then and simply started to
walk. Rather, she stomped.

Gabe stared after her. Frozen and dumbfounded by
her response, he simply stared, scowling. Mad. Terrified.

Not for the first time in his life, he didna know what
to do next.

Allie walked several feet, stopped, and stared up at
the star-studded sky. So many emotions zipped through
her that her brain hurt. She felt cold and hot at the
same time.

She wanted to throw something.

Or hit something.

She turned on her heel and marched back to Gabe.
She stopped when she reached him, boots toe-to-
toe. She looked up and frowned. "Don't pull me half-
ass into this, Gabe MacGowan. You're still asking for
my help? Although my role has changed considerably
since I arrived, you still want me to help? We'll do it
my way or I'm gone. Got it? Let me warn you, though,
it doesn't involve any ousting of any souls. If you don't
want my help, fine. I'll leave. And don't worry. I won't

charge you my usual fee. You'll only be out airfare and a few fish!"

She turned to stomp back off, but he caught her hand and held on. She could have jerked loose, but she didn't. She stood, facing away from him, and waited, heart pounding, breath coming hard.

God, she was mad.

And she wasn't exactly sure at *what*.

Gabe pulled, and she turned around. He continued to hold her hand.

She continued to let him.

Lifting her gaze, she met his. Gabe's chest rose and fell with heavy breaths, as though he had a pack of dynamite inside him somewhere that was close to exploding. She wasn't afraid, though. Not even a little.

He pulled her close, and lifted her chin with his knuckle. "Those are my ghosts, Allie Morgan. That's who I am. A recovering alcoholic with a haunting past."

Lifting her hand, Allie covered his and moved it to her cheek. "That's who you were, Gabe MacGowan. *Were*. The man I see now is far different from the boy back then. The haunting past? I can help with that. If you'll let me."

He searched her face, locked his gaze onto hers, and slowly shook his head. He muttered something in Gaelic, looked away, then looked back at her. Lifting his hand, he scraped her lips with his thumb, grasped her chin, and tilted it to the left, studied it, then tilted it a bit more and then lowered his head and brushed his mouth against hers.

Sensations soared within her, and Allie sighed against him, opening for him, longing to taste him. That same low growl, a desperate, urgent noise, sounded from deep within Gabe's chest as he slid a hand to the small of her back and pulled her tightly against him. His tongue brushed hers and Allie thought her knees would give out from under her.

She held his face, feeling the rough scruff of his unshaven jaw, slid her hand down his throat, the back of his neck, and their kiss became frantic, as though neither could be satisfied.

The warmth and roughness of Gabe's hand skimmed her lower back as he felt beneath her blouse, and then moved over her ribs and up to her shoulder blades, down her spine, and up again where he hesitantly brushed the side of her breast. Unable to stop it, Allie gasped.

Gabe jerked back, out of breath. He let her go and took a couple of steps back. "Christ, I'm sorry, lass. I couldna help myself."

"Well, 'tis a bloody good thing you finally did, you scalawag," said the friar, sifting out of nowhere. "As far as the helping of young Gabe here goes, we're all in."

Behind him, the rest of the Odin's Thumb spirits, minus Justin and plus Dauber, emerged as though stepping off an unseen escalator, all with a resounding and agreeing round of "aye."

Allie placed two fingers over her lips.

Good Lord, they'd been watching for who knew how long. She felt like hiding. Had there been a rock to climb under, she would have.

"Oy, no need to cover up, lass; we all seen," said Lord Killigrew. "Damn me, but the maids do know how to kiss in this century." He winked at Gabe. "Lucky bastard, you are."

"I wholeheartedly agree with you there," said Lord Ramsey. "Pity we were never able to sample the like, aye?" He grinned at Allie. "With all due respect, miss."

Allie felt her face grow warm, and she frowned. She

was nearly as mortified by being caught by the Odin's while lip-locked with Gabe MacGowan as she was the time her granny had caught her lip-locked with little Josh Canter in the fourth grade. Thank God Justin hadn't seen. He would never let her live it down.

Then she glanced around. The spirits looked like serious ghosts, flimsy-transparent with only the smallest amount of coloration as they moved over the grassy flat of the cliff. "Where's Justin?" she asked.

Mademoiselle heaved a sigh. "He stayed behind to visit Wee Mary. She was feeling dreadfully alone."

Dauber ambled close to Allie and leaned toward her ear. "Are you all right, love?"

Allie smiled at her old friend. "I am."

"Great!" said the friar. "It seems we have some discussions to handle regarding young Gabe's decision to sell the pub and inn, and I say Odin's is much more accommodating than this drafty old cliff."

A round of *aye*s sounded.

Gabe finally spoke up. "There is something else that needs discussing first and foremost." His gaze clamped onto Allie's. "There's a month's worth of potential buyers coming to view Odin's over the next few weeks. I canna get out of it. Realtor's contract."

Allie smiled. "Does that mean you've changed your mind about selling?"

Gabe rubbed first his eyes, then his jaw. He glanced at each of the Odin's souls, Dauber, then back to Allie. "I just dunna know if 'tis the right decision."

Allie smiled wide. "Well, that's a start." She looked at her ghostly cohorts. "It seems we have some serious business to discuss. Right, guys?"

Another round of *aye*s carried on the cool Highland air.

Allie glanced at her accomplices. She felt pretty confident things could be handled appropriately.

She *hoped*, anyway.

Once more, her eyes locked with Gabe's. Her body still hummed from their kiss, from his touch—so much she was amazed she hadn't keeled over yet. They'd made progress. *Good* progress.

She *hoped*.

She could barely wait to see what the morning would bring.

Much to Allie's chagrin, the very thing morning brought was not at all what she had expected.

Gabe's absence.

At least this time, though, he wasn't running away. Wee Mary had greeted her first thing upon rising to say Gabe had gone in to Inverness to have a meeting with the Realtor he'd signed the contract with.

To Allie, that was yet another step in the right direction.

So after her usual trip to Leona's for her pastry and coffee, Allie stopped at the red phone booth on the corner to make another call to her mom. The cold loch wind, particularly fierce for the morning, whipped her hair and stung her cheeks. Tears formed in her eyes from that cold blast and she brushed at them with her knuckles. Sealladh na Mara glistened in the early morning sun, with tiny shards sparkling atop the surface of the loch. Offshore, far into the sound, a large sailboat sat at anchor. She'd noticed that same vessel the night before, at the dance, just as the sun began to set. It had cast the loch and Sealladh na Mara into a fierce, reddish orange glow that had all but taken her breath away.

Funny, how a place could have that effect on a person.

On *her*.

Zipping her hoodie to the throat, Allie stepped inside the phone booth, pulled out her prepaid phone card, and dialed the numbers. After a four-second warning of how many minutes remained on the card, the number was connected. After three rings her mother answered.

"Hi, Mom," Allie said. "Are you busy?"

Her mom laughed. "Always. But I always have time for you. How's my baby?"

Allie thought it was great to hear her mom's voice. "I'm fine, Mom. It's beautiful here."

"I bet it is—oh Lord, here. Talk to Boe. She's dancing up and down to talk to you."

A second passed as her mom handed the phone off. "Hey, brat. You could have asked me to go with you."

Allie grinned. "Sorry. You were too busy petting the fishes." Boe, doing her internship as a marine biologist with a specialty on sharks, had been out to sea for over a month when Allie left for Scotland.

"Sharks, ding-dong, and we don't pet. We tag. We observe. We *research.*"

Allie gave a snort. "Tag. Pet. All spells crazy to me."

"You're not allowed to call anyone crazy."

"Oh, really? Did you get in the cage this time?"

Boe sighed. "I live for the cage."

In the background, Allie heard her mother say to Boe, "*Whose child are you, anyway?*"

Allie and Boe laughed together.

"Seriously, how long are you going to be there?" Boe asked.

Allie thought about it. "I'm not sure. There's a lot of work to be done here."

"Lots of spookies, huh?" said Boe.

Allie chuckled and turned to glance out of the phone booth—

"Whoa!" she shrieked.

She stared right into the smirking face of Justin Catesby.

"What's wrong?" Boe asked.

Allie placed a hand over her racing heart, frowned at Justin, who merely grinned that lopsided grin and crossed his arms over his chest, and she blew out a breath. "Let's just say the spookies, as you call them, while a handful to the max, aren't the problem. It's the man who employed me."

"Already I'm fascinated. What are the souls like?"

Allie stared at Justin through the glass. He'd pushed his tricorn back a ways, exposing a little more forehead. His long leather overcoat hung down below his knees, and the sword at his side almost gleamed in the sun. He gave her an arrogant grin.

"Well, the one I'm staring at right now," Allie started in a low voice, so Justin couldn't hear, "is one drop-dead-gorgeous sea captain from the seventeenth century."

"More," Boe said.

"Shoulder-length dark hair, wavy, with a close-clipped goatee, smoldering brown eyes, and a great build."

Justin smiled wide.

"And nice white teeth."

"I thought pirates had rotted teeth, or maybe gold ones."

"Too many movies, Boe," Allie said. "Justin's are nice, straight, and white."

"Justin, huh? Sounds nice. So is he your problem spirit?"

In the background, Allie heard her mom and younger sister, Ivy, say in unison, "Who's the problem spirit?"

Allie laughed as she continued to watch Justin strike multiple cocky poses, including withdrawing his pistols and holding them in a very 007-ish manner. She shook her head and he laughed. "While Justin is definitely a handful, he's not the problem. Like I said, it's the man who hired me."

"Talk to me, Sis," Boe said.

Allie sighed. "Too long of a story for now, but maybe later. Let's just say the mortal in the case has way more unsettled matters of the soul than the ghosts do."

"Ghosts? As in plural?" Boe asked.

"Yep. A friar. A French noblewoman. And two English lords."

Boe laughed. "Good God. I bet Dauber would be jealous. He is such a mother hen."

Allie smiled. Not long after Allie and Dauber met had Boe happened to pop in for a long weekend.

That was Boe's first experience with a spirited soul. In the beginning, she'd been resistant to believing Allie's claims to see ghosts. But Dauber had a few tricks up his sleeve, and it wasn't long before Boe's resistance to believe had been shattered.

As soon as it had, she'd been able to see Alexander Dauber to the fullest.

And she'd adored him ever since.

Allie's mom and other sisters soon followed suit.

"Well," Allie said. "Dauber's here. Mother-henning as we speak."

"Amazing," Boe sighed. "Hey, you know something?"

"What?"

Her sister paused, then said, "I had a dream about Dad last night. Strange, but I hadn't dreamt about him in a while."

Allie's chest tightened. She missed her father fiercely. "What was it about?"

"Remember the time we found that bag of dog

food, and thought it'd be huge fun to poke holes in it?"

Allie laughed. "And dog food spilled all over the clean clothes in the laundry room and Mom chased us outside with with the flyswatter?"

"And when Dad tried to intercept Mom, they both went down in the driveway?" Boe laughed.

Allie remembered the day well. "It was just a few days before he died." James Morgan had the absolute best smile, and he'd been laughing like a hyena that day, covered in mud.

"Yeah, I know. I miss him," she said, then muttered something under her breath. "Hey, Mom wants to talk again. Call me later, why don't you? I miss you so much I think I could sit and chat for hours. Oh, and Sika says hi." Sika was the nickname they used for their sister Ivy.

"Are you being careful?" asked Sara, Allie's mom, taking the phone back. "I worry about you being in a town full of people you don't know."

To that, Allie smiled. "Don't worry about me, Mom. The people here are super nice. You'd love it here. Sort of reminds me of your place. And I never get tired of hearing the West Highland accent."

"That makes me feel better," said Sara. "I miss you, you know."

"I know, Mom. I miss you, too." She glanced again at Justin, who'd finally given up trying to make her laugh and was now leaned against the phone booth. Or at least he seemed to be leaning. "Where's Emma?"

"She ran out to the market," Sara said. "She should be home soon."

Allie glanced at her watch. "I've got to go anyway, so just tell her I love her, okay?"

"Will do. Love you, baby. Take care."

And with that, they hung up.

Allie stepped out of the phone booth and Justin was still grinning from ear to swarthy ear. He fell into step beside Allie, and she looked at him. "What is up with you today?" she asked.

He traced his goatee with his thumb and forefinger, never once breaking his stare. "You find me drop-dead gorgeous, aye?"

Allie stopped, mouth open. "Oh! Stinkpot! How did you hear me?"

Justin lifted a brow. "Me first mate was deaf as a plank o' wood. I watched him read lips, so I picked up the habit, as well." He chuckled. "I find myself already sorry for admitting the likes to you. 'Twould have been quite useful, me reading your lips without you knowing I was doing so."

Allie mock frowned and continued walking. "You are a naughty man, Justin Catesby. Very, very naughty."

Justin Catesby could do nothing more than laugh.

And Allie could do little more than join him.

Chapter 15

After dinner had been cleared away and the last patron had left, Gabe, who'd finally made it home, Allie, Wee Mary, Gabe's mom, Laina, and all of the Odin's Thumb souls plus Dauber gathered in the main pub lobby to discuss the contract Gabe had acquired to sell the place, along with *options*. Options, Allie gathered, that Gabe was being somewhat resistant to. He'd mentioned his concerns that night on the cliff top, and they were true concerns. Ones Allie, and the others, could all understand.

But what concerned her more was that Gabe's bigger issues were with himself and Kait. His past haunted him fiercely, and until he could let it go and possibly forgive himself, Allie knew and warned the others that selling Odin's and leaving Sealladh na Mara, in Gabe's eyes, was the only answer.

A small crack had started in Gabe's reserve, though.

Allie planned to take a wedge and widen that crack to the very best of her ability.

Lord Ramsey rubbed his chin. "I'm not following. You signed a bloody contract to guarantee a sale?"

"Christ, man, why would you do such a thing?" said Captain Catesby.

Allie could tell Gabe was getting frustrated. He

rubbed the back of his neck and pinched the bridge of his nose. More than once.

He explained again. "Because. At the time—which was before I hired Allie—I felt selling was my only option. After you crazy fools scared off more than a half dozen potential buyers, I thought getting a guarantee per a Realtor would make sure Odin's would sell." He glanced at Allie. "I wasn't expecting to have my mind changed."

Allie grinned at him.

"We're no' leavin', are we, Da?" Jake's little voice said as he scooted across the lobby and threw an arm around Gabe's neck.

Gabe hugged his son and scrubbed his head. "Let's just say I'm thinkin' things over, lad."

Jake looked directly at Allie and smiled.

Gabe gave Jake a loving pat on the backside. "Now scoot back to bed, aye? You've school in the morning and you need a good night's sleep."

Jake then reached up, cupped his hand to Gabe's ear, and whispered something.

Allie couldn't read Gabe's expression. Surprise, maybe? She wasn't sure.

In the next second, the little guy was at her side, pulling on her arm so he could whisper something in her ear, too. She leaned down.

"Thank you, Allie," he said. "But we've still work to do, I think."

With that, he hurried back across the lobby to the stairs without turning back once.

Allie shot Gabe a look.

Green eyes studied her, bored right into her soul, so it seemed. It made her insides turn warm, and she wondered if anyone else could tell how flustered Gabe MacGowan made her.

She simply smiled and shrugged. How could she convey to Gabe something she herself didn't even understand? Later, when she could talk to Jake alone, she'd ask him more questions.

Wee Mary tapped the table with a nail. "So, lad, tell me more of this contract. 'Tis with the Realtor, you say? What does it mean, exactly?"

Gabe stretched his arms out over the table and clasped his hands. Allie noticed the thick veins running up his arms. He met Allie's gaze, then turned to his aunt. "I signed a contract with the Realtor. She gathers potential buyers and sets up the times for them to view the pub and inn. The contract is set so that she doesn't lose any money. Connected to that same contract is the one she makes with the potential buyers. They've signed a contract with her, as well. So I am obligated to allow them the chance to make an offer."

"So you basically signed away your right to say nay, aye?" Justin asked.

Gabe nodded. "Aye, indeed." He looked at everyone. "I've still no' made up my mind." He scowled.

Allie thought that too much pushing wouldn't do the situation any good, so instead she clapped her hands. "Okay. Let's let things settle overnight, and we'll talk again tomorrow." She met everyone's gaze. "How's that?"

"Right. Until then, we could plan just how to haunt the buyers, aye?" said Christopher Ramsey.

Allie frowned. "No, that's not what I meant." She glanced at Gabe. "Let's just think things over tonight. No hasty decisions. Okay?"

Several grumbled *aye*s filled the room.

For now, that was good enough.

"For the record, I'd like my opinion to be heard and known," said Justin. He looked straight at Gabe, and for a change, his expression was lacking mirth. He was dead serious. "I have known you your entire life, lad. I sometimes think I know you better than I know my own self, and there's one thing I know for a certainty. You and Jake belong here, with all o' us. At Sealladh na Mara." He cleared his throat. "I dunna want you to leave."

Each man held the other's gaze, and Allie could only imagine the years of memories running through both heads. She also couldn't help but wonder if Justin or the others had ever verbally spoken their feelings of Gabe and Jake staying, or if they'd simply dived straight in to the haunting.

Finally, Gabe wordlessly gave Justin a short nod.

"I fancied the head trick myself," said Lord Ramsey.

Everyone chuckled, and he winked at Elise. "Excellent performance, mademoiselle."

Mademoiselle Elise Bedeau's transparent cheeks stained pink and she gave a curt nod. "*Merci*. It was passing enjoyable. The look on that fop's face as my dismembered head spoke to him was quite memorable."

Everyone laughed.

"Gabe, do you have an appointment scheduled for your next buyer?" Allie asked.

He nodded. "Aye, in three days. Eight a.m. sharp."

Laina, Gabe's mother, spoke up. "Gabe, love, your father will be coming home that day. We were thinking of planning a welcome-home party." She winked at Allie. "He's been a longshoreman since the day I met him."

A few all-knowing *ahh*s sounded from the male souls.

" 'Twas on a long weekend young Gabe here came along," said the friar. "The very next year, his sister." He winked. "Busy lads, those longshoremen."

"Och, go on with ya, then," said Laina, blushing. A moment later, she murmured, "But you're right."

Another round of laughter rose.

"Oy, I'm tired. Sister, let's go, aye?" said Wee Mary.

"I can drive you both home," said Gabe, who started to rise.

"Nonsense, boy, sit down," said Mary. "We're just up the lane there." They rose and started to leave.

Gabe rose, too. "Auntie, dunna be so hard-headed—"

"Lad, sit. I had me appendix out, not knee surgery," said Mary. "Laina, tell your boy to stay put."

Lords Ramsey and Killigrew, as well as Captain Catesby, all rose at once. "We'll accompany the maids," said Killigrew.

Mary blushed. "Now, those escorts I'll accept. Come along, lads." She grinned at Allie. "*Beannachd leat*," she said in Gaelic.

"Aye, *beannachd leat*," repeated Laina, who waved. " 'Till the morn."

"Bye," said Allie.

Gabe walked both ladies to the door, dropped a kiss to each of their cheeks, and repeated those same Gaelic words.

"What does it mean?" asked Allie, rising and taking their glasses to the kitchen.

"I haven't the foggiest idea," said Dauber, scratching his head. "Are you two up for a bit of bones tonight?" he asked the friar and Mademoiselle.

As Allie entered the kitchen, she heard a resounding "aye" as well as "oui" behind her. She shook her head. How the spirited souls loved to gamble. Even if it was just for bragging rights.

Rinsing out the glasses, Allie placed them in the rack and dried her hands. Glancing out of the window, she saw wispy clouds sliding past a thumbnail moon that hung low over the loch.

" 'Tis beautiful, aye?" Gabe's deep brogue sounded close. He leaned on the counter beside Allie and stared out the window. He glanced at her. "When I was a wee lad, me da used to tell me stories of the kelpie who'd come to the wharf during a crescent moon to lure a mortal into the depths of the water to be its mate." He chuckled. "Used to scare the bloody hell out of me."

Allie smiled, then glanced at Gabe. He hadn't once tried to kiss her, much less touch her, since the night on the cliff. There was a hesitancy about him now, something making him hold back. It snapped in the air between them like a current of electricity.

She hadn't a clue what was wrong. But she decided that if he wanted to kiss her, he would. He'd unloaded a great deal of pent-up guilt to her that night over-looking the loch. Maybe he was ashamed? Maybe he wasn't sure he wanted to go any further with someone who would be leaving eventually.

"Me granny would say you were gatherin' wool," he said. "That means you're in deep thought. What's wrong?"

Allie shrugged. "Do you find it strange I'm here?" she asked. She turned, placed her hands on the counter behind her, and lifted herself up to sit. "I mean, I'm practically living under your roof, eating your food, interacting with your family, your spirits, working in your pub." She shook her head and crossed her ankles. "You hired me to oust your bothersome ghosts, but that's not why I'm here any longer. Don't you think that's weird?"

Gabe turned and leaned a hip against the counter, facing Allie yet only a couple of feet apart. He crossed his arms over his chest, and considered a moment. Then he nodded. "Aye. Almost as weird as, out of the entire bloody international and local Web sites listed for ghost busters—thousands, I recall—I randomly select a handful by name only and yours is one of them?" He whistled low. "Bloomin' crazy if you ask me."

Allie smiled. "That is weird, for sure."

Gabe stood, moved in front of her, placed a hand on either side of her thighs. With that profound stare, he studied her for several seconds. "I canna say where any of this is goin', lass, and I damn sure dunna know what will happen over the next month. Whether I decide to sell or no' sell, I'll still need your help, if you'll stay on." He leaned closer, still tall enough that he had to duck his head to look her in the eye. "Christ Almighty, I dunna know what I've done without you all this time. I think you were sent to me, lass."

Allie stared at him, her heart in her throat, that inner connection she felt with Gabe stronger than ever, and before she thought about it her hand lifted, and she brushed her fingertips gently over Gabe's lips. His eyes closed briefly.

Allie whispered, "I think you're right."

Inside, though, she was terrified.

In such a short time, Allie found herself falling for a guy. A guy who lived an ocean away from her home, her family.

A guy who wasn't sure about his own feelings.

She dropped her hand, but Gabe remained close, and without any words between them, that sensual electricity returned and snapped, and it all but made the air rush from her lungs. The way he looked at her, as though he'd found something precious and unique, mystified her. She'd been hurt before. Who hadn't? The thing was, before? She'd thought *that* guy had looked at her as though he'd found something precious and unique, too.

She hadn't been wrong, really, about *that* other guy.

Allie simply hadn't planned on him feeling the same way about another girl at the same time.

"Hey," Gabe said, shaking her out of her reverie. "Look at me."

She did, and couldn't help but drop her gaze to his mouth. When he smiled, it was a beautiful, even smile with lots of great white teeth showing.

But when he spoke? That same mouth veered to the left, just a fraction off-center. A little crooked.

Sexy? Good God, she adored it.

Add in that dead-sexy Highland brogue?

A slow, even smile spread across Gabe's face. "I know what you're thinkin', lass."

Allie blinked. "You do?"

"Aye, I do." He leaned into her, his lips so close but not touching hers. "I willna kiss you unless you want me to, Allie," he whispered. "And to be honest, I'm nervous as hell around you."

Allie's head whirled, almost as though she'd had too much wine. "You don't seem *nerv, nurv*," she started. That was one word she couldn't even mimic.

Gabe said it again. "Nervous, and aye, I am." He pulled back and looked at her. His arms were still braced on either side of her thighs, and he'd not moved an inch to touch her. Intensity etched into his features, his jaw flinched. "I've no' been with another woman since—" He looked down, then back up. "It's been a verra long time."

Allie blinked. She hardly knew what to say to that.

She wondered just how long *a long time* really was. Surely not as long as herself.

She gave a half grin. "A sexy guy like you? Come on, MacGowan. That's hard to believe." Her voice didn't sound at all as confident and witty as she'd meant it to be.

He leaned close again, his lips brushing her ear. " 'Tisna because I havena had the opportunity, lass." He breathed, silent. Then, "I havena had the desire." Pulling back, he looked at her hard. "For sex. For companionship. Christ, for anything." His eyes burned with . . . something. Fear? Hesitancy? "Until you."

Good Lord Almighty. What was she to say to *that*?

Lifting her hands, she slipped them around his neck and pulled his mouth to hers. "Well then," she mouthed against his lips, "lucky me."

"Hardly," he whispered back, and settled his mouth over hers. "Lucky *me*."

He touched her nowhere, only his lips to hers, and he stayed that way for several seconds, simply *inhaling, exhaling*. Allie could feel the power inside him, all but making him hum with desire to release, to explode, and yet he remained tranquil, in control. *Barely*.

He moved then, slightly, his tongue grazing her bottom lip before drawing it in and suckling it slowly in the most sensual kiss Allie had ever experienced in her life. Every time his tongue brushed hers, her body went numb, sensations within her purred, and she pulled him closer and kissed him back.

His control, she sensed, began to slip.

With a deep groan, Gabe slid his hands from the counter to her thighs, edged his hips between her knees, and deepened the kiss, still slowly, yet Allie could feel the desperation droning within him, right under the surface of his calm facade, and it made heat pool in places that hadn't heated in quite some time.

With a slowness that amazed Allie, Gabe slid his hands from her thighs, over her hips, and up the back of her sweater. Calluses made his hands rough, and the abrasion against her skin made her shudder and inch closer, and as Gabe wrapped his arms completely around her, his kiss turned frantic, as though he could swallow her whole and in one big gulp.

She kissed him back with just as much fervor.

And the more her hands explored, the nape of his neck, his Adam's apple, the hairline at his temple, the more desperate they both became. Gabe pushed his hands through her hair, held it steady, and turned it to the angle he wanted, and kissed, tasted, until finally, he once again abruptly stopped. With his forehead resting against hers, they both struggled to gain a decent breath. Finally, Gabe looked up.

His green eyes had turned stormy gray, and he searched her eyes, and Allie could tell he wanted to say something.

But he didn't.

Instead, he gave her one last kiss, slower this time, and then pressed his lips to her forehead. "Good night, Allie Morgan."

With that he pushed from the counter and left the kitchen.

Allie watched him leave, and pressed two fingers to her lips, closed her eyes, and smiled.

It was several minutes later and two glasses of water before she trusted her legs to carry her to her room.

Chapter 16

"Christ!" Gabe sat bolt upright in bed. He glanced at the clock. One a.m. Heart racing, forehead covered in beads of perspiration, and out of breath. Bending his knees, he rested his forearms there and dropped his head forward, trying to slow his breathing.

The chilled air from the open window hit his damp bare chest, and he swore. He hadn't left the bloody window open—

"Da?"

Gabe jumped, noticing that Jake stood directly by his side. His son stared, a blank look on his face, as though he were sleepwalking. "Go back to bed, lad."

Jake simply stared, turned, and glanced at the open window, and then met Gabe's gaze. "She needs me, Da."

Gabe rubbed his eyes. "Who?"

Again, Jake turned and looked at the window. "She does." He again slid a blank expression to Gabe. "She says you dunna need me anymore. She wants me to come."

A filmy, white mist rose within the room, seeping through the window and settling like heavy smoke in a bar. Gabe waved at it, squinting at Jake, but still it remained. "What are you talkin' about, son?"

Jake stared a moment, and then suddenly, his voice

wasna his own. "Make her leave, Gabe." The strange voice came from Jake's mouth. "Before something happens."

An internal chill stole over Gabe and he jumped from the bed.

Jake turned and ran for the window.

"Stop it now, lad!" Gabe yelled. "Come here!"

At the window, Jake turned, smiled.

And then he jumped.

The breath rushed from Gabe's lungs and his insides turned to ice. *"No!"* His heart slammed into his throat, he ran to the window and peered out. "Jesus Christ Almighty," he croaked. He tried to yell again, but his throat lacked the strength. "Jake!" he cried. *"Jake!"*

"Da! Wake up!"

Gabe opened his eyes and sat bolt upright in bed. Jake's hands were around his arm, shaking.

"Da, wake up now!" he yelled.

Christ, 'twas only a dream.

With his heart hammering in his chest, a heavy gust of relief washed over him, and he grabbed his son and pulled him into a tight embrace. Jake's hair, clean and fresh from his bath, smelled familiar, comforting. "Christ, boy," Gabe said, kissing Jake's cheek. He looked at him. "I'm sorry if I scared you."

Jake patted Gabe's cheek. "It's okay, Da," he said.

Gabe hugged him, Jake's small ear pressed against Gabe's cheek. He squeezed his eyes tightly shut and thanked God it *had* only been a dream.

Gabe opened his eyes, and with his son still tight in his arms, he looked over Jake's shoulder.

By the window stood his dead wife. She stared hard at him, black, endless eyes boring into Gabe's. Her mouth yawned into an exaggerated smile.

And then she faded away.

He felt himself shake in his wee son's arms.

Och, Christ Almighty. He was losing his bloody mind.

"Can we go downstairs and get some milk?" Jake asked.

Again, relief flooded Gabe's insides, just at hearing the lad's voice. He took a deep breath and let his son go. "We can go downstairs and get some water, aye?" he said.

Jake sighed. "Okay, then." He put his small hand in Gabe's. "Let's go."

Two nights later, again at one a.m., Gabe awoke. Each night interrupted by dreams. Awful dreams, ones Gabe would awaken from—think, rather, he'd awakened from—only to find the dreams weren't over at all.

And each night, after finally wresting himself awake, he'd stay up, check on Jake, and go to his workshop.

First, he'd walk up the stairs and stand at Allie's door. Christ, he wanted to go to her so badly, but he didna. He'd not told her about the dreams, about Jake being part of them, about how Kait had become more tangible. He wanted to fiercely, but hadna.

Kait's spirit was tormenting him, and he was beginning to fear she would do something harmful to Jake. 'Twas the real reason he now considered following through with leaving Sealladh na Mara. What if Kait could hurt his son? His own tormenting he could handle. But menace toward Jake? Christ . . .

He faced Allie's room now. And just like every other night, he simply stood there, in the dim light of Odin's corridor. Staring.

He placed the flat of each hand on either side of the jamb and leaned his forehead against the cool oak and closed his eyes. He knew she'd be in there, sound asleep. He'd even tried several times to convince himself that, if he *did* venture into her room, he'd only do so to *talk* to her. She comforted him. Soothed him. Made him feel alive for the first time since . . . Christ, he couldna even remember.

But he knew himself much better than that.

Knew his own body even better.

And what Allie Morgan did to him.

Drawing in a long, deep breath, Gabe let it out slowly. He'd not had a drink in more than four years. Four bloody years. He'd not missed it. Not at all.

Yet kissing Allie Morgan, feeling her skin beneath his palms, her body pressed to his, made him more intoxicated than anything that came from a bottle. Her blunt honesty, her humor, and her genuine love and affection for mankind—dead and alive—moved him. She'd taken to his family. His neighbors.

Him.

He opened his eyes, pushed away from the door, and eased downstairs. No sooner had he chosen a block of marble and his tools, and situated himself on the work stool than a voice interrupted.

"Keeping late nights again, eh, lad?"

Gabe turned and nodded at Captain Catesby. "Aye, so it seems." He inclined his head. "Conjure yourself up a stool and sit."

Wordlessly, the captain did.

For several minutes, Gabe worked on his marble, neither he nor Catesby saying a word.

The ghost didna stay silent for long.

"How bad are the dreams, lad?"

Gabe continued his chiseling, blowing, chiseling. "Bad enough." He glanced at his old friend. "Stop callin' me lad, Justin. We're the same age."

Justin shrugged. "I was there when you were pissin' your bairn cloths, boy. 'Tis a hard habit, watchin' you grow up and then treatin' you as my equal." He grinned. "Lad."

Gabe grinned. "I suppose."

Justin leaned forward, placing his elbows on his knees. The white cloth of his shirt ruffles slipped from the cuffs of his overcoat and hung down. "I am powerfully glad to know you've come to your senses about selling the place, by the by."

Gabe glanced at him but kept working. "How do you know that's my decision?" After that last experience with Kait, he again felt completely unsure.

"Because I know for a bloody fact that those dreams you're havin' are the cause of your wanting to leave."

Gabe stopped what he was doing and met Justin's gaze. "They're more than dreams." He scrubbed his jaw. "I'm afraid for Jake."

Justin gave a gusty, ghostly sigh. "You should talk to Allie about Kait, lad. She can help."

Gabe considered. "I dunno. Things have changed, Justin. Kait has left my dreams and is now more tangible." He looked at the sea captain. "She isna like the rest of you." He waved a hand. "You look as you did in life. Kait is . . . unimaginable. I'm afraid she'd frighten Allie or Jake."

Justin stroked his beard. "She wouldna hurt her own son, lad."

Gabe shook his head. "The vision I just experienced involved Jake. He said, *She wants me to come.*"

Justin clasped his hands. "You know, boy, Allie has a special gift. She touches souls unlike any I've ever encountered." He looked at Gabe. "She could try to reason with Kait's soul—"

"Bloody hell, no," said Gabe. "I willna allow it. Kait isna like the rest of you. She seems . . . touched by evil."

Justin rubbed his brow. "I say you should talk to Allie. I'm sure she could help."

They were silent for a moment before Gabe spoke again.

He blew on the small chunk of marble, taking on the first resemblances of a warhorse. "There are no children his age in the village to play with."

"He sees plenty at school. Besides—children are going to misbehave whether they're bored with no friends their own age about, or a gaggle of boys to sneak off and do mischievous things with." He shrugged. " 'Tis the nature of boys, methinks."

Gabe gave a sideways glance and continued his work. "Methinks you're speaking from experience."

Justin laughed. "I did give me mum a gray hair or two, indeed." He cleared his throat. "About the dreams. Tell Allie about them—"

"Nay." Gabe gave him a dark glare. "I dunna want her knowin', mate. I'm no' even sure how you know."

Justin stood and took off his tricorn. He ran a hand through his hair. "Because I've had to settle your boy more times than I can count after one of your dreams." He glared right back. "He hears them, you ken? He *knows* 'tis his mum who torments you."

Gabe set the chunk of marble down and stood. He hooked his hands behind his neck and stared at the floor.

"Mayhap she can help, boy," Justin said. " 'Tis what she does for a livin', aye? She's got a way with other-worldly souls—ways I've never seen a mortal possess before."

Gabe scrubbed his jaw. "So you just mentioned two minutes ago." He blew out a breath. "She's involved enough as it is, Justin. She'll be gone after a month's time, anyway."

Justin stopped and stared. "What do you mean, she'll be gone?"

Gabe lifted his gaze. "She's from America, man. She doesna live here." He turned his back and walked to the window. He hated to think of it, Allie's leaving. But inevitably, it'd come. He knew it. "Whatever my final decision is about Odin's, once the contract is null and void, she'll be leavin'. For good."

Justin simply stared for a moment, anger building in his ghostly eyes. "And you're just goin' to let her, then? Just bloody leave?"

Gabe returned the angry glare. "What would you have me do, Justin? She's no ties here. Her life is back there." He inclined his head in the direction of the sea. "An ocean away."

Justin braced his legs wide, tossed his hat onto the conjured stool he'd been sitting on, and folded his arms over his chest. "So your plans, then, laddie, are to dally with the lass whenever you like, aye? Take your ease with no regard to her?"

Gabe stared, anger rising enough to make his skin hum. "Dunna preach to me, Captain. What I do with her is me own business."

Justin glared. "Do you care for her, then?"

Christ, he didna know what he felt. Had he known her long enough to care? The thought of her leaving made an ache grow in his stomach. That meant something, in truth.

But *care*?

As in *love*?

Gabe swore and turned around, faced the wall. "Why are you so bloody concerned about her, Justin?"

When the captain didna answer, Gabe slowly glanced at him.

And then it hit him.

He looked hard at Justin. "What? *You* care for her?"

Justin did nothing but curse and look away.

Gabe gave a short laugh. "I canna believe I'm havin' this conversation with you. You *care* for her, Justin?"

"Mayhap I do."

Gabe paced, glanced at his friend, and paced some more. " 'Tis crazy, my friend—"

Justin turned, stormed across the room, and stopped, toe-to-toe with Gabe. He gave him a fierce frown. "No crazier than havin' a woman like Allie who in fact does care and then throw her out on her arse!"

Gabe had witnessed Justin Catesby angry before. Never had he seen him as he was now.

Justin pointed a finger at him. "You mind how you tread on her heart, boy. You mind it well." He strode to the stool, lifted his tricorn, and pulled it onto his head. He turned. "Or bad dreams will be the least of your concern."

With that, Captain Justin Catesby faded away.

Gabe stared at the spot Justin had just occupied. He walked over to his worktable, picked up the chess piece he'd been carving, cursed, pulled his arm back, and aimed for the door.

Just before he let it fly, he squeezed his fist tightly over it, cursed again, and set the piece back on the table.

Storming out of his workshop, he went to the sofa in the pub's lobby and flung himself into it. With narrowed eyes, he stared into the dying peat fire.

What in bloody hell was he to do? Allie was on his mind constantly. When he was around her, his idiot brain turned to porridge and could barely form a decent thought. When they kissed, he wanted more.

When he touched her?

He wanted it *all*.

Did that mean he cared for her? Or, for Christ's sake, that he *loved* her? He was a screwup. A recovering alcoholic who used to smoke like a friggin' freight train and whose first wife was so bloody unhappy she drowned herself in the damned ocean?

How the bloody hell would *he* know what love was?

With the heel of his hand, he rubbed his eyes. Exhaustion overtook him and his eyelids grew heavy. The longer Gabe stared into the glowing embers of the peat, the sleepier he became.

Until finally, he simply allowed it to happen.

As he drifted in and out of consciousness, he prayed that morning would come fast.

It didna. Not before another spirit visited with his twopence worth of advice.

"Ahem." A throat cleared, just as Gabe was about to drift off to sleep. He cracked open an eye.

Alexander Dauber stood before him, hands clasped behind his back, a somber expression upon his ghostly face.

Gabe sat straighter. "Aye?"

"I wanted to add one thing to Captain Catesby's concerns, sir," Dauber said.

Gabe blinked. "You heard?"

Dauber nodded with enthusiasm. "Oh, of course. We all did. 'Twas quite a ruckus, indeed."

Rubbing his chin, Gabe met Allie's friend's gaze. "And you have something more to add, right?"

"Indeed."

Gabe gave him a nod to start.

"I'll keep this short, as Captain Catesby said pretty much what we all were thinking," Dauber said. "But this is more on a personal level. I've known Allie since she was a young girl."

"Aye?"

Dauber glanced down at his boots, then met Gabe eye-to-eye. "The lass has been terribly heartbroken before. I was with her through that suffering and 'twas the most heart-wrenching thing to witness, I assure you." He scratched his brow. "The young man she'd given her heart to—Jared—completely chose another girl, out of the blue. While they'd not officially become engaged, they'd talked of marriage." He shook his head. "Allie was devastated when he broke off their relationship. Simply devastated. And she's not given her heart to another since." He sighed. "I know you've been through some mighty vicious times in your own young life, lad, and that you've conquered quite a battle. For that I commend you."

Gabe gave a single nod.

"But I beg you not to toy with her emotions, Gabe MacGowan. She is a giving soul. If one is lucky enough to win that young girl's love, he must surely know the jewel he's unearthed. 'Tis evident in everything Allie does."

Gabe stared, speechless. He already knew that.

"There's a reason why our Allie has such a strong passion for life, as well as for those whose demise arrived far too soon, or in an unnatural manner. A reason why she's so good with the dead."

That got Gabe's attention.

"Your month will pass quickly, lad. Don't waste time you simply don't have." Dauber began to fade. "Don't."

Gabe blinked at the empty spot of air Dauber had just occupied.

So Allie had a secret or two, as did he himself.

With a heavy sigh, he closed his eyes. He rubbed the sockets with both hands, and thought just how much he and Allie needed to have a long, long talk . . .

Chapter 17

The sun hadn't quite broken through the clouds, the wind was icy—yet Allie thought it to be a perfectly beautiful morning.

She supposed she liked Scotland quite a lot.

And now she had the answer to a single question that had plagued her for some time.

What did Gabe MacGowan do to maintain a chiseled six-pack and bulging biceps?

She followed the answer with her eyes. The man rowed. *Rowed.* As in, in the water, in a little skinny boat, with oars.

Wee Mary had let Allie in on that little tidbit, and had sent her to the best seat in Sealladh na Mara: Wee Mary's front porch.

Gabe hadn't a clue they watched.

Which was all the better.

"Quite a sight, aye?" Wee Mary said.

"*Oui*, indeed," said Mademoiselle, who'd joined them.

"Wow, look at him go," said Allie. "How long has he been rowing?"

Wee Mary smiled as she watched her nephew in the loch. "Och, he's always been into sports and such, but he started rowing when he was a wee lad—Jake's age, perhaps. He also sails, and as a younger lad played a good bit of rugby, as well, oh, and football." She grinned at Allie. "That'd be your American soccer, love."

Allie returned the grin. "Gotcha." She watched Gabe row, and even from a distance she could tell how much strength and effort it took. No wonder the guy was solid as a rock. "Does Jake row?" She couldn't remember ever seeing him in the loch.

"No, I'm afraid his da wouldna allow it. Shame, really," Mary said. She turned to Allie. "What do you know about Jake's mother, love?"

Allie shrugged and shielded her eyes as she watched Gabe. "Only that she and Gabe had a very rocky marriage, and that she died before Jake was a year old."

"Och," said Mary. "I see he's no' told you everythin'. Tsk-tsk." She glanced at Allie, who'd turned to listen. "He'll tell you, no doubt, all in his own good time. 'Tis the way of a man, no doubt. But I will tell you this much. Jake's mother drowned." She pointed to where Gabe rowed, just there, beyond the sound, where a string of tiny islands lay. Part of the Inner Hebrides. "When young Jake showed an interest in the rowin', Gabe refused. He's put him in other sports, and does quite a lot with the lad. But willna allow him in the sea."

Allie considered that. "Doesn't Jake know how to swim?"

Mary nodded. "Och, aye, Gabe made sure the lad learned. He took him to the youth center in Wester Ross three times a week just last year. The lad swims like a fish. But his da willna allow him in the loch." Again, she shook her head. " 'Tis a shame, but Gabe's been through a lot. I understand his hesitancy, with Jake's mum drowning there." She glanced at Allie. "Ye ken?"

Allie blinked. "Excuse me?"

Mademoiselle giggled. "She means, *Do you understand?*" She gave Allie a knowing look. "I've learned quite a lot just from sitting on this very porch."

"I'll bet." Allie smiled at Mary. "Yes. I definitely ken, then."

Wee Mary and Mademoiselle both laughed.

"Och, now, what sort of mischief have you gone and gotten your wee self into, lass?" boomed a deep, heavily brogued voice.

Allie turned to find a tall, lean, and quite handsome older man walking up the steps to Wee Mary's porch, wearing dark trousers, a dark turtlenecked gray sweater, and a dark skullcap. The wide smile and green eyes left little doubt who he was.

Mary turned in her seat and grinned. "Oh, you scalawag, 'tis about time your old arse washed ashore." She gave a nod toward Allie. "Your boy has picked up an American, Gerald."

Gerald's eyes sparkled mischief and he held Allie's gaze for several moments. Not quite as intense as Gabe's, but still—both men spoke volumes with just their eyes. "Aye, so I see." He swiped off his cap and gave a gentlemanly nod. "Nice to meet you, lass. Laina's told me all about you."

Allie nodded in return. "Nice to meet you, too." She noticed he had the same hairline as Gabe's, the same close-clipped hair, only Gerald's had tiny streaks of silver throughout, and silver at his temples. Still, quite a looker.

Gerald then nodded to Elise. "Mademoiselle, always a pleasure."

Elise giggled. "*Merci*, as with you, as well."

Gerald glanced out over the loch. "How long has he been at it?"

Wee Mary sighed. "About an hour and a half now. He should come in soon."

"Right. Tell him I'll see him later, then," Gerald said. He grinned wide. "I've got me bride to see, first." He nodded. "Lassies, a good morn to you."

With that he waved and left.

Allie glanced at her watch. Eight forty a.m. "I'd better run, too, and start getting set up for lunch."

"Aye, and tomorrow is the showing of the pub, right?" asked Wee Mary. "Bright and early if memory serves me."

Allie stood and glanced at Gabe once more. "Yes." She turned and gave Mary a smile. "We'll be ready."

Mary exchanged glances with Elise. "We'll all be ready."

Their giggles sifted over the crisp air as Allie made her way up the single-track lane toward Odin's Thumb.

She took in her seaside view of Sealladh na Mara as she walked, and really, breathtaking hardly described it. The quaint little cottages, whitewashed with dark roofs, and the craggy cliffs just beyond the loch, the brightly painted signs on the establishments lining the walk . . . not to mention the fresh, clean air, tinged with brine. Gosh, she couldn't imagine the beauty of it in the spring and summer.

Stopping in her tracks, she turned and studied the MacGowan ruins at the top of the cliff. She'd not been able to inspect it well enough that night with Gabe— she'd been too busy stomping around and acting like a bully.

And kissing. They'd certainly been busy kissing.

She'd hardly been able to think of anything else.

She continued on. Sweet God, the man could kiss. All that barely contained energy on the verge of igniting, he was like one big, intense, powerful stick of dynamite.

She felt it clear to her bones even now.

In the distance, a boat's horn blasted in the sound, and it carried on the wind and echoed through the village. Prawn traps were set at the far side of the loch, their white foam markers bobbing with the tide. So serene, peaceful.

And yet Gabe's wife drowned in that very water.

Allie walked faster, the uphill climb making her thighs burn, her lungs expand, and it felt *good*. Yet nothing she did could make thoughts of Gabe Mac-Gowan fade from her mind for long.

What would she do once she left?

There was so much Gabe hadn't told her, yet she knew with ferocity that he felt their connection as strongly as Allie. She could see it in his eyes, hear it in his voice, and by God, she could feel it in his touch.

Yet . . . there was quite a lot she hadn't told him, either.

Perhaps they were both a little fearful?

She wasn't a mushy, doe-eyed young girl with fanciful dreams of picket fences and knights on white horses. She knew firsthand the reality of heartache. Jared had shown her that. The actual heartache wasn't real anymore, but the memory of what it'd felt like certainly was, and Allie never wanted to experience anything like it again. She knew successful relationships required work.

Work, and honesty.

Gabe wasn't the only one with ghosts.

She had them, too.

And betrayal had been part of the reason her heart had been broken. *Another of her ghosts . . .*

Turning onto the walk, Allie headed up the way to Odin's. As she passed the bakery, she waved at Leona, who smiled and waved back. A bit farther up, Willy

MacMillan, the fishmonger, grinned and held up a freshly filleted cod.

Allie laughed, shook her head, and continued on her way. In a very short time she'd been accepted by the folks of Sealladh na Mara. They were kind, funny, and welcoming. They looked after each other.

Hey—they accepted a pub filled with various ghostly souls from various centuries as if they were their favorite relatives.

As she made it to Odin's, she stopped and glanced up at the sign. Colorful and bright, it stood stark against the whitewash of the five-hundred-year-old building itself, and the sign hung on a black wrought-iron bracket that groaned when the breeze blew it.

She suddenly felt as though she'd stood beneath the Odin's Thumb sign a hundred times before, and that she'd gone through its doors another hundred. It felt familiar.

Strangely enough, it felt like home.

Briefly, she wondered what Gabe would think of *her* ghosts.

A dangerous thought, she knew. But just as she couldn't help falling for Odin's proprietor—she could admit that now, even if only to herself—she certainly couldn't help falling for the seaside town filled with quirky, loving people, like the fishmonger who waved dead fish through the picture window.

As well as the quirky, loving spirited souls, of course.

A gloomy thought crashed over her as she pushed into Odin's. She might not be able to help falling for Gabe MacGowan and the folks—live and spirited—of Sealladh na Mara, but she'd better get over them, and *quick*.

Because in a month, she'd be gone.

And as she easily walked into Odin's, into the kitchen where she lifted one of Wee Mary's aprons off the wall hook and began getting lunch together, she told herself if she said it enough, her heart just might stay intact when it happened.

By six o'clock, Odin's Thumb was filled to the gills with patrons. Everyone who came brought a covered dish of food, and so there was always plenty to eat. As usual, a huge turnout of folks showed up to welcome home his da and the other longshoreman from his outfit who'd returned. "Another safe sea journey, aye?" passed round, and every time his da or one of the others replied, "Aye, unscathed and bloody starved!" a rousing round of cheers passed through the pub. Gabe never grew tired of hearing it. It meant his da was indeed home safe. And from the glow in his wee mother's eyes—eyes she couldna take off Gerald MacGowan— well, it was made that much more special.

To have a love like that? Christ. Gabe could barely imagine it.

His eyes immediately sought out Allie Morgan. Funny, that.

The lass sat at a table in the center of the pub, his mother and da on one side, Jake on the other, and the Odin's ghostly lot perched on stools as close as they could get to her.

More than once Justin Catesby had slipped Gabe a fierce scowl. They'd not spoken since that night in the workshop, but they needed to. He didna like fierce words to go unsettled—especially with family.

Aye. Justin and the others were family. They were to everyone at Sealladh na Mara.

Gabe watched his father rise, kiss the top of Laina's head, and make his way toward Gabe. In his hand, a tall glass of water, just like Gabe's. When Gabe had stopped drinking, his da, even though he didna have a problem, stopped social drinking, as well. He loved the man for that.

Gerald MacGowan took the bar stool next to Gabe, met his gaze, then glanced out at the Odin's crowd. "Your mother tells me you've been busy since I left," he said. "She dunna look much like a ghost ouster." He nodded. "Look at how they surround her." He glanced at Gabe, mischief in his eye. "Looks like you got scammed, lad."

Gabe chuckled and kept his eyes trained on Allie, who sat laughing at something Killigrew had said. "She's certainly something, aye?"

"Indeed she is," Gerald said. "You know she's got that grumpy fishmonger in her hands like putty."

Gabe smiled. "From the very first day she arrived."

Gerald nodded. "So you've changed your mind about leavin'?"

Gabe met his gaze. "I'm considerin'."

Gerald looked at him. "What happens after your contract is void with the Realtor?"

Gabe met his gaze. He knew exactly what his father meant. "She goes back home, Da."

Gerald simply nodded, took a long pull on his water, and nodded again. "She's a fine lass."

Gabe sighed. "I know."

Sliding off the stool, Gerald gave Gabe's shoulder a hearty slap and a smile. "Then that's all that matters, lad."

He went back to the table.

It was more than a few hours later when the only beings left in Odin's were the otherworldly souls, Gabe's parents, Wee Mary, and Allie. Gabe walked down the steps, having just put a sleeping Jake to bed, and joined the small group huddled around the large middle table in the pub. Gabe slid into the seat across from Allie. Her hair was pulled half back, and small curls framed her face. She wore a soft gray woolen jumper and a pair of jeans. Comfortable. Casual.

Perfect.

"So, you make a livin' oustin' spirits back in the States, then?" asked Gerald.

Allie nodded. "I don't really oust them, actually. I'm more of a . . . mediator. Or interpreter. Usually, the souls I'm hired to oust just need a bit of help finding the cause of their troubles. They need someone to talk to, who understands. And"—she grinned— "more likely than not it's the mortals who are the troublemakers. They hire me to get rid of the troublesome spirits invading their homes. I simply discover what the matter truly is, solve it, whether it be finding out their cause of death, what happened to their loved ones, and so on."

Gabe watched the play of the lamplight on Allie's face, how her lips formed words, and how she continuously talked with her hands. He found he liked that about her.

A lot. As much as how she spoke to his Odin's lot as though it were most natural thing to do.

"And how, my dear, are you able to decipher such?" asked Gerald.

Allie sort of shrugged. "Because I can relate, I guess, so I talk to them, find out who *they* are first, and some of the last things, places, dates they can recall."

Wee Mary smiled and patted Allie's hand. "No offense, love, but how can you relate if you've never been dead yourself?"

Allie laughed, but Gabe could immediately tell 'twas no' the same Allie laugh he was used to hearing.

"You know," she said, "I guess just being around so many ghosts, I just . . . adapted." She glanced at her watch. "Wow—look at the time." She smiled and pushed away from her chair. "I promised my folks I'd call tonight before it got too late." She smiled and started off. "I'll see you guys bright and early tomorrow, right? We've got some potential buyers arriving first thing in the morning."

With that, she waved and walked out of Odin's.

Gabe looked directly at Dauber. "What just happened?"

Dauber glanced around, then sighed. "She's quite all right, young Gabe. 'Tis simply a topic she's uncomfortable with in front of you, is all. She'll return."

"What is it?" Gabe said, and stood.

Alexander Dauber inclined his ghostly head to the front door. "I fear only Allie can be the teller of that tale. If you can wrench it from her, that is. But I'd give her a few moments to herself, were I you."

Gabe sat for a few minutes and listened to his father tell a couple rousing longshoreman tales before he pushed away from the table, excused himself, and headed straight out of Odin's front door.

It seemed they both had hidden ghosts whose bones needed rattling once and for all.

And he was in the mood to rattle.

Chapter 18

Tears streamed down Allie's face as she hurried up the walk. The night was clear and cold, and a thin mist slipped in from the sea. Angrily, she swiped at her cheeks but her eyes continued to leak. It only irritated her, and she cried more.

Why *that* conversation? Why had *that* topic been brought up? Why on earth had she never experienced a problem answering the same questions to others before? She'd been asked the very same questions dozens of times. She knew how to respond. So why an issue tonight?

She'd not told Gabe everything—that was why.

There'd been no way to divert it, either, that topic. She'd stepped right into it. Things she hadn't been prepared to tell anyone at Sealladh na Mara—mostly Gabe MacGowan—simmered right there at the brim of discussion, and she had no choice but to laugh it off like some lunatic, and right in front of the one person she didn't want to find out—

Strong fingers wound around her upper arm and Allie yanked to a halt. She didn't have to turn around to know who it was. Instead, she quickly swiped her eyes with her free hand, turned, and smiled.

"Gabe, you scared me! I'll be just a minute." She

nodded toward the red pay phone on the corner. "I'll call my mom and sisters and be right back."

He didn't let her arm go. Instead, he pulled her closer and studied her face, looking right at her damp cheeks. "Allie," he said, his voice calm, deep. "What are you goin' to call them with?"

She smiled. "My phone card."

Gabe continued to stare. He lifted his other hand. Her phone card was gripped between his middle and forefinger. "You left this on the table."

Allie took it and sighed. "I'm not a good faker."

Gabe gave a half smile. "Nay, you're no'."

She looked at him. "I'm usually not a crybaby, either." She blew out a gusty breath. "I just made an ass out of myself in front of your family, didn't I?"

With his index finger, Gabe tapped the end of her nose. "Darlin', you're standin' next to the biggest horse's arse in the northwestern Highlands," he said with that crooked way he talked. With his thumb, he wiped first one teary cheek, then the other. "No, you didna make an arse o' yourself. Dauber and I were the only ones who noticed anything out of the ordinary, anyhow. 'Twill be all right. Trust me."

Allie glanced down the walk, toward the wharf. She crossed her arms over her chest, and wanted badly to just go somewhere and talk, get the weight of her ghosts off her chest.

"Stay right here," Gabe said. "I'll be right back."

He turned and ran back to Odin's, ducked inside, and when he came back, he had a large, thick wool blanket. "We'll go sit by the wharf and you can talk me ears off, aye?" he said, draping the blanket over her shoulders and securing it with his arm.

How Gabe knew that was exactly what she wanted to do, she couldn't explain. But it was right, and it felt right.

Gabe felt right.

"Aye," Allie said, and leaned into him.

Minutes later they were seated on her favorite bench, just a few feet from where the sea lapped at the shore. That odd mist crept over the loch, illuminated by a thin slice of moon shining from over the hills behind Sealladh na Mara. Gabe lifted the blanket, draped it over them both, and pulled Allie close.

Then he allowed her to take her time.

Finally, Allie told a story she hadn't told a soul—save Dauber—in years. She took a deep breath.

And before she could begin, Gabe felt for her hand, found it, and laced their fingers together. He squeezed gently.

It gave her strength.

She looked at him. "When did you change from a rude, aloof man to such a sweet and considerate one?" she asked.

Gabe shrugged and squeezed her hand tighter. "Must be the company I'm keepin' lately."

"Indeed." She took a deep breath in, then let it slowly out before she began. "I haven't always been able to see spirits," she started. "But it wasn't until I died myself that I could not only see and interact but . . . relate."

She felt Gabe tense beside her. "What happened?" His voice was low, steady, and yet she could tell how her statement had affected him by how heavy his brogue had become. She'd noticed that about Gabe. The more excited, angry, or concerned, the thicker his accent became, as well. She found she liked it quite a lot.

If that were all she had to tell . . .

As if he understood, Gabe again squeezed her hand.

She continued. "I was two months short of turning eighteen years old when I walked into a convenience

store and startled a robbery. I was shot here." She
lifted her sweater and pushed down the waist of her
jeans, exposing the raised, four-inch scar just below
where her appendix used to be. "And here." She lifted
the other side of her sweater, to just below her lung
where another like scar rested. Gabe leaned forward
to look, and then he settled back against the bench.
The muscles in his jaw worked.

"I died twice, actually," she continued. "Once on
the floor of the Quickie-Mart, from blood loss and
respiratory failure from a collapsed lung, then again
in recovery, right after surgery." She looked at him,
and his gaze was fixed toward the sea. The moon
shone from the hills behind them and coated the right
side of his face in silver.

"Unlike a lot of people who experience near death,
I remember everything." She shivered, and Gabe must
have thought it was the cold because he lifted his arm
behind her head, tucked her close beside him, and
pulled the blanket close. He grasped her hand again,
and held tight.

It calmed Allie, his presence. And it made the telling of the rest not quite as difficult as she'd imagined.

"My father was right there, waiting. I'd missed him
so much that at that moment, nothing mattered—not
my mom, my sisters—nothing, except staying there,
with him. Even if it meant staying dead." She shook
her head, and Gabe leaned his head close, pressing
his lips to her temple. "I remember pacing in the recovery room, peering between the nurses and doctor
and anesthesiologist and respiratory therapist at my
body as they scrambled around, trying to bring me
back. My father paced with me, and then jerked me
around, hugged me tight, told me he loved me but I'd
better get my scrawny ass back to where it belonged,
that I was too young to die, that I couldn't leave my

mother and make her suffer another death. Still, I wouldn't listen. I tried to run, the people trying to save my life completely oblivious to the fact two ghosts were zipping between them, a father chasing his disobedient daughter." She breathed, and gave a short laugh. "And then the team quit. They stopped working on me." She glanced up at him. "They were done trying to bring me back and they called the time of death."

Gabe simply stared at her, waiting. He said nothing.

"I froze and stared at myself, lying on that recovery room gurney. I looked horrible. I wanted to go back, but I couldn't move." She smiled. "The last thing my father said was, *I love you, brat. Tell your sisters and mother I love them. And that I'm watching, and always near.* Then he pushed me. Pushed me so damn hard I squealed." She smiled. "He pushed me right back into my body. Later, the nurses would tell me how, just before my heartbeat registered on the monitor, they heard me squeal." Again, she laughed. "They said it scared the willies out of them." She shrugged. "It took me months to recover. No bones had been shattered—it was all internal injuries. I'd lost a lot of blood. But after, once I healed? I'd started college and had entered the chapel when I saw Alexander Dauber sitting on a pew alone." She smiled at the memory. "Gosh, he was funny. He glanced my way. I must have had a wide-eyed look, and he blinked, over and over, wiped his eyes, and blinked some more. After that, more spirits began to appear, many more than before, and I could do little more than just inter-act. I could feel them, their suffering, and I could fig-ure things out they couldn't figure out themselves. I could lessen their pain. Unsettle them, if you will."

She still hadn't told him the worst of it.

With a deep breath, Allie turned to the left, so she

faced Gabe directly. He looked at her, all serious and intense as usual, with his jaw clenching. She searched his eyes, noted every small detail of his face at close range, and she found she liked everything she saw—every laugh line at the corner of his eyes, his nose, his jaw. "When I was shot, the bullet hit a few things." She looked down, then lifted her chin. "I can't have children."

Gabe searched her eyes, then glanced out over the loch.

"I've accepted it, and I'm not looking for pity by telling you. But it makes me feel like . . ." She stuttered, and felt tears making her eyes burn. "Like I'm not a whole person because of it." She shrugged and wiped her eyes. "It's not something I bring up immediately upon meeting a new guy." She looked at him and tried to smile. "Tends to scare fellas off. Ya know? Makes people treat you differently if they know you've been through trauma." She sighed. "I don't like to be treated different, so I keep it to myself."

Gabe studied Allie Morgan, who sat sideways on a bench next to a Highland sea loch, legs pulled up and folded, baring her fears. The wind caught that glorious mane of curls and tossed them about, and she lifted her free hand to tuck the loose strands behind her ear.

He held her other hand tightly.

Lifting it, he brought it to his lips and pressed them there, and he watched Allie's eyes close, a soft sigh escaping her. He could feel her relief wash through her.

He wondered if she could feel his.

Christ, he thought she was about to tell him she was dyin'.

"I'm no' verra good at comforting words, Allie Morgan," he said, and she opened her eyes and looked at him. "But I know what it's like to not feel whole. Guilt can take a chunk out of your spirit just as clean and accurate as a surgeon's blade." He slid her close; her knees pulled up between them—just scooted her whole self closer, pushed that wild hair from her face, and traced her lips with his thumb. "You're the most complete person I know, Allie Morgan." He watched his thumb as it moved over her mouth. "You have a gift to touch and mend souls, lass—dead, alive, it doesna matter." He pushed her knees down then, placed both hands on her face, and pulled her so that their lips nearly brushed. "You've touched mine. And I'm tired of pretendin' you havena."

And truly, he could find nothing more to say that summed up just how special Allie Morgan was to him.

So instead of words, he kissed her.

As Gabe settled his mouth over Allie's, he inhaled, the smells of the sea combining with the clean, flowery scent that belonged solely to Allie. He held her jaw, used his thumb, and pulled her mouth open just a bit and tasted her slowly, savoring the softness of her lips, the warmth of her tongue, and it all but drove him crazy.

Her hands, slender and soft, slid around his neck and up into his hair, although he'd cut it so close there wasna so much for her to touch. Just the pressure of her hands on his head, pulling him closer and kissing him back with such desperation nearly sent him over the edge.

He knew the more he tasted, the more he'd want.

Resting his hand on her thigh, he felt her skin heat under his touch, and he slid his palm up, over her hip, and came to rest beneath her jumper on the soft skin at the small of her back. Allie groaned softly as they kissed, and when he felt her spine with his fingers, she groaned again and leaned into him.

"Christ, woman," he said against her mouth, then moved to her neck. "You're drivin' me bloody crazy—"

"No doubt you're drivin' her bloody crazy, what with all that slobberin' goin' on," a deep voice said behind them.

Both Gabe and Allie jumped, once again clunking their foreheads together. Gabe glanced over his shoulder.

Only to find his younger brother grinning at him like the idiot he was.

"Damn," Gabe muttered with a grin.

And before he could say another word, his brother leapt over the back of the bench, threw his stupid self down next to Allie, and put his bloody arm around her.

He gave Gabe's shoulder a push.

Lifting Allie's hand, his brother kissed it. "Sean MacGowan, lass, and I'd be more than happy to take care of this witless fool if he's botherin' you."

Gabe swore under his breath, and Allie laughed. "If he ever starts bothering me, you'll be the very first person I call." She smiled at Gabe, then turned to Sean and shook the hand he was still holdin'. "Allie Morgan and it's very nice to meet you."

Sean put a hand over his heart. "Och, an American. And such fine manners—wherever did you find her, Gabe? That accent is so sweet," he said, then lifted a brow. "Do you have sisters, then?"

Allie smiled. "Three."

Gabe hadn't even known that.

There was a lot he needed to learn about Allie Morgan.

"Great! When can they be here?" Sean said, and Allie laughed. Then Sean rubbed his arms with his hands and looked at Gabe. "It's bloody freezin' out here, man. You two are either goin' to let me in that blanket or head back to Odin's."

Gabe smiled, stood then, pulled his brother up from the bench beside Allie, and drew him into a fierce hug. Sean hugged him back. "Welcome home, little lad."

" 'Tis good to see you, old lad," said Sean. "I've missed you."

Gabe grinned and slapped his brother on the back. "Come on, then, you boneless schoolgirl. Let's get you back to the pub before you catch a chill."

Allie laughed and Gabe looked down at her.

The reality of Allie Morgan washed over him then, and how bloody lucky he was to have crossed paths with such a woman. To think a woman like that could, dare he hope, care for a man like him?

'Twas nearly unthinkable.

She stood and sidled next to him, and slipped her wee arm around his waist.

Over her head, Sean looked at Gabe and grinned.

Then he mouthed the word *perfect*.

Gabe pulled Allie close and returned his brother's grin. *I know,* he mouthed back.

And as they walked back to Odin's Thumb, on that cold, misty October eve, Gabe realized he'd been alone all this time, had made the mistakes he'd made and lived through a hell he mostly created for his own stupid self, and that maybe it had been for a reason. He hadn't known Allie Morgan would be the one to step into his life to try to stop him from leaving his and Jake's home, but he was damn thankful she did.

It was at that very moment Gabe decided with certainty that Sealladh na Mara was where he and Jake needed to stay. He'd not have to fight his ghosts alone—once he told Allie the rest of his own secrets.

He looked down at her, and she looked up at him, and he knew then he wanted to keep her.

Keep her forever.

He only prayed he could.

Chapter 19

An hour before her alarm was set to ring, and Allie's eyes popped open. *Five a.m.* She blinked, pulled the duvet up around her neck, and peered over her toes at the hearth. Once again, another slab of peat had been placed, a nice warm blaze making the room toastier than it would have been had the fire gone completely out.

She'd have to remember to thank Gabe later.

Studying the room in the amber light of the fire, Allie thought back to the night before, after she, Gabe, and Sean had walked back in to Odin's. Everyone was still sitting in the same place as when she'd left, and they cheered as the three crossed the pub to the table. Nothing was said about why Allie had left, and yet it was comfortable, inviting, easygoing.

She'd discovered Gabe's family was like that. Completely accepting, natural, and accommodating.

Allie really liked that.

Sean, who looked enough like Gabe they could nearly pass for twins except he'd grown his hair out a bit longer and was about an inch shorter, had walked right up to Wee Mary, kissed her neck, and was rewarded with a squeal and a swat to the backside, and then he did the same thing to his mother.

Allie realized quickly just what a charming flirt Sean MacGowan truly was.

Of course, she also realized just as fast where the MacGowan boys obtained their charm, because when Sean tried to walk past his father, Gerald pulled his six-foot-plus son into his lap and planted a big sloppy kiss right on his cheek. Everyone had roared with laughter.

Once released from Gerald's arms, Sean had bowed to Mademoiselle Bedeau, who'd blushed a ghostly pink, greeted the other spirited souls of Odin's like family, who returned the greeting likewise, and had entertained the group with what Wee Mary had called *youthful naughty shenanigans* from university. Wee Mary was right. Naughty hardly described Sean MacGowan.

For the first time since arriving at Sealladh na Mara, Allie saw Gabe *relax*. A change, just as recent as their talk at the wharf, seemed to come over him. His demeanor was more laid-back, he *laughed* more. And God, what a great laugh he had. Not to mention that adorable, slightly crooked mouth when he spoke.

Gerald MacGowan then enlightened Allie on a few shenanigans pulled by a little Gabe MacGowan, including a few mishaps involving pollywogs, hedgehogs, and a little girl named Cassidy who'd once lived up the lane. Gabe covered his face with his hands and laughed, along with the rest of his family, and had turned to her and said, "Dunna believe everything they tell you, Allie Morgan." and then his eyes had danced with mischief.

She learned quite a lot about Gabe MacGowan in the two hours she'd sat amongst his loved ones. And she discovered the more she learned, the more she *liked*. He had a sister named Merriweather—Merri for short—who seemed to be just as mischief as Gabe. Allie hoped to meet her.

Rolling over, she pulled her knees up to her stomach and watched the peat burn in the hearth. The earthy scent wafted through the room and she inhaled, and thought a better smell couldn't possibly exist. Maybe because that same scent had clung to Gabe's clothes, and Allie had inhaled a good bit of it while nearly sitting on his lap as he kissed the socks off her.

Closing her eyes, Allie easily called forth the memory of Gabe's thumb grazing her lips, the way he stared so deeply into her eyes and making sure her head was at just the perfect angle before tasting. Sweet God, the man could kiss, more erotic and sensual than Allie ever thought she'd experience. Perhaps those sensations happened because of the man himself. Gabe MacGowan did nothing without thought, purpose, and yet spontaneity at the same time.

Their first kiss still lingered in her memory—and the way Gabe had been *before* that first kiss. Wide-eyed and seemingly in another place, Allie wondered what had caused him to be out of bed and so out of sorts at that time of night. Rather, morning. She remembered it had been around one a.m. Had a dream awakened him?

All she knew was the fun, joking, lighthearted Gabe MacGowan was something to consider. Just watching him laugh at his brother, or at something he and his brother conspired to do, made her smile. Laina and Gerald had shaken their heads and laughed. Pride shone in both of their eyes, and it made Allie happy to know that while during Gabe's tormenting struggle through his marriage, the loss of his career, drinking, his wife dying—and all the recovery he'd accomplished after, he'd had a close-knit, supportive family system to see him through it.

She'd be willing to bet he was glad for it, too.

Briefly, and not for the first time, Allie considered

what might become of her and Gabe. How on earth could she just walk away from him and everything wonderful in Sealladh na Mara? Not that she'd been asked to stay, of course, but their relationship—if she could call it that—was so fresh and new. To even think of staying, or Gabe asking her to stay, seemed too far-fetched at the moment.

But would they be able to carry on with a big fat ocean between them? Would she be able to easily get over him if they simply parted ways once the contract for Odin's was up?

Pulling a pillow over her face, Allie groaned. She was thinking way too much, and too fast. She needed to calmly swallow a big chill pill and take things easy. Go with the flow. See how things worked out over the next few weeks.

Flinging back the duvet, Allie gathered her clean clothes and toiletries. She looked in the mirror over the dresser and stared at her reflection. Truth be told, the Odin's lot could completely handle the hauntings— which was exactly what they'd decided to do to dissuade any potential buyers with a mind to buy a pub— while the contract ran its course. She wasn't needed. Not really. Yes, she could conduct a pretty frighteningly haunting experience, but it could all be done without her presence. Especially since Gabe was now on the same page as everyone else.

That was a feat all its own.

Allie felt as if she were on an extended vacation.

She smiled. That was the good thing about being a money saver and having your own small business, being your own boss.

No one to answer to.

She squinted at herself in the mirror. "Yeah, you should definitely stay," she said. "See how things go."

She turned and slipped out of her room and into

the bathroom across the hall. She'd get ready, go over to Leona's for a pastry and coffee, and get back to Odin's.

They had a scheduled haunting in the pub at nine a.m. sharp, followed by lunch preparations.

She didn't want to miss a minute of it.

An hour later and Allie started up the walk toward Leona's. Pushing open the door, she drew up short as a man walked out, the two nearly colliding. At first, she thought it was Gabe, but quickly recognized Sean instead.

He smiled and held the door for her. "Och, what a fine morn to find such a bonny lass to be stuck in a doorway with. Leona, love, look who I've found."

"Saints, boy, you're such a flirt," Leona said, shaking her head. She smiled. "Come in, Allie. I've your pastry waiting for you."

Sean bent his dark head over her waxed paper. "Leona's meat and cheese pie. A girl after me own heart." He cocked his head and wagged a brow. "Are you sure it's me old decrepit brother you're interested in, lass?"

"Are you jokin', boy? Have you seen the way those two look at each other?" Leona said. "All but caught the pub on fire last night."

A gleam of mischief shone in Sean's eyes when he grinned. "You should have seen the wee bench by the wharf. Smolderin', 'twas."

Allie shook her head, but she could feel the heat rush up her neck. "You guys are bad."

"You guys," Sean mimicked. "God, that American accent is so adorable."

"Och, wee Sean, you've more than a run for your money in your brother. That rogue Justin Catesby has the eye on her as well."

Allie wasn't surprised when that comment didn't startle Sean MacGowan—or slow him down—at all.

"Well then, seems I'll have to work extra hard, aye?" he said. "Come, Allie Morgan from America. Let's go break our fast together." He winked. " 'Twill be good to make the old decrepit brother jealous."

Allie laughed. "Okay, let's go." She handed Leona three pounds for the pastry and coffee. "Don't forget. Haunting at nine sharp."

Leona's smile proved just how much she enjoyed being part of the Big Odin's Fiasco. "Wouldna miss it for the world, love. I'll see you there."

Sean held the door and Allie ducked out of Leona's. Together they walked down to the wharf and sat on the bench facing the loch.

"So, tell me about these sisters of yours," Sean said, taking a big bite of his pastry. He barely finished chewing. "What are their names? Are they as bonny as you?"

Allie slid a glance his way, took an enormous bite of her own pastry—which turned out to be the exact same one Sean had—chewed, and swallowed.

"Bloody hell, you're no bigger than a bird but can eat like a man," Sean said with pride. He smiled. "I like that. Now go on. Tell me." He took another bite.

"I'm the oldest. Next there's Emma, she's twenty-eight; then Boe, she's twenty-six; and Sicka—her name's Ivy, but we call her Sicka—she's twenty-four." She grinned. "They're all ten times more gorgeous than me."

He shook his head. "I dunna believe a word of it." He smiled and inclined his head. "Do any of them have that glorious mane of curls you have there?"

Allie chewed, watching Sean closely. As he ate with gusto he had the most devilish tilt to the corner of his mouth. "You're not very shy, are you?"

He didn't break his amused stare. "Nope," he said through another mouthful of pie. "No' in the least."

Allie shook her head, balled up her empty wax

paper, and sipped her coffee. When she slid Sean a glance, he was still staring at her.

"What?" she asked.

Funny how she felt completely comfortable around a guy she'd known less than nine hours.

"You're a true miracle, Allie Morgan," he said. "I canna tell you the difference I see in Gabe, just since the last time I saw him."

That somehow made Allie tingle inside. "When was that?"

"About three months ago." He shook his head and wadded up his own empty pastry wrapping. " 'Tis like night and day." He continued to study her, an approving grin lighting his handsome face. "You're good for him." He winked. "I suppose I'll have to settle for one of your gorgeous sisters, aye?"

Allie laughed. "You're crazy." Like Gabe—actually, like everyone else at Sealladh na Mara—Sean's accent was so pleasing to hear. *About* sounded like *aboot*, *ago* sounded like *agoo*, and there was that ever-present, always pleasing to the ear *aye* that Allie thought she'd never grow tired of hearing.

"I can only imagine wee Jake adores you, as well," Sean said. "He's a great little kid."

"He is," Allie agreed. And she meant it. She loved kids, and some of her favorite spirited souls were children. "He's been wanting to take me up to the family homestead."

"Och, the MacGowan keep," Sean said. "One of me favorite places to go. Maybe we'll take a run up there before I leave."

"I've seen it at night but not during the day," she said.

Sean laughed. "I'll bet. That wily brother of mine."

Allie remembered the memory. She'd never forget it.

"So, is Gabe still havin' those horrible nightmares?" Sean asked. "Christ, they're bloody terrifying, what with his dead wife appearin' to him and such."

Allie's eyes widened. "What?"

Suddenly, Sean's face blanched. "Christ, you didna know?" He swore under his breath. Something Gaelic, and a word Allie hadn't heard before.

Allie shook her head. "I knew he'd been having horrible nightmares about his wife but not that he'd been seeing his wife's spirit. That's a whole new ball game."

Sean rubbed his chin, much as Gabe did. "He's goin' to kill me if he finds out."

Allie grabbed his hand. "No, tell me. Please. I may be able to help."

Chapter 20

Allie could see the hesitancy in Sean's eyes, and she immediately felt bad for pressuring. But if Gabe was still dealing with issues—not only horrible dreams but, according to Sean, seeing Kait's spirit— then he needed help. Kait, apparently, needed help, too. Desperately.

Allie's help, if Allie had anything to do with it.

She gave Sean's hand a squeeze, then turned loose. "How bad are the dreams?" she asked.

Sean scratched a place beneath his eye, stared at Allie, then sighed. "I suppose if he's to trust anyone, it should be you. Your friend Dauber told me just this morning you have a way with spirits and such. Maybe you can help me brother, since he's so lack-witted he'd rather suffer than ask for anythin'." Leaning forward, legs spread in total guy fashion, he rested his elbows on his knees and looked at the spot of gravel between his boots. "The only reason any of us ever learned anythin' is that wee Jake told me mum once whilst spendin' the night at her house one weekend. Och, 'twas about six months ago now." He rubbed his jaw. "The lad wakes up to Gabe shoutin' sometimes, wavin' his arms about and swearin', with a terrified, wild look in his eye, Jake says." He shook his head. "I've never seen it myself, though. I've been away at university for nearly four years now, and if he was havin' those dreams before that, he didna tell me about it."

Allie looked out over the loch. Gulls screamed overhead, and large gray clouds rolled in like smoke from a chimney. She rubbed her arms. "I think he's still having them," she said, recalling the night of their first kiss. "I ran into him downstairs about one in the morning and he was certainly not himself. And a few other times he's been awake, in his workshop, at . . ."

Sean turned to her. "Aye?"

Allie slowly looked at Gabe's brother. "One a.m. He goes to bed but always seems to be awake at one a.m." She stood, and Sean did the same. As the wind blew, she pushed her hair behind her ear. "I'm not one to hide things from people. I like the truth. I'm in favor of the truth." She grasped his forearm and squeezed. "But in this case, I want to try something."

In unison, they turned back up the walk and started toward Odin's. "What?" asked Sean.

"Find out if Gabe is having nightmares, or actually having experiences with Kait's soul."

Sean looked at her. "Seriously? Do you think she's haunting me brother?"

Allie shrugged. "Well, if it *is* Kait's soul, hopefully I can help." She smiled. "It's what I do—deal with ghostly souls in need of settling. I can only imagine poor Kait died having serious issues at hand. Her soul is probably tormented by her past. But if it's truly nightmares, then . . . I don't know. We'll see."

Together they hurried up the walk, past the Royal Post, past Leona's, and past Willy the Fishmonger's. As they neared Odin's, Sean pulled Allie to a stop and gave her a quick kiss on the cheek. "A finer lass couldna have come along at a better time in Gabe's life. Thank you for helpin' me brother. He's a lucky man."

Allie smiled. "I'm lucky, too, and I hope I can help."

Sean's grin touched his eyes. "You already have, lass." He inclined his head. "Now hurry. We've a hauntin' to accomplish."

Gabe looked in the mirror, ran his fingers over his hair, and straightened his tie. 'Twas almost a joke, getting all set up for a potential sale only to purposely thwart it.

He was a fool for ever signing such a contract.

And an even bigger fool for ever wanting to sell Odin's and leave Sealladh na Mara. He'd been fearful that Jake would suffer from his nightmares—from his own mother's soul. But mayhap Allie could help. *Once he finally told her . . .*

He looked at his reflection. It only took the wily planning of a wee witch with a headful of blond curls to change his mind.

Change his *life.*

Downstairs, his auntie, Leona, his da and mum, his brother, and Allie Morgan took their places amongst six scheming, cunning, lovable spirits trying to save their home. Had Jake not been at school, he'd be in the midst of it, as well.

After today, they had six more appointments to thwart and the contract to sell Odin's would be null and void.

Never to be placed on the market again.

His only fear now was that one of those potential buyers liked the idea of a haunted pub and inn. Sealladh na Mara in fact had a reputation throughout the Highlands, but most of the folks in search of a B and B or pub to purchase were those no' from the area. While the idea of a haunted pub appealed to them, usually, a truly haunted pub did no'.

He could only hope.

Through the mirror, a shadow darted across the floor. Gabe glanced over his shoulder, only to find nothing. Just his bed.

He turned around, and when he did, his blood ran cold.

Staring at him through the mirror, seemingly directly over his left shoulder, was *Kait*.

With an intake of air, Gabe turned around. Nothing.

This time when he looked back to the mirror, there was also nothing. He gripped either side of the dresser with his hands, squeezed, and hung his head down. He stared at the floor between his feet as he spoke. "Damn it, Kait, what do you want with me?" He took in a long breath. He wasna scared of her, but it unnerved him to see his dead wife—especially in the form she presented herself in. The way she'd used Jake to frighten him, too, angered him. For two solid nights he'd not dreamt of her, nor had she come to him.

She was here now.

Either that or he was in fact goin' crazy.

"What do you *want*?" He lifted his head. Again, she stared back at him, and his gaze didna waver from hers. 'Twas the first time she'd done it in broad daylight, and she looked horrid, with hair missing in patches, what was there woven with seaweed, and her eye sockets a dark cavern of black. He frowned, anger building. "I want you to go, Kait. You dunna belong here anymore," he said between clenched teeth. "Go, and leave us alone!"

Kait simply stared, before that wide, dark mouth opened. No lips to form words, no tongue, just a big, gaping hole. Still, her voice came through.

She looked straight at him. "Make her leave."

Just then, someone knocked at the door.

Gabe blinked, and Kait's image in the mirror disappeared.

With a heavy sigh, he took one long, deep breath and let it slowly out. "Aye, 'tis open."

The door cracked open and his brother poked his head in. "Och, you look gorgeous, bro. Now stop curlin' your hair and paintin' your toes and come on, aye?"

Gabe shook his head.

Mostly to rid his thoughts of what had just happened.

What continued to happen.

As he punched Sean in the shoulder and they left, Gabe couldn't help wondering if the dreams would ever end.

And if Kait would ever leave him.

The two MacGowans walked down the corridor side by side. Sean glanced at him. "I had breakfast with your wee lass this morn. She eats like a rugby player."

Gabe chuckled, the tension already easing away. "I fancy that about her."

Sean laughed. "Aye, 'tis a fetchin' trait." He scratched his head. "I wonder if all American lasses are like Allie Morgan? Are you sure you want her, lad? Because if you dunna, I'll gladly have her myself."

"I want her."

Sean laughed. "Well, 'tis good to hear it, then. Besides." He winked as they took the stairs. "She's got sisters." He held up fingers. "Three of them."

They both hit the landing and Gabe stopped short.

His mother and da sat together at a small table in one of the alcoves. Leona sat at the bar. Wee Mary had taken a position at a table close to the front door—probably for the best view—and Allie was behind the bar as though serving.

She smiled at him and shrugged.

He thought her adorable.

And whoever came to look at the place had no bloody idea just what sort of morning they were in for.

With a grin, he shook his head. "Right. Let's get this done, aye?"

A round of *aye*s rose from his accomplices.

It nearly cleared his mind of the incident with Kait. Sean took another bar stool, and with a resigned sigh, Gabe took his place at the front door.

Minutes later, a dark blue midsized car pulled up to the curb. A tall, slender man stepped out, closed the door, and shielded his eyes as he glanced out at the loch. Gabe watched as he stood there for a moment, probably taking in the spectacular view.

Gabe went through the door and walked out to greet the man. He felt bad for what Wee Mary called *shenanigans*, but 'twas the only way to keep the pub without losing loads of pounds from the Realtor.

"Right. Mr. MacGowan? I'm Stanley Mann." He stuck out his hand and Gabe shook it. "Jolly nice village. Lovely view."

"Aye," Gabe said. He inclined his head. "Right this way, then."

Stanley Mann took in a deep breath, patted his chest, and exhaled. "Fabulous air. Fabulous."

Gabe held the door and Stanley Mann walked through.

He might even have squealed.

"Perfect!" he said, and clapped his hands once. "Lovely interior. Did you decorate it yourself?"

Gabe wished Stanley would just keep quiet and look round. "Aye."

"Fabulous."

He also wished Stanley Mann would stop saying *fabulous*.

"Oh, hello," he said, waving to Allie, who gave him a wide smile and waved back.

Thankfully, she kept quiet. No doubt if Stanley Mann heard her adorable American accent, they'd never get him to leave.

The lanky man ran from corner to corner, inspecting details in the wood, the furniture, the lamps. One thing Gabe had to say for Stanley Mann—he had great taste in pubs.

Finally, blessedly, the Odin's lot came out of hiding.

First, the lights began to blink. Stanley Mann noticed immediately. "Oh dear. A glitch in the wiring, mayhap?" he said, glancing at the lamps.

Next, Lords Ramsey and Killigrew sifted through the hearth, swearing and charging the other with threats of a duel. They began to circle Stanley Mann, whose eyes had grown so wide Gabe could see the whites completely round the color.

The other patrons, of course, carried on conversation, drank, and laughed amongst one another. Pretending not to see a thing.

Only when Stanley Mann began to wail did they all look up. "My good sir!" he shouted, his voice cracking. "What is this witchery?"

Witchery?

Gabe put his hand over his mouth to pinch it shut before he laughed out loud.

He cleared his throat. "What's wrong, Mr. Mann?"

Just then the two lords placed a frantic Mann between them, turned, and walked eight paces.

Stanley Mann turned his head first at Killigrew, then at Ramsey. "What are you doing? What's going on?" he cried.

Just before the two devilish lords stopped, turned, and aimed their pistols.

Stanley Mann didna wait for them to fire—even

though 'twould have been a fake firing of pistols anyway.

He *ran*. No good-bye, no threats of a solicitor, nothing.

Just . . . *ran*.

The lords, of course, along with Sean, roared with laughter. Justin, the friar, Mademoiselle, and Dauber emerged from thin air, shaking their heads.

Allie scooted from behind the bar and came to stand beside Gabe. She leaned into him. "Poor guy. I feel sorry for him."

"Aye." Gabe looked down at her, just as she looked up.

She grinned. "One down. When's the next appointment?"

"No' until next week. Then three, back-to-back."

A wicked gleam shot through her eyes, and Gabe tapped her nose. "That look frightens me, lass."

She smiled and wiggled her brows. "It's high time you had a couple of days off, Gabe MacGowan."

Gabe thought there was nothing more he wanted than a day off with Allie Morgan. "With both Wee Mary and Katey out of work, I just canna, lass," he said. "I'm sorry."

"Oh yes, you can, lad," said Mary, who trotted right up. "I'm no' an invalid and I'm goin' stir-crazy just sittin' on me porch all day. Sean here said he'd help me, as did your mum and da."

Gabe locked his gaze on Allie's. "I canna leave Jake, lass," he said.

"Jake has his own plans, lad," said Sean. "I'm home for a week, so we're goin' off for the whole of Saturday, if it's okay with you, so you two can have a day of it alone."

"Go on, boy," said Gerald, pulling his wife close.

"I've no' seen you take time off in years, so go. We can handle Odin's whilst you're away."

Gabe slid a quick glance at Allie, who lifted one fine brow.

"It seems as though I'm the one bein' conspired against now, aye?" he said.

Everyone chuckled.

He pulled Allie close. "Right. A day off it'll be, then." He whispered, "Are you ready for *my* Scotland?"

Chapter 21

Two nights later, Friar Drew Digby paced before the hearth in Odin's lobby, hands clasped behind his back, cowl down, teeth worrying his lip.

He had the most adorable friar-bowl haircut Allie had ever seen. Reddish blond, it was soft and swung as he walked.

So did his long woolen cloak.

"I just don't know," he muttered, and not for the first time. " 'Tisn't proper. 'Tisn't proper at all."

Gabe, Allie, and Sean sat at the center table. Allie slipped a glance at Gabe. He was pinching the bridge of his nose. Sean had a wicked grin on his face and he kept pinching his mouth shut with two fingers to keep from chuckling out loud.

"I know my Allie and her word is her bond," said Dauber. "If she says all will remain proper while she and Gabe leave, then I believe her."

Justin Catesby snorted. " 'Tisna your Allie you should worry about," he said under his breath. " 'Tis that tadpole there."

The two men, Justin and Gabe, glared at each other.

"Bleedin' hell, they sleep under the same roof every night," said Baden Killigrew. " 'Tisn't a bit different."

Allie smiled at Baden, who blushed.

"I say one of us should follow them," said Christopher Ramsey. He slid Allie an evil, older-brother grin. "Mayhap *two* of us."

Allie frowned and mouthed *I'm going to kill you.*

Christopher Ramsey barked out a laugh. " 'Tis a jest, nothing more," he said. "They're grown adults, Drew. And it is the twenty-first century, after all. Let them go in peace."

"*Oui*," said Mademoiselle. "I think it's perfectly romantic they escape away . . . *alone.*"

Sean yawned and stretched. "I say each of you should take a turn checking on the lovebirds," he said, that evil mischief gleaming in his eyes. "There is the lass's reputation to uphold."

Several ghostly murmurs agreed throughout the room, and Allie laughed. "I'm sure my reputation can hold its own."

"That's enough," said Gabe. He glanced at the friar. "Drew, if you can find us, you may certainly check up on us like the good man of the cloth you are," he said. Then Gabe's grin turned wicked, as did his voice. "But dunna interrupt."

Another round of laughter echoed throughout Odin's.

All, that is, except Justin Catesby. He got up, walked to Gabe, and leaned close to his ear. Allie could hear every word, even though it was whispered.

"Lad, if you take advantage of that girl there, you will have me to answer to," Justin said. He and Gabe stared without saying anything more.

Then Justin Catesby strode across the lobby and disappeared through the front door.

Literally.

Allie jumped up. "I'll be right back."

Gabe held her arm. "Lass, let him go. He's just worried about you. 'Tis Justin's way."

Allie leaned down and kissed Gabe on the nose. "I know. But we need to talk. I'll be right back."

As she hurried from the pub, she heard the whistles, ghostly and mortal, of Gabe getting ribbed for receiving a kiss.

Outside, it was warmer than usual, and a westerly wind had begun to drift gently over the loch. For a change, her sweater kept her warm enough. The moon, fuller now, stood behind the hills but shed a silvery glow over Sealladh na Mara.

With her arms crossed over her chest, Allie simply called for the captain. "Justin, I know you can hear me, so please. Walk with me?"

Before the last word left Allie's mouth, Justin Catesby appeared. Slightly transparent, but dashing still the same, he gave her a low bow. "Certainly, lass, you know I could never say your nay." He raised and looked down at her. "And why would you leave the warmth of the pub to walk outside in the cold with a spirit?"

Allie shrugged. "It's not that cold out tonight, really, and"— she glanced at him—"Justin, I just want to talk. We need to clear some things up. I don't like that you and Gabe are mad at each other because of me."

He extended a hand, down the walk, indicating for Allie to lead the way. So she did. Justin fell in beside her. "I just want the verra best for you, Allie Morgan," he said, his voice rich, deep, and a bit scruffy. "You're an advocate for the ghostly souls of the earthbound world. No' many like you, I'll warrant. I fancy you quite a lot."

Allie smiled up at him. "Thank you. I think."

Justin chuckled. "Forgive my bluntness. I speak my mind quite freely, in case you havena noticed yet."

"Oh, I've noticed," she said. "Slightly hard thing to miss."

He laughed. "So it is." He looked at her for a long moment. "I make you uncomfortable."

She shook her head. "Not at all. I do appreciate the kind way you look out for my well-being." She smiled. "It's what friends do for each other, you see."

He grabbed his tricorn, slipped it from his head, and shoved his fingers through his hair. "Och, damn. I've been labeled *friend*." He winked. " 'Tis the silent relationship killer."

She laughed. "Where on earth did you hear that?"

"Young Sean. He's quite knowledgeable with modern love, you know."

Allie shook her head and smiled. "I'd use caution when taking love tips from him."

Justin laughed softly. "Indeed."

They walked in silence for a moment; then Justin cleared his throat. "You've a way with souls, Allie Morgan. 'Tisna often a soul like myself crosses paths with a woman like you. You're almost of both worlds—one who would fit in either, by the by. I would be a liar if I said I hadna hoped to have a chance to win your affection. And I'm many things." He looked at her. "But no' a liar."

Allie stopped, Justin stopped, and she looked up at him and smiled. "You are a very sweet, caring, soul, Justin Catesby. Ridiculously handsome, too."

He grinned and shook his head. "But?"

Allie glanced back up the walk, toward Odin's. "But I hold something special—something completely unexpected yet familiar, here"—she placed her hand over her heart and looked at Justin—"for Gabe." She sighed. "I couldn't make it go away, even if I tried. I'm sorry."

Justin's eyes softened as he gave a winsome smile. "Dunna be sorry, lass. I will cherish your friendship always, and I am always and forever naught but a call away."

"Thank you, truly. And Gabe loves you. You're

part of his family." She slid the ghostly sea captain a glance. "And you love him, too. So I don't want you two fighting anymore. Savvy?"

Cocking his head, he gave her a nod, then studied her for several seconds. "And what of you, Allie Morgan? Will you leave here? Leave Gabe and his family and Sealladh na Mara behind once the contract has become void?"

Allie crossed her arms over her chest. "God knows I don't want to. I suppose we'll have to see how things go." She shrugged and smiled. "It may be too early to tell."

He nodded. "So right." With a grin, he inclined his head back toward Odin's. "Let us make our way back, then. And whilst we walk, why dunna you tell me about your bonny sisters . . . ?"

"Good-bye, Allie Morgan," said Jake, throwing his arms around her neck and hugging fiercely. The sun had broken through the clouds, and it cast a golden glint to Jake's auburn hair. He pulled back and gave her a very serious look—a difficult feat seeing that his cowlick made the hair at that particular point of his hairline stand straight up. "Dunna worry. I'll handle things here at Odin's whilst you and Da go on holiday."

Allie smiled. "I have no doubt you will. Now, you and your uncle Sean have lots of fun Saturday."

Jake nodded.

Allie narrowed her eyes. "Are you still going to take me up to the MacGowans' keep?"

His wide blue eyes sparkled. "Aye—and Uncle Sean and Da says we're goin' to take the ferry over to Skye, as well. You'll love it there!"

"I can't wait." She squatted down, to look at Jake

eye level. "And don't you worry. I'll take good care of your da."

Jake leaned forward, pushed her hair aside, and whispered in her ear, "Watch him during the night especially. He has bad dreams."

Allie drew back and looked at him. "I will watch him very closely."

Jake looked around, then met her gaze with one that seemed too wise for his six-year-old self. "If you can, Allie, could you try and mend me mum's soul? She scares my da, I think."

Allie's insides turned cold just hearing little Jake's words. But she nodded and squeezed his shoulder. "I will. Now go and have fun with your crazy uncle."

Jake jumped up and ran to his father. Gabe lifted him and pulled him into a bear hug.

Jake glanced at Allie over Gabe's shoulder and smiled.

Allie thought it the sweetest thing she'd ever seen.

Once Gabe set Jake down, the little boy ran to his uncle, who scooped him up sideways and scrubbed his head. Jake, of course, burst into laughter.

"You two have fun," said Sean, that wicked gleam back in his eyes. "Dunna do anythin' I wouldna."

Gabe grinned. "Well, that leaves verra few options, aye?"

Sean shrugged and laughed.

"You can reach me on my mobile if anythin' comes up," Gabe said, then looked at Jake. "You mind your uncle and granny and grand. We'll be back sometime tomorrow."

Jake nodded and wiped his nose on his sweater sleeve. "I will, Da." Then he whispered in Gabe's ear, and Gabe turned and looked at Allie.

She wondered what Jake had said.

With Wee Mary, Gabe's parents, Sean, Jake, and the Odin's ghostly souls watching on, Gabe threw his and Allie's bags into the back of the Rover, opened the door for her, and inclined his head. "Ready?"

Oh, she definitely was.

After a stern look from the friar, a sly grin from Justin, and a wink from Dauber, and waves from the two dueling lords and the mademoiselle, as well as the rest of the MacGowans, she and Gabe left Sealladh na Mara.

Allie hoped, as she glanced at the sexy, sweet, funny Highlander beside her, that she would indeed be able to mend his soul. And she was willing to face whatever it took to accomplish it.

Even if it meant challenging a lost, malevolent—possibly dangerous—soul bent on making Gabe's life as miserable as that soul's once was.

And, apparently, continued to be.

Allie turned and glanced behind her. Sealladh na Mara grew smaller, a handful of white flecks against a gray-blue sea. And in the distance, off to the right, the ancient ruins of the MacGowans' keep dominated the coastline.

Gabe's hand covered hers, and together, their fingers entwined. The sensation of Gabe's calluses against her skin warmed her, and she looked at him and smiled.

"So, have you chosen a place to escape to?" Allie asked. "One where the friar can't find us?"

Gabe stared straight ahead, eyes fixed on the road, but a slow smile slid into place on the most handsome face Allie had ever seen. "Absolutely. You'll love it." Then he looked at her, and his eyes locked on hers. "Trust me."

And Allie did.

Chapter 22

The one thing Gabe quickly learned about Allie Morgan was that no matter where she went, souls took notice.

Live ones, and no'-so-live ones.

Gabe couldna blame them a bit.

And the one thing he'd always known about ghostly souls was they did just what they wanted. If they chose to let you see them, you would. If no', you wouldna. And it seemed everywhere he and Allie went, those ghostly souls recognized her as their champion and approached.

He wondered if he'd ever get her to himself.

They'd visited an ancient Norman kirk, a favorite of Gabe's, and Allie's wide blue eyes had scanned the old stones, seemingly amazed at the architecture and doubly amazed at the age.

A French-Norman knight had emerged from the wall, introduced himself as Sir Geoffrey de Gables, and had proceeded to ask Allie if she could discover how he might have come to the western Highlands of Scotland. She promised she'd look into the matter once she got back to Sealladh na Mara.

Gabe had been to that particular kirk scores of times and not once had that old knight shown himself. He couldna help but wonder just how jam-packed the mortal world was with otherworldly souls.

Apparently, Sealladh na Mara wasna the only unique place in the Highlands.

And he felt especially certain the reason the old knight appeared this time was because of Allie Morgan.

According to Dauber, 'twas her own unique brush with death and, thanks to her da, a fierce and sudden reentry back into the world of the living that made her soul so receptive to spirits. No' to mention her soul was by far the sweetest he'd ever encountered.

After visiting a circle of standing stones, where four druids sifted from the rock to ask Allie a few questions on the possibility of time travel, a small croft museum where an eighteenth-century Highlander, complete with pipes, insisted he play Allie several melodies, Gabe decided he should try to avoid all things *old* and just move on to their destination.

The Highlands—probably anywhere in Scotland—was apparently wall-to-wall loaded with spirited souls.

Allie scooted as close as her seat belt would allow and grinned. "Stop pouting. They were all very nice and interesting."

Gabe grunted. " 'Tis a good thing, then, we skipped Culloden. We'd no' have left before the gloaming."

"Well, it's barely after noon, so we've plenty of time left. What's the gloaming?"

Gabe slid his hand to hers. Damn, he didna think he'd ever touched such soft skin. He wrapped his fingers through hers and looked at her briefly. " 'Tis that moment in time where the last rays of the day slide into dusk. The Scots believe 'tis a magical time, the gloaming." He lifted a brow. "You never know what you might encounter."

Allie slipped her thumb over the top of his hand. "That is just plain sexy, Gabe MacGowan."

And it was.

Gabe had decided to put everything behind him for

the day. All he wanted was to be with Allie, learn more about her, her mother and sisters, where she grew up. He could hardly blame the spirits for being so drawn to her.

He certainly was.

While he drove, Gabe studied her with small glances—inconspicuous, he thought. Allie's hair, free and wild today, stood out against the thin black sweater and leather jacket she wore. Faded, frayed jeans clung to her long legs. The hiking boots on her feet were probably all that kept her slim, delicate body from drifting away.

Something about those rough hiking boots strapped to such a feminine body appealed to Gabe. She wasna afraid of anything, to go anywhere, try new things— she'd even had a bit of haggis at lunch.

He thought the stuff nasty, and he was a Scotsman.

Gabe noticed something else, as well. And the more he was around her, the more evident. 'Twasna just Allie Morgan's exterior that was lovely. Inside, her beauty all but stopped his breath. She had a deep, inner love for all souls, an appreciation for life, and he truly thought she'd give her life to help another.

So verra unlike anyone he'd ever encountered. So verra unlike Kait.

Not wanting to let go of Allie's hand, he rubbed his chin against his shoulder and mentally escaped that train of thought. 'Twasna fair of him, really. Kait had been young, her life abruptly changed, and she'd been in such a dark place when she died that he could only imagine how horrible it must have been for her.

Especially with a partying drunkard for a husband.

"Oh, Gabe! Pull over!" said Allie, looking out her window. "Please!"

Gabe glanced, and couldna help but grin. He pulled over, parked, and before he could walk round the car,

Allie was out, hurrying to the fence where a handful of Highland cows munched on grass.

"They're so gorgeous!" she said, holding out her hand toward them and making a smacking sound to draw them near. She briefly looked over her shoulder at Gabe. "Don't you think so?"

The Highland sun shone through Allie's long, springy curls. They hung over her shoulders and down her back, and when she looked at him, the sheer joy of those long-haired cows made her eyes sparkle. That lovely smile, which stretched from ear to ear, touched him, and he couldna quite believe the feeling.

He, Gabe MacGowan, was touched by a grinning ghost ouster over a pair of silly cows.

He'd never admit it to anyone.

Walking up behind Allie, Gabe reached for her arm and gently tugged. When she turned, her eyes collided with his and she smiled—this time for *him*.

Behind her, the cows *moo*ed their protest.

Too bloody bad. Let them find their own ghost ouster.

He'd found his and he wasna in the mood for sharing.

Allie thought the Highland cows—rather, *haidee coos* as Gabe called them, absolutely darling. With their long, shaggy hair and wide horns, their pudgy noses moist and cool, she thought they were the cutest things she'd ever seen.

Until her arm was tugged and she turned to face the sexy Highlander standing behind her.

Much cuter than the *coos*, she thought.

Gabe wore a pair of sexy shades, so those intense green eyes were covered. But Allie could tell by the clench of his jaw that those eyes were boring into hers. She shielded her eyes with her hand and grinned. A dark green long-sleeved shirt, brown leather jacket, and well-worn jeans and boots made Gabe MacGowan look mysterious, carefree.

Definitely cuter than the *coos*.

She continued to inspect him until a smile lifted the corner of his mouth. Then he turned and hung his head, the smile widened until nearly all his white teeth showed, and he looked back at her. The sexiness of the total guy gesture made her smile.

Allie wiggled a finger. "Come here."

He moved closer, dropped her arm, and placed both hands on her hips. "Aye?"

Lifting her hands, she slid off Gabe's shades. The sun made his eyes a brighter green, flecked with gray. Without unlocking gazes, she slipped the glasses into the pocket of his jacket.

They stood there together for the longest moment, simply staring. She for one couldn't help it. Gabe's rugged beauty stole her breath. She loved his strength, his intensity, his humor, and the boyishness that had suddenly emerged. All of it shone through his eyes.

Lowering his head, Gabe settled his mouth over hers and, with an agonizing slowness, kissed her. One of his hands left her hip and buried itself into her hair, his strong fingers angling her head just so before tasting her lips, one at a time, then brushing her tongue with his. The sensation made her groan against his mouth, and her hands then rested on Gabe's hips, pulling him close until her back rested against the large, wide, concrete fence post.

Gabe's lips moved to her throat. "I'm no' made of iron, lass, so be careful where those hands go, aye?" he said against her skin.

That sensation made her shiver.

"Sorry," she whispered, and she felt him softly laugh.

Then he pulled back his head and stared at her. "The *coos* are gettin' quite a show." He glanced at them over her shoulder. "I think they're makin' me nervous."

Behind them, the *coos* mooed.

Gabe and Allie chuckled.

"Ready to go?" he asked. Then gave her a quick kiss, thought better of it, apparently, and kissed her long.

"Now's good, I think," she muttered.

Gabe laughed, took her by the hand, and pulled her to the Rover. Then they were on their way.

As they drove, Allie shifted her glances between the beauty of the northwestern Highlands, and the beauty of the northwestern *Highlander.*

Both were pretty darn gorgeous.

Allie couldn't quite get enough of Scotland's landscape, from the craggy rocks and the fields of faded heather to the random stone wall rambling across the moors.

And when it came to the Highlander beside her? God, she didn't think she'd *ever* get enough. And that *scared* her.

Gabe wouldn't tell her where they were headed, and since she didn't know much about Scotland, she just went along for the ride, soaked up the flashing scenery, and enjoyed Gabe's company. He told her funny stories of him, Sean, and their sister, Merri, when they were kids, and Gabe, being the oldest, usually got in the most trouble. When they were *caught*, he added.

She knew the feeling well, being the oldest herself.

They came upon a small, intriguing little town with a name Allie couldn't pronounce to save her life, and Gabe guided the Rover through a couple of traffic lights before pulling into a small alcove of shops. Gabe parked, turned, and grinned.

"I've a little something to show you, lass," he said. "Interested?"

Allie lifted a brow. "Always."

They got out, crossed the small parking lot, and entered a local gift shop that Allie soon discovered contained local artists' crafts for sale. As they walked in, a small bell tinkled at the door, and a middle-aged woman wearing a lovely tartan skirt and white blouse looked up from the register, saw Gabe, and smiled.

"Well, hello, Mr. MacGowan. How are you this fine day?"

Gabe returned the smile and gave a nod. "Verra well, thanks."

"Oh, we've just put in a new order for you, lad. I was going to drop it into the post, but since you're here I'll just give it to you before you leave, aye?"

"Aye, thank you."

Allie gave Gabe a questioning look, the corners of his mouth pulled into a grin, and he placed his hand on the small of her back and guided her to the back corner of the shop. They stopped before a glass wall display case.

Allie glanced at it. "Gabe, why are we—"

She quickly turned back to the display case, and the small plaque that read HAND-CARVED, ONE-OF-A-KIND PIECES MADE TO ORDER BY LOCAL ARTIST.

Allie blinked. She found several rows of various-sized marble chess pieces. Articulately carved into the shapes of warriors from various centuries.

Allie placed her fingers over her lips.

They were Gabe's chess pieces.

Allie peered through the glass. "You little devil." She looked at him. "They're absolutely amazing, Gabe."

He gave a casual shrug, but Allie could see the pride in his smile. "Friends of mine are responsible, actually. I'd given them a set, for all their help, and they'd directly taken them to several of their favorite stores to show the managers." He rubbed his chin. "They're sold all over Scotland, England, and Wales."

"And Ireland, dunna forget," said the clerk up front.

Gabe looked down at Allie and grinned wider. "And Ireland."

"Canna keep the stock available," said the clerk. "Orders come in weekly."

So Gabe was an artist of hand-fashioned marble chess pieces. *Amazing.*

Allie slipped her hand into Gabe's. "You must be so proud. They're all beautiful."

He stared at her for a long moment. "I'm verra pleased you're pleased."

They left, after Gabe received his new order, and pulled out of the quaint little village. A small town that took several miles before Allie could finally pronounce the name. Drumnadrochit. Gabe had laughed at her first attempt, and she'd had him repeat it several times before she finally got it right. Before long, the road began to wind and curve until eventually, Allie could see water. Hills, covered in the faded brownish purple of heather, rose behind the water, and there, in the distance, a ruined castle perched high on a cliff.

"Where are we?" she asked.

Gabe grinned. "You'll see."

Several minutes later, Gabe turned the Rover onto a long private drive and started the ascent. Tall Scotch pines, oaks, and rowans, as Gabe pointed out, rose behind a small white cottage at the top of the hill. They parked the Rover and Gabe shut off the ignition.

He turned to her and grinned. "You're no' afraid

of monsters, are you, Allie Morgan?" he asked. He wagged his brows.

Allie cocked her head. "Monsters?"

Gabe grinned, got out, and came around and opened her door. He pulled her to her feet, turned her around, and pulled her against him, her back to his front. Allie glanced up, and the sun shot through the canopy of trees above them, dotting everything with little patches of light. The air, a bit cooler, smelled clean and crisp in contrast to the warmth of Gabe behind her.

Gabe leaned his head, brushed his lips to her ear, his breath on her skin making her shiver; then he whispered, that deep brogue washing over her, "Close your eyes, Allie Morgan."

Without question, she did.

"Now move with me, lass," he said, urging her forward, his hands guiding her hips. "I willna let you trip or run into anythin'." Again, his mouth moved to her ear. "Trust me."

"I can barely concentrate on moving my feet when you do that thing to my ear," she said.

Gabe laughed softly. "Sorry. I canna seem to help myself. Now just take regular steps. We'll be there soon."

Although Gabe was driving her completely wild with his hands on her hips, his chest against her back, and the scruff of his chin against her neck, Allie moved. How she managed it, when all she wanted to do was dissolve into a puddle of mush at his feet, she couldn't decide. Her heart soared at their nearness, at the thought of being alone.

At the thought of controlling themselves.

She could just imagine the friar popping in at the most inopportune time. It made her smile.

"No peekin'," Gabe warned.

"I willna," Allie answered.

Gabe laughed, and Allie felt the low rumble in his chest at her back.

After a few minutes of walking in that heavenly state, with Gabe MacGowan's hands gripping her hips, he finally angled her, and then pulled her to a stop.

His strong arms slid around her abdomen, he pressed close against her and rested his chin on her shoulder. "Open your eyes, Allie Morgan."

Slowly, she did, and she gasped.

The beauty of it literally took her breath away.

High atop a craggy, pine-covered cliff they stood, with a wide loch that seemed to stretch for miles in either direction below them. The sunlight glistened off the water, making it sparkle like a thousand shards of glass. On the other side of the loch, more heather-clad hills and hardwoods whose leaves had begun to change color.

"Again, I ask," he said in her ear, and a shiver ran over her spine at the warmth of his breath on her skin, "are you afraid of monsters?"

Allie leaned against him as her answer struck. "You mean Nessie?" She smiled and turned in his arms. "This is Loch Ness?"

Gabe grinned. "Aye, a portion of it, anyway." He looked at her. " 'Tis one of my favorite places. I thought you might like—"

Allie hushed him with her mouth. Slipping her hands over Gabe's neck, she pulled his head down and kissed him. At first surprised, Allie felt Gabe's body relax, and he pulled her tightly against him and kissed her back. His hands, flat against her back, lowered, sliding over her backside, and pulled her even closer.

She knew then how much Gabe really liked kissing her.

At that contact, Gabe groaned, a low sound coming from deep within him, and his kiss deepened, tasting every corner of Allie's mouth, her tongue, and he groaned again and pulled back. He looked at her, green eyes now a tumultuous green gray, their bodies so close Allie could feel his heart beating.

After a moment, he smiled. "I take it you like the loch?"

Allie smiled. "Absolutely."

It was only then, glancing behind Gabe, that she noticed the back of the cottage had an enormous railed deck that ran to the edge of the cliff, overlooking the loch. An outdoor stone fireplace sat off to one side, and what looked to be the frame of a wooden sofa, minus cushions, stood before the hearth.

She looked at him, only to find Gabe watched her closely. "Whose place is this?" she asked.

Gabe glanced out over the loch, shrugged, and grinned. "Mine."

Chapter 23

Allie simply blinked. "Yours?"

Again, Gabe shrugged. " 'Tis small, so it didna take me long to build. I bought the land on a foreclosure."

"You built it? As in"—she held up her hands and wiggled her fingers—"*built* it?"

The pride in Gabe's eyes flickered. "Aye, I suppose I did. With some help from me da, Sean, and friends."

"It's gorgeous, Gabe," she said. "When did you have time to build it? You're at Odin's nearly every day."

He glanced up at the cottage's roof, at the deck, and back to the loch. He didn't look at her. "When I was dryin' out."

Without hesitation, Allie stepped into his arms, lifted her hands to his jaw, and forced him to look at her.

He did.

"Then it's almost as amazing as you, Gabe Mac-Gowan."

He nodded, and the smile on his sexy lips reached his eyes. "You're wily with the words, Allie Morgan." He glanced down. "You have a way of makin' a man forget he screwed up." He kissed her, soft, slow, and long. When he lifted his head, his green eyes were stormy. "Thank you."

Allie had to remind herself to breathe. God, the way he looked at her made her feel completely alive. She grazed his jaw with her fingertips. "Are you going to show me the monster?" she asked.

One side of his mouth quirked and he lifted a dark brow.

She narrowed her eyes. "Dunna be a perv, Mac-Gowan." She jerked a finger over her shoulder, toward the loch. "The monster oot *there*."

Gabe's quirky grin turned into a full-blown smile, just before he threw back his head and laughed. In the dappled sunlight filtering through the canopy, he rubbed his jaw and his eyes twinkled. "You, Allie Morgan, are somethin' else." He shook his head. "Aye, let's go look for the monster, then."

After a tour of the cottage—which, although small, as Gabe had said, was immaculate and charming, with two small bedrooms, a fireplace, kitchen, and living room—Allie stood, staring. Completely furnished, it was the perfect getaway home.

"I had a friend from across the loch stop over, air it out, and take off the coverings," Gabe said, looking around. "His wife was kind enough to send us a bit of food, too." He pointed. "I met them both whilst building it. They have a cottage, just there." He pointed across the way and up to the left. "The Munros. Nice couple." He looked at her. "They'll probably stop over this evening, if you've a mind to mingle."

"I'll be happy to mingle," said Allie, and briefly thought of how, not very long ago, she'd admitted to Dauber that she wasn't much of a mingler at all. Funny, how some things change according to the people who unexpectedly pop into your life. Imagine her, Allie Morgan. A *mingler*.

"Och, I've got somethin' for you," Gabe said, unzipped one of the two large duffel bags he'd brought, and withdrew a long pair of . . . *rubber boots*?

He handed them to her. "Your very own Wellies."

She laughed and took them, turning them around to inspect. Just a tall, rubber pair of boots. "Thanks. You shouldn't have."

Gabe laughed, too. "Aye, well, you'll be glad you have them once we start walkin'. 'Tis a requirement of being a true Scotsman, aye? A sturdy pair of Wellingtons to get you through the forest and muck."

Gabe laughed at her expression. "You'll see."

So she pulled on her Wellies. They fit perfectly.

How else could one possibly go in search of the most infamous and elusive monster in the world?

Gabe and Allie spent the rest of the afternoon hill walking, taking a path Gabe himself had taken many times whilst drying out. Christ, that had been the most difficult of times. Ethan, his neighbor across the loch, had been building his cottage at the same time and had been a huge help. Along with two brothers, a handful of cousins, and Gabe's brother and father, they'd all pitched in and seen Gabe through the worst time of his life.

The worst time in Jake's life, as well.

His mum swore Jake was too young to know what was happening, and too young to remember, but the thought still plagued Gabe. There his wee son was, in the care of his grands because the parents were too wrapped up in their own miseries no' to be selfless enough to raise him with the proper care. Gabe had always loved Jake, from the moment he first laid eyes on him.

He thanked God every day he had left that destructive life behind.

And for the family and friends who pulled him through it.

Allie's hand reached over then, and took his. So much smaller than his, softer, delicate, yet Gabe felt a powerful strength radiating from her. It frightened him.

She looked up and smiled, the sun falling through the leaves and onto her face. She had the smallest of freckles on her nose, and when she smiled, her eyes squinted into the most adorable half-moons. She took his breath away every time he looked at her. He couldn't remember ever noticing such detail on a woman before.

Truth be told, that frightened him, too.

He was beginning to think he was a bloody chicken.

"Tell me about your family," Gabe said, wanting to relieve his mind of old ghosts. "Sean says you claim your sisters are even more gorgeous than you." He pulled her close. "Which I refuse to believe."

Allie giggled. "Emma is two years younger than me. She's smart, very serious, tall, and has my mother's hair—a lovely auburn. Like Jake's. And she has hazel eyes." She thought a minute. "Boe—short for Boe-dine, which she *hates*, and she cringes whenever one of us calls her that—is the wild child of the bunch. My father insisted on naming her after his grandmother. Four years younger than me, strawberry blond straight hair with blue eyes like mine," Allie said, batting her eyes. "She is a marine biologist."

"Really?" Gabe said. "Interesting."

"Tell that to my mother. Boe's specialty is sharks and it freaks my poor mom *out*."

They came to an enormous fallen pine, and Gabe stopped and smiled down at Allie. "And the last sister?"

Allie sat, and Gabe followed. "Ivy. We've always called her Sika, though. She looks more like my father, with dark hair and green eyes. Quite a looker. She helps run the B and B my mother owns. She's a gourmet chef and good *God*, that girl can cook."

Gabe picked a piece of loose bark, studied it, and tossed it onto a patch of mossy ground. "You miss them, aye?"

Allie nodded, stretching her legs out and studying her Wellingtons. "Yes, I do."

"So why do you stay in Raleigh?" he asked.

Brushing the tree bits from her hands, she rested them on her thighs and blew out a sigh. "I guess I don't know. After my dad died, my mother tried to make a living in Raleigh with us girls, but it was hard on her. The memories were difficult, and my mom had always been a stay-at-home mother. She searched and searched for something she could make money at and still give her daughters a good life." She smiled. "She's a great mom. And when she inherited a B and B from her great-aunt, she jumped at the chance." She shrugged. "That chance happened to be in Maine."

"Long way off."

"Yes. So I worked hard at my grades and got a full scholarship to NC State University. My mom and sisters stayed, of course, in Maine."

Gabe cleared his voice, lifted her hand, and studied her long fingers. "Can you tell me how 'tis that a gorgeous woman like yourself isna taken?" He looked at her and waited.

"You're crazy," she said quietly, but she smiled. "The usual story, I guess. My heart's been broken, so I've been majorly cautious, involving myself in loads of work. Before that, I was busy in school, and I suppose most guys probably thought I was a little weird. I never partied, never went to clubs, didn't belong to any school organizations or athletic departments. I had friends, but I wasn't *involved*. You know? I was *that* girl." She shrugged. "Maybe because I'd sort of found my *calling*, if you will. With spirits."

Gabe gave what he hoped was a comforting smile. "Lucky me."

She shook her head and stared at her feet. "Crazy."

He didna want to bring it up now—he'd wanted to wait, until later. But he found he couldna help himself. "Will you continue to stay there, Allie Morgan? In Raleigh, alone with your ghosts?"

A soft breeze wafted through the trees, and it lifted a long strand of curls from Allie's shoulder. She tucked it behind her ear and shrugged. She didna look at him. "I don't know, Gabe."

Now she looked at him, those wide blue eyes full of question. "I could say a few things that would probably make you take off running for the hills."

Gabe's heart lurched. He dared to hope for anything. He didna want to sound like a wee lad who'd never had a girl. Didna want to sound overly anxious. So he calmly took a breath and looked at her. "So try me, Allie Morgan."

Allie stared out across the forest, then up at the tall canopy of trees overhead. God, she must be insane to risk telling Gabe her feelings. Guys didn't want feelings.

But then again, not all men were like Gabe MacGowan.

Just because she held out hope he would be interested, even a smidgen interested, in what she *felt*, didn't mean Gabe was anything but macho. He was definitely that. He wasn't a shouter; she hadn't seen him get into any fistfights yet, but still—he was one proud Scotsman. Strong, a powerhouse of muscle, and fearing nothing that she could see, Gabe, to her, was the perfect guy. He had his imperfections—and he'd been man enough to be honest and share them with her. He was a strong but loving father—a single father at that and doing a fantastic job. He loved his family and treated the females in his life as if they were pieces of gold.

Yeah, Gabe MacGowan had numerous marks that made him a very fine man.

She glanced at him.

He was grinning.

She heaved a gusty sigh. "You're making me nervous."

He glanced away, but in his voice she could still hear him smile. "Sorry."

Another sigh, and Allie kicked at a clump of dirt. "I guess, Gabe, you've sort of gotten to me. Somewhat. Well, a lot, really. Actually, I can't stop thinking of you." She swore under her breath—one of the nice Gaelic ones Wee Mary and Laina had taught her—and turned to him. "You, your son, your family—those bloody Odin's ghosts. Sealladh na Mara." She kicked another dirt clod, her voice sounding angry to her own ears. "I guess I've fallen for all of it, Gabe. Every last bit of it." Then she muttered, "For you."

Gabe sat silent—didn't say a single, solitary word for God knew how long. It seemed like bloody forever.

Oh, gosh. I've even started talking like him now.

Only the wind through the treetops rustled the leaves, making a crisp, crackling noise that would normally soothe and relax.

Allie could hear the hands of her Timex *tick-tick-tick*ing as the seconds rolled by. That tiny sound rose above the wind and leaves, just to annoy her. To irritate her.

And scare her to death.

Tick. Tock. Tick. Tock.

Had she just made the wrong decision? Gabe was too silent, was taking too long to respond. And she was too chicken to take a peek. God, she wished mightily she could take it back and stuff it into her big ole mouth.

Just when she thought she might scream out loud, Gabe took his knuckle, hooked her chin, and turned her face toward his. Usually so open, she now felt embarrassed. Or afraid to see the rejection in his eyes. She just wouldn't look . . .

"Open your eyes, lass," Gabe said, his voice deep, his words perfectly gauged. He cleared his throat. "Now."

Slowly, she did.

And fixed her gaze directly over Gabe's shoulder, to the nice rowan bush he'd shown her earlier.

"Look at *me*."

Allie shifted her gaze. Gabe's eyes, those mesmerizing, intoxicating eyes, had turned smoky, yet with so much depth and clarity Allie thought she could see all the way through them. She didn't say a word, just locked on to Gabe.

And then he spoke.

"You thought that would have me runnin' for the hills?"

He moved his knuckle over her cheek, and then gently gripped her jaw with one hand. He lifted it, just a bit.

"I dunna know how, lass, because I damn well wasna expectin' it," he started, and Allie noticed just how thick his accent had grown. "But it happened." He scooted closer. "That night, when we first kissed, and you told me to breathe, and to look at you?" His gaze dropped to her lips, as though maybe he was remembering that kiss, and then lifted back to her eyes. "I knew then. I know it now without a doubt."

Allie sat completely still. She couldn't move. Couldn't breathe.

"I'm in love wi' you, Allie Morgan," he said, and his deep voice cracked, just a fraction. "Christ knows I'm in love with you." He leaned to her then, and his lips brushed hers as he spoke. "You make me feel alive, whole again. And I desperately dunna want you to go away."

Allie's heart soared. Inside, she quivered uncontrollably, and pressed her lips to Gabe's. That small motion grounded her. *He* grounded her. With her eyes still open, she whispered, "I am so in love with you" against his mouth. "I don't want to go, either."

Gabe laughed, threw his arms so fiercely around Allie that they both tumbled backward off the log.

Allie squealed as they landed on the soft, mossy forest floor, laughing.

After a moment, Gabe gently pushed Allie to her back and braced himself on his elbow above her. He looked down at her, and his eyes moved over her face, studying it closely, before meeting her eyes with his. He lifted his hand and brushed her lips with his thumb. "I know this is right," he said. "I feel it here." He took her hand and pressed it over his heart. "With every bloody thump, I feel it."

Allie's eyes burned with tears and by God, she fought hard for them to stay in their ducts. But they slipped out and trailed down her face.

Gabe brushed them with his finger, and then lowered his head. Against her mouth, he whispered in Gaelic, "*Tha gaol agam ort.*" He kissed her. "I love you." Again, he kissed her, long, thorough. "I dunna want to ever let you go."

Allie kissed him back, loving the feel of his lips against hers, the pounding of his heart pressing against her chest, and those sweet, brogued Gaelic words washing over her.

She knew Gabe MacGowan was a man of his word. He meant *everything* he said.

She wrapped her arms around him and clung tightly. Finally, she'd found *home*.

Chapter 24

Gabe's heart had never felt lighter. He had Allie Morgan in his arms, on a soft Highland forest ground, and the sun was shinin'.

She loved him.

His mobile vibrated on his hip. Actually, between his and Allie's hips.

"Well, well," Allie said, wiggling her brows. "Can't say I've ever had that reaction from a guy before."

He grinned, shook his head, and reached for it. Bracing himself on one elbow, he checked the caller—Sean—and flipped open the phone. "Aye?"

"Drew says you'd best take care with our Allie," he said with a laugh. "Honestly, Gabe. Control yourself, lad."

Gabe frowned and glanced round. "How the bloody hell does Drew know what we're doin'?"

Allie snorted.

Sean laughed.

Allie thumped his chin. He rubbed it and gave her a mock glare. She simply smiled.

"So things are goin' well, aye?" asked Sean.

Gabe looked at Allie. *His* girl. "Aye. How's Jake?"

"Fine. We're goin' bikin' here in a bit. So we're off. Try and behave. Or Drew's goin' to tell Mum and Da."

Gabe rolled his eyes. "I'm thirty-two years old, for Christ's sake."

Sean laughed. "Doesna matter and you know it. You kids be good now."

With that, Sean disconnected.

Gabe shook his head and hooked his mobile back on the clip.

"What?" Allie asked, raising herself up on her elbows.

Gabe reached over and plucked a leaf from her hair. "Apparently Drew and the others dunna trust me so much."

"I can't imagine why."

With a laugh, he gently threw her back to the ground and kissed her until she couldna breathe.

So involved in their kissing, they completely missed the heavy boots smashing up the trail.

"Damn me, but it looks like fine sport, that," a deep voice said close by.

Gabe and Allie jumped, and for the third time since meeting, their heads clunked together whilst kissing.

A sign, Gabe thought.

He recognized the voice right away.

He opened his eyes and glanced down at Allie. She took it in stride, the getting caught. She grinned at Gabe, looked over his shoulder, her eyes widened, and she waved the cutest little wave he'd ever seen.

"Hi," she said.

The voice spoke again. "Och, I should have known. An American. Do you need a hand, lad?"

Gabe shook his head, pushed up, and helped Allie stand. He turned around and looked his friend square in the eye.

That wasna exactly the truth. He did have to look up a wee bit.

He had a verra big friend.

Before he could make a move, his friend had pulled

him into a fierce hug. He nearly squeezed the life out of him.

He thought he heard Allie giggle.

Finally, Gabe was set free. The big lad looked him over thoroughly, then slapped him on the shoulder.

Gabe nearly went flyin' over the bloody log.

"Bleedin' priests, man, 'tis good to see you." His gaze drifted to Allie, lingered in appreciation, and he nodded. "Fetchin' lass, MacGowan." He flashed Allie a big smile. "Where's your manners, lad? Introduce me."

Gabe pulled Allie close. "Allie, this is Ethan Munro from across the loch. Ethan"—he inclined his head—"this is Allie Morgan."

Ethan smiled, gave Allie a low bow, and came up grinning. "From America." He took her hand and kissed the top of it. "My pleasure, lass."

Gabe watched his Allie, and her eyes narrowed, just a bit. She could tell Ethan wasna *right*. She had a special perception with souls. With *all* souls. Of course she'd notice, but maybe no' right away. Ethan was dressed much like himself, but that long hair and the war braids at the temples might give a clue or two away.

He'd just have to wait and see.

"To the cottage, then?" Gabe said, and inclined his head.

And the three of them started off back through the forest.

Allie couldn't help it. She was sandwiched between two of the sexiest men she'd ever laid eyes on. Of course, one she loved and the other she'd only just met, but still.

Good *God*.

She kept stealing little teensy glances at Ethan Munro. Easily six feet and a half, he . . . sort of looked normal, other than being so big and bulked with muscle. His hair was exceptionally long—clear to the middle of his back, dark, wild looking, with a tiny braid at each temple. Part of her wanted to ask if he was an actor, because he definitely looked as though he could play some big medieval hunk in a sweeping Scottish historical.

He glanced down and caught her staring.

And winked.

Ethan and Gabe continued to talk, and that was another thing that made Allie pause. Ethan's speech was different. Heavily accented like Gabe's, but there was something else, something she couldn't put a finger to. And not just the accent, but the *words* he chose. He said, *I vow 'tis a most comely time of year, what wi' the leaves turning color*, and it just wasn't right. It sounded right on him, but out of century, maybe?

Had he not lifted her hand and kissed it, she would have thought him a ghostly soul.

Finally, the cottage came into view and they all stomped their feet on the grating near the deck.

"My wife and I would like you to come for supper this eve, if you've a mind for it," Ethan offered. " 'Tisna often we're here without the boys. A few of my kinsmen are on their way over now." He winked at Allie. "We're *grilling.*"

Allie nearly choked at the proud expression on his face. *Kinsmen?*

Gabe glanced at Allie, and she gave him a nod.

"We'll be there, Munro," said Gabe. "How's the time, and what can we bring?"

Ethan smiled at Allie. "Bring nothin' but this

fetchin' maid you've snagged and come round six." With a wave, he started off down the lane. "By the by, then."

Allie watched the big man disappear into the forest. She shook her head and turned to Gabe. "There's something strange about him."

Gabe pulled her into his arms and grinned. "Aye. He's no' near as sexy as me and he's a bit daft," he said, twirling a finger round his temple. "He canna help it, lass."

Allie burst out laughing, and then fell into the easy, toe-curling kiss of her very own Highlander.

They stood there, beneath the canopy of trees on the shores of Loch Ness, for quite some time like that.

Allie decided it suited her just fine.

After a snack of chocolate-dipped *digestibles* and a pot of tea—compliments of Ethan and his wife—Allie and Gabe showered *separately*, dressed, and started for Ethan's. Since they had time, they took their time, and explored the quaint town of Drumnadrochit. Although Gabe said it was quite touristy, he took her through the Loch Ness Visitor Center, which had numerous accounts of Nessie sightings and the research involved through the years. They stopped at the Urquhart Castle ruins and walked through, with Gabe telling Allie of several trips he'd had as a *wee boy* to the great loch's ruins.

He told her a Highland story or two, as well, involving fairies and warriors and ghostly knights.

And of course, they couldn't visit an ancient ruin without spirited souls flagging Allie down, introducing themselves and whatever other soul who might be around, and asking a question or two about their past.

Somehow she could always find out just what they needed.

At Urquhart, a young knight, maybe seventeen years old, approached Allie and Gabe, gave a low bow, and asked Allie if she could help him locate his lost love.

To Gabe's chagrin, Allie noticed, she *could*.

After collecting the boy's name, year of birth, and as many details surrounding his death that he could remember, Allie promised to return and do what she could. The young knight gave her a wide smile, another bow, and drifted back into the depths of the castle's stones.

Gabe had simply watched.

As they returned to the Rover, Allie glanced over. "What?" she asked, smiling.

At the Rover, Gabe stopped at her door and propped himself against the window. "You amaze me, Allie Morgan."

Allie just smiled.

Next, they were winding up the lane, on the other side of the loch, to Ethan's. At the top, they parked the Rover, and Gabe ran over to help Allie out—though she needed no help whatsoever but couldn't remember the last time a man helped her from a vehicle, so allowed it—and started up the steps to the cottage. A thin trail of smoke rose from behind the house, and on the breeze carried several deep, loud bouts of laughter.

Gabe nodded in that direction. "Och, they're round back. Let's go there, aye?"

So down the steps and round the back they went. A deck, very similar to Gabe's with an outdoor fireplace and furniture, seemingly had no room left for one more person.

The size of the men on the deck took up so much room, Allie didn't think she could squeeze in.

Good *God*.

"Are you friends with the entire local rugby team?" she whispered to Gabe.

He chuckled. "Worse. Just wait and see."

As soon as the first man caught sight of Gabe, an uproar of thick Highland brogue rose through the air, and Gabe gave Allie a gentle shove. "Back up, darlin'. I dunna want you to get squished—"

Allie gladly backed up, although she didn't think anyone would squish her. Not the way they were squishing Gabe, anyway. Five of the biggest guys Allie had ever seen—especially gathered at one location—crowded around Gabe and took turns putting him in bear hugs and slapping his back. Several things in Gaelic were spoken, but nothing Allie knew. Heck—she only knew a few swears compliments of Wee Mary and Gabe's mother.

Suddenly, one of the huge men strode straight toward her, and although she'd never met him in her life, Allie could tell he was one naughty Highlander. The mischievous gleam in his eyes revealed that much. Like Ethan, he had an abundance of hair, a brawny physique, and a devilish smile.

He walked right up to her, grasped her hand in his, and brought his lips down. When he raised his head, a wicked grin lifted his mouth. "Aiden Munro, lass." His smile widened. "Ethan's cousin. I beg you, tell me you're that little lad's sister."

Allie laughed. "Sorry. Definitely not sister."

"Bloody hell."

Allie patted his arm. "Don't worry. There'll be others."

Aiden's eyes lit up. "Och, damn, another American lass. Ethan's married to a bonny one. Fine lot, you are."

"Aiden Munro, you big ole flirt," said a female voice. "Stop bothering our guest."

Thank God. A girl to talk to.

Through the crowd of rugby players, Allie caught sight of Gabe. He peered through the men around him, shrugged, and grinned.

Gabe MacGowan was no small man. At six feet two inches, and packed with muscle, Allie thought him to be pretty darn big.

But he was surrounded by giants.

"Allie? I'm Amelia, Ethan's wife," she said. A beautiful woman with long, straight blond hair and the most uniquely shaped eyes Allie had ever seen rested her hand on her belly—a belly that looked the slightest bit pregnant—and grinned. "Why don't you come over here, away from that shower of testosterone? I've got some iced tea."

Allie chuckled. "Very nice to meet you, and thanks, I'd love some." She glanced back at the wall of muscle. Something was said in Gaelic, and all heads turned to stare directly at her.

They all had the same serene smile on their faces.

All, that is, except Aiden.

His expression still reminded Allie of a wolf, after finding a nice, juicy rabbit for dinner.

Aiden then threw back his head and laughed.

"What'd they say?" asked Allie, hoping Amelia had heard and that she knew Gaelic.

Amelia grinned. "Sounds to me like you've won the heart of bad boy Gabe MacGowan." She handed Allie a glass of tea. "And from the sound of it, he couldn't be any happier."

Chapter 25

An hour later, after the absolute craziest food fest involving the largest eating machines had run its course, not a crumb remained and everyone sat on Ethan's deck, enjoying the fire crackling in the hearth and good-hearted conversation.

Involving Allie.

"So, lass," Ethan Munro said, "Gabe tells us you're a cherished advocate for spirited souls." He nodded. "Vastly honorable occupation, methinks."

Allie blinked.

Gabe chuckled.

Aiden grinned. "Tell us about it, aye?"

Allie slid a glance over the group and gave a sheepish grin.

Gabe squeezed her hand—the one he held clutched between them.

So she did. Keeping the facts minimal, of course. They wanted to know where she was from, where she lived, and what her favorite movies were.

Amelia, sitting across from her on the love seat with Ethan, grinned. Ethan rested a hand over her slightly swollen abdomen, and every once in a while they'd exchange a loving look.

It nearly made Allie cry.

Usually, her inability to have children didn't bother her so much. She'd had time to accept her fate and was awfully grateful to be alive.

Gabe slid his hand to rest on her knee, and the warmth from his skin seeped through her jeans. It comforted her, and made her happier than ever that she'd been given a second—rather, a third—chance to live out her life.

Hopefully, she'd get to live it out with the man beside her.

"Amelia, why dunna you tell Allie our story, aye?" said Ethan's younger brother, Rob.

"Come on, sister," said Aiden.

Amelia sighed. "Are you up for one crazy story, Allie?" she asked.

Allie nodded. She doubted quite seriously Amelia or anyone else could top anything she'd ever seen, heard, or personally done.

Quickly, she discovered just how *wrong* she could be when it came to being the holder of the crazy story.

After Amelia finished, Allie sat for a second or two, blinked, rose from her seat, and paced in front of the long sofa that miraculously held four Highland knights. *Who'd all been born in the fourteenth century.*

She couldn't help but stare in fascination.

Every time her gaze passed over Aiden's, he grinned.

Finally, she sat down again beside Gabe. She looked at Ethan. "I didn't think I could be shocked. But that story?" She shook her head. "I thought I noticed something off about you earlier."

Everyone roared.

Five warriors, enchanted in a ghostly state of existence for centuries? For one hour a day—the gloaming—they'd gain substance. And for all of those centuries, they had no idea why. All they remembered was that just before a fierce battle between clans, Ethan Munro had been accused of murdering his new bride.

Amazing.

"And then Amelia came along," said Ethan, who slipped his free arm around her and pulled her close. "This little wildcat stormed my keep to write a novel, unafraid of anythin'," he said, and then looked at her. "And stole my heart."

"Lucky bastard," said one of the warriors.

They all roared again.

Allie looked at Amelia. "Your novel?"

Amelia gave a short nod.

"Amelia's an American novelist," said Gabe. "She writes under *Amelia Landry*, and she wrote about her experience at the Munro keep. It's in fiction form but 'tis their story, just the same."

Allie smiled. "Wow, that's fantastic. I'd love to read it. I'll make sure to pick it up."

Amelia waved a hand. "Don't you dare. I've got some spares around here, probably." She elbowed her husband gently. "Ethan or one of the others always has a copy on them."

Gilchrist, Ethan's youngest brother, grinned. "Chicks dig it."

Everyone laughed.

Afterward, the guys all rose and hurried off to inspect a motorcycle one of them had purchased, leaving Allie and Amelia alone.

Amelia sighed, got up, and came to sit beside her. She held Allie's gaze with a kind look. "It's amazing, isn't it?"

Allie wasn't quite sure what she meant. "You mean your story?"

With a smile, Amelia shook her head. "I guess you don't see it. But I do." She cocked her head. "It might not be any of my business, and if so, just tell me to hush. But I'm so proud of Gabe, and his love for you is so blatantly obvious. It's a blessing, you two finding each other." She paused. "What do you know of his and Ethan's first meeting?"

Allie felt a kindred spirit in Amelia and found she didn't mind talking to her at all. "Only that Gabe was going through a terrible time *drying out*, he calls it, and that Ethan and the others helped him through it."

Amelia rubbed her cheek with one finger and looked at Allie. "Ethan is a friendly, outspoken man. He isn't afraid to show his feelings, whether it be for me, his kin, or a friend." She crossed her jean-clad legs at the ankle. "So when Ethan noticed Gabe across the loch, he made his way over one afternoon and introduced himself."

Allie nodded.

"And Ethan, in his outspoken way, told Gabe— more than once—he looked like *bloody hell*." Amelia gave a soft laugh. "Ethan came home with two black eyes, a bloody nose, and a swollen jaw."

Allie's eyes widened. "Gabe beat him up?"

"They beat each other up. Beat the living tar out of each other, my granny would say. I don't know who looked worse, but they must have duked it out for quite a while before deciding enough was enough." The smile touched Amelia's eyes. "And they've been fast friends ever since."

"It sounds as though Ethan and the guys pulled him through some rough times," Allie said. "It must have been horrible."

"He looks amazing now," said Amelia. "Back then, when he first came, he was skinny, unshaven—yeah, it was horrible. I felt so sorry for him. Having the guys, and their unique situation, helped, I think. Plus Gabe's dad and brother are fantastic." She shrugged.

"Everyone pulled together." She patted Allie's leg. "But my Lord, look what you've done to him now."

Allie grinned. "I haven't done anything. I've known him for a very short time, actually."

"Really?" Amelia said, grasping Allie's hand and squeezing. "I don't see that."

Allie glanced at Ethan, his kinsmen, and Gabe down on the car park as they looked over the bike.

Although it was dark, the outdoor light cast enough light for Allie to notice Gabe had turned his gaze in her direction.

He smiled, the whites of his teeth stark against the low light.

"I guess I don't see it, either," Allie said.

And she didn't.

"You and Gabe will have to visit us at the keep sometime," Amelia said. "There's plenty of room and lots of fun places to explore."

Allie glanced at her belly and smiled. "That sounds exciting. How much longer before you can't explore anymore?"

Amelia waved a hand. "Pah, this is my third, and I've still got four more months to go. Easy peasy. You guys come whenever you like."

Allie smiled and looked at the other woman who'd fast become her friend. "It's been great meeting you," she said.

Amelia met her gaze. "Likewise. You know, in a sea of testosterone, us girls have to stick together. Big-time. And you know," she said, pinching her thumb and index finger close together, "we're only this far apart on the map. So let's not be strangers."

They laughed, and while the guys finished being guys, Allie dared to imagine what it would be like to be a part of this kind of life permanently.

The clean, cool Highland night air rushed over her,

like an accidental touch, or a profound whisper, as someone urgently, from the glens and crags and depths of the loch, leaned close to her ear and said, *Stay, Allie Morgan, you belong. You belong with Gabe. You belong here.*

Allie wrapped her arms about herself and inhaled again, hearing the water of Loch Ness ripple and lap at the shore below, and the leaves rustle above.

She indeed felt content. Gabe made her feel whole.

And she prayed with fervor that the haunting whispers of the glen were right.

Gabe pulled Allie close as they said good-bye to the Munros. Ethan's kin had all nearly slapped the breath from his lungs with their version of farewell, but Gabe felt lucky to have such an unusual lot of friends.

They'd all loved Allie on sight.

He'd expected no less.

As they climbed into the Rover, Gabe glanced down and noticed a copy of Amelia's book, *Enchantment*, clutched in Allie's hands. He was sure she'd find it just as fascinating as he had.

As long as she found it fascinating some *other* night. *Not tonight.*

They waved, leaving the big lot of lads, plus wee Amelia, on the deck. Ethan pulled his wife close and kissed her temple, one hand protectively sitting atop Amelia's blooming belly.

Gabe wondered briefly if that bothered Allie. Somehow, even if it did, he thought she'd never tell him. He wished mightily that he could change things for her.

As they drove along, he snatched glimpses of her profile in the dark, with only the stereo's neon green numbers casting an iridescent glow to Allie's face.

Beautiful.

Turning the Rover onto a single lane, he headed toward a favorite place of his he felt sure Allie would love. They seemed to love quite a lot of the same things—which amazed him. She was simple, loved the outdoors, didn't mind hard work, and sweet God, she could kiss.

Which is all they'd be doing tonight regardless of their opportunity to be alone.

He'd given his word.

And while not at all a scaredy-cat—a term Ethan had used but Gabe felt sure he swiped from Amelia—he wouldn't give his word to five big lads from the fourteenth century who'd proudly hacked off a head or two and then take that word back.

A fool he wasna.

No' to mention that while Allie drove him close to insanity, with her warmth, her soft skin that smelled of flowers, the way she kissed and her bonny form pressed tightly against his, he *respected* her. He so completely respected her he'd push his own urges aside to care for her wishes.

He just prayed she didna wish the same thing he did.

"They're really nice," Allie said, turning sideways to look him straight-on. "I really liked them."

Gabe nodded. "Aye, and they took right to you, as well." He smiled and inclined his head. "I see Amelia gave you one of her novels. You'll enjoy it. 'Tis an amazin' story."

She looked at him and smiled. "This isn't the same way we came." She cocked her head—an endearing gesture she did frequently that Gabe decided he liked. "Are you taking me somewhere secluded to make out?"

He raised a brow. "Aye, darlin', I most certainly am."

Allie laughed softly and slipped her hand into his. "Good. I was hoping you were."

Only his Allie would be so vulnerably open. He liked that about her, too.

Easing the Rover down the narrow gravel path, Gabe came to a stop and lifted the emergency brake. He inclined his head. "Quite a view, aye?"

Allie's eyes moved across the loch, the moonlight making her pupils shine. "Breathtaking."

"Aye," he agreed, although to a different scene altogether. He opened the door. "We have a clear view of the sky from here that we canna see from our porch because of the trees."

Together, they leaned against the hood of the Rover and watched the stars. Gabe slid up onto the hood and pulled Allie to rest against his chest. He draped his arms around hers and held her, his chin on the top of her head.

He felt content.

Aside from *wanting* her so badly, that is.

"What did you study at university, lass?" he asked, thinking a nice, safe nonkissing topic would help him keep his hands to himself.

She laughed softly. "Strangely enough, astronomy."

And then Allie Morgan proceeded to point out several constellations, stars, planets.

On her own, she turned in his arms to face him. His hands settled against her hips, and, God help him, she slid her wee hands to *his* hips. In the darkness, with the moonlight and the sounds of Loch Ness, Allie Morgan smiled and leaned against him. She pressed her mouth to his and inhaled as she slowly tasted him, and Gabe moved his hands over her back and pulled her to him, so close he could feel Allie's heart pounding against his. Her hands came up and grasped either side of his face, her fingers rubbing against the day's stubble on his jaw.

Without hesitance, she kissed him long, thorough, and he let her take the lead. When she finally stilled against his lips, kissed him softly once, and opened her eyes, she first looked at the mouth she'd just tasted, and then at his eyes.

"I love you, Gabe MacGowan."

He smiled, shook his head, and then laughed. "She loves me!" he shouted, and his deep, booming voice bounced off the waters of Loch Ness and echoed through the glen.

Allie laughed and placed her hand over his mouth. "Shh, you crazy thing," she said, her eyes shining.

"I love you, Allie Morgan," he said against her fingertips. "I love you."

Chapter 26

Allie thought she and Gabe would get tired, grow sleepy, stop talking, or kiss some more.

Or just throw caution—and her reputation—to the wind and give in.

They both wanted it. Good Lord, the profound strength Gabe had exerted to *not* lose control when they had been on the forest floor was almost as much of a turn-on as the control getting lost.

She was thirty years old, for God's sake. She wasn't a virgin. She hadn't had many lovers—okay, so there was just *one*. But that *one* had lasted for a couple of years, and she thought they were going to get married. Little did she know he'd dump her for another woman.

But she and Gabe didn't give in. Not yet, anyway. Instead, on the high banks of Loch Ness, on the porch Gabe built with his own hands, they snuggled.

Guys hated that word. *Snuggle*. It was a girl thing to do, invented, probably, *by* a girl. It meant *to snug*. In other words, in a guy's mind, to *snuggle*, or to *snug*, meant *no sex*.

Allie thought Gabe hid his loathing for snuggling rather well. Either that or, dare she think, he was one of the few men who actually *liked* it?

Either way, snuggle, in fact, is just what they did.

After they kissed some more.

The night wasn't as cool as it had been recently, and the outdoor fireplace, along with a few blankets, kept Allie and Gabe toasty warm. They talked. About family, about childhood, about places they'd like to visit, things they each enjoyed doing—they just *learned.*

Allie was fairly positive that making love with Gabe would be earth-shattering. He'd probably have to teach her all over again how to actually make love— it'd been quite a long time for her.

Gabe kept talking, and Allie wanted to keep kissing. She wanted to touch, skim her hands over his rocky biceps, slip her hand under his shirt, and feel the ripped abs she'd seen that night when he'd had just a button-up shirt on, unbuttoned.

The thought made her mouth go dry.

Gabe made her mouth go dry.

What, exactly, were they waiting on, anyway? Frustrated? To have Gabe so close and be so casual?

Ugh!

"Allie?"

"Yes?" she asked, smiling through her clenched teeth.

Gabe, lying behind her and on his side so she could fit on the deck sofa with him, looked at her, relaxed. With his head propped on the heel of one hand, the other rested casually over her stomach, he grinned. "What's wrong, lass?"

How could he be so calm?

She certainly wasn't. She felt as if someone had lit her virtual fuse and it was getting shorter and shorter by the second. Good Lord! They'd been lying nearly on top of each other for over two hours and she was about to yank her hair out. She probably needed to just go either jump into the cool October waters of Loch freaking Ness or take a cold shower in the cottage.

She opted for the cold shower.

Because of that whole monster thing.

She lifted Gabe's hand from her stomach, set it onto his own thigh, and rolled off the deck sofa.

Literally. She hit the wood, stood up, brushed off her backside, and began walking to the back door of the cottage.

"Allie, where are you goin'?"

She stopped, breathed a few times to mask her . . . whatever it was, and turned and smiled. "I'm *gooin'* to take a shower." She smiled extra wide for good measure.

"But you just took one, lass. Before we went to Ethan's."

"Not a cold one. I'll be back."

Then she turned and slipped into the cottage.

Since no one had thought to leave on a lamp, the interior of the cottage had only a slight silvery glow from the moon as it poured in through the two large picture windows facing the loch. Finding the small hallway, she made for the room she'd set her overnight bag in. Once there, she yanked off her jacket and flung it onto the bed. "It's so hot in here," she muttered under her breath while digging through her bag.

"Allie, stop, love."

She squealed and jumped. Turning around, she pasted on a smile she hoped the dark would conceal.

Especially if it looked as fake as it felt.

"I'll just be a minute," she said, and brushed by Gabe, who stood just outside the door to the room.

Allie didn't even make it to the bathroom door.

Gabe grabbed her hand as she tried to pass, and she jerked to a stop. Without a word, he rounded on her, placed his fingertips on her stomach, gently pushed until her back touched the wall. He braced his weight with a hand to either side of her head and stared down at her.

Even just standing there, with him so close and she with her emotions soaring, Allie's breath came hard. She tried to slow it down, but her chest rose and fell and she knew Gabe noticed.

He *looked*.

Once more, he asked, "Lass, what's wrong with you?"

She attempted to duck under his arm. He lowered it and trapped her again.

Allie rubbed her forehead and then looked Gabe dead center in the eyes. "You might be able to control yourself, Gabe MacGowan, and remain calm and collected and unaffected by, well, you know. Me." She narrowed her eyes. "I'm not quite that strong. I'm the type of person whose emotions can't just be bottled up. For long."

"I see," he said, his voice smooth and nonflustered.

Allie frowned and ducked under his arm once more and this time, she made it. She scooted down the short hallway toward the bathroom, but again, she didn't make it.

"Enough, lass," Gabe said as he spun her around. Once more, she found herself pressed against the wall. "Do you think I find any of this easy?" His breathing came a bit faster now, frustrated, maybe even angry. He dropped his voice to a whisper, leaning closer to her ear as though making sure no one else heard his confession but him. "Dunna think for one bloody second I'm no' dyin' inside to touch you." His gaze dropped, and one hand grazed her hip, eased over to where her sweater didn't quite cover her stomach, and slipped a knuckle over the sensitive skin by her navel.

Allie sucked in a sharp breath, just at the contact. His gaze then slowly lifted back up to her throat, her mouth, and then to her eyes. "I'm starved for you, Allie Morgan, wild-hungry to taste you." His voice dropped lower still, his brogue thick, and this time, with his eyes still fixed to Allie's, he brushed his lips over hers. "To take you." He closed his eyes shut, hung his head, and *breathed.* Then he looked up again. "Dunna you understand, lass? If I started to touch you, I'm no' sure I'd ever have the power or desire to stop."

Allie wet her lips and stared into Gabe's stormy green eyes. "Maybe I wouldn't *want* you to stop, Gabe MacGowan." She dared not touch him, for she could already feel the wound-up barely contained explosion within Gabe's body. Her voice dropped to a whisper on its own. "Maybe I want you just as badly." She laughed softly. "*Need* you."

Gabe's eyes closed, and he swore. "I promise, love," he said, his voice hoarse. He looked at her. "It's more than that. It has to do with me no' losin' control. 'Tis something I vowed never to do again."

Suddenly, it hit Allie like a ton of bricks.

It had to do with his sobriety. Not just about keeping her reputation intact. It had to do with making sure he stayed in complete control of his urges, including the ones that tempted him to drink.

Inwardly, Allie cringed. Could she be any more selfish?

Outwardly, she threw her arms around Gabe's neck, kissed his cheek, and hugged him tightly. "I'm sorry," she said against his throat. "I'm—I wasn't thinking."

Gabe's arms went around her, one hand cradling the back of her head. His body shook, and his breathing was ragged, but he managed a soft laugh. " 'Tis all right, love. 'Twill be fine." He kissed her temple. "Let's just rest up before morning. 'Tis nearly midnight."

So together they held each other in the moonlit hall of the cottage, and through Allie's desire she realized Gabe's sheer determined strength, and she discovered she loved him even more than before.

He pulled back and looked at her. "I'm a strong man, Allie Morgan, but no' strong enough to sleep with you in my arms and behave."

Allie didn't say anything. She just smiled.

And Gabe left her, went to the spare bedroom, and shut the door.

Sometime later, after Allie had drifted off to sleep, she awakened with a start. She lay there in the small room of the cottage, gathered her bearings, and stared into the darkness. She felt sure she'd heard—

"No!" Gabe's voice called out, frantic, angry. "Damn you, Kait, *no!*"

Allie threw the covers back and hit the floor running. Though the same moon shone silvery light through the picture windows, she still stumbled through the shadows until she reached Gabe's room. Without hesitation, she opened the door and hurried in.

She stopped dead in her tracks. The icy temperature nearly robbed her breath. Allie immediately recognized the coldness. An intense, restless spirit was close by. It was a telltale sign.

She stifled a gasp. A filmy, transparent soul stood next to Gabe's bed. *His wife . . .*

Allie kept her eye trained on the malevolent spirit and approached Gabe with caution. The moonlight fell across him, and he writhed in his bed, out of the covers, still wearing his jeans but bare-chested. He spoke in Gaelic, so much of what he said Allie didn't understand. What she did understand, though, was Gabe MacGowan was terrified.

Then the soul moved its stare from Gabe to Allie, and she felt a coldness settle over her that she'd not experienced in all her years of dealing with souls. Chunks of hair were missing; pale, puckered skin covered a too-skinny frame, one eye socket sat empty and blackened, and the mouth, crooked in a way that suggested a broken jaw, flailed open, shadowy. Frightening.

Allie could feel the despair and hatred pouring off the soul in heavy, suffocating waves.

She drew a deep breath and knelt down beside Gabe. She rested her hand on his biceps and stared at his wife's spirit. "Leave him," Allie ordered. "Please, Kait, leave him alone." She stared, unafraid, at the spirit. "If you'll let me, I can help you—"

A terrible groan sounded from the soul, threatening, overwhelming, and yet no words formed.

Gabe's wife simply screamed. And with the one eye remaining looked at Allie, pointed, and her flailing mouth smiled.

And then the soul vanished.

Chapter 27

"Gabe! Wake up!"

Gabe jerked and sat up. His heart hammered in his chest, his breath quickened, and he rubbed his eyes with the heels of his hands.

Christ, another dream . . .

A soft hand stroked his, and he jumped back. Startled, he stared into a pair of wide eyes.

"Gabe, it's Allie. Look at me. *Breathe.*"

The cobwebs of the nightmare still clogged his brain, and he slid his hand round the back of his neck. He did breathe. He closed his eyes and his body began to shake.

"Gabe, look at me."

That same soft hand rested against his cheek, grasped his jaw, and turned his head. "Gabe."

Gabe opened his eyes and recognition set in. He heaved a sigh, took a deep breath, and heaved another. "Christ."

Allie. It was *Allie.* She eased onto the bed, leaned against the short headboard, and pulled Gabe to her. He went willingly, slid his arms around her waist, and settled into her softness. Her arms went round him and she held on tightly. He felt her mouth press against the top of his head. Neither said anything for quite some time.

Then Allie spoke.

"This is why you're awake at the same time every morning," she said, her voice gentle. "She comes to you."

Gabe inhaled Allie's scent, and it calmed him. "Aye. And I should've told you. I was goin' to that night at the wharf, but Sean interrupted." He sighed again. "I suppose I was hopin' to handle it myself, or that she'd see I'd moved on with my life, and leave me and Jake alone."

Allie's soft fingertips trailed his hairline, his ear. "She's not going to, Gabe. She's so miserable, so angry."

In the silvery light, he glanced up. "At first, 'twas just dreams—or so I thought. Then they became so bloody real, I couldna tell if I was dreamin' or if her spirit was haunting me." He squeezed her tighter. "Her soul came to me the other day during the waking hours. She knows you're with me, Allie. She's told me several times to make you go. She doesna like you."

"There's always a first for everything," she said, and Gabe could feel her smile in her voice.

He leaned up on one elbow. "I think she's dangerous, Allie. I dunna want you near her." He rested his head next to hers. "I can handle it."

"You're not doing such a swell job, MacGowan," Allie said. She turned and looked at him, and gently brushed the areas beneath both eyes. "Look at you. You're being tormented, Gabe. And honestly, I can help."

A rush of fear swept over Gabe at the thought of Allie interacting with Kait's soul. He rolled off the bed and walked to the large picture window. Pressing his forehead against the cool glass, he watched the treetops sway from the wind.

"When I walked into the room it was like ice," Allie

said, behind him but not touching. "She's torturing you, Gabe, and she'll keep torturing you until her spirit is eased. She's so sad, so full of guilt and pain—and she doesn't know why." Allie placed a hand on his back. "She'll continue, and maybe get worse, until her soul is mended—"

Gabe turned and took Allie by the shoulders. He leaned toward her and locked his gaze on hers. "Listen to me, lass. I dunna need your help with me dead wife." He gave her a gentle shake. "Do you hear me? I want you to leave it be." He'd not be able to live with himself if something happened to Allie.

She smiled and searched his eyes. "But I can't. I'm involved. And I cannot bear to see a soul suffer. She appears frightening because she's troubled, Gabe. Unlike the Odin's lot, who appear as they did in life, Kait appears as she probably did after death took its toll. She cannot help herself. Whether by guilt over the mistakes she made, her uncertainty, or a truth that is unknown—it's all made her soul demented." She shook her head. "No matter her mistakes, and no matter how much she has tortured you, you must understand that no soul deserves to toil forever like that. She needs my help."

Gabe heaved a frustrated sigh. He brushed a stray curl from Allie's face, then held her head with both hands. He leaned close, brushed a kiss across her lips, and gave her a hard look. "I love you for wanting to help me, Allie Morgan, and Christ, for wanting to help Kait. But I canna allow it. Her soul is dangerous." He pulled her into a fierce hug, and he buried his face into her neck. "Just then, before you chased Kait away, I couldna wake myself up. 'Twas like I lay trapped." He traced her jaw. "I dunna know how she's able to use me strength against me, but she is and I couldna live with myself if she hurt you. Leave it alone, I'm beggin' you. I'll be fine."

Allie's arms wrapped around his waist, and she rested her head against his chest. He wanted to put Kait from his mind, didna want to think of Allie getting involved in something so dangerous.

He let his hands slide down Allie's back, over her hips, and just enveloping himself with her presence comforted him.

And it was then he noticed just how verra little Allie had on.

"Christ, woman," he said against her ear. "Are you tryin' to kill me yourself?" He nuzzled her neck. "What in bloody hell are you wearin'?"

Allie gave a soft laugh. "It's a tank top and shorts, silly. Perfectly acceptable bedtime attire."

Obviously, Allie failed to realize what a thin top and a cold room could do to a woman's body. With a groan, he set her back.

Before he took her against the bloody picture window.

He looked at her and stifled a groan. " 'Tis passed now, Kait's presence. She never stays for verra long. Go back to sleep. We'll get up early and take our time drivin' back to Sealladh na Mara."

"Okay." She stared at him a moment, her eyes searching his, and although she smiled and didna mention Kait or the dream again, he knew 'twas on her mind. And that she was strong enough and willing to face whatever evil Kait had to offer, just to help him? Christ Almighty, what a woman.

His woman.

Gabe watched her leave the room and close the door. In the hall, her soft footsteps led her to her own room.

He closed his eyes and prayed the moon would sink, and the sun would rise soon.

With a groan, he flung himself back onto the bed, threw an arm over his eyes. Before sleep took him, visions of Allie beneath him, her bare skin glistening from the faint light of the moon, and the sweetness of her body as it moved with his overtook all thoughts of malevolent ghosts and night terrors . . .

The ride home the next morning was beyond breathtaking. Before she and Gabe left the cottage, they'd taken an early morning stroll through the wood and down to Loch Ness, where an eerie mist had slipped along the shore and blanketed the water. She'd borrowed one of Gabe's big sweaters, and together they walked the pebbled beach, looking for the infamous waterhorse.

Nessie had decided to keep to herself that morning.

Afterward, they'd driven into Drumnadrochit for breakfast, and then they'd started home. Gabe drove past another small ruin, a field dotted with white fluffy sheep, and then through Wester Ross.

At a craggy rock, they'd witnessed a majestic stag with a full rack of antlers, staring out across the moors. With the mist slipping through the air and the cool stillness of the morning, it nearly took Allie's breath away. Every sight felt new, memorable, beautiful.

As did the man beside her.

She'd never forget the strength he'd shown the night before. It made her feel proud that, even in the midst of an electrical current of pent-up desire, Gabe Mac-Gowan held true to his sobriety vow. God, she'd always remember it.

As soon as the sign for Sealladh na Mara came into view, Allie felt at home.

Strange, given she was born in Raleigh, North Carolina.

The day had turned overcast, the wind had picked up, and the few small fishing boats anchored in the loch bobbed with the tide. The whitewashed buildings of the village stood stark against the grayness of the midmorning, but the flower boxes, filled with pansies and geraniums, lent a surreal color to the bleakness.

Come to think of it, the bleakness really wasn't all that bleak.

Gabe hadn't said anything more about Kait or the dreams and ghostly visits that had plagued him for God only knew how long. He'd made it quite clear how much he *didna* need Allie's help.

He just didn't realize Allie's potential. Mending souls is what she did for a *living*, and she accomplished it by actually being able to understand the spirits' issues. And if anyone's soul needed mending, it was Kait MacGowan's. Why would Gabe willingly want to suffer if he didn't have to?

Talk about suffering. Suffering was being held against Gabe MacGowan's bare chest with his lips pressed against your neck, and then being told to go to bed.

That was suffering.

She glanced over at him. Jaw tight, eyes trained on the road ahead, that little space between the brows pinched. Fingers gripping the steering wheel as if holding on for dear life.

But then Gabe must have sensed her stare, and when he turned his head he flashed a wide, white smile. His green eyes softened and Allie all but melted.

She'd decided earlier, while suffering in Gabe's arms against his bare, six-pack abdomen, that she was going to help Gabe by helping Kait's soul—whether Gabe wanted her to or not. The poor woman had been miserable in life, and was even more miserable in death. And the more miserable a soul became, the more malevolent it became. It couldn't help it. Allie didn't think Kait MacGowan deserved it. Gabe's wife had been young. She'd made mistakes. *Everyone* makes mistakes.

Besides. Kait was Jake's mother. Allie felt pretty sure little Jake wouldn't want his own mother suffering an eternity of misery.

The Rover pulled onto the one-track lane of Sealladh na Mara and started the incline toward Odin's Thumb. No sooner had they pulled to a stop than the door swung open and a middle-aged woman wearing a gray suit ran out.

Screaming.

Gabe's head turned and his gaze followed the woman as she ran across the street, jumped into a red two-door, and sped away. "Christ."

Just then, Sean came hurrying out of Odin's. Gabe and Allie stepped out of the Rover, and met the grinning younger man on the walk.

Sean glanced at the red car speeding up the lane. "Right. There goes another one."

Gabe rubbed the back of his neck. "Another one?"

Sean nodded. "Two since you left. The Realtor called directly after and asked if the two appointments could be moved up." He shrugged. "We handled it."

Gabe scratched his temple. "I dunna even want to know about it—"

"Da!"

They turned and Jake came barreling out of Odin's, followed by the five residing souls, plus Dauber.

Jake leapt into Gabe's arms and the two hugged tightly.

"How's me lad, aye?" Gabe said, and kissed his son on the cheek. "Have you been well behaved?"

Jake grinned. "Not so much."

Gabe laughed. "Well, with your uncle Sean around I canna say I blame you." He kissed him again and set him on the ground.

Then Jake made a beeline for Allie. She squatted down and Jake ran straight into her arms. When she hugged him, she caught Gabe's eye, and he smiled.

The sight nearly made her melt.

Against her ear, Jake whispered, "Have you mended me da's soul yet, Allie Morgan?"

Allie squeezed the little boy tightly, loving his clean scent and sweet concern over his father. "I think I may have," she said. When Jake lifted his head, he smiled. "I knew you were the one."

The profoundness of Jake's confidence struck her, and Allie nearly teared up. She stood, and Jake took her hand in his.

Gabe watched on, smiling.

"I see you two had a couple of verra close calls," Sean said with a grin. "I thought Drew was going to go mad."

"I nearly did go mad," the friar said, stepping forward and giving a mock glare. "I'm quite happy to see you two return safely."

"You had a lovely trip, *oui*?" said Mademoiselle, her powdered wig teetering just a bit to the left. "Did you meet anyone interesting?"

Allie caught the eye of Captain Justin Catesby. He shook his head and laughed. Turning to Gabe, he gave a short nod. "Glad to see you home again, lad. And I thank you for keeping your word."

Lords Ramsey and Killigrew watched on, devilment shining in their eyes.

She could only imagine what sort of naughtiness they'd conjured in the hours they'd been gone.

Just then, the door opened and Wee Mary poked

her head out. The delicious scent of pot roast wafted out and mixed with the brine of Sealladh na Mara, and Allie's stomach growled.

"Boy, dunna you feed the lass properly?" said Justin. "I can hear her bloody innards protesting from here."

Everyone roared.

Allie held her stomach. "Well, thank you very much, Justin, for that announcement." She led Jake by the hand and past the mischievous lot of souls and into Odin's.

Wee Mary looked up at her and grinned.

And Allie grinned back.

And as they all pitched in and prepared for the Sunday pot roast crowd, Allie thought things could hardly be more perfect.

And the only thing left to do was to help right one lost soul's mistake in life, and help her find the peace she so desperately craved.

Even if Kait didn't realize it.

Nearly two weeks went by, and Allie was beginning to wonder if she'd frightened off the malevolent soul of Kait MacGowan.

Allie knew the spirits listened to her more closely than they did anyone else. Yes, she was still mortal, but because she'd died *twice*, they seemed to respect her a bit more, value her consult. At least, she liked to think.

Earlier, before they'd turned in, Gabe had finally admitted that his dreams had stopped, and Kait had shown herself no more. Gabe didn't have to admit it, though. Allie had been able to tell by Gabe's demeanor and attitude over the past two weeks.

It'd been an amazing transformation.

As Allie rested, duvet pulled to her chin and the

smoky peat burning in the hearth, she thought of that amazing, transformed man. Funny, joking, and laid-back, Gabe MacGowan had done something he hadn't done in years. *Live life.*

And she'd been lucky enough to witness it.

Before Sean had gone back to Glasgow, he, Gabe, and Jake had taken her on the ferry to Skye and Iona. The day had been absolutely breathtaking, with the sun shining full and bright. The air had remained crisp and cool, especially with the brisk sea wind. The white, fluffy clouds stood stark against a cerulean sky, and the sun had reflected against the choppy water like hundreds and hundreds of finely cut diamonds under a brilliant flash of light.

Although Jake had crossed over to Skye and Iona many times, he kept his uncle busy, darting here and there, wanting to sit on top deck, wanting to sit on bottom deck, wanting to get close to the bow, wanting to sit by the captain.

Excited by everything he saw.

Allie thought it adorable.

She ran with him a good bit, too. Heck, *she* wanted to sit by the captain.

But Jake's father had other things on his mind. He'd grabbed Allie, and they'd stood at the *Caledonian*'s railing as they'd crossed to the isles. Gabe had gathered her in his arms, her back to his front, his chin resting atop her head. The sea had washed over them, and Gabe had nuzzled her neck and brushed kisses against her ear.

By the time they'd reached Skye, Allie thought she might have to take a wee dip in the seawater to douse her desire.

The man certainly could get her worked up.

They'd then spent one day visiting the Isle of Skye, where they'd viewed the MacLeod stronghold, and the spectacular cliffs. Another day, they'd visited the isles of Mull and Iona, with the colorful red, yellow, and blue buildings of Mull's Tobermory, and the ancient cloister and abbey at Iona. Serene and moving, the nearly 180 medieval-carved stones and crosses stood sturdy and proud against the fierceness of the Hebrides.

And Allie had never been more thrilled than to share it all with Gabe MacGowan. And she'd never thought she'd ever find a love so intense and real . . .

Allie's eyelids grew heavy, and she had no idea how long she'd been asleep before a small voice awakened her.

"Allie, come quick!" cried little Jake. He grabbed her hand and pulled. "Please, Allie. *Now!*"

Allie jumped up and hit the floor running, Jake right on her heels.

Without even asking, she ran straight for Gabe's room.

Chapter 28

When Allie threw open Gabe's bedroom door, her heart nearly stopped. The lights flickered, and Gabe lay sprawled out on the bed, unmoving, pale.

And hovering over him, Kait's ghastly spirit.

She wished Jake hadn't seen his mother's soul in such a state, but he had. He was just as receptive to spirits as anyone else in Sealladh na Mara.

"Go find the others," Allie instructed Jake.

He took off down the corridor.

Slowly, she stepped into the room and eased in close to Gabe's bed. God Almighty, she'd swear he was dead if not for the very slight rise and fall of his chest. Behind his lids, his eyes rolled restlessly back and forth. She didn't know how, but Kait had him.

She needed to do something *now*.

"Kait," Allie said, making her voice calm, steady. When the spirit ignored her, Allie raised her voice. "Let him go, Kait. Now."

The decayed shell representing Kait's body turned her head and screamed. The sound, inhuman and unnatural, made Allie nauseated. She covered her ears until the sensation passed, and then she addressed her once more.

"Kait! You won't change anything by harming him," she yelled, forceful and angry now. "Let him go, Kait, and let me help *you*." Somehow, through so much torment and misery, Kait's soul had gained an unnatural strength. Not physical strength on Kait's part, but rather using the power of her mind to control the strength within Gabe.

Allie had never experienced anything like it before.

The remaining eye on Kait's ghostly face bored into Allie. That mouth, so gruesome and exaggerated, stretched open wide. Still, she said nothing.

"Do it for Jake, Kait," Allie continued, stepping closer. The icy wind in the room picked up and whipped through Allie's hair. "He loves you, Kait. I can help mend your soul!"

"Bloody hell," yelled Justin from the doorway. "Get out of there, lassie!"

A quick glance told her Dauber, Captain Catesby, the friar, and the others had all gathered behind her. Mademoiselle Elise Bedeau gasped.

"I can't," Allie whispered to herself. "I won't leave him." Tears stung her eyes, and Allie stepped around the bed, closer to Kait's hovering form. "I love him. Do you hear me?" she said firmly at Kait's soul. "I won't let you take him." Sitting on the side of the bed, Allie lay across Gabe's body. It felt cold to the touch, and it looked as though he barely breathed.

"I know you've suffered a long time," Allie said, now looking directly up at the semitransparent form of Gabe's wife. "I can help you, Kait. You don't have to suffer anymore."

"No, Jake!"

Allie glanced at the door in time to see Jake hurtling across the room toward them. His face was scrunched in anger, fists flailing.

"Get away from my da!" he hollered. "Leave my da alone!"

Suddenly, Jake's body stopped so fiercely, it seemed as though he'd hit a brick wall. He stumbled back and stared, disbelieving.

"No!" Allie cried. "Kait, no!"

Gabe's dead wife looked at Allie then, and before Allie knew what was happening, she unwillingly moved her body from Gabe's, and with a force she hadn't expected, Kait slammed her against the wall.

Dauber, Justin, and the two lords rushed into the room. Dauber stood over Jake while the others approached the floating form of Kait MacGowan.

"Cease, Kait!" shouted Justin. "You've no place here anymore. You must leave him. Leave *them*."

Allie tried to speak, to tell Justin to hush, but she couldn't breathe. An invisible hand squeezed her throat, and she felt hers fingertips go numb.

Gabe pushed up onto his elbows, glanced at Jake on the floor, and Allie against the wall. He shook his head, as though trying to clear his vision, and then he turned a hard stare onto his dead wife.

"Kait, I understand now." He glanced at Allie, fear in his wide green eyes. "Let her go, lass. Let her go now and I'll make sure 'tis done."

The hideous, flimsy form shifted, hovered, and came to float beside Allie.

"Leave," the soul hissed in Allie's ear. "You'll no' have them. *Ever . . .*"

A fierce wind pummeled through the room and out the window. The lights stopped flickering, and Allie's breath came out in a rush. Her knees gave out from under her and she crumpled to the floor.

Kait's dispirited soul had vanished.

Jake and Gabe reached Allie at the same time.

"Da!" Jake said.

Gabe pulled his son close, and with his free hand

he grabbed Allie's chin, a bit roughly, and turned it side to side. His eyes searched her face, then settled on her eyes.

"Are you hurt?" he said, his voice hoarse, and when she didn't answer, his voice became harsh. "Did she hurt you?"

Allie shook her head. "No, I'm fine," she said. "I'm fine, really." She lifted her hand and placed it over Gabe's.

He pulled her into a fierce embrace, his son on one side, Allie on the other, and Allie threw her arms around him and snuggled close. She felt Jake's little hand rest on her back.

" 'Twill be all right, Allie Morgan," said Jake, patting her. "Right, Da?"

The spirits of Odin's Thumb stood about them, Dauber included, and watched.

Gabe raised his head and met Allie's gaze. "Right, lad. 'Twill all be fine. I promise."

Allie held on, and even as she felt Gabe's kiss atop her head, and his arm pull her closer, fear tightened her throat. She wanted to comfort Jake, to tell him his mother couldn't help the state she was in and that she just needed help. But before she could, Gabe spoke.

"Jake, go with the others to the lobby, aye?"

Jake glanced up, first at Allie, then at Gabe. "Och, Da—"

"Go now, lad," Gabe said firmly. "I'll come see to you after I have a private word with Allie. Aye?"

"Aye," Jake said. He slowly got up and patted Allie's head. When he leaned to her cheek to kiss it, he whispered, " 'Twill be all right. My da says so. He promised."

And with that, he ran to the door, a reluctant group of spirited souls trudging behind him.

At the door, Dauber glanced over his bony shoulder

and gave Allie a winsome smile. Almost as if he knew what was going to happen. It made her heart sink a little more.

And then Dauber left.

Gabe rose, walked to the window, and slammed it shut. He paced, thankfully unharmed, in a pair of drawstring sleep pants. Nothing more.

He rubbed the back of his neck and didn't say anything for quite some time.

Allie got up and sat on the edge of the bed while he continued to pace silently.

"I'm sorry I ever brought you here," he finally said. He didn't look at her. " 'Twas a mistake, lass." He did look then. "A bloody mistake."

Allie didn't know what to say. A lump formed in her throat, and it took several times to swallow past it. "You don't mean that," she said quietly.

Anger flared in Gabe's eyes. "Aye, I do mean it." He looked away, swore, and stopped. Turning, he crossed the room and pulled her up. "I want you to go home, Allie Morgan." He glared at her. "I dunna want you here anymore."

Breath wouldn't come. Even though she knew he was saying it out of fear for her safety, it knocked the wind from her. After a few tries to suck in a little air, Allie looked at Gabe, searched his face, and could think of nothing better to say than what she'd said before. "You can't mean that—"

He gave her a shake. "I do mean it! Stop sayin' I dunna mean it when I do!" With his hand around her wrist, Gabe pulled.

"What are you doing?" she cried. "Gabe, stop it!" She followed him, only to keep from being dragged along. Up the stairs and to her room they went, and at the door, he slung it open and pulled her inside. He dropped her arm.

"I want you to pack your belongings now, Allie," he said, barely looking at her. "I'm sending you home."

Allie stared at him. "I love you."

His face hardened, jaw tight and flinching. "Get packed now, Allie."

Tears burned the backs of her eyes and throat. He wasn't thinking rationally, and she knew it, but it still hurt. "It's two in the morning, Gabe."

"I'll take you to Wee Mary's. You'll wait there until the morn. You're no' stayin' here." He gave her a hard stare. "Now get packed. We'll leave in an hour."

And with that he stormed out and slammed the door.

Allie stared at the solid oak door and wiped the tears as they fell from her face.

She swore in Gaelic and punched the pillow.

Gabe MacGowan loved her. She *knew* that. And she also knew he was sending her away because he feared for her life.

To see his face in anger, seemingly directed at her? Yeah, that hurt. But she knew it wasn't *really* directed at her.

Gabe was absolutely terrified. Who wouldn't be? She'd met a few malevolent beings before, and they were the most unsettled and dispirited of souls. Kait's was one of the worst she'd ever experienced, and it left little wonder why Gabe feared his dead wife would do something to Allie, or maybe even to Jake. It was completely possible.

Allie understood all of that perfectly.

Pushing off the bed, she dropped to her knees and pulled the empty suitcase out from under the bed, yanked her clothes out of the drawers, and packed.

What Gabe MacGowan *didn't* realize about Allie Morgan was that, like the spirited souls she advocated for, she couldn't be made to do anything she didn't want to do. Or vice versa.

And by God, she didn't want to leave Odin's Thumb, Sealladh na Mara, or Gabe and Jake Mac-Gowan.

And all the family in between.

She loved them. Loved them all.

And she was *in love* with Gabe.

They had unfinished business.

They were unsettled.

And she wasn't going to stop until she'd made it all right.

Allie raced around the room and grabbed what few things she had, pulled on a pair of jeans and a long-sleeved tee, and finished stuffing her suitcase. She glanced at her watch. Only fifteen minutes had passed since Gabe's order to pack.

Pulling her hair into a ponytail, she dug out her NCSU baseball cap, threaded her hair through the hole in the back, and settled it on snugly. She ran across the hall, brushed her teeth and washed her face, and then hurried back over to the room. Zipping the suitcase, she pulled it to the stairs, picked it up, and trotted to the first floor.

There stood all the Odin's lot, waiting, their faces long and sad.

She'd let them stay long and sad. If any of them knew what she was up to, they'd probably tattle.

The friar pushed his cowl back and looked at her with unshed tears. "My dear, this is so sudden. I'm certain Himself will change his mind."

"*Oui*, miss. I think you should consider having speech with him once he's calmed down a bit," said Mademoiselle Bedeau. She snugged the ribbon beneath her chin and sniffed. "Perhaps had we known

Kait's soul was coming to Gabe. We thought he was having naught but bad dreams."

"Kait's soul has just begun appearing to Gabe," said Justin. "Until now, it has only been nightmares." He looked at Allie. "Settle down, lass. We can talk some sense into the lad."

Allie smiled at all the Odin's spirits. They'd all become friends. And no way was she letting on to what she was about to do. Justin, for one, wouldn't allow it, if he knew. She looked at them all. "You have been wonderful," she said with a sigh, "but I don't think there's any changing of Himself's mind. You didn't see him up there." She inclined her head. "He meant it when he told me to leave."

Justin Catesby met her gaze. "And he always means what he says, aye?"

Allie gave a soft smile. "He does."

Glancing around, and not seeing Gabe, Allie thought the best thing to do would be to just leave. If she had to endure little Jake's tears, she just might not be able to accomplish what needed to be done.

To settle Kait's soul whether she wanted it settled or not . . .

With a winsome grin, because she didn't know when the next time she'd see the inside of Odin's would be, Allie said her good-byes. "You talk to Dauber. Apparently he knows how to shift places rather well. And you can come to see me anytime you please."

Mademoiselle Bedeau hiccupped. The friar sniffed. The two lords gave a solemn bow of the head and Justin kept his back turned.

"Come on, Dauber," Allie said. "Let's go."

And with that, they did. She'd have to let Dauber in on her plan, of course, or that busybody would be wondering why she hadn't boarded the plane to take her home.

* * *

Gabe returned from taking Jake to his mum and da's and started up the steps to the second floor of Odin's. His head pounded.

He didna want Allie Morgan to leave at all. Christ Almighty, he loved her.

But she had to.

Kait's spirit had crossed a barrier she'd not crossed until tonight. Haunting Gabe was one thing.

Threatening the life of the woman he loved was quite another. Now he also feared for Jake's well-being, too.

When he got to Allie's room, the door sat ajar. He pushed it open, only to find it verra empty. He wasted no time in rushing downstairs. When he got there, the Odin's lot, minus Justin Catesby and Dauber, stood near the door.

"Where's Allie?" Gabe asked.

"You told her to leave," said the friar. "So she did."

The others glowered at him.

"I didna mean for her to set off in the middle of the night alone," Gabe said, glancing round. "Where'd she go?"

"To Wee Mary's," said Lord Killigrew. "She walked."

Gabe didna wait to find out anything else. He hadn't meant for Allie to just *leave*.

Pushing back out of Odin's, Gabe ran up the walk and round the corner to the small lane Wee Mary lived on. He raced to the door and knocked.

Wee Mary peered out, a frown affixed to her face. "Aye?"

"Can I come in, Auntie?" Gabe said.

Wee Mary's eyes narrowed. "Dunna *Auntie* me, boy. If 'tis Allie you're wantin' to see, then too bad. She doesna want to see you at all."

Gabe blinked. He hadn't expected that.

Wee Mary cocked her head. "Unless you've come to your bloody senses and changed your mind about her leavin'?"

Gabe rubbed his eyes. "Nay, I havena changed my mind." He met Wee Mary's gaze. "I . . . just want to say good-bye, aye?"

Mary's frown deepened. "You should have said your good-byes before you tossed her out on her wee ear!"

Gabe sighed and pinched the bridge of his nose. "I have my reasons."

Wee Mary wasna letting him through that door for love or money.

Again, he heaved a sigh. "The cabbie will be here at nine sharp to pick her up. Her tickets are at the airport in Inverness." He looked at his wee little aunt and gave a solemn smile. "Make sure she goes, Wee Mary, aye? Her life depends on it."

Chapter 29

"Och, come away from the window, love. He might see you," said Wee Mary.

Allie watched Gabe leave. The look of misery etched in his features made her heart hurt. She'd been on the other side of the door as he'd pleaded with Wee Mary to let him inside. Allie had drawn all her strength together to keep from throwing open the door and catapulting herself into his arms. Even in the dark and in the low light from the porch, his face looked drawn and she could see that the dark circles beneath his eyes were back. She prayed it wouldn't be long before that look disappeared from his handsome face forever.

When Gabe rounded the corner, Allie moved from the window.

"Now, love," said Wee Mary, patting her arm and tugging her to the sofa. "Have a wee rest. You've several hours before the cab arrives."

Mary crossed the room, scooted down the hall, and brought back a pillow and blanket. She set them on the sofa beside Allie and glanced over at her two companions. "Now you lads will have to find somethin' to do with yourselves whilst she rests. She's got a busy day ahead of her."

Dauber and Justin stood a few feet away. Allie

smiled. "That's okay, Wee Mary. I don't mind if they stay. Conjure up a couple of stools, guys, so you're not just standing over me."

And so they did.

Wee Mary reached with her hand and gently grasped Allie's chin, lifting her head to meet her gaze. "That boy loves you, lass. I could see it in his face how badly he didna want you to leave. So dunna go gettin' yourself hurt, aye? I'd never forgive myself for schemin' behind Gabe's back if you did."

Allie grabbed Wee Mary's hand and gave it a gentle squeeze. "I know, and I appreciate your help. I promise to be safe."

Wee Mary nodded. "Good, then." She cocked her head. "But tell me, lass. Why is it you have to go out on the water at such an hour as one in the mornin'?"

Allie sighed. "Because I'm pretty sure that's what time Kait died."

Wee Mary shook her head. "That girl was indeed in a frightful mess when she lived, mopin' about, wouldna work, and hardly paid little Jake a bit of attention after she had him. Of course she and Gabe together, with both of their miseries and bad choices combined . . ." She let her words trail with a slight shake of her head. "I felt sorry for her, actually. But what made her become so horrid in death?" She glanced at Justin and Dauber. "Look at these two. Gentle as kittens, they are, and look just as scrumptious now as they did in life. Neither would hurt a fly."

Justin lifted a brow.

Allie leaned back against the sofa. "I think it's guilt, Wee Mary. Guilt for turning her back on her son when she was alive, and from what I've learned about dispirited souls, the more guilt they experienced in life, the more they experience in death, as well. And in death, the guilt makes them despondent—they can't change the past." She glanced at Justin. "They become malevolent, with even a bit more power than your average happy-go-lucky unsettled soul. It uses a mortal's power against them. To make them do something against their will."

Wee Mary tsked. "Och, lass, then be even more cautious, aye?"

Allie smiled. "I will. Now get some sleep. And thank you again."

Wee Mary returned the smile and headed back to bed.

"How can you know you'll be able to reach her?"

Allie looked at Justin. His voice had lost the usual charisma it carried. He was dead serious.

"There's not been a malevolent soul Allie couldn't reach," said Dauber. "I've seen her deal with the nastiest of souls."

Justin's jaw clenched, much in the same way as Gabe's. He regarded her for several seconds. "That soul of Kait's is verra dangerous, lass. Had I known that she was appearing before Gabe as she was this eve, I would never have allowed you such closeness with her. She's gained power, Allie. She can hurt you."

Allie pulled one of the sofa's soft throw pillows to her chest and wrapped her arms around it. "I don't believe in pure evil, Justin. I just don't. And where Kait is concerned?" She shook her head. "I think what's happened is her guilt has grown and grown to such enormity, and that watching Jake grow up without her, and watching Gabe turn his life around and be such a huge influence in Jake's life, has made her become even more embittered and guilt-ridden. All of those unsettled emotions have taken over her and her true soul is lost." She met his gaze. "She can't help it."

Justin leaned back, stretched out his long legs, and

crossed one booted foot over the other. He stroked his goatee as he stared at her. "I dunna think I've ever come across such an extraordinary woman before—in life or unlife—as you, Allie Morgan." A small grin lifted his mouth. "You amaze me."

Allie felt herself blush. "You're crazy, Justin Catesby."

"And you, Allie Morgan," he said, his face again serious, "had better be glad I'm a mere spirit and no' a live man." After a moment of studying her in silence, he gave a slight smile. "Gabe MacGowan is a lucky lad, indeed."

Allie simply smiled in response. "I'm pretty darn lucky, too," she said. "How many other girls get to have such an assortment of fantastic friends?"

Justin sighed. "Again with the friends. I swear, lass, were I no' already deceased, you'd be the death of me." He glanced at Dauber, who'd been sitting quietly. "Quite tenacious, aye?"

Dauber exchanged a look with Allie. "You don't know the half of it."

Allie rested her head back and closed her eyes. She knew she wouldn't be able to fully give in to sleep, but she'd need rest to get through the next twenty-four hours.

She prayed she wouldn't screw things up.

Never had Gabe tested his self-control more than now.

Except, of course, each and every time he'd been alone with Allie Morgan. To touch her, kiss her until his heart nearly hammered out of his chest? That hadna been a test of self-control; that had been pure torture.

Sleep wouldn't come. After being sent home by Wee Mary, Gabe had come back to Odin's, paced for

nearly an hour before retreating to his workshop. All
he could think about was Allie. He'd sent her home.
He'd told her it was a mistake to have brought her to
Sealladh na Mara.

It was only partially true.

Christ knows he didna want her to leave. But after
witnessing what his dead wife was capable of doing?
Jesus, he'd no' realized Kait had gained so much
power. He could handle being tormented in his sleep,
as well as the frequent visits by his dead wife. But
to have his loved ones threatened? No' if he could
help it.

Aye, Allie Morgan needed to leave Sealladh na
Mara and never come back.

He didna have to bloody like it.

Gabe glanced at the chiseled chunk of marble in his
hand. He'd nearly ground it into a heap of powder.

Glancing at the clock over the workbench, Gabe set
his marble aside, stood, and stretched. He wasna sure
if Kait could find Jake or Allie on her own—she
seemed to appear only where he happened to be. He'd
thought it safe to take Jake to his parents, and Allie
to Wee Mary's to await her cab.

He wanted one last look at her. A self-destructive
act, he knew. It would tear him up inside to see her
leave. But Christ, it wasna safe here. Not anymore.

Gabe crossed the floor to the small sink in the corner and washed the marble dust from his hands. He'd
fancied the idea that having Allie by his side would
ease the hauntings of his wife to at least a tolerable
level. He could live with it. He would have lived with
it, had Kait no' turned her malevolence toward Jake
and Allie. He couldna control her dispirited self and
by Christ, he wouldna have the two things he held
dearest to his heart in Kait's destructive path.

With a deep breath, he collected his thoughts and

left. 'Twould be dawn soon; he'd row until almost time for Allie to leave; then he'd return, make sure she left Sealladh na Mara safely, and then prepare for Odin's lunch crowd.

His heart heavy, Gabe dressed and made for the wharf.

Sobriety was a piece of cake compared to losing Allie Morgan.

"Here, love. Have some tea, aye? 'Twill calm your jitters a wee bit."

Allie smiled and accepted the tea from Leona's mother, Cora, where the cab had taken her after picking her up from Wee Mary's. It would be her hideout from Gabe until time to leave. "Thank you, Cora. And thanks for going along with our big plan."

"Och, 'tis my pleasure, lass. Gabe was always a favorite lad of mine round the village, and he's a fine young man now and I'd love nothin' more than to see him happy. Now make yourselves at home and I'll be just in the kitchen if you need me." With a smile, she left.

"I daresay 'tis a long afternoon," said Justin. "The whole bloody thing unnerves me, though. I'll be happy to see it done."

"It sounds like you have confidence in me," said Allie, sipping the steaming cup of tea.

Justin gave her a half grin.

"I'm not sure if it's a good idea for you two to go along, though. It might upset Kait, and the less irate her spirit is, the better chance I have of reaching through to her."

Justin and Dauber both gave her a frown. Justin leaned forward. "If you think for a solid bloody second I'd allow you to traipse out into the loch to lure an unsettled soul such as Kait's, you're mad."

"I agree," said Dauber. "It's not even an option, young lady."

With a heavy sigh, Allie agreed. "I know, I know." She gave them a smile. "You guys are great for hanging out with me here. I really appreciate it."

And she meant it, too. After turning her head and looking out the rear of the cab, and seeing Gabe standing at the end of the lane, watching her leave? She might not have been able to see his features clearly, but she'd *felt* him. Sorrow had rolled off him in thick waves and she'd sensed it clear to her bones. It'd hurt—actually physically *hurt*.

It pained her more to know she caused Gabe such grief.

Hopefully, though, she'd be able to erase that sorrowful look from his handsome face. No more would he be tormented, nor would little Jake have to suffer, either. And if everything went as planned, poor Kait's soul would be released from its own tormented prison, as well. *Soon.* Very soon.

"No' soon enough, to my notion," said Justin.

Allie scowled. "Stay out of my thoughts, Catesby."

He barked out a laugh. "As you wish, lass."

"Why don't we play a round of cards?" suggested Dauber. "Allie, do you have your deck?"

Allie pulled her duffel bag close, unzipped it, and fished out the cards she'd purchased at the petrol station. "Right here."

"Great," Justin said, cracking his knuckles and conjuring his and Dauber's own deck. "I have a score to settle with you regarding our last game and we've all afternoon to do it."

With that, Allie settled her thoughts on playing cards with two sweet-spirited souls who tried their very best to lighten the mood and take her mind off what was to come.

*   *   *

Gabe listened to the message on Allie's voice mail requesting the caller to try back again, for the fifth bloody time, and hung up the phone. He'd only wanted to hear her voice, to make sure she'd landed safely and that she had made it back home.

'Twas obvious, she was ignoring him.

He probably acted like a stalker. Kicking her out of his life and then begging her to pick up the phone? *Insanity*.

There'd been no other choice.

Glancing at the clock, he was surprised to find it already half past one in the morning. Kait must have known he'd sent Allie home and was giving him a brief break in tormenting.

That, he guessed, would go on forever, the tormenting, as long as Allie was out of his life.

Maybe 'twas what he deserved after all?

Deciding to wait until later in the morning to try Allie's phone again, Gabe clicked off the light and left the office.

No sooner had he made it to the kitchen than a pounding at Odin's front door made him jump. He hurried down the short hallway, flung open the door, and nearly fell over when he saw his mum on the other side, wringing her hands, her face pale and drawn. He grasped her arms gently.

And before he could even ask what the matter was, she told him.

" 'Tis Jake, lad—he's gone!"

A cold fist grabbed Gabe's throat. "What do you mean, he's gone?"

His mother sniffed, and her voice cracked. "I dunno—I heard him get up, and I thought he was getting a drink of water, and when I checked on him—"

" 'Tis okay, Mum." He gave her shoulders a quick squeeze. "Calm down. I'll find him."

Gabe turned to grab his jacket from the hook on the wall, and Justin's sudden appearance made him swear. "Damn it, man, what's wrong with you?" Gabe said, pushing his arms into the sleeves of his leather jacket.

Justin Catesby's expression brought Gabe up short. "What is it?" he asked, his heart plummeting.

Justin's jaw tensed. "Your son and woman are both in the loch," he said. "And you'd better hurry or you'll see neither alive again."

Gabe stared at Justin. "What do you mean, my woman? She left."

Justin shook his head. "Nay. She didna. Now hurry."

Gabe simply ran. With his mother's sobs trailing after him and his heart pounding out of his chest, Gabe pushed out of Odin's at a full run and made for the wharf.

Chapter 30

As Allie rowed with all her strength, the wind picked up and blew with such an unnatural force that it all but made the small dinghy capsize.

Allie felt pretty sure that was Kait's intention. She was doing her best to keep Allie from reaching Jake.

She'd underestimated not only Kait's soul's power, but her own inability to deal with such a malevolent soul.

And that thought alone made her heart sink.

Just up the shoreline from Sealladh na Mara, a small, nondescript island of trees sat in the loch. With the full moon hanging over the crags, a bright, luminescent light spilled over the pines and hardwoods, and onto the water.

Kait had lured Jake onto the water, and Allie's muscles burned with each pull of the oars as she tried to reach him. Kait wanted her son back, wanted Jake to join her. Allie should have *known* that. So Jake had taken Gabe's rowboat and was headed straight for the island. Over the wind, Allie yelled to get his attention. "Jake! Wait!"

Things had gone terribly wrong. She'd not had even the slightest suspicion Kait would lure her own child into the sea. Allie had left Cora's as planned, taken her husband's small dinghy, and rowed out into the loch in the direction Kait was last seen the night she'd died. She'd expected the dispirited soul to come to her, had fully anticipated on a struggle, a fight, but hadn't counted on little Jake being in danger.

How very wrong she'd been.

And she'd sent Justin to get Gabe, and Dauber to be with Jake.

Soaked to the bone, Allie rowed fiercely toward the island and Gabe's little son. The wind surrounded only her, thank God, and as she rowed, she kept her eye trained on Jake. The moon loomed exceptionally low and cast so much light that Allie could fully see him. Not his features, but *him*. Miraculously, she grew closer.

And that's when Kait's fury unleashed, and she appeared.

In a silvery slip of rotting hair and skin, Kait's gruesome features seemed even more frightening in the moonlight. Still transparent, the black space where one eye used to be glared sightlessly as Kait hovered over Allie's boat, and then she appeared close to her face. Allie held her place, awaiting an attack. She glanced at Jake. Relief washed over her to see the little guy still in Gabe's rowboat. She decided to say what she'd come to say to Kait.

"Kait," she hollered over the wind, continuing to row toward Jake, "you have to let go! I know it wasn't your fault! Please, let Gabe and Jake live in peace—"

NO! I want him! I want my son!

Allie drew a deep breath. "You didn't kill yourself on purpose, did you, Kait?" she yelled. "Trust me! I can help you!"

Go away! I want my boy—

"I won't go away!" shouted Allie. "I love them

both, too! If you love Jake, you'll let him live! You don't want him to die in the water like you did, do you? It's cold here, and awful!"

Only the wind whipping overhead made any noise. Allie stared into the ghastly face of Gabe's dead wife. "I know you must have felt so much despair, Kait. It was a bad time in your life, wasn't it?" Allie waited, still keeping an eye on Jake, who simply sat in the rowboat, watching. "We all make mistakes, Kait—"

He wanted me to die . . . told me to do it . . .

Allie knew Kait meant Gabe. The amount of pain and anguish she sensed in Kait's dispirited soul nearly choked her. No wonder she'd become so vicious and malevolent. "Gabe didn't mean it, Kait. No one wanted you to die!" she shouted over the wind. So close to Jake now . . .

I didna mean to . . .

Then Kait glanced with her one good eye toward Jake, and her voice changed a little; the wind died somewhat. *I miss my son so verra much . . .*

"I know you do," Allie said. "But leave him here—"

He hates me now because of you!

And just that fast, Kait's mood changed.

And in the next breath, Kait shifted from Allie's presence to Jake's, and Allie watched in horror as the wind changed directions, surrounding the little boy who stood up in the boat, then jumped into the loch.

"No!" Allie cried out, and without thinking of anything else, she dived into the icy water. With her arms and legs pumping, she swam toward where Jake had jumped in, and when he went under, so did she. Blindly, Allie felt for him. The water was dark—so dark that she couldn't see anything except the moonlit surface above. In her mind, she cried for Gabe to hurry, and she screamed and pleaded for Kait to listen.

Kait! Please, I beg you, let your son go. He loves you and he loves his dad and family here. You can make things right now, by letting him go! All of the mistakes can be forgotten! You can rest your soul! Allie screamed to Kait in her mind. *Your dying was an accident, wasn't it?*

Just then, Allie felt an arm, and she grabbed on to it and started kicking toward the surface. They weren't under far, but Kait had indeed lured them beneath the sea's surface and had a grip on Allie so forceful she nearly couldn't swim at all. Her lungs burned and her muscles screamed, but she kicked and kicked. *Let us go!* she screamed to Kait once more. *With your soul healed, Jake's memory of you will be healed, as well! He loves you, Kait, and he keeps your picture by his bedside . . .*

Kait suddenly let go.

Allie didn't ponder why. She broke the surface of the water, little Jake in her arms, both of their teeth clacking from the cold, and Allie began to swim. The shore of the island lay a mere twenty feet or so, but it felt like twenty miles. When she found her footing, she shoved toward the pebbles and sand, dragging Jake behind her. Gripping him around his waist, she heaved one last time and pushed him up onto the beach. Dauber was there, pacing and wringing his hands.

"Alll-lie," Jake said, his voice quivering from the cold. "Tell my mum I do love her, and I didna m-mean to say I hated h-her in private. I didna mean it!"

Allie, her own lips quaking, gave Jake what she hoped looked like a comforting smile. "I will, sweetheart. Your dad's on his way—"

"Allie!" cried Jake.

Just as Allie was suddenly pulled back toward the water and swept back under.

Allie struggled, but Kait's soul was too strong. Jake's little voice drifted away as Allie dropped farther under the surface of the loch.

Gabe sped to the little island, the boat's small spotlight adding a beam to the surface of the already lit-up water. Never had he felt so scared in his entire life as he did now.

"Just there," Justin said. "To that small isle."

The boat's beam picked up a small figure at the shore. "Jake!" Gabe yelled. "Jake!" His heart leapt with relief.

"Da!" his son hollered back. The boy jumped up and down. "Hurry!"

Gabe killed the engine and ran the boat up onto the pebbled shore. Before it stopped he jumped out, grabbed his son, and pulled him into a fierce hug.

"Da, let me go!" Jake cried, wiggling and pushing away.

Gabe let go and held his son's shoulders steady. "What's wrong with you, boy?"

"Allie's in the water, Da!" he cried, pointing and running to the water's edge. "She went below!"

"Stay with him," Gabe told Justin and Dauber, and then ran to the boat, reached into the supply box below the bow, and grabbed an underwater lantern, then turned and dived into the freezing November water.

Christ, please let her be alive . . .

Gabe swam out several feet, then plunged below the surface of the water. Kicking, he swept the beam of light frantically as he searched for Allie. It was dark as night; he saw very little other than floating bits of sea life.

He turned to the right, to the left, sweeping the lantern beam in every direction. He kicked to the surface, drew in a lungful of air, then went below again. The salt water stung his eyes but he ignored it. He had to find Allie. *Now.*

Then a thought crossed his mind.

Kait! Please, let her go! he thought. *'Tisna her fault, Kait. She only wants to help!*

Suddenly before him was Kait's form. Sea-sodden and deathly, she hovered close, inspecting, weighing. Waiting.

I'm sorry for all of it, Kait. I didna mean for you to die. I dunna blame you and I know it was an accident . . .

Out of air, Gabe kicked to the surface and drew another breath. Below, Kait waited on him, floating, staring, saying nothing.

Please give her back to me, Gabe said. *Jesus, please give her back. She can help you. You've got to forgive yourself, Kait, and I beg you, please forgive me . . .*

Kait met his gaze, then lowered her head and drifted away, out of the beam of Gabe's lantern. He swept the beam through the water, and just when he thought his lungs would burst, he saw her.

Christ Almighty, she looked dead.

She'd saved his son's life.

Kicking hard toward her, Gabe grabbed Allie by the waist and pushed toward the water's surface. As soon as they broke free, he kicked harder, swimming for the shoreline. Finally, he found footing and dragged her to the beach. He tossed the lantern and laid her on her back.

She didna move. Didna breathe.

Jake, Dauber, and Justin, now accompanied by the friar, Lords Ramsey and Killigrew, along with Mademoiselle Bedeau, stood around him, silent.

"Allie!" Gabe shouted, and grabbed her by the shoulders and shook. Still, she didn't move. "Allie, please! Come back to me, love!" He shook her some more. "Allie!"

All at once, she sputtered, and Gabe turned her onto her side as she spewed seawater, choking and coughing and sucking in large gulps of air. Before her eyes found his, she grabbed his hand and pushed something into it.

"It's Kait's," she said, her voice quivering from the cold. "She led me to it. It's for Jake."

Gabe lifted Allie onto his lap and pulled her into a fierce, although wet, embrace. With his free hand he pulled his son close, too. Over Jake's shoulder, he opened his hand and peered at the object Allie had given him.

'Twas a small heart on a chain. A locket. He'd open it later, for inside he knew he'd find a small picture of Kait on one side, and an infant Jake on the other. Kait had worn it constantly, despite her misery for life.

And she'd been wearing it the day she died.

Over Jake's shoulder a slip of mist appeared. No complete form, just a simple wisp of mist. A sensation of peace settled over Gabe, and Jake turned his head. Allie snuggled close.

"Thank you," Gabe whispered, knowing the form was Kait, that she was no longer malevolent, and that her hideous form had disappeared.

Jake stuck out a hand and as the form began to fade, he waved. "Bye, Mum."

And the mist sifted into the night.

"Let's get you three home and in front of a fire, aye?" said Justin, who'd knelt beside Allie. "All of your lips are blue and I swear I cannot steer that bloody vessel of yours, MacGowan."

Gabe stood, pulling his two beloveds with him. He

held them both so close he could feel their hearts beating. He pressed his lips to Allie's temple and kissed her. "Are you okay?" he asked softly. "You're freezing."

"I'm fine now," she said, her arm resting against his chest. "Much better now."

"I'll never let you go again, Allie Morgan," he said. "Christ, I'll never let you go."

Gabe loaded his son and woman into the boat, pulled out the only thing to wrap around them—a tarp—and headed toward Sealladh na Mara's wharf.

He and Jake—and Kait's soul—were finally free.

And Kait's soul had been mended by a selfless, loving soul who simply wouldna give up. *His* Allie. She'd no' turned her back on Kait, even in her darkest moment. She'd made Kait realize she'd no' meant to die on purpose, and that her son still loved her. It made Gabe love Allie even more.

The Odin's Thumb lot disappeared, along with Dauber.

And Gabe, Allie, and Jake headed home.

The rest of the night settled down to a slow pace. After they'd all had hot showers and gotten warm clothes, Wee Mary and Laina seated them all before large bowls of steaming porridge and tea. Once their tummies were full, they all gathered in the lobby before a roaring peat fire. With the Odin's lot, plus Dauber, gathered around, they warmed up, talked, and once Jake fell asleep between Allie and Gabe, Laina took him up and put him to bed. When she returned, Allie told them what she'd learned from Kait.

"She was a very sad soul, and the guilt for neglecting little Jake when he was born ate at her in life and in death." She shook her head and looked into Gabe's eyes. "She didn't kill herself. She just simply wanted to escape the misery for a while and thought she could handle the boat. When she lost an oar, and stood up to reach for it, she capsized and went into the water. With her drinking, her senses had become slow and dull." Allie held Gabe's hand, their fingers laced. "She fought, but she drowned. And that misery and guilt is what made her so despondent."

"I think you reached her," Gabe said, putting his arm around her and pulling her close. "She seemed at peace, finally."

"Do you think we'll ever see the poor lass again?" asked Wee Mary.

Allie shrugged. "It's hard to say. We might not see her, but she may very well show herself to Jake." She glanced at Justin, Dauber, and the others. "But I felt her guilt ease, and it wouldn't surprise me a bit to one day come across a very different soul of Kait Mac-Gowan."

After a little more chatting, Wee Mary and Laina rose. "Well, lads and lassies, we best be off," said Mary. "Sister, shall you stay at my house tonight?"

"Oh, goody, a sleepover," Laina said. "Aye, sounds fine to me."

"Lads, an escort?" said Mary.

Lords Ramsey and Killigrew both jumped up. "Aye, our pleasure," they both said.

"We'll have a nice hand of cards awaitin' you," said Justin, making his way to the corner alcove—a favorite card-playing spot, so it seemed. "Ladies, good night."

Gabe rose and walked his mother and auntie to the door. With a kiss and hug from each, he saw them out the door, their ghostly escorts in tow.

When he returned, Gabe sank down onto the sofa beside Allie and pulled her close, her head resting on his chest. She could hear his breath moving through his lungs with each intake and exhale of air, and his heart beating against her ear made her own beat faster.

He slipped his arms around her waist and rested them against her stomach. "I want to do something tomorrow, and I'd like you to be included."

"What's that?" she said.

"Kait had a small burial in Sealladh na Mara's cemetery after her death, but I'd like to have a ceremony at sea." He kissed her head. "You're an amazin' woman, Allie Morgan. You've given my son a reason no' to hate his mum, even after everything he saw. He understands she loved him—just no' herself. You're the most unselfish person I've ever known." He turned her then, grasped her chin, and looked at her. "There's something else I want to do."

Allie wiggled her brows. "Do tell, before the friar overhears and separates us."

Gabe chuckled, the deep sound rumbling in his chest. " 'Tis a surprise, lass. We'll go tomorrow afternoon. Aye?"

Allie smiled. "That's most definitely an aye."

Gabe's eyes sparkled mischief.

He didn't say anything else.

Chapter 31

The next morning, nearly the entire town had turned out for Kait's burial at sea. Before they'd left, Allie had called home, had spoken to her mother and Boe, and this time Emma, as well, and let them in on everything going on at Sealladh na Mara. Frightened at first because of the terrifying experiences with Kait, and then thrilled to hear of her relationship with Gabe and Jake, Sara Morgan had cried on the phone for her eldest daughter. Tears of fear and joy at the same time. Allie had promised to call them later, once she returned to shore.

Gabe had kept Jake out of school, and with the help of Jeff, the ferryman, loaded nearly the entire village of Sealladh na Mara onto the vessel, and gone to the very spot where Kait had drowned. The sun slipped out from behind the clouds and shone brightly, making the water dance and sparkle. Friar Drew Digby had led a small sermon, sending Kait prayers of peace and serenity, and little Jake read a small letter he'd written to his mum. After a word of prayer, they'd laced the sea's surface with flowers; Jake placed his small note in a bottle, capped it, and dropped it in, as well.

Allie had slipped a peek at Gabe, whose expression revealed little—except to her. She could sense his acceptance of Kait's actions, her mistakes—as well as his own. That day, he didn't just forgive his wife, but he forgave *himself*.

It made Allie's heart soar.

After the ceremony, the ferry chugged back to Sealladh na Mara, where the folks hustled back to their businesses, and life went on as usual for a Friday midmorning.

Except for the ferryman, Jeff. Who simply waited at the wharf, smoking a pipe.

There was something decidedly different in the air. Allie could tell. She just couldn't tell *what*.

Back at Odin's, Wee Mary and Laina took over the kitchen. Gabe grinned, brought Allie her coat, and pulled her to the door. "My sweet auntie and mum have the lunch crowd taken care of."

"Where are we going?" Allie said, laughing.

Gabe stopped, slipped her jacket on her, and kept his eyes trained on hers. "You'll see."

He slowly buttoned her peacoat, and at the top, his fingers stilled, his gaze deepened, his green eyes grew smoky. He leaned into her, and his mouth settled over hers in a slow, erotic kiss. When he pulled back, Allie's heart slammed into her chest.

"Let's go."

And so they did.

Gabe grabbed her hand and led her at a fast pace down the walk, past Leona's, who stopped them, handed Gabe two white paper bags of *something*, two thermoses of *something*, and then shot them both a knowing smile filled with *something*. They continued on.

At the wharf, Jeff the ferryman gave a nod and led them to the small dock where the ferry sat anchored. Allie threw a questioning look at Gabe, who merely smiled, shrugged, and led her on board. He took her straight to the bow, deposited their foodstuff in a small container, and pulled her into his arms.

Allie settled against his chest, his chin resting on her shoulder, and the scruff of his jaw brushing hers made her just snuggle closer. So she did. His lips smiled against her ear. "Do you notice anything special, lass?"

Allie sighed. "Yeah, the friar's not here, trying to pull us apart."

Gabe kissed her lobe. "Exactly."

Allie's knees turned mushy.

With a few short blasts of the horn, the ferry began to move.

Although it was still very chilly, the sun shot warm rays of light through the sparse clouds, and the wind felt crisp against Allie's skin. With Gabe's warmth around her, she wasn't cold a bit.

When he kissed her neck, as he was doing now? Quite the opposite.

She was burning up.

The ferry skirted the shoreline and traveled north, and the dramatic scenery took Allie's breath away. Gabe showed her several landmarks, including a circle of ancient standing stones, high on a cliff. He promised to take her there.

She couldn't wait.

"Allie, turn round."

She did, and leaned her back against the railing. She looked up, wondering at the look of intensity that clenched his jaws, turned his eyes darker. She cocked her head. "What's wrong?"

Gabe looked down at her, his eyes searching her face. With his thumb, he slid it along her jaw, over her chin, and across her lips. He watched his movement with a look of fascination in his eye. Finally, he lifted his gaze back to hers. "I never thought I'd be truly happy. Content, aye. I could be content with my family, my son. Sealladh na Mara. But happy and fulfilled, in here?" He lifted her hand and placed it over his heart. "No' until I met you, Allie Morgan."

Allie's heart sang at his words. She started to tell him so, but a finger over her lips hushed her.

"I am so in love wi' you it makes me ache inside," he said, his brogue deepening. "You've swept into my life, Jake's life, my family—we've all been affected by you, lass. Especially me."

Allie blinked. His brutal honesty and admission of things guys usually wouldn't admit to stunned her. Gabe was a man's man. He was big, scruffy, not so much the sensitive type but more the totally honest type, she supposed.

He was being honest now.

It made her breath catch.

Just then, the horn blasted, and Jeff the ferryman's voice came over the intercom, gruff, deeply brogued, and clear. "Turn to starboard, Allie Morgan!"

Allie glanced at Gabe, whose jaw flinched. His eyes twinkled. And she turned to starboard.

There, on a nearby island—more like a large copse, really—stood two large poles jammed into the ground, and stretched between them, a big sign. The words MARRY ME, ALLIE MORGAN were painted in bright red.

She gasped and covered her mouth. The longer she stared at that white sign with red lettering that said MARRY ME, ALLIE MORGAN, the more tears built in her eyes. She felt herself shaking, and she gripped the rail of the ferry hard to try to stop that shaking. It didn't work.

"Allie," whispered Gabe against her ear, kissing the lobe, his warm breath making goose bumps rise on her skin. "Say aye, love. Marry me. I swear you willna regret it."

Slowly, Allie turned and leaned against the rail. Her breath came fast, and as she looked into Gabe's eyes, she knew how deeply she'd fallen in love with the Highlander.

But it still frightened her. She wasn't a whole woman.

"You know I can't have children," she said, scared the reminder would change his mind. "It's not a misdiagnosis, Gabe. I've had surgery. I can't conceive. Ever."

Gabe took both hands and placed them on either side of her jaw. He tilted her head to better look at her and studied her for several seconds. It seemed like hours.

"You were sent to me, Allie Morgan. Sent to me and Jake. You were made just for us, and I would be honored for you to be my son's mother." He brushed his lips over hers and whispered, "Christ, I'm in love wi' you. Please say aye."

Allie's heart soared, and she wrapped her arms around Gabe's neck and pressed her lips against his.

How could she reject a proposal like that?

She *couldn't*.

"Aye, Gabe MacGowan, I'll marry you," she said, and kissed him. Then she pulled back. "It is more than an honor for me to be Jake's mother."

Gabe embraced her tightly, grasped her jaw with one hand, tilted her head just so, and met her gaze. His green eyes had softened, and they stared right into her soul. "You've made me complete, Allie Morgan."

And then he turned to the little window where Jeff the ferryman sat behind the ship's wheel, gave a thumbs-up, and Jeff let out five long blasts on the horn.

Gabe shouted and punched the air as the horn blew. "Aye! She said *aye*!" He laughed and swung her around, her feet leaving the wooden deck. "Woo-hoo! I'm gettin' married!"

Allie laughed and marveled at the change in Gabe MacGowan. It literally stole her breath.

He stopped then, settled her against the rail, and held her close. His eyes searched hers, and he gave her a smile that reflected in his eyes. "You've made me a happy man, you ken?" he said. "You've mended my soul, Allie Morgan." He grasped her hand in his, and withdrew something from the pocket of his leather jacket. Gently, he straightened her finger and eased on the most beautiful ring Allie had ever seen. A silver band with a square setting and a modest solitaire diamond, it fit her perfectly in every way. " 'Twas my granny's, and I'd be honored if you wore it."

She stroked the antique ring and smiled up at him. "I love it."

Then he kissed her. Slow, deep, and so sensual Allie thought the friar would pop up at any second. Gabe's hand stilled on her hip, and he rested his forehead against hers. "*Tapadh leat*," he whispered in Gaelic.

"What's that mean?" she asked.

He looked at her, his eyes filled with joy. "Thank you."

Allie kissed Gabe then, and they stayed wrapped tight in each other's arms until the ferry reached Sealladh na Mara's wharf.

Hand in hand they walked up the lane, back to Odin's Thumb. When they walked in, Allie was surprised to see it packed with *everyone*. They stared, silent. No one said a word.

And then the entire crowd, ghostly and mortal, erupted in a deafening cheer.

Thanks to Jeff the ferryman, and his blasting horn, the village of Sealladh na Mara knew Allie's answer.

Gabe grinned, then laughed, and pulled Allie close. "She said aye!" he hollered, just in case anyone missed the blasts.

And once the crowd settled in at Odin's Thumb, including the spirited souls sitting amongst the townspeople, they all cheered again. Wee Mary and Laina rushed over, raining kisses on Gabe's and Allie's cheeks.

Little Jake jumped down from his seat in the alcove, next to Justin, and rushed across the floor to Allie. He threw his arms around her waist and hugged her tight.

Allie bent down, and hugged him proper. The little guy wrapped his arms around her neck and whispered in her ear, "I am ever so happy to have you as my other mum. And I thank you for mending me da's soul, Allie Morgan."

Allie didn't think her heart could fly any higher. The two men she loved most stood beside her. An entire family had accepted her into their fold as their own, as well as the entire village of Sealladh na Mara.

Not to mention her new spirited friends, as well.

Wee Mary clunked a glass against the table. "We've got a weddin' to plan!"

Cheers went up, and Allie suddenly realized she had a lot of work to do.

She glanced up and met Gabe's gaze, and she knew then she probably didn't have a whole lot of time to do it in.

Which was completely okay by her.

Chapter 32

Four weeks later

G abe paced at the front of the small Norman kirk, wearing his best kilt. The entire village had turned out for the event, as well as all the Munros, and Allie's mum and sisters. Lovely lasses, all of them.

No' nearly as lovely as his Allie.

His father had his on, too. A kilt, that is. He watched as Gabe paced.

Watched, and *smirked*.

Gabe stopped. "What is so bloody funny?"

"Shh!" hissed his da. "Watch your tongue in the house of God, lad." He grinned. "You're quite nervous, aye?"

"Of course I'm nervous." He rubbed the bridge of his nose. "What if she changes her mind?"

Silence.

When Gabe looked up, his da had changed his expression from quirky to serene. He smiled.

" 'Tis more than fine to see you so happy, son," said Gerald. "I canna think of a better mate for you."

He gave his da a nod. "I canna, either." He glanced at his watch for the hundredth time. "What's takin' so long—"

Just then, a haunting melody of a pipe drifted into

the kirk, and the priest stepped out of a side room and took his place. He nodded at Friar Digby, who joined him.

Together, they'd complete the ceremony.

Gerald took his place next to Gabe, and waited.

Gabe could barely breathe. He wondered briefly if his dress dirk was sharp enough to impale himself on . . .

Finally, the lads and lasses came through the door.

Allie's sister Emma walked with Ethan. She looked like a wee sprite wearing a blue gown beside that big oaf. And the Munro, the jackass, was smiling from ear to ear. At least he'd pulled some of that hair back. They started the procession down in the old stone church, with tiny candles lining both sides of the aisle. Candles were lit everywhere, in the alcoves, windows, and walls.

Next, Allie's sister Boe came through the door on the arm of Sean. Those two would definitely have to be watched.

Finally, Ivy Morgan came through with none other than Jake. His son looked handsome in his kilt, and he held the arm of Allie's youngest sister with the seriousness of any grown lad.

They all took their places, Ethan looked down and winked at Gabe, Sean barely contained a smirk, and Gerald lightly elbowed him.

Then the music changed.

If Gabe thought the first tune to be haunting, the one now playing topped it by meters. Allie appeared in the doorway of the kirk, and Gabe's heart hit his ribs so hard he nearly gasped.

Christ, the woman was beautiful.

She'd flown back to America briefly, and whilst there she'd chosen a gown. It was simple, elegant, an off-white silk with thin straps that clung to her narrow hips and flat stomach, and with that mass of blond curls pulled up and a tiny veil just to her chin, she simply took Gabe's breath away . . .

Dauber guided her down the aisle to him. The priest said his prayers, Dauber gave Allie away, and she and Gabe then faced each other.

Drew Digby said a few words, too, although he was a friar-in-training.

Then they joined hands. Allie's felt warm against his, and he could barely concentrate on what the priest said, he was so consumed with her.

"Do you take this woman forever, lad? To treat her with kindness and respect, and to love through all times, good and bad?"

Gabe stared into Allie's eyes. "Aye, indeed I will."

"And do you take this man forever, lass? To treat him with kindness and respect, and to love through all times, good and bad?"

Allie's eyes welled up with tears, but she smiled through them. "Yes. I will."

"Indeed, you both are truly husband and wife." The priest looked at Gabe. "You can kiss her now, boy."

The priest's words were still on Gabe's ears as he lifted Allie's veil, met her gaze, and kissed her. Shorter than what he'd like, the kiss, he smiled against her mouth and lowered his lips to her ear. "More later, love."

She sighed against him, and he thought his knees would give out from under him.

"I give you Mr. and Mrs. Gabe MacGowan," said the priest, and Gabe and Allie made their way to the end of the aisle.

As he passed Justin Catesby, the ghostly sea captain gave him a smile and a short nod. Gabe returned the gesture.

Outside, the sun was beginning its descent. The

wind had died, and the air wasn't quite as cool as it had been.

All in all, it was the most perfect day of Gabe's life.

After everyone had gathered in the little kirk's yard, congratulations went all round. Jake came up to him and Allie and motioned for the both of them to lean over. They did, and Jake whispered, "This is the best day of my life. I've got a new mum and a new da, too."

Gabe hugged his son.

Indeed, he was right.

Gabe did feel like a brand-new man.

When he looked at his wife, receiving hugs and congratulations from his people, he knew she was to blame for it.

Allie's mum, Sara, approached with all three of Allie's sisters. The wee woman took Gabe by both hands and pulled him into an embrace.

"Welcome to the family, son," she said, and looked at him. "It's good to have you."

Gabe smiled down at Allie's mum. "I am ever so grateful to have met your daughter."

"You won't think that when you hear how loud she snores," said Boe. "I should know. I had to share a room with her."

They all roared.

Emma and Ivy, along with Boe, exchanged a hug with Gabe, and then embraced Allie.

They looked more than adorable, the Morgan women.

Merri, Gabe's little sister, came next. She hugged Gabe, then threw her arms around Allie's neck. She whispered something in his bride's ear. Allie chuckled, and he'd have to remember to ask her later what his mischievous sister had said.

"Let's all go back to Odin's!" hollered Wee Mary. "Everyone's invited!"

A cheer went up in the crowd, and everyone in fact did go back to Odin's for the reception.

The trail of car lights seemed to stretch for miles.

Gabe pulled his new wife close.

He could hardly wait for the reception to be over.

Epilogue

Allie didn't think she'd laughed so much in her life. Odin's Thumb Inn and Pub was packed wall-to-wall with the wedding party.

Her mother was dancing with Justin Catesby, if that told the story of it.

Sara Morgan and her daughters had always known about Allie's ability.

They didn't realize they had it themselves.

Rather, they didn't know they could see and interact with spirited souls, other than Dauber, until arriving in Sealladh na Mara.

They'd adjusted faster than what Allie had imagined.

"We're so happy for you." Boe, Emma, and Ivy gathered around her in a sisterly hug. "And my God, your husband's hot!"

"Boe!" cried Allie, and then glanced at Gabe. "He is, isn't he?"

And he was. In his dress kilt, he was more than impressive.

He had really nice calves.

"His friends aren't so bad, either," said Ivy. "They're all so huge."

"Did you know Ethan's married to Amelia Landry?" said Emma. "I've read all her books. She's fabulous."

"Nice, too," said Allie. She glanced around. "Love

you guys, but I've gotta run." She gave them all kisses. "See ya later."

As she scooted by, making a beeline for Gabe, Justin and her mother stopped her.

"Allison, you're going to trip in that dress if you don't stop running," Sara said, grinning at Justin. "You didn't tell me you had such handsome friends."

Allie grinned at Justin. "Don't fill his head with that stuff, Mom. He's already hard to live with."

Justin chuckled.

Allie kissed her mom's cheek. "Gotta run. I'll see you guys later."

And with that she scurried off.

Gabe had already slipped out the back door and was waiting on her, with the Rover packed.

She'd almost made it to the kitchen when the rest of Odin's lot stopped her. The friar looked exceptionally happy with himself. "You look rather fetching today, young Allie," he said. "I am most happy for you and Gabe."

"Aye," said Lords Ramsey and Killigrew. "And you've fetching sisters, as well."

Killigrew wiggled his brows.

"*Oui*, you look beautiful," said Mademoiselle Bedeau. "I am very happy for you."

Allie smiled. "You guys are the best. Thanks. Gotta run!"

And with that she hurried to the kitchen.

And when she got to the door, Wee Mary opened and held it while she scooted through it.

"Thanks, Wee Mary!" Allie called over her shoulder. "See you soon!"

"No' too soon, I hope!" Wee Mary said, laughing. "And dunna worry—I'll do me best to keep the Munro clan from followin' you!"

Gabe waited at the Rover with the door open.

"Hurry and get in. If those Munro lads find us we're in for it."

Allie wasted no time diving in.

As they drove away, they laughed. Gabe checked his rearview mirror several times. "I think we're safe." He looked at her. "You're too far away."

Allie glanced at the console between them. "I'd rip this bloody box out if I could."

Gabe laughed. "No doubt."

"You don't think anyone will really follow us, do you?" she asked, turning around and looking through the back of the Rover.

"I hope no'."

Allie hoped the same.

Less than an hour later, they arrived at the cottage on Loch Ness. A full moon hung over the crags, casting a silvery glow to the mysterious black loch. Gabe got out, came around, and helped Allie out. He immediately picked her up in his arms and walked up the deck to the back sliding glass doors. With one hand, he dug in his pocket, found the key, and unlocked the door.

Once inside, he held her close, nuzzled her neck, and whispered against her ear, "I'll be right back."

He gently set her down and went out the door.

Minutes later he returned with their bags.

Then he turned to her and stared. The only light filtered in from the open windows, bathing the interior in a ghostly gray. He stepped toward her and lifted a hand, brushing aside a stray curl. With a finger, he traced her jaw. "I canna believe you're mine," he said, and his voice sounded deeper and more gruff than usual.

Allie found she couldn't say anything at all.

Gabe stared hard at her, seemingly drinking her in, and he let that hand drop to her arm, slid it down, and then draped it over her hip and pulled her to him.

Without closing his eyes, he kissed her. One hand came up and pulled several pins from Allie's hair, and he let them drop to the floor with a clink, one by one. Finally, it all tumbled down, her hair, and his eyes grew dark.

His fingers trailed down her bare back, down her spine, and skimmed over her backside, the rough calluses of his hands catching on the silk of her gown. "You're so beautiful I can hardly breathe," he said.

Just before he kissed her again.

With a hand on her jaw, Gabe turned her mouth to just the right angle and settled his lips over hers. Gentle at first, and with his hands moving over her back, he began to taste more. Allie slipped her arms around his waist and kissed him back.

Together they moved, until Allie's back rested against the wall in the living room. Gabe pulled back, just a bit, and stared down at her as though it were the first time he'd ever laid eyes on her.

Allie's heart lunged when Gabe's hands moved over her hip and to her thigh, and he leaned into her and kissed her, and he grasped her thigh and pulled it up, wedging himself in, holding her in place.

She didn't want to move a muscle.

Slowly, and without words, he lifted a hand to her straps, lowering them each and stroking her collarbone, her shoulders, and then he leaned toward her, mouth to ear. "I've no' been with anyone, Allie," he confessed. "No' since I've vowed to sobriety." His hand moved slowly over her thigh, up her hip, and brushed her breasts. Her intake of air sounded harsh.

"I've no' wanted anyone," he said, his other hand lifting her jaw and meeting her gaze. "No' until you. And Christ, I want you badly."

Allie's hands covered his; one on her thigh, one on her hip. "I am yours to have forever," she said, and slipped a hand round his neck and pulled his mouth to hers. "Forever, aye?" she said against his lips.

He smiled, and then he slowly let her leg drop, and he moved to the sofa, slung the pillows on the floor, along with a few blankets. He threw peat into the hearth and the earthy slab ignited. Resting back on his knees, he stared into the flames. He glanced over his shoulder. "Come here."

She did, and while on his knees, Gabe slid his hands around her waist and pulled her into an embrace, his cheek to her stomach. His hand caressed her bottom, and he pulled her down slowly.

As she lay there, he undressed. His chiseled muscles flexed in the moonlight, catching planes and angles of shadow that made him appear dangerous, mysterious.

Barely bound power, unleashed.

He was breathtaking, with ripples in his stomach and heavy, muscular thighs, and a broad back with knotted chunks of rock. He pushed her down all the way, her head resting on a pillow, and he simply gazed at her.

Without a word, he touched her. At first, hesitantly, a stroke of her chin, her eyebrows, and her lips. Then her hips, and his eyes grew dark and stormy when he eased the dress down, exposing her bare skin. She wiggled all the way out of it, her shoes, too, and just lay there, with Gabe looking at her.

It was the most intense, erotic moment of her life.

The sigh on his breath caused butterflies to beat furiously against her stomach as he moved his hands over her, and she arched into him as his mouth came down on hers. Slowly, he tasted her, touched her, and everywhere his hand caressed, his tongue followed.

And Allie's hands moved over his taut body, his forearms, and when his tongue grazed hers, traced her bottom lip, and then swept it with a long kiss, she groaned against him, and reached for him.

He didn't hold back.

Moving over her, he stared into her eyes as he settled his hips between hers. Bracing his weight, he looked down at her, at every place he'd kissed, touched.

He was in complete control.

Until Allie touched *him*.

Taking him in her hand, she stroked him and looked into his eyes. "I want to feel you inside me, Gabe MacGowan." With her free hand she pulled his head close. "To make us whole." She kissed him, stroked him. "To make us one."

Gabe groaned and covered her mouth with his, nudged her hips apart, and moved into her, filling her, and when he looked into her eyes, he kissed her lips softly. "I willna close my eyes, love. I want to watch you."

He began to move, gentle at first and then frantic, and she wrapped her legs around him and took him in, moved with him, the power within Gabe building so fierce it all but sparked electricity.

All at once, Gabe groaned, low, deep, and feral, and Allie arched and met his release with her own as a thousand lights flickered behind her eyes. So intense was the release that it left her gasping, her heart racing out of control.

Gabe slowed his movements, touching her everywhere, and his mouth came down on hers. So gentle, it hardly seemed real. He whispered against her mouth, "I love you, Allie MacGowan. Now we're one forever and I'll never let you go."

Allie ran her hands over his back and pulled him close, kissing him and touching him everywhere. "I love you, Gabe MacGowan," she said. She pulled back and looked into his fathomless green eyes. "I've been waiting for you forever. I think you were born just for me."

They smiled, content, and when Gabe came to her an hour later, there were no words needed. He reached for her, and she willingly went.

And together, they mended their souls.

Forever.

ACKNOWLEDGMENTS

I'd like to give heartfelt thanks to the following people for helping to make *MacGowan's Ghost* possible.

As always, Jenny Bent, my superagent, who always looks out for me, and my wonderful editor, Laura Cifelli, who always keeps my writing in check. And Lindsay Nouis, whose superb editing really helped my vision of this book bloom.

My kids, Kyle and Tyler, who have encouraged me and made me laugh along the way.

Kim Lenox, my silly-crazy and full-of-ideas sister writer. We talk every day, and good Lord, we now both have discovered picture messaging on our cell phones. Hel-looo, technology! Kim, I don't know what I'd do without you!

You remember my demented nursing pals, right? Well, thank God, they're still demented and the most supportive, funny, crazy, and sweet bunch of friends I could ever ask for. Thanks to Betsy (the ringleader of the Dementeds and the funniest person I know), Molly (who knows more swear words than any sailor alive—and shares them frequently), Eveline (Queen of the Monkeymail and *hys-ter-i-cal*), Val (when Val laughs, *everyone* laughs, because it's so funny when she laughs), Allison (she wears toe socks to work and we fight over who gets to marry Brendan Fraser in our next life), and Karol (my *snacksista*—she still eats the tar out of candy corn, but we *tore up* the jelly beans this year, too). You guys are absolutely the best bunch of friends *ever*!!! And you've made life so much more fun.

Donnie and Fiona Hossack from the Waterside House B&B in Ullapool, Scotland, for answering all sorts of Highland questions regarding the setting of the moon and the school system. Thank you!

Professor Adam Tomkins from the School of Law at Glasgow University for kindly answering all things pertaining to law students and their careers.

My crazy Denmark Sisterhood, whom I adore. I so look forward to our front-porch get-togethers (we shall remain tight-lipped and mum about those get-togethers, right, girls?).

As always, my mom, Dale, who I wish lived right next door but is supportive four hundred miles away just the same, and my dad, Ray, who is so funny! Thanks, guys, for all your support.

To all my sisters- and brothers-in-law, and brothers and cousins and aunties and uncles who support me, buy my books, and give them to friends and other relatives. *Thank you!*

And finally, a sincere thank-you to my readers. Without you, this incredible journey would not be possible.

Read on for a sneak peek
at another delightful and enchanting
love story from Cindy Miles,

THIRTEEN CHANCES

Available in September 2009 at
penguin.com and wherever books are sold.

The White Witches Souls for Eternity Convention
Northwestern Wales
All Hallows Eve, 1895
Somewhere in the dead of night . . .

"Okay, ladies, open your scrolls!"

Willoughby's fingers tightened on the parchment and she glanced up at the head mistress, Mordova, who impatiently awaited the opening of the Souls' Scrolls. A breeze wafted through the copse of trees, and dead leaves flitted to the ground. Somewhere close by, a field of dried corn crackled as the brisk autumn wind slipped between the stalks. Above, a harvest moon, large, full, and bright, shone through the canopy of birch and oak, bathing everything it touched in shimmering silver. Several bonfires flickered with orange flame.

"Willoughby!"

Willoughby jumped, startled, then glared at her sister. "*Don't* do that, Millicent."

"Well, then open the bloody scroll!" another sister, Agatha, said under her breath. "I'm dying to see our assignment!"

Four Ballaster sisters gathered round and leaned their heads close together as Willoughby, the eldest, slowly unrolled the scroll.

Four Ballaster sisters drew in sharp breaths.

The gathering of White Witches ceased looking at their own scrolls and turned to stare at Willoughby.

"It's *them*!" squealed Millicent, the middle Ballaster sister, pointing at the scroll. "Christian and Emma! Oh, Willoughby! Do you know what this *means*?" She clapped her hands in excitement.

"Yes, Willoughby Ballaster," said Mordova, who'd come to stand before them. "*Do* you know what this means?"

Willoughby looked up, and before she could say a word the head mistress continued.

"It means you and your sisters have the most difficult of assignments." She turned, her long, silvery hair gleaming in the moonlight, and addressed the rest of the witches. "For those of you new to the convention this year, Christian and Emma's souls have longed to be together for centuries, and for centuries they've been denied"—she waved an elegant hand—"all because they inadvertently cursed *themselves*." She tsked and shook her head. "Poor Christian of Arrick-by-the-Sea. A gallant and fierce Crusader, he vowed in the throes of death that he would forever await his Intended's love. And true to his vow, he is here, earthbound, yet a spirit, in truth." She clasped her hands together and paced. "And Emma, upon Christian's departure for the Crusades, performed an ancient incantation the poor lamb had no business of performing." She stopped and again shook her head. "Mortals. Always convinced they have the control to conjure magic."

Willoughby and the other Ballaster sisters stared on with the rest of the conventiongoers. Head Mistress Mordova faced first the crowd, then the Ballasters—particularly focusing on Willoughby.

"In an attempt to keep her true love safe in battle, Emma concocted an ancient Welsh spell by using an aged, outdated book of incantations. Sadly, she didn't pronounce the verse correctly and it, for lack of a better word, backfired."

"What happened?" said a quiet voice in the crowd.

Mordova gave a winsome smile, and firelight cast her face in shadows. "Every seventy-two years Emma's reincarnated soul returns to Arrick-by-the-Sea for reasons completely unknown and unfathomable to her. Drawn like a moth to light, she is, only she doesn't know why. Nor does she recognize her true love."

A resounding sigh echoed through the moonlit night.

Mordova continued. "So every seventy-two years, Christian awaits his true love, his Intended, his eternal soul mate. Eleven times thus far he has made Emma fall in love with him all over again." The head mistress heaved a gusty breath. "And due to that discombobulated scrap of magic, something inadvertently happens and Emma dies, only to be reborn, her soul forgetting everything. Meanwhile poor Christian's heart is severely broken each time, and I fear 'tis nigh to being unrepairable soon."

Silence filled the night air.

Willoughby met the gazes of her sisters, gave a nod, then cleared her tightened throat. "Head Mistress, we, the Ballasters, proudly accept this assignment." She looked out over the expectant faces of the coven and raised her voice. "We'll see that Christian and Emma are reunited once and for bloody all!"

A thunder of clapping sounded through the wood, accompanied by laughter and whoops and whistles. Many of the other witches walked up to Willoughby and the other Ballaster sisters to offer wishes of good luck—and a few homespun spells, if needed. When the crowd thinned, Mordova stood before the Ballasters, staring.

Willoughby lifted her chin. "Can the Council not help?"

The head mistress shook her head. "We are administration. We oversee, but do not give aid."

Willoughby sighed. "Figures."

"I know you girls have pure hearts and good intentions," Mordova said, her amber eyes shiny in the firelight. "I say this not to intimidate, but to encourage: take heed, I beg you. Not one of your predecessors has succeeded in reuniting Christian and Emma's souls, and they had many more centuries of experience at spellmaking than you young Ballasters. The undoing and redoing of such a discombobulated incantation is precarious at best. 'Twill not be an easy task, and can be rather heartbreaking—as well as dangerous. I warn you: beware of the magic you use. Be absolutely sure of each and every word chosen in any spells you conduct, for one misspoken word could mean the end of their chances. *Forever.*"

1937 Castle of Arrick-by-the-Sea
Northwestern Wales
Once again in the dead of night . . .

"We simply weren't prepared!" Agatha cried. "Whatever did we do wrong?"

"Another chance gone!" said Millicent, fretting her hands. "Oh, dear, Willoughby, what shall we do now?"

"Perhaps we should contact the head mistress?" said Maven.

Agatha snorted. "She cannot help, sister. Remember? She's *administration.*"

Willoughby rubbed her chin with an index finger and stared out at the castle ruins. Through the moonlit night, she saw Christian, walking the battlements. He'd just lost Emma for the twelfth time.

Willoughby could feel his pain from where she stood.

Something needed to be done once and for all.

She thought hard and paced.

"Just look at him, the poor dove," whispered Maven. "I cannot bear to see his anguish again. We must do something!"

"Indeed. Willoughby, where did we go wrong?" said Agatha. "Our spell was perfectly orchestrated. We planned it for seventy-two years!"

"Aye, and we should be thankful there's no retribution from it." Willoughby shook her head. "We're approaching this whole thing a bit too timidly, I think, especially when working with an incantation as discombobulated as Emma's. And conjuring from afar simply won't do. We need to be closer, for one. More aggressive. None of this peering from behind the tree line and conjuring spells from the wood business." Willoughby nodded to herself. "We shall become the new owners of the manor house near the castle. 'Tis for sale and we've the funds to purchase and restore it." She met each sister's puzzled look. "I know what else needs to be done, but 'tis risky."

Maven raised a brow. "How risky?"

Willoughby stroked her chin. "The riskiest."

Three other Ballasters gasped.

"You don't mean the—" started Millicent.

"Whsst!" Willoughby placed two fingers over her lips. " 'Tis the dodgiest of incantations and mustn't ever be spoken aloud." She gave a stern look to the others. "You know the one I mean, aye?"

"Aye," the others said together in a hushed whisper.

"I'm uncertain and not at all comfortable about it, Willoughby. No one has ever, in the history of the White Witches, succeeded. Using this spell will mean it is Christian and Emma's very last chance," said

Maven. "Their eternal love relies on this one scrap of magic. If it fails—if *we* fail—'tis over."

"Forever," whispered Agatha.

Willoughby again glanced out at the ruins and watched the silhouette of the fierce Crusader as he paced the battlements. He stopped, turned, and stared out to sea.

"Well then," Willoughby said with determination, and met her sisters' eyes. "We mustn't fail, aye? We'll waste not another second. Time's of the essence, girls. Thirteen is a lucky number and we've seventy-two years left to conjure the chanciest of charms!" She inhaled with gusto and puffed out the air slowly. Under her breath, she said on a sigh, "By Morticia's wand, let's not screw this up."

MacGowan's Ghost

CINDY MILES

A SIGNET ECLIPSE BOOK

SIGNET ECLIPSE
Published by New American Library, a division of
Penguin Group (USA) Inc., 375 Hudson Street,
New York, New York 10014, USA
Penguin Group (Canada), 90 Eglinton Avenue East, Suite 700, Toronto,
Ontario M4P 2Y3, Canada (a division of Pearson Penguin Canada Inc.)
Penguin Books Ltd., 80 Strand, London WC2R 0RL, England
Penguin Ireland, 25 St. Stephen's Green, Dublin 2,
Ireland (a division of Penguin Books Ltd.)
Penguin Group (Australia), 250 Camberwell Road, Camberwell, Victoria 3124,
Australia (a division of Pearson Australia Group Pty. Ltd.)
Penguin Books India Pvt. Ltd., 11 Community Centre, Panchsheel Park,
New Delhi - 110 017, India
Penguin Group (NZ), 67 Apollo Drive, Rosedale, North Shore 0632,
New Zealand (a division of Pearson New Zealand Ltd.)
Penguin Books (South Africa) (Pty.) Ltd., 24 Sturdee Avenue,
Rosebank, Johannesburg 2196, South Africa

Penguin Books Ltd., Registered Offices:
80 Strand, London WC2R 0RL, England

First published by Signet Eclipse, an imprint of New American Library,
a division of Penguin Group (USA) Inc.

First Printing, February 2009
10 9 8 7 6 5 4 3 2 1

Copyright © Cindy Homberger, 2009
All rights reserved

Also Available

from

Cindy Miles

Highland Knight

Bestselling mystery novelist Amelia Landry
journeys to the Scottish Highlands to stay in a
remote 14th-century tower, hoping to re-awaken
her imagination. She finds the inspiration she
seeks in the ghostly form of Laird Ethan Munro—
who has spent six centuries trying to discover why
he is neither alive nor dead.

Ethan senses that Amelia may be the one he has
been waiting for. Only she can uncover the truth
behind the curse and free his heart...

**Available wherever books are sold or at
penguin.com**

Also Available

from

Cindy Miles

Spirited Away

Knight Tristan de Barre and his men were murdered in 1292, their souls cursed to roam Dreadmoor Castle forever.

Forensic archaeologist Andi Monroe is excavating the site and studying the legend of a medieval knight who disappeared. But although she's usually rational, Andi could swear she's met the handsome knight's ghost.

Until she finds a way to lift the curse, however, their love doesn't stand a ghost of a chance.